The Man
in the
Gray Flannel Suit

The Man
in the
Gray Flannel Suit

SLOAN WILSON

THORNDIKE PRESS • THORNDIKE, MAINE

Library of Congress Cataloging in Publication Data:

Wilson, Sloan, 1920-
    The man in the gray flannel suit.

    1.Large type books.   I. Title.
[PS3573.I475M3   1985]   813'.54   84-24002
ISBN 0-89621-591-1 (lg. print)

Large Print edition available through arrangement with
Simon & Schuster, Inc.

Cover design by Eileen Rosenthal

This book is dedicated by my wife
and me to her father,
CARL E. PICKHARDT

ACKNOWLEDGMENTS

I'm grateful to Elise Pickhardt Wilson, my wife, for the help she gave me in writing this book. She mowed the lawn, took care of the children, and managed the family finances so that I could find time to write. She never made me feel that writing is justifiable only if it is successful. During a two-year period of almost all work and no play, she made life worth living for everyone in my house. Many of the thoughts on which this book is based are hers.

Both she and I are thankful for assistance rendered by many others. During dark hours when there was no realistic reason to suppose that the manuscript was ever going to get finished, Richard L. Simon, my publisher, administered miraculous transfusions of skill and courage. He emboldened me to have a try at this book in the first place, and now that the work is done, leaves me feeling as though he had fought at my side through a long war. There is no greater friendship.

For editorial advice and encouragement, I'm also deeply indebted to Norman Cousins. My mother, Mrs. Ruth Danenhower Wilson, proved that she is, among other things, a good editor. Kenneth Payson Kempton at Harvard was the first teacher to show me that a writer doesn't necessarily have to be a fool. Lester Anderson at The University of Buffalo helped in many ways. And last but not least, I'm grateful to the people in my office at The University of Buffalo. They did much of my University work while I was otherwise occupied.

S.W.

So I said
To the man who knew:
"Where are they going?
And what do they carry?
And why do they hurry so?"
A.F.W.

1

By the time they had lived seven years in the little house on Greentree Avenue in West-port, Connecticut, they both detested it. There were many reasons, none of them logical, but all of them compelling. For one thing, the house had a kind of evil genius for displaying proof of their weaknesses and wiping out all traces of their strengths. The ragged lawn and weed-filled garden proclaimed to passers-by and the neighbors that Thomas R. Rath and his family disliked "working around the place" and couldn't afford to pay someone else to do it. The interior of the house was even more vengeful. In the living room there was a big dent in the plaster near the floor, with a huge crack curving up from it in the shape of a question mark. That wall was damaged in the fall of 1952, when, after struggling for months to pay up the back bills, Tom came home one night to find that Betsy had bought a cut-glass vase for forty dollars. Such an extravagant gesture was utterly unlike her, at least since the war. Betsy was a conscientious household manager, and usually when she did something Tom didn't like, they talked the matter over with careful reasonableness. But on that particular night, Tom was tired and worried because he himself had just spent seventy dollars on a new suit he felt he needed to dress properly for his business, and at the climax of a heated argument, he picked up the vase and heaved it against the wall. The heavy glass shattered, the plaster cracked, and two of the lathes behind it broke. The next morning, Tom and Betsy worked together on their knees to patch the plaster, and they repainted the whole wall, but when the paint dried, the big dent near the floor with the crack curving up from it almost to the ceiling in the shape of a question mark was still clearly visible. The fact that the crack was in the shape of a question mark did not seem symbolic to Tom and Betsy, nor even amusing — it was just annoying. Its peculiar shape caused people to stare at it abstractedly, and once at a cocktail party one of the guests who had had a little too much to drink said, "Say, that's funny. Did you ever notice that big question mark on your wall?"

"It's only a crack," Tom replied.

"But why should it be in the form of a question mark?"

"It's just coincidence."

"That's funny," the guest said.

Tom and Betsy assured each other that someday they would have the whole wall re-plastered, but they never did. The crack remained as a perpetual reminder of Betsy's moment of extravagance, Tom's moment of violence, and their inability either to fix walls properly or to pay to have them fixed. It seemed ironic to Tom that the house should preserve a souvenir of such things, while allowing evenings of pleasure and kindness to slip by without a trace.

The crack in the living room was not the only reminder of the worst. An ink stain with hand marks on the wallpaper in Janey's room commemorated one of the few times Janey ever willfully destroyed property, and the only time Betsy ever lost her temper with her and struck her. Janey was five, and the middle one of the three Rath children. She did everything hard: she screamed when she cried, and when she was happy her small face seemed to hold for an instant all the joy in the world. Upon deciding that she wanted to play with ink, she carefully poured ink over both her hands and made neat imprints on the wallpaper, from the floor to as high as she could reach. Betsy was so angry that she slapped both her hands, and Janey, feeling she had simply been interrupted in the midst of an artistic endeavor, lay on the bed for an hour sobbing and rubbing her hands in her eyes until her whole face was covered with ink. Feeling like a murderess, Betsy tried to comfort her, but even holding and rocking her didn't seem to help, and Betsy was shocked to find that the child was shuddering. When Tom came home that night he found mother and daughter asleep on the bed together, tightly locked in each other's arms. Both their faces were covered with ink. All this the wall remembered and recorded.

A thousand petty shabbinesses bore witness to the negligence of the Raths. The front door had been scratched by a dog which had been run over the year before. The hot-water faucet in the bathroom dripped. Almost all the furniture needed to be refinished, reupholstered, or cleaned. And besides that, the house was too small, ugly, and almost precisely like the houses on all sides of it.

The Raths had bought the house in 1946,

shortly after Tom had got out of the army and, at the suggestion of his grandmother, become an assistant to the director of the Schanenhauser Foundation, an organization which an elderly millionaire had established to help finance scientific research and the arts. They had told each other that they probably would be in the house only one or two years before they could afford something better. It took them five years to realize that the expense of raising three children was likely to increase at least as fast as Tom's salary at a charitable foundation. If Tom and Betsy had been entirely reasonable, this might have caused them to start painting the place like crazy, but it had the reverse effect. Without talking about it much, they both began to think of the house as a trap, and they no more enjoyed refurbishing it than a prisoner would delight in shining up the bars of his cell. Both of them were aware that their feelings about the house were not admirable.

"I don't know what's the matter with us," Betsy said one night. "Your job is plenty good enough. We've got three nice kids, and lots of people would be glad to have a house like this. We shouldn't be so *discontented* all the time."

"Of course we shouldn't!" Tom said.

Their words sounded hollow. It was curious to believe that that house with the crack in the form of a question mark on the wall and the ink stains on the wallpaper was probably the end of their personal road. It was impossible to believe. Somehow something would have to happen.

Tom thought about his house on that day early in June 1953, when a friend of his named Bill Hawthorne mentioned the possibility of a job at the United Broadcasting Corporation. Tom was having lunch with a group of acquaintances in The Golden Horseshoe, a small restaurant and bar near Rockefeller Center.

"I hear we've got a new spot opening up in our public-relations department," Bill, who wrote promotion for United Broadcasting, said. "I think any of you would be crazy to take it, mind you, but if you're interested, there it is. . . ."

Tom unfolded his long legs under the table and shifted his big body on his chair restlessly. "How much would it pay?" he asked casually.

"I don't know," Bill said. "Anywhere from eight to twelve thousand, I'd guess, according to how good a hold-up man you are. If you try for it, ask fifteen. I'd like to see somebody stick the bastards good."

It was fashionable that summer to be cynical about one's employers, and the promotion men were the most cynical of all.

"You can have it," Cliff Otis, a young copy writer for a large advertising agency, said. "I wouldn't want to get into a rat race like that."

Tom glanced into his glass and said nothing. Maybe I could get ten thousand a year, he thought. If I could do that, Betsy and I might be able to buy a better house.

2

When Tom stepped off the train at Westport that night, he stood among a crowd of men and looked toward the corner of the station where Betsy usually waited for him. She was there, and involuntarily his pace quickened at the sight of her. After almost twelve years of marriage, he was still not quite used to his good fortune at having acquired such a pretty wife. Even with her light-brown hair somewhat tousled, as it was now, she looked wonderful to him. The slightly rumpled cotton house dress she was wearing innocently displayed her slim-waisted but full figure to advantage, and although she looked a little tired, her smile was bright and youthful as she waved to him. Because he felt it so genuinely, there was always a temptation for him to say to her, "How beautiful you are!" when he saw her after being away for the day, but he didn't, because long ago he had learned that she was perhaps the one woman in the world who didn't like such compliments. "Don't keep telling me I'm pretty," she had said to him once with real impatience in her voice. "I've been told that ever since I was twelve years old. If you want to compliment me, tell me I'm something I'm not. Tell me that I'm a marvelous housekeeper, or that I don't have a selfish bone in my body."

Now he hurried toward her. "Hi!" he said. "It's good to get home. How did things go with you today?"

"Not so well," she replied ruefully. "Brace yourself."

"Why, what happened?" he said, and kissed her lightly.

"Barbara's got the chicken pox, and the washing machine broke down."

"Chicken pox!" Tom said. "Do they get very sick with that?"

"No, but according to Dr. Spock, it's messy. The other two will probably get it. Poor Barbara feels awful. And I think we're going to have to buy a new washing machine."

They climbed into their old Ford. On the way home they stopped at a drugstore, and Tom bought Barbara a toy lamb. Barbara was six and wanted nothing but toy lambs. When they got to Greentree Avenue, the little house looked more monotonous than ever, and Tom saw that the front lawn needed cutting. Janey, followed by his son, Pete, ran to meet him as he opened the front door. "Barbara's got the chicken pox, and we're *all* going to get it!" she said delightedly. "Mother says so!"

Lucy Hitchcock, who lived next door and who had been staying with the children while Betsy drove to the station, was sitting in the living room watching a puppet show on television. She got up to go, and while Tom was thanking her, Janey saw the parcel he was holding in his hand. "What's that?" she demanded.

"A present for Barbara because she's sick."

"Did you bring anything for me?"

"No. You're not sick yet."

"That's not *fair!*" Janey said, and began to howl. Without making any inquiries, Pete began to howl too.

"Barbara's *sick!*" Tom said.

"You always bring her presents and you never bring me any," Janey retorted.

"That's not true," Tom said.

"No television!" Betsy said. "If you children don't stop this nonsense immediately, no television for a week."

"Not *fair!*" Janey said.

"This is your last chance!" Betsy said. "Be quiet."

". . . fair," Janey murmured.

"All right, that does it," Betsy said. "No television for a week!"

Redoubled howls came from Janey and Pete, until Betsy relented on condition that they both be quiet for the rest of the evening. Mournfully the children followed Tom upstairs. He found Barbara in bed, with her small face already a mass of sores. "Did you bring me a present?" she asked eagerly.

He gave her the parcel. "A lamb!" she said delightedly when she unwrapped it. "Another lamb!"

"I didn't want another lamb anyway," Janey said. "Lambs are silly."

"They're not silly!"

"Quiet! Not another word!" Betsy said, coming into the room with a glass of water and medicine for Barbara.

Tom went downstairs and mixed a Martini for Betsy and himself. When Betsy came down, they sat in the kitchen, sipping their drinks gratefully while the children played in the living room and watched television. The linoleum on the kitchen floor was beginning to wrinkle. Originally it had been what the builder described as a "bright, basket-weave pattern," but now it was scuffed, and by the sink it was worn through to the wood underneath. "We ought to get some new linoleum," Betsy said. "We could lay it ourselves."

"I heard about a new job today," Tom said. "Public relations. United Broadcasting Corporation."

"How much does it pay?"

"Probably a good deal more than I'm getting now."

There was an instant of silence before she said, "Are you going to try for it?"

"I might."

Betsy finished her drink and poured herself another. "I've never thought of you as a public-relations man," she said soberly. "Would you like it?"

"I'd like the money."

Betsy sighed. "It would be wonderful to get out of this house," she said.

3

The next morning, Tom put on his best suit, a freshly cleaned and pressed gray flannel. On his way to work he stopped in Grand Central Station to buy a clean white handkerchief and to have his shoes shined. During his luncheon hour he set out to visit the United Broadcasting Corporation. As he walked across Rockefeller Plaza, he thought wryly of the days when he and Betsy had assured each other that money didn't matter. They had told each other that when they were married, before the war, and during the war they had repeated it in long letters. "The important thing is to find a kind of work you really like, and something that is useful," Betsy had written him. "The money doesn't matter."

The hell with that, he thought. The real trouble is that up to now we've been kidding ourselves. We might as well admit that what we want is a big house and a new car and trips to Florida in the winter, and plenty of life insurance. When you come right down to it, a man with three children has no damn right to say that money doesn't matter.

There were eighteen elevators in the lobby of the United Broadcasting building. They were all brass colored and looked as though they were made of money. The receptionist in the personnel office was a breathtakingly beautiful girl with money-colored hair — a sort of copper gold. "Yes?" she said.

"I want to apply for a position in the public-relations department."

"If you will sit down in the reception room, I'll arrange an interview for you," she said.

The company had a policy of giving all job applicants an interview. Every year about twenty thousand people, most of them wildly unqualified, applied for jobs there, and it was considered poor public relations to turn them away too abruptly. Beyond the receptionist's desk was a huge waiting room. A rich wine-red carpet was on the floor, and there were dozens of heavy leather armchairs filled with people nervously smoking cigarettes. On the walls were enormous colored photographs of the company's leading radio and television stars. They were all youthful, handsome, and unutterably rich-appearing as they smiled down benignly on the job applicants. Tom picked a chair directly beneath a picture of a big-bosomed blonde. He had to wait only about twenty minutes before the receptionist told him that a Mr. Everett would see him. Mr. Everett's office was a cubicle with walls of opaque glass brick, only about three times as big as a priest's confessional. Everett himself was a man about Tom's age and was also dressed in a gray flannel suit. The uniform of the day, Tom thought. Somebody must have put out an order.

"I understand that you are interested in a position in the public-relations department," Everett said.

"I just want to explore the situation," Tom replied. "I already have a good position with the Schanenhauser Foundation, but I'm considering a change."

It took Everett only about a minute to size Tom up as a "possibility." He gave him a long printed form to fill out and told him he'd hear from the United Broadcasting Corporation in a few days. Tom spent almost an hour filling out all the pages of the form, which, among other things, required a list of the childhood diseases he had had and the names of countries he had visited. When he had finished, he gave it to the girl with the hair of copper gold and rang for one of the golden elevators to take him down.

Five days later Tom got a letter from Everett saying an interview had been arranged for him with Mr. Gordon Walker in Room 3672 the following Monday at 11:00 A.M. In the letter Walker was given no title. Tom didn't know whether he were going to have another routine interview, or whether he were actually being considered for a position. He wondered whether he should tell Dick Haver, the director of the Schanenhauser Foundation, that he was looking for another job. The danger of not telling him was that the broadcasting company might call him for references any time, and Dick wouldn't be pleased to find that Tom was applying for another job behind his back. It was important to keep Dick's good will, because the broadcasting company's decision might depend on the recommendation Dick gave him. In any one of a thousand ways, Dick could damn him, without Tom's ever learning about it. All Dick would have to do when the broadcasting company telephoned him would be to say, "Tom Rath? Well, I don't know. I don't think I'd want to go on record one way or the other on Mr. Rath. He's a nice person, you understand, an awfully nice person. I'd be perfectly willing to say that!"

On the other hand, it would be embarrassing to tell Dick he was seeking another job and then be unable to find one. Tom decided to delay seeing Dick until after he had had his next interview.

Walker's outer office was impressive. As soon as Tom saw it, he knew he was being seriously considered for a job, and maybe a pretty good one. Walker had two secretaries, one chosen for looks, apparently, and one for utility. A pale-yellow carpet lay on the floor, and there was a yellow leather armchair for callers. Walker himself was closeted in an inner office which was separated from the rest of the room by a partition of opaque glass brick.

The utilitarian secretary told Tom to wait. It was extremely quiet. Neither of the two girls was typing, and although each had two telephones on her desk and an interoffice communication box, there was no ringing or buzzing. Both the secretaries sat reading typewritten sheets in black notebooks. After Tom had waited about half an hour, the pretty secretary, with no audible or visible cue, suddenly looked up brightly and said, "Mr. Walker will see you now. Just open the door and go in."

Tom opened the door and saw a fat pale man sitting in a high-backed upholstered chair behind a kidney-shaped desk with nothing on it but a blotter and pen. He was in his shirt sleeves, and he weighed about two hundred and fifty pounds. His face was as white as a marshmallow. He didn't stand up when Tom came in, but he smiled. It was a surprisingly warm, spontaneous smile, as though he had unexpectedly recognized an old friend. "Thomas Rath?" he said. "Sit down! Make yourself comfortable! Take off your coat!"

Tom thanked him and, although it wasn't particularly warm, took off his coat. There wasn't anyplace to put it, so, sitting down in the comfortable chair in front of Walker's desk, he laid the coat awkwardly across his lap.

"I've read the application forms you filled out, and it seems to me you might be qualified for a new position we may have opening up here," Walker said. "There are just a few questions I want to ask you." He was still smiling. Suddenly he touched a button on the arm of his chair and the back of the chair dropped, allowing him to recline, as though he were in an airplane seat. Tom could see only his face across the top of the desk.

"You will excuse me," Walker said, still

smiling. "The doctor says I must get plenty of rest, and this is the way I do it."

Tom couldn't think of anything more appropriate to say than "It looks comfortable. . . ."

"Why do you want to work for the United Broadcasting Corporation?" Walker asked abruptly.

"It's a good company . . ." Tom began hesitantly, and was suddenly impatient at the need for hypocrisy. The sole reason he wanted to work for United Broadcasting was that he thought he might be able to make a lot of money there fast, but he felt he couldn't say that. It was sometimes considered fashionable for the employees of foundations to say that they were in it for the money, but people were supposed to work at advertising agencies and broadcasting companies for spiritual reasons.

"I believe," Tom said, "that television is developing into the greatest medium for mass education and entertainment. It has always fascinated me, and I would like to work with it. . . ."

"What kind of salary do you have in mind?" Walker asked. Tom hadn't expected the question that soon. Walker was still smiling.

"The salary isn't the primary consideration with me," Tom said, trying desperately to come up with stock answers to stock questions. "I'm mainly interested in finding something useful and worth while to do. I have personal responsibilities, however, and I would hope that something could be worked out to enable me to meet them. . . ."

"Of course," Walker said, beaming more cheerily than ever. "I understand you applied for a position in the public-relations department. Why did you choose that?"

Because I heard there was an opening, Tom wanted to say, but quickly thought better of it and substituted a halting avowal of lifelong interest in public relations. "I think my experience in working with *people* at the Schanenhauser Foundation would be helpful," he concluded lamely.

"I see," Walker said kindly. There was a short silence before he added, "Can you write?"

"I do most of the writing at the Schanenhauser Foundation," Tom said. "The annual report to the trustees is my job, and so are most of the reports on individual projects. I used to be editor of my college paper."

"That sounds fine," Walker said casually. "I have a little favor I want to ask of you. I want you to write me your autobiography."

"What?" Tom asked in astonishment.

"Nothing very long," Walker said. "Just as much as you can manage to type out in an hour. One of my girls will give you a room with a typewriter."

"Is there anything in particular you want me to tell you about?"

"Yourself," Walker said, looking hugely pleased. "Explain yourself to me. Tell me what kind of person you are. Explain why we should hire you."

"I'll try," Tom said weakly.

"You'll have precisely an hour," Walker said. "You see, this is a device I use in employing people — I find it most helpful. For this particular job, I have twenty or thirty applicants. It's hard to tell from a brief interview whom to choose, so I ask them all to write about themselves for an hour. You'd be surprised how revealing the results are. . . ."

He paused, still smiling. Tom said nothing.

"Just a few hints," Walker continued. "Write anything you want, but at the end of your last page, I'd like you to finish this sentence: 'The most significant fact about me is . . .' "

"The most significant fact about me is . . ."

Tom repeated idiotically.

"The results, of course, will be entirely confidential." Walker lifted a bulky arm and inspected his wrist watch. "It's now five minutes to twelve," he concluded. "I'll expect your paper on my desk at precisely one o'clock."

Tom stood up, put on his coat, said, "Thank you," and went out of the room. The utilitarian secretary already had a stack of typewriting paper ready for him. She led him to a small room a few doors down the hall in which were a typewriter and a hard office chair. There was a large clock on the wall. The room had no windows. Across the ceiling was a glaring fluorescent light which made the bare white plaster walls look yellow. The secretary walked out without a word, shutting the door silently behind her.

Tom sat down in the chair, which had been designed for a stenographer and was far too small for him. Son of a bitch, he thought — I guess the laws about cruel and unusual punishment don't apply to personnel men. He tried to think of something to write, but all he could remember was Betsy and the drab little house and the need to buy a new washing machine, and the time he had thrown a vase that cost forty dollars against the wall. "The most

significant fact about me is that I once threw a vase costing forty dollars against a wall." That would be as sensible as anything else he could think of, but he doubted whether it would get him the job. He thought of Janey saying, "It isn't *fair!*" and the worn linoleum on the kitchen floor. "The most significant fact about me is . . ." It was a stupid sentence to ask a man to finish.

I have children, he thought — that's probably the most significant fact about me, the only one that will have much importance for long. Anything about a man can be summed up in numbers. Thomas R. Rath, thirty-three years old, making seven thousand dollars a year, owner of a 1939 Ford, a six-room house, and ten thousand dollars' worth of G.I. Life Insurance which, in case of his death, would pay his widow about forty dollars a month. Six feet one and a half inches tall; weight, 198 pounds. He served four and a half years in the Army, most of it in Europe and the rest in the South Pacific.

Another statistical fact came to him then, a fact which he knew would be ridiculously melodramatic to put into an application for a job at the United Broadcasting Corporation, or to think about at all. He hadn't thought about this for a long while. It wasn't a thing

he had deliberately tried to forget — he simply hadn't thought about it for quite a few years. It was the unreal-sounding, probably irrelevant, but quite accurate fact that he had killed seventeen men.

It had been during the war, of course. He had been a paratrooper. Lots of other people had killed more men than he had. Lots of bomber crews and artillerymen had, but, of course, they never really knew it. Lots of infantrymen and lots of paratroopers had, and most of them knew it. Plenty of men had been dropped behind the enemy lines, as Tom had been on five different occasions, and they had had to do some of their killing silently, with blackjacks and knives. They had known what they were doing, and most of them were healthy enough not to be morbid about it, and not to be proud of it, and not to be ashamed of it. Such things were merely part of the war, the war before the Korean one. It was no longer fashionable to talk about the war, and certainly it had never been fashionable to talk about the number of men one had killed. Tom couldn't forget the number, "seventeen," but it didn't seem real any more; it was just a small, isolated statistic that nobody wanted. His mind went blank. Suddenly the word "Maria" flashed into it.

"The most significant fact about me is that I . . ."

Nonsense, he thought, and brought himself back to the present with a jerk. Only masochists can get along without editing their own memories. Maria was a girl he had known in Italy during the war, a long time ago, and he never thought about her any more, just as he never thought about the seventeen men he had killed. It wasn't always easy to forget, but it was certainly necessary to try.

"The most significant fact about me is that for four and a half years my profession was jumping out of airplanes with a gun, and now I want to go into public relations."

That probably wouldn't get him the job, Tom thought. "The most significant fact about me is that I detest the United Broadcasting Corporation, with all its soap operas, commercials, and yammering studio audiences, and the only reason I'm willing to spend my life in such a ridiculous enterprise is that I want to buy a more expensive house and a better brand of gin."

That certainly wouldn't get him the job.

"The most significant fact about me is that I've become a cheap cynic."

That would not be apt to get him the job.

"The most significant fact about me is that as a young man in college, I played the mandolin incessantly. I, champion mandolin player, am applying to you for a position in the public-relations department!"

That would not be likely to get him far. Impatiently he sat down at the typewriter and glanced at his wrist watch. It was a big loud-ticking wrist watch with a black face, luminous figures, and a red sweep hand that rapidly ticked off the seconds. He had bought it years ago at an Army post exchange and had worn it all through the war. The watch was the closest thing to a good-luck charm he had ever had, although he never thought of it as such. Now it was more reassuring to look at than the big impersonal clock on the wall, though both said it was almost twelve-thirty. So far he had written nothing. What the hell, he thought. I was a damn fool to think I wanted to work here anyway. Then he thought of Betsy asking, as she would be sure to, "Did you get the job? How did it go?" And he decided to try.

"Anybody's life can be summed up in a paragraph," he wrote. "I was born on November 20, 1920, in my grandmother's house in South Bay, Connecticut. I was graduated from Covington Academy in 1937, and from

Harvard College in 1941. I spent four and a half years in the Army, reaching the rank of captain. Since 1946, I have been employed as an assistant to the director of the Schanenhauser Foundation. I live in Westport, Connecticut, with my wife and three children. From the point of view of the United Broadcasting Corporation, the most significant fact about me is that I am applying for a position in its public-relations department, and after an initial period of learning, I probably would do a good job. I will be glad to answer any questions which seem relevant, but after considerable thought, I have decided that I do not wish to attempt an autobiography as part of an application for a job."

He typed this paragraph neatly in the precise center of a clean piece of paper, added his name and address, and carried it into Walker's office. It was only quarter to one, and Walker was obviously surprised to see him. "You've still got fifteen minutes!" he said.

"I've written all I think is necessary," Tom replied, and handed him the almost empty page.

Walker read it slowly, his big pale face expressionless. When he had finished it, he dropped it into a drawer. "We'll let you know our decision in a week or so," he said.

4

"How did the interview go?" Betsy asked him that night as soon as he got off the train. "Tell me *all* about it!"

"I don't know," Tom said. "I wouldn't get my hopes up. I'm one of about forty people being considered."

"You'll get it," she said. "I'm *sure* you will."

"Don't get your hopes up."

"I talked to a real-estate agent today," she replied. "He said we could probably get fifteen thousand dollars for our house, maybe more. And he's got some *wonderful* places selling for about thirty thousand!"

"For Pete's sake!" Tom said. "Aren't you rushing things a little?"

"It doesn't do any harm to *plan,* does it?" she asked with an injured air.

"You better just pretend nothing's happened at all," he said. "Then you won't be disappointed if nothing does happen."

Tom tried not to think about the interview with Walker. Probably it would be a week or two before he heard from United Broadcasting, he figured, but as things turned out, a letter from Walker arrived at Westport only three days later. Betsy took it from the mailman, ripped it open, and immediately called Tom at the Schanenhauser Foundation. "It's here!" she said. "The mailman just brought it! Walker wants to see you at eleven o'clock next Tuesday for another interview."

"Fine," Tom said noncommittally.

"That means things must be getting pretty serious, doesn't it? I mean, they wouldn't want to see you again if you didn't make a pretty good impression last time."

"Maybe."

"Don't be stuffy," Betsy said. "I feel like celebrating. Tonight we're going to have steak and sparkling Burgundy, and to hell with the cost."

She hung up before he could object. She's probably right about one thing, he thought — I don't think Walker would want to see me if he didn't have anything for me. It was time to talk to Dick Haver, his boss at the foundation, Tom concluded.

Dick Haver was a tall, tweedy man who had been a college professor. "Why do you want to leave?" he asked Tom that afternoon when Tom had explained the situation.

"Money," Tom said. "I have three children and I need more money than I think I can make here in the immediate future."

Haver smiled wanly. "How much do you think you need?" he asked.

"I'd like ten thousand," Tom said. "And later, I'd like to think I could make more."

"You could here — in time," Haver said.

"How much time?"

"Five or six years maybe. Up to now, you've been doing fairly well."

"I'd like a place where there would be more opportunity for rapid advancement," Tom said.

"Don't make your decision too quickly," Haver replied. "I'll talk the matter over with some of the others here, and we'll see if we can do a little more for you. I'm not at all sure you'd like it over at United Broadcasting."

"Why not?"

"It's just a feeling I have," Haver said. "Think it over and make your own decision, of course."

"Nuts!" Betsy exclaimed that night when

Tom told her about his conversation with Haver. "The old goat is just trying to hang onto you! He'll come up with an offer of some piddling raise you should have gotten two years ago, and every time you want another one, you'll have to threaten to quit!"

She sipped her sparkling Burgundy reflectively a moment. "You know what you ought to do now?" she said. "You ought to go have a talk with Grandmother. After all, she told you about the job at the foundation in the first place, and she might have ways of finding out whether Haver really will have anything big for you. Anyway, she ought to know you're thinking about leaving — she'd be hurt if she found out about it from anyone else."

"I guess so," Tom said reluctantly. "I'll take a run up to see her Saturday."

Early Saturday morning he drove to South Bay alone, because by that time all three of the children had chicken pox and Betsy had to stay with them. South Bay is a small town not far from Stamford. When Tom approached it, he got a curious feeling of homecoming which was still strong, despite all the years that had passed since he had lived there. The wide, elm-shaded main street had changed since the war. Brightly painted one-story houses filled the fields where Tom had hunted rabbits as a boy, and even the old nine-hole golf course had miraculously become something called "Shoreline Estates," in spite of the fact that it was a good two miles inland. The road leading from the main street to his grandmother's house had changed little, however. The great brick and stone mansions were not quite so well kept as they had been when Tom had ridden his bicycle past them, but they still seemed comfortable, solid, and much more permanent than the recently built structures on the golf course, which looked as though they were quite capable of disappearing as quickly as they had come. At the end of a row of big houses, the road narrowed and started up a steep hill. The old Ford groaned as Tom shifted it into second gear. There were two sharp turns in the road made necessary by massive outcroppings of rock which gave the hill the appearance of a mountain. It was on the second of these turns that Tom's father, Stephen Rath, had been killed thirty years ago, before Tom was old enough to remember him. Stephen Rath had been driving down the road very late one night at what must have been a vicious speed and had slammed into the rock so hard that his automobile had been completely demolished. Tom had never found why his father had been driving down that narrow road so fast at such an odd hour, and long ago he had learned to stop wondering about it. Now as he passed the rock, he glanced away from it, as he had ever since, at the age of five, he learned that it was the place where his father had been killed.

Stone posts topped by iron urns three feet high marked the entrance to the driveway of his grandmother's house. Beyond them were the carriage house, which itself was bigger than Tom's home in Westport, and the rock garden in which his mother and he had spent so many sunny mornings long ago. In the corner of the rock garden stood a heavy stone bench, now almost entirely surrounded by bushes which once had been kept neatly trimmed. At the sight of it, Tom was beset by the same old mixture of emotions from which he always suffered when he visited the place, as though each object there were possessed of a special ghost which leaped out at him as soon as he passed through the gates. His mother had spent countless afternoons sitting on that bench and watching him as he played. Once, when he was about seven years old, he had noticed two lines of verse carved in bold script across the back of the bench. With his forefinger he had traced out the letters grooved in the warm stone and had asked his mother what they meant. Now, almost thirty years later, he could still remember the bitterness in her voice as she read: "The lark's on the wing; the snail's on the thorn: God's in his heaven — all's right with the world!"

He looked quickly away from the bench which had become so strangely surrounded by bushes, and continued along the driveway. It led to the top of the hill, on the highest point of which was the old mansion itself, a tall Victorian structure with a tower at one end that had been designed to appear even larger and more grandiose than it was. The wind that almost always blew there seemed full of voices.

"It's a dwarfed castle," he remembered his mother saying bitterly the year before she died of pneumonia, when he was fifteen years old. "When your father first took me here before we were engaged, he joked about dwarfs in armor behind the parapets at the top of the tower. . . ."

"Here, it's for you!" he remembered another voice saying, the voice of his grandmother. She had been holding a beautifully polished, old-fashioned, deep-bellied mandolin out to him — he couldn't have been

44

more than ten or twelve years old at the time. "Your father used to play it," she had said. "Maybe you'd like to learn."

Now Tom paused at the top of the hill. There was a breath-taking view of Long Island Sound, with the bright water mottled by the shadows of clouds. The grass on both sides of the driveway had grown long. Looking at it, Tom remembered the days when it had been kept as carefully as a putting green and felt the first pang of the rising annoyance he feared every time he went there, the rage at his grandmother's refusal to sell the place, and her calm willingness to pour into it what little was left of the money she had inherited from her husband and father.

"I love this place, and I'll keep it as long as I can pay the taxes on it" she had said when, shortly after the war, Tom had suggested that she move.

He left his car by the front door. Edward, a tall old man who long ago had served as her butler and now acted as a man of all work, let him in. "Good morning, Mr. Rath," he said deferentially. "Mrs. Rath is waiting for you in the sunroom."

Tom found his grandmother seated in an armchair, dressed in a long white gown. In her hand was a gnarled black walnut cane which looked almost like an extension of her withered fingers. She was ninety-three years old.

"Tommy!" she said when she saw him, and leaned eagerly forward in her chair.

"Don't get up, Grandmother," he said. "It's good to see you."

The old lady peered at him sharply. He was shocked at how much she had aged during the past two months, or perhaps it was just that he persisted in remembering her as a younger woman and was surprised now, each time he saw her. And she in turn was shocked to see Tom, whom she remembered as a young boy. She continued to stare at him, her old eyes bright and disarmingly kind.

"You look tired, Tommy," she said suddenly.

"I feel fine."

"You're getting a little stout," she said bluntly.

"I'm getting older, Grandmother."

"You ought to go riding more," she said. "The Senator always said riding is the best exercise. He used to ride for an hour almost every morning."

There it was, her terrible projection of the past into the present, which was more a deliberate refusal to face change than a passive acquiescence to senility. And there too was her elaborate myth about the Rath family's accomplishments. "The Senator" was the phrase she always used for her dead husband, Tom's grandfather, who had served one term as a State Senator in Hartford during his early youth, and who had spent most of the rest of his life doing absolutely nothing.

"I've got a few things I want to talk over with you," Tom began, trying to change the subject.

"You mustn't get stout," the old lady went on relentlessly. "Your father never got stout. Stephen was always slender."

"Yes, Grandmother," he said. Sometimes he imagined that she deliberately dwelt upon painful subjects, for she enjoyed talking about his father with him, presenting a caricature of a hero, elaborated by all kinds of distorted facts, hidden among which Tom often caught glimpses of what he suspected were unpleasant truths. What were the facts about his father? Tom had had to piece them together from trifles. "I don't know why, but Stephen never played the mandolin after the war," the old lady had told him once long ago. "At college he was in the Mandolin Club, and even as a boy he played beautifully, but after the war he never did it any more."

47

His father had been a second lieutenant during the First World War. He had been sent home from France several weeks before the Armistice for unexplained reasons and had for a while worked with a large investment firm in New York. As far as Tom could make out from the dim echoes of rumor which survived, Stephen Rath had either quit work or been fired about two years before he died, and during his remaining days had simply lived a life of leisure in the big house with his wife, mother, and son. Presumably he had not been happy; he had never played the mandolin any more. Tom suspected that there must have been quite a chain of events leading up to the night when Stephen had backed his Packard out of the carriage house and careened down the road to the waiting rocks at the turn. But of all this Tom could learn nothing from his grandmother's conversation. According to the old lady, Stephen had been a great military hero, and over the years she had advanced him by her own automatic laws of seniority to the rank of major.

"I hear you're getting ahead very well at the foundation," the old lady was saying now.

"I think I may leave the foundation, Grandmother," he said. "That's what I want to talk to you about."

"Leave? Why?"

How difficult it was to explain to an old lady who had never earned a penny in her life, and who had never even bothered to conserve what she had inherited, that he needed more money! He said, "I may have an opportunity offered me that's too good to turn down."

"I was telling Mrs. Gliden the other day how well you're doing at the foundation," the old lady said. "I told her it might not be long before you were chosen as director. I hear that man Haver may be leaving."

"Where did you hear that?"

"I don't remember," the old lady said. "There is a rumor. . . ."

That was the trouble — he never could be sure whether his grandmother was simply ensnaring him in her dreams of family glory, or whether the old connections with prominent people which she treasured so carefully actually resulted in useful information. But on the face of it, the thought that he might be chosen to head the Schanenhauser Foundation was ridiculous, regardless of whether Haver was leaving or not. There were at least twenty people who would be chosen first.

"Are you thinking of going into government?" the old lady asked unexpectedly.

"No — I'm thinking of going into busi-ness."

"Your great-grandfather was very success-ful in business," she said. "At one time he owned a fleet of twenty-eight vessels. Are you going into shipping?"

"No," Tom said. "This will be a little dif-ferent, Grandmother. There's nothing defi-nite about it yet, but I've mentioned it to Dick Haver, and I thought you ought to know."

"I'm sorry you have to go into business," she said soberly, "but I suppose it's neces-sary. Business is such a bore — The Major never could stand it, and neither could The Senator. But I suppose it's necessary. Come, let's talk about something more cheerful. How do you think the place looks?"

"Fine," he said.

"I can't afford to keep the lawns up, but the house itself is in as good repair as ever."

"It looks beautiful."

"I hope that when I go, you and Betsy will be able to live here," she said. "I'm trying to keep it up for you. I don't want you to men-tion it to a soul, but I had to take a small mortgage on the place to have the roof fixed and to have an oil furnace put in. Edward is getting old, and he can't shovel coal any more."

A furnace, Tom thought — I'll bet that the price of a furnace for this place would send all three of my kids through a year of college. He felt the old double, contradictory anger rising in him, the familiar fury at his grandmother for dissipating money which ordinarily would come to him eventually, and the accompanying disgust at himself for lusting after an old lady's money. He tried to feel the gratitude which, after all, was due the person who had brought him up, and paid for his education, and treated him with kindness and love.

"She's selfish, but I could forgive her that," Tom remembered his mother saying about the old lady. "What I can't forgive is the arrogance, and the deliberate pretenses she inflicted on her son, and everyone around her. Poor Steve was raised on lies. . . ."

His mother hadn't been talking to him when she had said that; she had been talking to a minister who visited her quite often after her husband's death, and the minister had noticed that Tom, who was only twelve years old then, had come into the room, and he had said, "Hush — the boy's here. How are you, Tom? It won't be long before you'll be going to high school!"

Now Tom wondered whether he should try to work with the old lady's lawyer to straighten out whatever might be left of her estate. When he had come home from the war, he had, after tortuous examination of his own motives, asked his grandmother whether he could help manage things for her, and she had turned him down abruptly. She had never mentioned money to him in all the years he had lived with her, except to say that it didn't matter, that it was a frightful bore.

"If you want any help, let me know," he said now. "I don't think it's wise for you to be taking out mortgages — there might be ways to avoid it."

"The bank was very helpful," she said. "I haven't got many more years to go, and I think the lawyer has arranged for me to be taken care of quite nicely. The important thing is to keep this house in shape for you and Betsy."

"I doubt whether we'll be able to afford such a place," he said. "Not many people can these days."

"Nonsense!" she replied. "You're going into business, aren't you? Perhaps you'll be able to improve it. The Senator always wanted to put another wing on the south side of the house. Come, and I'll show you where."

She walked with astonishing agility and

pointed with her cane to show just where the billiard room should go, and a glass-walled conservatory for raising orchids.

There were really four completely unrelated worlds in which he lived, Tom reflected as he drove the old Ford back to Westport. There was the crazy, ghost-ridden world of his grandmother and his dead parents. There was the isolated, best-not-remembered world in which he had been a paratrooper. There was the matter-of-fact, opaque-glass-brick-partitioned world of places like the United Broadcasting Company and the Schanenhauser Foundation. And there was the entirely separate world populated by Betsy and Janey and Barbara and Pete, the only one of the four worlds worth a damn. There must be some way in which the four worlds were related, he thought, but it was easier to think of them as entirely divorced from one another.

5

The following Tuesday Tom left the Schanenhauser Foundation at ten-thirty in the morning to keep his appointment with Walker. It was not necessary for him to give any excuse for leaving his desk, but he felt vaguely guilty as he told his secretary he probably wouldn't be back until noon. He walked quickly up Fifth Avenue and across Rockefeller Plaza, so preoccupied with his own thoughts that he hardly noticed the people he passed. When he got inside the United Broadcasting building, a starter wearing a fancy, silver-braided cap directed him into one of the waiting gold-colored elevators.

"Floor please?" the elevator operator said. He spoke in a deep voice with a slight Italian accent. Tom glanced at him. The man was wearing a plum-colored uniform and had his back turned toward him. He was a stout, dark-complexioned man about thirty years old with thick black hair only partly covered by a plum-colored cap shaped like an army overseas cap. Across the back of his thick neck, just visible above his collar, was a long, thin white scar. There was something startlingly familiar about the slope of his narrow shoulders and the deep voice. Tom stepped to one side to get a better look at him, but the elevator was getting crowded, and he couldn't see the front of the man's face.

"Floor please?" the elevator man repeated as people filed into the car. "Floor please?"

"Thirty-six," Tom said. The man turned toward him, and their eyes met. The elevator operator's face was fat, almost round, and he had a thin, incongruously dapper mustache. His eyes were black and unblinking. He stared at Tom for several seconds. There might have been a quickly suppressed flicker of recognition, but Tom couldn't be sure. The face seemed impassive. Tom looked away. The elevator doors rumbled shut, and the machine shot upward. There was an instant of silence before it stopped, and the doors rumbled open. Tom started to get out.

"This is twenty," the operator said in his deep voice.

Tom edged back into the elevator. When

he got out at his floor, he felt oddly flustered. Down the hall he saw a men's room and went there to wash his face and comb his hair before going to see Walker. It was absurd to attach such importance to a chance encounter with an elevator man. Even if it were someone he had known, what possible difference could it make?

A few minutes later Tom found Walker reclining as usual in his adjustable chair. Sitting in front of Walker's desk was a handsome, angular man whom Walker introduced as Bill Ogden. Ogden shook hands with Tom rather stiffly and said almost nothing during the remainder of the interview. Apparently he was there simply as an observer.

"We've gone over your qualifications and are now prepared to talk in more specific terms," Walker said, smiling cheerily. "I think I should begin by saying that this isn't just an ordinary job in the public-relations department we're considering. What we're looking for is a young man to work with Mr. Hopkins, the president of the company, on a special project. . . ."

He paused, apparently expecting Tom to say something. "That sounds very interesting," Tom said.

Walker nodded. "As a matter of fact, this

position wouldn't really be with United Broadcasting at all, except in a purely technical sense," he continued. "You would be working directly for Mr. Hopkins on an outside project completely unrelated to the company. One reason we think you might be suited for the job is that you would be working quite closely with the foundations. We hope that the project will eventually be sponsored by the foundations."

"Just what kind of a project is it?"

"Mr. Hopkins has been asked to start a national committee on mental health," Walker said.

There was a brief silence, during which Tom heard a fire engine, deprived of its siren because of the need to reserve the sirens for air raid warnings, go chortling down the street far below, uttering shrill but unsirenlike mechanical screams. "A committee on mental health?" he asked stupidly.

"Mr. Hopkins plans to get together forty or fifty national leaders from many different fields and devise a program to encourage people all over the United States to work for mental health," Walker said.

"What kind of a program?" Tom asked incredulously.

"We don't know yet. Perhaps it will be a

drive for better mental hospitals, or community guidance clinics. Something which would do for mental disease what the March of Dimes has done for polio."

"Sounds like a good idea," Tom said, realizing he was expected to register enthusiasm.

"What Mr. Hopkins wants now is a young man to begin helping him with research for the speeches he will have to make to kick the project off. Later he will want someone to help him draw up a prospectus for an organization and to start getting the people together. Are you interested?"

"I certainly am!" Tom said heartily. "I've always been interested in mental health!" That sounded a little foolish, but he could think of nothing to rectify it.

"This wouldn't be a very high-paying job," Walker continued. "We were thinking of a figure somewhere near seven thousand dollars."

Tom knew then that Walker had talked to Dick Haver at the foundation and learned what he had been making. The union of bosses is the most powerful union in the world.

"I'd been hoping for more than that," he said. "Ordinarily, salary wouldn't be an important consideration for me, especially in connection with a job of this kind, but I have increasing personal responsibilities. I feel I should be making ten thousand dollars a year."

"Wouldn't that be quite a jump from your present position?" Walker asked bluntly. Ogden, who had been sitting almost motionless, put his hand in his pocket and took out a package of cigarettes.

"It would," Tom said, "but there would have to be considerable incentive for me to leave the foundation."

Walker, lolling comfortably in his chair, glanced at Ogden, who had just finished lighting a cigarette.

"We don't have to make any decisions now," Ogden said, in a casual, almost bored voice.

Walker nodded. "Perhaps the next step would be to have him meet Mr. Hopkins," he said to Ogden, as though Tom were not in the room.

"All right," Ogden said.

"Could you have lunch with Mr. Hopkins at twelve-thirty, day after tomorrow?" Walker asked.

"Certainly," Tom said.

"Meet me here, and I'll take you up and introduce you," Walker concluded.

Tom thanked him and hurried out of his office. When he got in the elevator, he glanced at the operator, but it was a thin man he had never seen before. In a telephone booth in the enormous lobby downstairs he called Bill Hawthorne, who had told him about the job in the first place. "Come on down and give me some briefing," he said. "I'm supposed to have lunch with Hopkins day after tomorrow!"

"With Hopkins!" Bill said in an awed voice. "Say, for a guy who hasn't even been hired yet, you're doing all right!"

They went to a bar two doors down the street and ordered Martinis. "Now tell me all about your boy Hopkins," Tom said. "Walker tells me he's starting a project on mental health. What's it all about?"

Bill sipped his drink thoughtfully. "What do you already know about Hopkins?" he asked.

"Not much," Tom said. "I've hardly heard of him. Somebody told me he started with nothing and he's making two hundred thousand a year now. That's about all I know — I don't think I've ever even seen a picture of him."

"Precisely," Bill said professionally. "Precisely."

"What the hell do you mean by that?"

"I mean it looks like the public-relations boys have cooked up a big deal to put Hopkins on the map, and you've stumbled into it."

"I don't get it," Tom said.

"Figure it out for yourself. Here's Hopkins, about fifty years old, and the president of the United Broadcasting Corporation. As you say, he makes about two hundred thousand dollars a year, and that doesn't count stock deals and all the rest of it. Inside the company he's the biggest shot in the world. The top comedians and all the famous actors are scared to death of him. But outside the company he's nothing. Taxi drivers don't call him "Sir." Waiters in restaurants more than five blocks from Radio Center don't give him a special table. Little boys don't gape at him. Don't you see how tough it must be?"

"I'm weeping," Tom said.

"All right. Here's a guy who works fifteen or twenty hours a day — inside the company he's famous for it. He's a regular *machine* for work. And he's competent. Give him almost any business, and he'd double the profit in a year. And people like him — he knows how to drive people and still make them like him. But what's he get out of life?"

"Money."

"Of course! But if he made only a quarter as much money, he'd still be able to buy everything he wants. Hopkins is a guy of simple tastes. He has only one or two places in the country, and a small yacht, and three automobiles. He was able to afford all that long ago and could go on affording it if he quit work tomorrow. So what's he keep working fifteen or twenty hours a day for?"

"Must be nuts," Tom said.

"Nuts nothing! The poor son of a bitch wants fame! And he's in a position to buy it. So he calls in Ogden and Walker and says, 'Boys, make me famous. One year from today I want to be famous, or you're fired!'"

"Oh come on," Tom said, laughing. "You know damn well that's nonsense."

"Perhaps it wouldn't work that way exactly," Bill said, obviously enjoying himself. "He'd say, 'Gentlemen, I believe that for the sake of the company, the major executives must direct more attention to their personal public relations, and I hope that in the immediate future we can work something out.'"

"I doubt like hell that a man in his position would say that either."

"Okay — be a stickler for detail. What would really happen is that somebody would

62

suggest that Hopkins head a committee on mental health — these guys are asked to do that sort of thing all the time. Usually they refuse. But this time Hopkins figures he's got a chance for the national spotlight. You're right about one thing — he'd never say anything about it. He wouldn't have to. He'd call in Walker and Ogden, and they're paid enough to *know* what he's thinking without being told. The only thing they'd all say is that it's every citizen's duty to do something about mental-health problems. They'd be nauseatingly noble about it. But all the time they'd know damn well they were doing it to give Hopkins a shot of publicity, and that's the reason why you, my boy, will be on the United Broadcasting Corporation's pay roll, and why every cent that Hopkins spends on this project will come off his company expense account!"

"Why mental health?" Tom asked. "Why a subject like that?"

"Figure it out for yourself. What would you do to make Hopkins famous? You can't play up the success he's had in business, because nobody much cares, and because newspapers and magazines don't like to publicize radio and television companies any more than they have to — they're all in competition for advertising. You've got to play up something about his personal life, not his business. And you can't have him marrying chorus girls, or winning a prize for water skiing — you've got to keep it dignified. What would you do?"

"All right, I'll give the answer you want," Tom said. "I'd advise him to start a national committee on mental health, or some other public-service thing, and I'd publicize hell out of it."

"Precisely," Bill replied, finishing his drink and ordering another one. "You would follow the newest maxim of the public-relations boys: 'If you want good publicity, do something good!' It's all very profound. Want another drink?"

"I think I'd better stay sober," Tom said. "And I also think there's something wrong in your theory."

"You're going to be a *good* public-relations man!" Bill said admiringly. "You're defending him already!"

"Nuts!" Tom replied. "I just want to take all the possibilities into account. You say he's doing this because he wants publicity — yet all his life, he's apparently detested publicity. Certainly he could have had it long before now if he'd wanted it. Why has he waited all this time, and what's made him change?"

"All right, all right, there may be more to all this than meets the eye," Bill said. "Maybe he personally doesn't want publicity. But maybe the board of directors is worried about the bad name the company's getting by making the television shows just as bad as the radio programs. There's been a rumor going around lately that United Broadcasting is just trying to make money and is half-hearted about improving people's minds. One thing the company could do is actually to improve the programs, but it would be cheaper to tell all the company's top executives, and particularly the president, to go out and acquire a reputation for doing good. After all, Hopkins will always be identified as the president of the United Broadcasting Corporation, and if he's doing something good, and kind of intellectual, that would be about the least expensive way the company could get respectable."

"Maybe," Tom said.

"Or perhaps it's more complicated," Bill continued. "Hopkins has had a taste of power inside the company. Maybe he likes it and wants more. He can't get any more inside the company. So it's just possible that he's made up his mind to go into politics. He'd have to do some public-service thing first — right now he'd be political poison. But after he was known all over the country as the man who started the very successful mental-health committee, who knows? You may be the first campaign man in the Hopkins-for-President drive!"

"Haven't we left one possibility out?" Tom asked.

"What?"

"That he might be sincere. That he might want to do some good. That after concentrating on his personal fortune all these years, he may have come to the point where he wants to do something for the public welfare, with no strings attached."

"It's possible," Bill said doubtfully. "But it would be awfully dull if it were true!"

"Do you really know him?" Tom asked. "Do you really know what kind of a guy he is?"

"Hell," Bill said. "I've been working for this damn outfit for four years, and I've never laid eyes on the guy. There are all kinds of stories about him — they used to say he had two children and had been home twice in the last twenty years. I think his son was killed during the war — anyway, nobody talks about that any more. They say he needs less sleep than Edison did. They say he's got his whole filing system memorized, practically, and can quote from any important letter or contract in it. Some say he's got a little blond girl on Park Avenue. Some say he's sleeping with some actress who flies in from Hollywood once a month. I've even heard it said that he's queer. But nobody who passes that stuff around really knows him. The only people I know who actually work with him are Walker and Ogden, and of course they never talk about him. To tell the honest truth, I have no idea in the world what kind of man he is, except he must be pretty damn smart to be where he is."

"He ought to be interesting to work for," Tom said.

"Maybe," Bill replied, "but I ought to tell you one more thing: everybody says he's tough as hell. If you can't do what he wants, he'll fire you without batting an eye. I don't *know* that's true, mind you, but it's what everybody says."

"Sounds fair enough, if you can do what he wants," Tom said. "If you do it real well, is he quick with the raises?"

"I don't know. You'd be surprised how a company this size can pinch pennies — they even got an order out the other day cautioning us all to put our office lights out when we weren't using them and asking us to quit stealing pencils. But I'd say it's always a good bet to work for a man making two hundred thousand a year. At least you've got a long way to go before you start competing with the boss!"

"If I can get the job, I think I'll take it," Tom said.

Bill finished his drink and lit a cigarette. "If you don't, you're crazy," he said.

6

Tom thought Betsy would be excited when she heard he had a luncheon date with the president of United Broadcasting, but as soon as he stepped into his house that night he knew something was wrong. The house looked as though a herd of wild horses had stampeded through it. Soiled laundry was scattered about the living room. In the kitchen a mixture of dirty luncheon and breakfast dishes littered the table and counters.

"Betsy!" he called from the living room. "Where are you?"

"Up here," she said in a weak voice.

He raced up the stairs and found her lying fully clothed on the bed. "What's the matter?" he asked.

"I feel awful," she replied. "It hit me right after you left this morning, but I didn't want to call you up and bother you. Go see if the kids are all right."

He stepped into the room the three children shared. The beds were unmade, and a tangle of clothes and toys littered the floor. The three children were crouched over a glass of water paint. Pete was naked, and Barbara and Janey wore only underclothes. All three showed the ravages of chicken pox on both their faces and bodies, but they glanced up at Tom cheerfully.

"Momma's sick," Janey said delightedly. "We've been taking care of her."

"You're not very well yourself," Tom said. "You're supposed to be in bed."

"We're *painting!*" Janey said indignantly.

Tom went through some drawers and got them pajamas. He helped them put the pajamas on and tucked them into bed before returning to Betsy.

"I went to sleep," Betsy said. "I was trying to keep an eye on them, but I went to sleep. They've really been angels — I told them I wasn't feeling well, and they've been talking in whispers all day."

Tom felt her forehead and found it was dry and hot. He searched through the medicine cabinet in the bathroom and returned carrying a thermometer.

"You're sure that's the one you're supposed to put in your *mouth?*" Betsy asked suspiciously.

"Sure," he said. "Stick it under your tongue."

While they were waiting the required two minutes, Janey suddenly called in a loud clear voice, "Daddy, is Momma going to die?"

"No," he said.

"Well, if she *does* die," Janey continued speculatively, "who will take care of us?"

"She's not going to die!" Tom said.

"But if she did . . ."

"I'm not going to!" Betsy blurted, trying to keep her lips closed around the thermometer.

"Anyway," Janey said, "I guess Grandmother would take care of us, wouldn't she?"

"Don't worry about me, kids," Betsy said. "I'm going to be fine." She held the thermometer up to the light.

"What is it?" Tom asked.

"A hundred and three."

"Have you ever had chicken pox?"

"Oh, God!" she said. "Of course, I must have had it! All children get it!"

"Do you remember having it?"

"Not exactly," she said. "I just assumed . . ."

"We better call the doctor," he said.

He telephoned Dr. Grantland. He always disliked calling him, because although Dr. Grantland was only about forty-five years old, he suffered from rheumatism and asthma, and it always seemed a shame to bother him. After the telephone had buzzed for a long while, the doctor answered wheezily.

"Do you want me to come over?" he asked after Tom had described Betsy's symptoms.

"If it isn't too much trouble," Tom said.

The doctor wheezed alarmingly before saying bravely, "All right, all right. I guess I can make it."

While they were waiting for the doctor, Tom told Betsy he had a luncheon engagement with Hopkins. "Who's he?" she asked.

"The president of United Broadcasting."

"That's nice," she said weakly. "Oh, Tommy, my head hurts!"

"What are we going to have for supper?" Barbara called. "Mother just gave us soup for lunch and we're hungry!"

"I'll get you supper in a few minutes," Tom said. "The doctor is coming to see Mother."

"Is he going to give her a needle?" Janey asked enthusiastically.

"I don't know."

"If he does, can we watch?"

"No!" Tom said. "You stay in bed."

"I can't stand it," Betsy said. "Chicken pox! Why didn't I get it when I was a child?"

"You won't be very sick," Tom said.

"I will too! And I know why I didn't get it when I was a child — because Mother took such damn good care of me. She never let me play with other children because she was afraid I'd catch something."

"I don't see why we can't watch her get the needle," Janey called. "She always watches when the doctor gives it to *us!*"

"Quiet!" Tom said. "I'm going downstairs and pick up a little before the doctor comes."

He threw the dirty laundry down the cellar stairs, then went to the kitchen and mixed himself a Martini. Before he had finished it, the doorbell rang, and Dr. Grantland was there.

"Oh, dear," he said as Tom let him in, "I think this asthma of mine is getting worse every day."

"I'm terribly sorry," Tom said. "Betsy's upstairs. Can I carry your bag for you?"

"No," he said bravely. "I can manage."

Tom followed him upstairs. The doctor sat down on a chair beside the bed, opened his bag, and took out a nebulizer with which he sprayed his own throat. "Ah," he said gratefully. "That certainly helps."

"My head hurts and I have a temperature of a hundred and three and I feel awful," Betsy said. "Tom thinks I have chicken pox."

"Have you ever had it before?" the doctor asked.

At that moment the three children came into the room, their scabbed faces wreathed in smiles. "Are you going to give her a needle?" Janey asked.

"Heavens!" the doctor said, and started to wheeze. "You certainly have been exposed!"

"I guess I never had chicken pox," Betsy said grumpily. "Mother always kept me away from other children, and I never got *anything.*"

"Remove your upper clothing," the doctor said.

"Are you going to give her a needle?" Janey repeated.

"Go back to bed!" Betsy ordered. "This minute!"

"I'll stay in your room with you and tell you a story," Tom said to the children. "Get in there now, and I'll be right in."

The children withdrew to their own room. Tom ducked downstairs, grabbed his drink, and joined them.

"Tell us about Bubbley," Barbara said.

Long ago he had made up a story about a little dog named Bubbley who swallowed a cake of soap and blew bubbles when he barked. Barbara always wanted it recited over and over again in precisely the same words he had used the first time.

"There was this little dog named Bubbley," he began wearily, after taking a long sip from his glass.

"No!" Barbara said. *"Once upon a time* there was a little dog named Bubbley."

"All right," he said irritably. "Don't interrupt."

"Well, tell it *right!"* Barbara said.

Pete, who was only four years old, looked at his father solemnly with his thumb in his mouth. "I *hate* the story about Bubbley," he said quietly to himself.

"You keep still!" Barbara said venomously to him.

"One day he swallowed a cake of soap," Tom said. "And ever after that . . ."

Before he had finished the story, the door opened, and Dr. Grantland came in. "I guess she's got chicken pox all right," he said. "Could you give me a glass of water?"

"Sure," Tom said, "but before you go, could you take a look at the kids?"

The doctor glanced at the children with

distaste. "I'm not a pediatrician," he said.

"I know," Tom replied. "We had a pediatrician look at them two days ago, but I thought that since you were here . . ."

"I only look at children in emergencies," the doctor said. "All my patients have to be twelve years old or more."

"I'll get you a glass of water," Tom said.

The doctor followed him downstairs. When Tom gave him a glass of water, he slipped a pill into his mouth and swallowed it.

"Thank you," he said gravely. "Now about Mrs. Rath. All we can do is let this thing run its course. Here are some prescriptions which will help a little, but there's not a great deal we can do. Make sure she gets plenty of rest. She should stay in bed for a week, maybe more."

"I'll try to find someone to look after the kids," Tom said.

Two hours later, when the children had had their supper and the house was cleaned up, Tom started telephoning to find a woman to act as housekeeper. No one he knew was available, but an elderly woman named Mrs. Manter who was recommended by a friend said that as a special favor she would come for sixty dollars a week, provided Tom would call for her in his car not earlier than nine in the morning and take her home not later than six in the afternoon. That would mean he would not be able to get to work until eleven in the morning and would have to leave the office at four o'clock in the afternoon, and it would also mean that the family budget would have to be scrapped, but there was no choice. He hoped Dick Haver wouldn't think he was just taking it easy because he expected to get a new job.

The next morning Mrs. Manter turned out to be a stern-faced farm woman about sixty-five years old who weighed at least two hundred pounds and had a voice without any volume control.

"I'm awfully glad you could come," Tom said when he picked her up. "You know how it is when the woman of a family gets sick and there are sick children to be cared for."

"DON'T TELL ME!" she thundered. "I HAD EIGHT KIDS MYSELF, AND ONCE WHEN THEY WAS ALL DOWN WITH MEASLES, I BROKE MY LEG!"

"Why, that's terrible," Tom said.

"MY HUSBAND WAS AWAY," she said so loudly that he immediately made up his mind she was deaf and couldn't hear herself.

"WHAT DID YOU DO?" he yelled.

"YOU DON'T HAVE TO SPEAK SO LOUDLY!"

she shouted back. "I can hear! I just put my knee on a chair and tied it that way. Found I could get around the house quite well, dragging the chair with me."

Tom drove her quickly to his house, introduced her to Betsy, who looked dazed, and rushed for the train.

7

When he got to his office he explained to Dick Haver why he was going to have to keep the hours of the semiretired during the next two weeks.

"That's all right, Tom," Dick said pleasantly. "I understand. By the way, some of the people over at United Broadcasting called me up the other day to ask about you. Anything definite developed there yet?"

"I haven't made up my mind what to do," Tom said, figuring he'd better leave an opportunity to say he didn't want to go to United Broadcasting if Hopkins ended by not wanting to hire him.

"We'd like to keep you here if we could," Dick said, "but I don't want to try to influence you too much. There are a few things you might want to take into account when you make your decision, however."

"I certainly would appreciate any advice. . . ."

"If you stay here, you can expect fairly steady small salary increases," Dick said. "If you go there, you might make a great deal in a short while, and on the other hand, you might find yourself without a job. It's extremely unlikely you'll remain in your present financial position for long if you go to United Broadcasting — you'll either go up or down. . . ."

"It's hard to figure," Tom said tentatively.

"I happen to know Mr. Hopkins," Dick said.

So they told him all about the job, Tom thought. Probably he knows more about it than I do — a whole lot more.

"He's a fine man," Dick continued. "He's one of the few authentic business geniuses in New York today. If you get a chance to work with him, it will be a great privilege."

"That's what I think," Tom said.

"On the other hand," Dick went on thoughtfully, "I understand that they don't really want you to work for United Broadcasting — they want you for some private project Ralph Hopkins is dreaming up. There are some dangers for you there. . . ."

Dick paused. "What do you mean?" Tom asked.

"He might get sick of his project and abandon it — a man like Ralph Hopkins is always starting things, trying them out, and discarding the ones that don't work. If that happened, he might drop you — or he might let you try out at United Broadcasting. But the important thing for you to remember is that when you start work on a private project for a man like Hopkins, you don't have any clearly defined ladder to climb. You're just going to have to play it by ear, hoping Hopkins will not lose interest. You won't have any real profession — your profession will be pleasing Hopkins. And if you fail in that, the experience you've had with Hopkins won't necessarily prepare you for a very good job anywhere else."

"I can see that," Tom said.

"What I'm trying to say," Dick continued, "is that working for Great Men is a profession in itself, and the trouble is that when you're through with one Great Man, you can't always find another."

He's making it sound as though I'm going to be a professional toady, Tom thought. He's trying to persuade me not to go. He said nothing.

"I think I ought to add," Dick said, "that when you leave, if you leave, we'll have to replace you, and it might not be possible for us to find a position here for you if you returned to look for a job."

"Of course," Tom said.

Dick smiled. "Make your own decision," he said. "Whatever you do, I wish you luck."

Tom thanked him and went to his own desk. If he had really wanted to keep me he could have offered me a big raise, but that would have encouraged everybody else to threaten to leave, he thought. He couldn't do that. Or, if he wanted to keep me, all he would have to do would be to give me a bad reference. He could do it over the telephone and I'd never know about it, but Dick would never even think of that. The union of bosses is powerful, but, within its self-prescribed limits, marvelously scrupulous. Tom glanced at his watch and saw it was almost time for lunch. On his desk was a long report from a college trying to explain what it had done with a half-million-dollar grant the Schanen-hauser Foundation had given it a year ago. Tom started to read it. He decided he wouldn't go to lunch. He worked right through the day, unobtrusively making sure that Dick Haver knew it.

When Tom got back to Westport that night he found the house spotless, and an enormous steak dinner in the oven awaiting him.

"THERE'S AN APPLE PIE IN THE BREAD BOX," Mrs. Manter shouted. "THE CHILDREN HAVE ET THEIR SUPPER AND ARE IN BED."

"Fine," Tom said. "How is everybody?"

"YOUR WIFE'S NOT REALLY SICK AT ALL," Mrs. Manter said. "TAKE ME HOME NOW — IT'S ALMOST SIX O'CLOCK."

Before taking her home, Tom ran up the stairs to see Betsy, who was lying on a neatly made bed looking wilted. "How are you?" he asked.

"Exhausted," she said. "Just watching that woman makes me exhausted. Do you know what she did? She washed clothes by hand in the bathtub, and she scrubbed all the woodwork in the kitchen. She mowed the lawn. She made cookies. And the children mind her like trained seals. She tells them to keep quiet and they don't say a word."

"Maybe we can learn something," Tom said.

"The children are in their room now keeping quiet."

"I'll take her home," Tom said. "Can you manage till I get back?"

"I won't tell the children she's gone," Betsy said weakly.

At seven the next morning Tom awoke

83

with the knowledge that he had to prepare breakfast for the children, get Mrs. Manter, and go into New York to have lunch with the president of the United Broadcasting Corporation. He was dismayed to find that no freshly pressed suit was in his closet, and that the one shirt in his drawer which didn't have a frayed collar lacked two buttons.

"Betsy!" he said. "I can't go in to see Hopkins looking like a bum!"

"I forgot!" Betsy replied. "I was supposed to pick up your things at the cleaners the day before yesterday. So much has been going on!"

"What will I do?"

"Go down and get breakfast," Betsy said. "I'll be pressing your gray flannel suit and sewing on buttons."

"Are you strong enough?"

Betsy struggled out of bed. "You don't have to be very strong to lift a button," she said.

Dressed only in his shoes, socks, and underpants, Tom went to the kitchen and fried eggs. The children, feeling much better in spite of the fact that their faces had not yet healed, insisted on having breakfast in the kitchen, instead of in bed. Tom remembered the formal breakfasts his grandmother's butler had served during his own childhood, with silver covers on dishes of eggs and sausage, and, seeing himself in his underwear serving his children, he thought, Things sure are different for them — one thing they won't have to get over is gracious living.

By the time he was dressed, Tom found himself surprisingly nervous at the prospect of meeting Hopkins. He felt almost the way he had before combat jumps during the war. "Wish me luck," he said to Betsy, after he had delivered Mrs. Manter and was leaving to catch his train.

"You'll get the job," Betsy said confidently.

That was the way she always was. During the war, he was sure, she had never worried about him — she was perfectly confident that he'd come back unhurt. Her confident letters, which sometimes had arrived when he was certain he would never survive the next jump, had made him acutely lonely and he felt the same way now as he bent over and kissed her.

There's no damn reason in the world to be nervous, he thought, later in the morning, as he walked toward the United Broadcasting building. After all I've been through, why should I be nervous now? He wondered what

Hopkins was like. What did a man have to be like to make so damn much money? It's never just luck that lets them make it, he thought, and it isn't just who they know — I won't let myself fall into the trap of thinking that. Hopkins has got something, something special, or he wouldn't be making two hundred thousand a year. What is it?

All I have to do is be myself, he thought. Just treat him like anybody else. I wonder what it's like to have all that money? I wonder what it's like never to have to worry about frayed shirt collars, and cracks in the living-room wall, and holes in the kitchen linoleum, and how to pay a woman to take care of your children when your wife is sick? I wonder what it's like to know there's plenty of money to send your kids to college? What's it like to be a success?

Buck fever, he thought — I've got buck fever. I've got my sights on the guy, and my hands are beginning to shake. The son of a bitch. Why shouldn't he like me? He may be tough all right, but I wish he'd been along with me a few years ago; I would like to have seen how tough he was when the sergeant opened the door of the airplane two thousand feet up and said, "Guess we're getting close, sir. Are you ready?"

I'll bet old Hopkins has fought battles, Tom thought, but his battles paid off. Suddenly the ridiculous old resentment rose in him, the crazy anger he had felt so many times when he'd been scared and seen some poor inoffensive colonel who never had to jump sitting behind a desk, drinking coffee maybe, and wisecracking with a sergeant about when they were going to get their next leave. When he'd seen something like that, especially when he'd seen it a few hours before he knew he had to take off, this crazy anger had risen in him, and for no reason at all he felt the same way now. Then he was in the gold elevator, going up, high into the sky. He looked at the operator and was absurdly relieved to find it was not the man whose face and voice had been so strangely familiar.

"Hello!" Walker said as Tom entered his office. "You're right on time!"

Tom smiled. "I try to be punctual," he said primly, and felt absurd.

Walker put his small puffy white hands on his desk and painfully eased his enormous bulk from his reclining chair. "We'll pick up Bill Ogden and go on up to see Mr. Hopkins," he said.

Ogden looked more like a fashion plate than ever. "Glad to see you," he said to Tom, but he didn't sound glad at all — he didn't sound as though he had ever been glad about anything except the happy circumstances which had caused him to be handsome and slender and well dressed and in a position of at least a little authority.

With Ogden leading the way and Walker puffing along behind, Tom got back into the gold elevator. Following Ogden, he stepped out at the fifty-sixth floor. The corridors there were wider, he immediately noticed. The floors were carpeted more richly, and even the light fixtures on the ceiling were of a heavier brass than on the floors below. In the air, he felt, there was almost the smell of money, impregnating everything, like musk.

Hopkins' outer office was a large room, in which two pretty girls and one gray-haired woman sat at big typewriters which looked like cash registers. There were five comfortable chairs made of molded plywood arranged in a circle around an ash tray on a pedestal. Three doors, all of them shut, led from this outer office. One of these doors was especially broad and obviously led to the final retreat of Hopkins himself.

"Mr. Hopkins is busy," the gray-haired woman said to Walker, and smiled. Everybody in this building smiles, Tom thought — even Ogden managed a thin little twinge of the lips whenever he spoke. It must be a company rule.

They sat in the chairs surrounding the ash tray, and Tom saw a row of carefully framed photographs on the wall in front of him. One was of Winston Churchill debarking from an airplane. Something was written in a bold script across the bottom of the photograph, but Tom was not close enough to read it, and somehow it would have been unthinkable to get up and inspect the photograph closely.

"He has Mr. Givens with him," the gray-haired woman said. "They'll be through in a moment." She smiled again, and both Ogden and Walker smiled back at her.

Ten minutes later a tall, distinguished-looking man emerged from the largest of the three doors and walked briskly through the outer office toward the elevators.

"You can go in now," the gray-haired woman said.

Following Ogden, Tom entered a large rectangular room with big windows on two sides of it. The view of the city was breath-taking — the floor seemed almost like a platform suspended in mid-air. At the far end of the room, behind a huge rectangular desk, sat

Hopkins. He was small, not more than five feet three or four — somehow Tom had expected him to be seven feet tall. He was pale, slender, and partly bald. His eyes were deep set, the face narrow, and the nose short like the nose of a child. His smile was curiously boyish. He was dressed in a brown worsted suit.

"Hello!" he said, getting up from his chair and walking briskly around the end of the desk. "Good morning, Gordon! How are you, Bill! And you're Tom Rath! I certainly do appreciate your taking the time to have lunch with us!"

His manner was both warm and deferential. He shook Tom's hand heartily, and without making it necessary for him to say more than "How do you do?" kept up a steady patter of conversation.

"I hear you're working with the Schanenhauser Foundation," he said. "My, that's a fine outfit! I've done a little work with Dick Haver on committees. . . ."

He moved toward the door and, after insisting that everyone precede him out, walked beside Tom to the elevator, still talking. Gradually, Tom found himself relaxing. It was ridiculous to be nervous with this friendly little man who seemed so anxious to please him. Now that Tom had met him, the conversations he had had with Bill Hawthorne seemed absurd.

When they got on the elevator, Tom saw immediately that the operator was the familiar-appearing man he had seen before. The elevator man glanced at him, then quickly looked toward Hopkins.

"Good morning, Mr. Hopkins!" he said in his deep voice, and shot down to the ground floor without any intermediate stops. Hopkins insisted on being the last man out of the elevator. As they walked out of the building, Tom glanced over his shoulder and saw the elevator operator standing there at the door of his car watching them. Tom looked away quickly. Hopkins led the way across Rockefeller Plaza to another building, at the top of which was a club with a large dining room overlooking the city. They sat down at a corner table, and a waitress took orders for cocktails.

"I understand that Bill and Gordon here have told you something about the new project we're thinking of starting," Hopkins said when the drinks had arrived. "What do you think of it?"

"I don't know any of the details yet, but it certainly sounds interesting," Tom replied, trying to combine wariness, sagacity, and enthusiasm.

"We don't know the details ourselves yet," Hopkins said. "It all started when a group of doctors called on me a few months ago. They apparently felt that there is too little public understanding of the whole question of mental illness, and that a campaign like the fight against cancer or polio is needed. I was impressed by the statistics they gave me. Do you know that more hospital beds are occupied by the mentally ill than by all the cancer, heart, and polio patients put together?"

"I've heard that," Tom said. "Did the doctors have any specific program to suggest?"

Hopkins smiled. "I'm afraid it's up to us to develop a program," he said. "What would you do?"

"I suppose we could, in general, divide the operation into two parts," Tom said, "publicity and action."

"Which do you feel is the more important?" Hopkins asked mildly.

"I don't think their importance can be rated," Tom said, "for the purpose of publicity would be to get action."

"That's very true," Hopkins said, as though he had just heard something very profound. "What kind of action do you think we should try to get?"

A waitress came and replaced the empty cocktail glasses on the table with full ones. "Of course, I'm just talking off the top of my head," Tom began, "but theoretically I suppose we could urge people to donate more money for research on mental illness, we could try to get them to vote more state and federal funds for mental hospitals, and we could suggest some kind of direct action at the local level, such as the organization of community psychiatric clinics."

"How would we do that?" Ogden asked in an unmistakably bored voice which contrasted sharply with Hopkins' enthusiasm.

"I suppose we'd have to consult with a lot of people to determine that," Tom said quickly. "I certainly couldn't tell you now."

"Of course," Hopkins said reassuringly. "None of us can spell anything out at this stage."

Walker sat looking amused and saying nothing. Tom's nervousness was returning. A waiter took orders for food.

"I hear you live out in Westport," Hopkins said to Tom. "I live out that way myself — I just got a place in South Bay."

"South Bay!" Tom said. "I was born there. My Grandmother lives out there now."

It was ridiculous, but Tom found it some-how impossible to think of Hopkins in South Bay. It seemed to Tom that everyone in South Bay either was something like his grandmother and her friends, or was a buyer of one of the unlikely-looking houses which had been built on the golf course. Certainly Hopkins fitted neither category.

"We just built a little place down by the water," Hopkins said. "It's a beautiful town, isn't it?"

He must have bought the old yacht club's land — I heard it was for sale, Tom thought. I wonder what kind of a place he's got. Aloud he said, "I think you'll like it there — I've always thought South Bay the nicest town within commuting distance."

"Stop in next time you visit your grand-mother," Hopkins said. "We'd be delighted to see you."

He sounded as though he meant it. Tom suddenly saw himself and Betsy and the three children, all with the chicken pox, descend-ing on the Hopkins household. What kind of a wife did Hopkins have? Bill Hawthorne had mentioned all sorts of rumors, but it didn't seem possible that they could be true.

"Do you play croquet?" Hopkins asked.

"Yes," Tom said, though he hadn't played

for fifteen years. He had a vision of himself playing croquet with Hopkins, using solid gold balls and silver mallets.

"We'll have to have a game sometime," Hopkins said. "I used to play tennis, but I'm getting a little too old for it. . . ."

Throughout the meal, Hopkins continued to chat as though the luncheon were strictly a social occasion, rather than an opportunity for him to inspect a prospective employee. Before dessert was served, however, he glanced at his watch. "My!" he said. "I've got to be getting back to the office! Would you people excuse me?"

Before the others could stand up, he waved cheerily and dashed toward the elevators.

"Coffee?" Walker asked Tom.

"Please," Tom said.

There was a heavy silence, while Tom wondered what, if anything, had been decided. What was the next step? Would Hopkins and Walker and Ogden all get together now and decide whether to hire him, and if so, when would he hear?

"Cigarette?" Ogden asked.

Tom accepted one. It seemed funny they didn't give him some kind of hint about what to expect. Maybe Hopkins hadn't liked him and had kept up the friendly patter just to get through a difficult lunch. Maybe he would get a letter in a couple of days which would begin, "We tremendously enjoyed talking with you, but we're sorry to say there have been some changes of plan. ..."

Walker painfully pulled himself to his feet. "Got to be getting back," he said. "Nice to have seen you, Mr. Rath."

He sounded friendly, but noncommittal. Ogden made no motion to get up. "See you," he said to Walker and poured himself another cup of coffee.

Maybe he'll tell me now, Tom thought. Maybe he'll just be frank and say, "I'm awfully sorry it didn't work out. ..." Still, how could he know what Hopkins had thought? He hadn't had a chance to speak to Hopkins while Tom wasn't there. Maybe they have some signal, Tom thought. Thumbs down.

"It was a very nice lunch," Tom said tentatively. "Thank you very much. ..."

"Glad you could come," Ogden said. "More coffee?"

Coffee was the last thing Tom wanted, but apparently Ogden didn't want him to leave yet. He accepted the coffee and waited. Ogden sat staring expressionlessly out the window, and for a long while said absolutely nothing. The tension mounted. Tom couldn't make up his mind whether Ogden was just being completely matter-of-fact about the luncheon, or whether this was an act of deliberate cruelty.

"We'll be in touch with you before long," Ogden said finally. "Mr. Hopkins has got to go to the West Coast tomorrow, and we may have to wait until he gets back before making any final decision. Meanwhile, I wouldn't count too heavily on anything. It's not entirely definite yet that we're even going to tackle this mental-health project."

"I understand that," Tom said, and hurriedly added, "I've got to be getting back to my office now — thanks again for the lunch."

He almost fled from the table. When he thought of Hopkins, it seemed certain that he would get the job, for if Hopkins hadn't liked him, why would he have been so friendly? But Ogden had been careful to pave the way for a letter ending the whole thing. Anyway, I met Hopkins, he thought. He seems like a nice guy pretty much like anybody else. Whatever it is that makes him worth two hundred thousand dollars a year is certainly well hidden.

8

When he got back to his office he found a slip of paper on his desk saying that his wife had called and that it was important for him to call her back. He put the call through immediately.

"It's your grandmother," she said. "She fell and broke her thigh. At her age, Tommy, bones don't knit. She wants to see you, and you better go out there right away. I would have gone myself, but I still feel pretty rocky, and the doctor's with her — it's not a real emergency."

"I'll go right out," Tom said.

The next train to South Bay was a local one, which stopped almost every five minutes. Tom sat on a soiled green seat in the smoker staring out the window. He didn't want to think. At first there were only the dark caverns of Grand Central Station to see, with the dim figures of tired-appearing men in overalls occasionally illuminated by naked electric-light bulbs. Then the train emerged into the bright sunlight and was surrounded by the littered streets and squalid brick tenements of Harlem. Tom had passed them twice a day for years, and usually he didn't look at them, but now he didn't want to think about his grandmother and he didn't want to think about Hopkins, and the tenements absorbed his attention. There was one grimy brick building with a huge billboard showing a beautiful girl thirty feet long lying under a palm tree. "Fly to Miami," the sign said. Directly under the girl's head, about six feet below the edge of the billboard, was an open window, outside of which an orange crate had been tied. In the orange crate was a flowerpot with a withered geranium, and as the train passed it, an aged colored woman with sunken cheeks leaned out of the window and poured some water from a milk bottle into the flowerpot.

"Ticket?" the conductor asked. He was a stout, red-faced man. Tom gave him his commuter's ticket.

"We don't go as far as Westport," the conductor said.

"I'm getting off at South Bay."

"Westport tickets are no good on this train," the conductor said. "You'll have to buy a ticket to South Bay."

"But South Bay is on the way to Westport," Tom objected.

"I don't make the rules," the conductor said.

Tom paid for a ticket to South Bay. The whole damn world is crazy, he thought. Grandmother is hurt and probably dying, and she brought me up, and I should be thinking only the kindest thoughts about her, and I can't.

She's dying, he thought. She's lived ninety-three years, and it's all been a free ride. She's never cooked a meal, or made a bed, or washed a diaper, or done a damn thing for herself or anybody else. She's spent at least three million dollars, and her only comment has been that money is boring. She's had a free ride for ninety-three years, and I'm damned if I'll cry about the end of it.

Yet to his astonishment he suddenly felt like crying. She doesn't want to die, he thought. I'll bet the poor old lady's scared.

Suddenly he remembered a night soon after his mother had died when a particularly violent thunder squall had struck the old house. Although he had been fifteen years old

100

then, he had been afraid to stay in his room alone. He had gone to his grandmother's room, and she had played double solitaire with him half the night. If she wants me to, I'll stay with her, he thought. I guess Betsy can get along without me for a few days.

As soon as the taxi let him out at the front door of the big house, old Edward opened the front door for him. "The doctor's in the living room, Mr. Rath," he said. "He was hoping to see you before he went."

"Tell him to wait," Tom said, and raced up the stairs to his grandmother's room. The door was closed. Cautiously he opened it, in order not to awaken her if she were asleep. There was her big four-poster bed, with the old-fashioned crocheted canopy. The old lady was lying in the precise center of the bed, propped up on pillows. She was looking out the window at the Sound, where a fleet of small sailboats was racing in the distance. She turned her head quickly and smiled at him. "I'm glad you're here," she said "They're trying to take me to the hospital."

"I'll talk to them," he said.

"My leg broke. I didn't fall and break it — it just broke, and then I fell."

"I'm sorry, Grandmother," he said. "We'll get you fixed up in no time."

"Don't be ridiculous," she said. "I'm going to die, and I prefer to die here. I detest hospitals."

"I'll talk to the doctor," he said.

"Never mind that. I want you to make sure they don't take me to the hospital. They keep giving me drugs, and I don't want to wake up in some iron cot with a lot of supercilious nurses telling me what to do."

"I'll do my best," Tom said.

"The Senator died in this bed, and I want to die here too."

"I'll talk to the doctor now," Tom said.

"Stay here. There's plenty of time. I've got lots of things I want to tell you and I may be asleep when you come back up. Do you know I've left everything I've got to you?"

"I didn't, Grandmother," he said. "I'm very grateful."

"There's not much," she said. "For the last ten years I've been living off capital. And there's a small mortgage on the house. You won't get much."

"Try to sleep now," he said. "We can talk about business later."

"We might as well get it over with now. Did you know that most of your grandfather's estate was lost long ago?"

"Yes, Grandmother."

"How did you know?"

"I guess you must have told me. I think I've always known it."

"I'm sorry things have happened this way," she said. "The Senator and I had so much. I've always been sorry we couldn't do more for you."

"You've given me a great deal," he said.

There was a long moment of silence during which she seemed to be breathing with difficulty, but she kept her eyes intently on his face, and he saw she didn't want him to go.

"I want you to do something for Edward," she said. "He has to be kept in his place, but he's been loyal. He's old and should be provided for."

"I'll try, Grandmother," he said.

She closed her eyes. "How do you think the house looks?" she asked drowsily.

"Beautiful."

"I have tried to keep it up for you," she said. "The west wing . . ."

The sentence trailed off, and Tom saw she was asleep. After waiting a few minutes to be sure, he went downstairs. His grandmother's doctor, an elderly man named Worthington, was waiting.

"I'm afraid your grandmother isn't very well," he began.

"How long do you think she can live?"

The doctor took off his glasses and started polishing them with his handkerchief. "She's broken her thigh," he said, "and I think the pelvis may be fractured too. She took a bad fall. She says her leg just snapped and she fell, and it may actually have happened that way. We won't be able to tell about the pelvis till we take her to the hospital and get her X-rayed."

"She doesn't want to go to the hospital," Tom said. "Is there really much point to it?"

"We've got to get X-rays," the doctor replied, sounding shocked. "And we can't give her proper care here!"

"Won't she die pretty soon, anyway?"

"She will if she doesn't get proper care!" the doctor said angrily. "With the proper care, we might be able to keep her going for quite a little while."

"She'll be miserable in a hospital."

"I'll call an ambulance," the doctor said. "There's no question that she has to go."

"I don't think she'll allow you to take her."

"We'll fix it so she won't know a thing about it," the doctor said. Picking up a black bag, he climbed the stairs to the old lady's room. Tom didn't try to stop him. So she's going to wake up in an iron bed in a strange room after all, he thought.

9

Florence Rath died only eight days later, complaining not so much of a broken thigh and a fractured pelvis as of the refusal of the doctors to obey her.

"They *know* they can't cure me, so why don't they send me home?" she asked Tom every day, and he was never able to invent a plausible answer.

Perhaps on the theory that she might be sent home if she made herself unpleasant enough, she made as much trouble as possible and constantly insulted everyone.

"The nurses are so *common!*" she said loudly to Tom, "and the doctors aren't much better. They all look like a lot of *druggists!*" She made the word sound like an unpardonable obscenity.

For the entire eight days, she constantly demanded services of everyone. Every few minutes she called a nurse to ask her to smooth her covers, or to change the water in the many vases of flowers with which she had surrounded herself. She asked doctors to make telephone calls for her and even asked one elderly physician to go out and buy her a paper. The night nurse simply disconnected her call bell.

Never once, however, did the old lady complain of pain or show any fear of death. She made no attempt to solicit pity, and it would have been impossible to feel truly sorry for so imperious a figure. Tom wasn't much surprised to find that in spite of the demands and insults she hurled at them, the doctors and nurses loved her. Tired and harried as they were, they ran errands for her and sat listening to the endless stories she told of the exploits of "The Senator" and Tom's father, "The Major."

She died in her sleep, two hours after Tom had left the hospital to go back to Westport. He had visited her every evening on the way home from work, after having arranged for a taxi to take Mrs. Manter home. By that time Betsy was able to care for the children a few hours by herself.

When the hospital called him to say the old lady had died, Tom said, "Thank you for calling," very quietly, and put the telephone receiver carefully back on its hook.

"What is it?" Betsy asked.

"Grandmother's dead," he said.

He went into the kitchen and got himself a drink. He was tired — for the last eight nights he hadn't been getting to bed until after midnight, and even then he hadn't been able to sleep. Everything seemed uncertain. He hadn't heard a word from United Broadcasting. He had no idea whether his grandmother would leave even enough money to cover her debts. While she was in the hospital, he had asked her for the name of her lawyer, but she had seemed offended.

"Wait," she had said. "I'll tell you when the time comes."

And she had told him, the afternoon before she died. The lawyer was Alfred J. Sims, a name Tom had never heard before in his life.

Now the thought that there was a large house with an old man in it who had worked for his grandmother half his life and who now presumably expected a pension from him worried Tom. The thought that Hopkins might decide not to hire him worried him, and the fact that Dick Haver seemed to be growing increasingly impatient over the whole situation worried him. Every day Dick asked him whether he had heard anything from United Broadcasting — he seemed to take a wry pleasure from the question. And beyond these worries, Tom faced accumulating small debts. Mrs. Manter's wages, the down payment on a new washing machine, and the daily taxi bill had wiped out his cash on hand, and he was charging everything he could, from groceries to medicine. Soon there would be his grandmother's hospital bill and funeral expenses. He wondered how long it would take to settle her estate.

"Isn't it funny she never told you her lawyer's name before?" Betsy asked.

"She never talked about business."

"Don't you think you should get a complete accounting from the lawyer? I mean an accounting for all the money she lost — it seems awfully funny that she lost so much. For all we know, the lawyer's been cheating her for years."

"I'll get a complete accounting," he said.

That night he slept hardly at all. In the morning he telephoned Sims, who apparently had only a residence in New York and no office. The lawyer's voice was high pitched, with a pronounced Boston accent. "I've been expecting to hear from you," he said. "Your grandmother's death was a great shock to me.

Her papers are all in order, and I don't think you need expect any difficulty."

Sims's house was a brownstone structure on Fifty-third Street. After telling Dick Haver he wouldn't be in all day because of his grandmother's death, Tom took a taxi there. A uniformed maid opened the door and ushered him into a dimly lit study lined with books. Sims, a gaunt-faced man about sixty years old, was sitting in a wheel chair behind a desk littered with papers.

"I'm glad to see you, Tom," he said. "Excuse me for not getting up. And excuse me for using your first name — I've known your family far too long to use anything else."

"I'm glad to meet you," Tom replied.

"Your grandmother was a great woman," Sims said. "She's the last of her kind."

"I know," Tom replied abstractedly. He was staring at a photograph of a young man, a rather faded photograph which he was quite sure was of his father. The photograph was in a leather frame on Sims's desk.

"You recognize the picture?"

"My father?"

"Of course. Your father and I were good friends. We were classmates at college, and we were in France together."

"I never saw that picture before," Tom

said. He picked the frame up and inspected the photograph more closely. It showed a man five or six years younger than himself. The man wore a tweed cap, and he was smiling boyishly. Tom put the photograph down. Somewhere in the back of the house a clock struck the quarter hour.

"Now about your grandmother's estate," Sims said, picking up a folder with a blue cover from his desk. "As I presume you know, you are the sole heir."

"She told me," Tom said.

"And I presume you also know that there isn't much in the estate."

"How much?"

"This may come as something of a shock to you, but when the estate is completely settled, I don't think you'll have much except for the house. There are some securities of course, but there's also a mortgage on the house, and there'll be an inheritance tax. And I suppose you'll want to do something about Edward."

"I'll have to see," Tom said. "Just what is the value of the securities?"

"I haven't checked the current market value recently, but there will be about twenty thousand dollars. Not much more. If your grandmother had lived a few more years, I don't know what we would have done."

"And the mortgage? How much is that?"

"Ten thousand dollars."

"I don't understand it!" Tom blurted out. "Do you have any idea how much Grandmother inherited from her father and from Grandfather, and how she managed to lose it?"

"What has she told you?"

"Nothing!"

"But you knew she had lost a great deal."

"She told me just before she died, and I guess I've always assumed it, from the way she had to economize."

Sims sighed. "What do you know about your father?" he asked.

"What kind of man was he?"

"He was delightful," Sims said. "He was possibly the most charming, talented man ever born. That's why I wish you could have known him — you would be proud of him."

"What happened to him?"

"I don't know — it's pretty hard to explain what happens to people. When we were in college together, Steve could do anything. During the first few weeks we were overseas, he was the best officer I've ever seen. He was the last man I'd ever expect to have a nervous breakdown, but that's what he had. In those days we called it shell shock. They sent him home, and after he had spent a few months in a hospital, he got a job with Irvington and Wells — that used to be just about the best brokerage house on the street. He tried awfully hard there — I guess I'm one of the few people who really knows how hard he tried, and how much he wanted to succeed — but he wasn't well. He couldn't concentrate on anything, and sometimes he got so nervous during conferences that he'd have to get up and walk out of the room. Old Wells loved him like a son — everyone loved your father — but finally he had to ask him to take some time off and try to get himself under control. Your father had just been married a few months, and it was a great blow to him. He and your mother lived with your grandmother, and the idleness didn't do him any good. He asked your grandmother if he could handle her estate, and your grandmother thought it might give him confidence to let him try. He made some bad mistakes — that can happen to anyone. Your grandmother was patient, but he got panicky — he was determined to get back everything he'd lost. He started taking long shots on the stock market and losing more and more. I tried to reason with him, but getting back all the money he had lost seemed a matter of life and death with him. I talked it over with your grandmother, and she finally decided she had to take what was left of her estate out of his hands. The night she told him that, he started driving off somewhere and was killed."

"Was it suicide?"

"I don't know. He left no notes. When we looked into things, we found he had recently taken out some life insurance that had a suicide clause in it. The insurance company paid. We also found that his losses had been worse than we knew. Four fifths of your grandmother's estate was gone."

Sims paused. "In 1928, I managed to build up the estate a good deal, and we were lucky enough to get out before the crash," he continued. "I must admit, though, that I never could get your grandmother to live on a budget — she aways felt that she was entitled to a certain standard of living, and that she would maintain it as long as she had a cent. I don't know what she would have done if she had been forced to sell that house — I'm glad I never had to find out."

"Thanks for telling me all this," Tom said. "I don't know why, but I feel a lot better knowing."

"Your father's death was a great shock to

your grandmother," Sims said. "She was determined never to tell you about it. And she never wanted any member of her family to have anything to do with her money after that, either. That's understandable, of course, but she carried it to extremes. She never wanted you to meet me — she was afraid I'd tell you about your father. I think she'd be angry it she knew I was telling you now."

"She gave me your name," Tom said.

"She knew you finally had to know. Anyway, there's nothing for you to be ashamed of. He was a fine man."

Sims wheeled his chair to a cupboard near his desk and took out a bottle of sherry. Tom noticed that his hand shook as he poured it into two glasses. Suddenly the older man looked up and smiled. "You see," he said, "I understand your father. The war hit me too. Not only my legs — my hands."

"It almost happened to me," Tom said.

"You were in the last one?"

"Not Korea. The one before that."

"But you came out all right."

"I wasn't in sustained action," Tom said. "We didn't have trench warfare. I don't think I could have taken that. I was usually thrown in for a few days and then taken out."

"I remember now," Sims said. "I know what you were in. It scares hell out of me just to think of it."

The sherry tasted good. When they had finished it, Sims said, "I've prepared a dossier on the whole estate — a complete history of it, in fact. I'll have it typed up and mailed to you. It may take several months to get the will through the probate court. If you need cash in the meantime, I can arrange for a bank to give you a loan on the securities."

"I may need cash," Tom said. "I'm broke. And until the house is sold, things are going to be tough."

"Don't sell it too fast," Sims said. "Your grandmother has twenty-three acres of the best land in South Bay. It ought to be worth something."

10

That night when he got home to Westport, Tom found a letter from United Broadcasting. "We're sorry to have taken so long before getting in touch with you," it said, "but Mr. Hopkins has been on an extended trip to the West Coast, and it has not been until now that we have been in a position to discuss final arrangements with you. Mr. Hopkins enjoyed meeting you, and if you would care to drop into my office Friday at 11 A.M., I hope we can work something out." The letter was signed by Ogden.

"It's good news, isn't it?" Betsy asked.

"I guess so."

"You don't sound very excited."

"I'm confused," Tom said. "I don't see how we can do everything we're supposed to do."

He had already told Betsy about his conversation with Sims. They both sat thinking about the necessity to make some sort of decision about old Edward, and how to sell the big house most advantageously, and how to keep it up meanwhile, and how at the same time to start a new job.

"The trouble is," Tom said, "I have no idea what we're going to net on the estate, and it may be months before we know. That old house is pretty much a white elephant, I'm sure, but until we sell it we won't have any idea whether we're going to end up in the hole, or with quite a lot."

"You worry about United Broadcasting," Betsy said. "I'm feeling pretty well now. I don't need Mrs. Manter any more, and I'll make all the arrangements about your grandmother's house. Don't worry about it for the next month. I've already talked to Edward and told him we wanted him to stay on for another month, until we know what arrangements can be made. He's going to live there as a caretaker."

"You've already spoken to him?"

"He telephoned here for instructions."

Tom sighed. "The funeral's tomorrow," he said, "and the next day, I'll see Ogden and make some kind of decision there. After that I'll worry about Grandmother's house."

The day after the funeral when Tom went into the United Broadcasting building, he did not think at all about the familiar-appearing elevator operator until he saw the man standing outside his elevator, smoking a cigarette. Instinctively wishing to avoid him, Tom quickly walked into another elevator. When he got to Ogden's outer office, a secretary told him he might have to wait quite a long while, because someone from out of town had come in unexpectedly to see Ogden. Tom sat in a comfortable leather chair. His thoughts kept returning to the elevator operator. It was ridiculous to be preoccupied with such a matter, he told himself; what possible meaning could it have? Still, it was maddening not to be able to place the man's face and that deep, familiar voice. With an effort Tom forced himself to think about his coming interview with Ogden.

"Have you made up your mind whether you want to work with us?" Ogden asked when Tom finally got in to see him.

"I don't really know enough details to make a decision," Tom said. "We haven't discussed salary."

"We discussed it, but I guess we didn't reach an agreement," Ogden said casually. "I understand your salary at the Schanenhauser

Foundation has been seven thousand a year. We are prepared to offer you eight."

Tom hesitated. It didn't seem feasible for him to bargain with United Broadcasting, but it also didn't seem possible that Hopkins would worry about two thousand dollars more a year if he really wanted him. "I've had a long talk with Dick Haver," Tom said finally, "and I understand my prospects are fairly good at the foundation. . . ."

"We don't believe in starting people at high salaries," Ogden said. "If new employees prove themselves here, their compensation is adjusted accordingly."

Tom visualized himself going back to Dick Haver and saying he had decided not to go to United Broadcasting. Dick would probably let him wait a long while for a raise after that. Still, if Hopkins really wanted him, now was the time to hold out.

"I'm sorry," Tom said. "There is always a certain amount of risk in starting a new position, and I feel I should be compensated for it. I want ten thousand a year."

"We wouldn't feel justified in giving you that," Ogden said easily. "We don't like to quibble about these things, for we feel that if a man really wants to work for United Broadcasting, it isn't necessary. Nevertheless, we

119

might stretch a point and give you nine thousand. I'm afraid we couldn't do more than that now."

If I still held out, I might be able to get more, Tom thought, but he dreaded the possibility of another week's indecision while Ogden and the others conferred. "All right," he said. "I'm very pleased to accept the position. I feel it will be a great privilege to work for Mr. Hopkins."

"Fine!" Ogden said. "We're delighted to have you. Can you start in a week?"

"I ought to give the foundation at least two weeks' notice."

"We need you right away — Mr. Hopkins has a speech he has to prepare. I'll see if we can fix it up with Dick Haver."

"If Dick approves, it's all right with me," Tom replied.

"One more thing," Ogden said. "You'll be working with Mr. Hopkins, but you'll be responsible directly to me. And for the first six months you'll be on a temporary basis."

"I understand."

"Good luck," Ogden said, concluding the interview. "We're looking forward to a very happy relationship."

When Tom got home that night there was a long bright-red Jaguar convertible parked in the driveway of the little house in Westport. In the living room Betsy was seated on the sofa, talking to a short thin man dressed in a soft tweed suit.

"This is Mr. Swanson Howard," she said to Tom as he came in the front door. "He wants to talk to you."

"How do you do, Mr. Swanson," Tom said.

"It's Swanson Howard, not Howard Swanson," the man said, getting to his feet. He was almost a foot shorter than Tom.

"Of course," Tom said. "I'm glad to meet you."

"Anybody want a drink?" Betsy asked.

"Martini?" Tom suggested to Howard.

"A little Scotch on the rocks," Howard said.

"I'm afraid we don't have any Scotch," Betsy said.

"A Martini will be fine then," Howard replied, and lit a cigarette. "I was very sorry to hear of Mrs. Rath's death."

"You knew her?" Tom asked.

"I knew of her." Howard looked around the room, and Tom imagined that his eyes dwelt on the crack in the wall, and the soiled upholstery on one of the chairs. "I understand she left you her house," Howard said.

"That's right."

"Do you plan to move into it?"

Betsy came from the kitchen, carrying a tray with a pitcher of Martinis and three glasses. "I'm sorry, but there aren't any olives or pickled onions or lemon peels or *anything* to go in it," she said. "Anyway, we've got the essentials."

Howard accepted a drink, but kept his eyes on Tom.

"We expect to sell it," Tom said.

"I might be interested in buying the place," Howard said casually, and took the first sip of his drink. Betsy sat down suddenly in the nearest chair.

"The estate won't be settled for quite a while," Tom said.

"I understand that of course, a place like that isn't easy to sell, as I'm sure you know. The property needs a lot of work. The house is old-fashioned, and far too big for most people. The taxes are about twenty-two hundred dollars a year, and it would cost about twenty-four hundred a year to heat the place. And of course it couldn't be run without servants. You won't find many prospective purchasers for a property like that, and it will be expensive for you to hold for long."

"You seem to know a lot about it," Tom said.

"I like the place. I like the view. We might be able to work something out."

"Do you want to make an offer?"

"My offer would probably sound low to you," Howard said. "It would be based solely on the value of the land. Although I might live in the house, I'd figure it had almost no market value."

"How much would you offer?"

"Twenty thousand dollars."

"I'll have to consider it," Tom said. "I won't be able to give you an answer for a long while."

"I'm afraid I'd have to know within a week or so," Howard said. "We're considering several properties." He took an engraved card from his pocket and handed it to Tom. "Hearthside Restaurants, Inc.," it said in large letters, and in smaller letters at the left-hand bottom corner, "Mr. Swanson Howard." In the right-hand corner was an address on Thirty-third Street in New York and a telephone number.

"Would you be buying the house as a residence for yourself?" Tom asked.

"Of course. If we can get a decision within a week or so."

"I'll be in touch with you," Tom said.

Howard thanked him for the drink, smiled

mechanically, and left. A moment later the engine of the Jaguar roared — apparently he had a cutout on the exhaust.

"What do you think?" Betsy asked excitedly. "You'll hold out for more, won't you?"

"I don't know," Tom said, stretching out exhaustedly on the couch. "By the way, United Broadcasting hired me today. The salary's nine thousand, and I'm on a temporary basis for six months. I'm supposed to start in a week."

"That's wonderful!" Betsy said. "Oh, Tommy, let's put this damn little house on the market tomorrow! Everything's going to be wonderful for us — I can just feel it!"

The front door slammed, and Barbara rushed in, followed by Janey and Pete. "Momma!" Janey said excitedly. "There are some boys across the street with knives, and they said they're going to *stick* us!"

"They're probably rubber knives," Betsy said.

"They're *real knives!*"

"Play upstairs then," Betsy said. "Your father and I are talking."

"They said they were going to chop off our hands and our legs and our heads and everything!"

"They were just fooling," Betsy said. "Upstairs!"

"But they *weren't* fooling!"

"UPSTAIRS, or I'll call Mrs. Manter!"

The three children immediately went upstairs.

"The name Mrs. Manter still works," Betsy said gratefully. "I don't think you ought to sell Grandmother's house to that man. He's in too much of a hurry. With a salary of nine thousand we could afford to hold it for a while."

"I don't know," Tom said. Unaccountably, he felt depressed and pessimistic. "Suppose we turn down this offer," he said, "and suppose that after six months, they tell me I'm through at United Broadcasting. And suppose we can't sell Grandmother's place. Then what do we do?"

"Don't be absurd," Betsy said. "I'll bet that at the end of six months you get a big raise at United Broadcasting. Hopkins seemed to like you, didn't he?"

"Sure, he seemed to like me. Hopkins seems to like everybody. With the money he makes, why shouldn't he? I tell you, Betsy, I'm uneasy. I don't like this guy Ogden, and it's him I'm really going to be working for. I don't like being responsible for old Edward.

What are we supposed to do, pay him a salary for the rest of his life, or give him a lump sum? You can't throw an old man like that out on the street. And I'm worried about Grandmother's house. It would cost us at least six thousand a year to hang onto it, counting mortgage, taxes, minimum repairs, and a caretaker of some kind. You'd have to have a caretaker there, or it would go to hell in no time. Are you going to keep a house that costs you six thousand dollars a year on a salary of nine thousand? And what happens when you lose the job paying you the nine thousand?"

"You can't look at things like that," Betsy said. "You've got to plan on things going all right. I've never seen you lose your self-confidence!"

"I haven't lost it, but maybe it's time we started being sensible. All we've ever thought about is getting out of this house. The more I think about it, the more I think that's crazy. This house is plenty comfortable enough. With nine thousand a year, we could afford some life insurance. Did you ever stop and think what would happen to you if I dropped dead some morning?"

"Don't think about it!" Betsy said. "I'd drop dead right alongside you."

"Then what would happen to the children?"

"What's gotten into you, Tommy? I've never heard you talk like this before!"

"I think we've both always assumed that Grandmother would be waiting to catch us if we tripped," he said. "Maybe it's time we grew up. She's not there any more."

"All right, get some more insurance," Betsy said, "but when we sell Grandmother's place, we can still afford a better home."

"Can we? Let's say that after we take care of old Edward, we net twenty thousand dollars out of Grandmother's house. Let's say I hang onto my job, and over the years get a few small raises — I'm beginning to doubt like hell I'm going to get rich quick on a mental-health project. Let's say, though, that in ten years I'm making fifteen thousand. How are we going to send the kids to college?"

"On fifteen thousand it would be easy!"

"Maybe — but we've never lived on a budget yet. For a while, all three kids will be in college at the same time. We ought to figure at least three thousand dollars a year for each child at college. That's nine thousand a year, *after* taxes. That means we'll need thirty-six thousand dollars to send three kids through college. Do you think you could take that out of my salary?"

"We'd manage it somehow. Anyway, they wouldn't need three thousand a year."

"I needed it, and that was fifteen years ago, almost. We've never talked about this, Betsy, but I figure we owe our kids the same kind of education we got, and that's what Grandmother's money really should be used for."

"You plan to live the rest of our lives *here?*"

"We could do worse."

"I don't give a damn," she said. "I won't be noble. Not unless you make me."

"Think it over," he said.

"I *have* thought it over. It's not fair to the children to bring them up in a neighborhood like this!"

"What's wrong with this neighborhood?"

"It's *dull.*"

"You mean 'The Senator' wouldn't like it?"

"That's cruel," she said. "Anyway, 'The Senator' is your ancestor, not mine. I mean that I don't like it, and I'm not ashamed to admit it!"

"It's time we forgot the Rath family's dreams of glory, and *your* family's dreams of glory too," he said. "It's time we started being sensible."

"My family never had any dreams of glory!"

"Didn't your father borrow ten thousand dollars to throw that coming-out party where I met you?"

Betsy flushed. "Where did you hear that?"

"He told me himself. He was very honest about explaining to me that I wasn't marrying any money."

"Dad borrowed it to keep a promise," she said. "Ever since I was a little girl, he promised me a big coming-out party, and when the time came, he couldn't afford it. So he borrowed the money. That's the kind of a man he was. And he paid every cent back."

"It was nice of him," Tom said, "but don't you think that was a crazy promise to make to a little girl? Hell, when you were a little girl, you didn't care! He was making a promise to himself."

"It was a lovely party," Betsy said. "I'll never forget it. And if I hadn't had it, I might never have met you."

"Most expensive damn introduction in the world!" Tom said. "We've got to get that kind of stuff out of our minds."

"I haven't even *mentioned* a coming-out party for Barbara and Janey," Betsy said. "All I want is a decent house, without a damn-fool crack in the wall like a question mark, and without everything coming apart."

"We can have the wall replastered," Tom said. "I'm going to bed."

He took a half tumblerful of Martinis up with him and lay for a long while sipping it in the dark. When it was finished, he went to sleep. He had no idea how much later it was when Betsy awoke him by shaking his shoulders hard. "Go away," he said. "I'm asleep."

"Wake up!" she said. "I've got a wonderful idea!"

She almost rolled him out of bed. The light was bright in his eyes. "Tell me in the morning!" he said.

"No!" she said. "Now!"

He struggled to a sitting position and rubbed his eyes. "What time is it?"

"It's only about one o'clock. Ever since you've been asleep, I've been sitting downstairs thinking, and suddenly I got it!"

"Got what?"

"This idea!"

"Go to sleep."

"No! You've got to listen to me!"

"I will if you get me a drink," he said.

She rushed downstairs and came back with a glass half full of gin and ice. "There's no more vermouth," she said, "but this ought to fix you."

He sipped it and made a face.

"Now!" she said. "Will you listen?"

"Is there a choice?"

"What I want to do," she said, "is to sell this house and move into Grandmother's house. Not for good, you understand — just until we can figure out what to do with it."

"That's wonderful," he said. "Grandmother wanted us to add another wing. Do you plan to do that too?"

"Be quiet. Now you stop and figure, Tommy. We've got twenty-three acres in South Bay, the only twenty-three acres with a view anything like that. Even around here, good one-acre lots sell for as much as five thousand dollars apiece. If we divided that land up, we might get as high as a hundred thousand dollars!"

"Sure," he said. "But there are a few other things to consider. Things like zoning restrictions. Things like building roads, so people could get to their lots. Things like wells and sewers."

"Exactly," she said. "And we couldn't figure all that out while we were living in Westport and you were working in New York. But if I were living in Grandmother's house, I could *see* the zoning board, and show contractors the place, and all the rest of it."

"And what if it didn't work?"

"We'd still be there to sell Grandmother's place. And we'd have the money from selling this house. And we could let Edward stay with us."

"Let's talk about it in the morning," Tom said.

"We can't give Edward a pension — we never could afford it. And I bet he'd rather stay right in the old house."

"Talk about it in the morning," Tom repeated.

"And there are even more possibilities! Let's say we took all our available money, from selling this place and from Grandmother's estate and everything. Let's say we took it all and converted Grandmother's carriage house into a dwelling. It could be a *charming* place. Let's say we did that and sold it with one acre of land for forty thousand dollars. Places like that go for *at least* that, and I bet we could fix the old carriage house up for twenty thousand. That would give us a profit of twenty thousand. We could use that to build *another* house and sell that for profit. We could put up a whole housing development, one house at a time. Maybe we could make *more* than a hundred thousand!"

"I'm dizzy," Tom said. "To do that, you'd need capital. You'd have to know the real-estate business and the building business. And you should be able to devote full time to it."

"I can learn, and I will devote full time to it."

"And in the end we'd lose our shirts," Tom said. "I know it."

"In the end we might have a hundred thousand dollars and the pick of the new houses for ourselves."

"Dreams of glory," he said. "I've spent my whole life getting over them."

"Look, Tommy," she said. "You said I should think, and I did. You know what you are? You're spoiled. You've spent most of your life feeling sorry for yourself because you knew Grandmother wasn't going to leave you a lot of money. You're spoiled and you're licked before you start. In spite of all you did in the war, you're not really willing to go out and fight for what you want. You came back from the war, and you took an easy job, and we both bellyached all the time because you didn't get more money. And what's more, you're a coward. You're afraid to risk a goddamn thing!"

"Thanks for the character reference," he said.

"You've gotten to the point where you disrespect anybody who does what you can't do," she said. "You sneer at the United Broadcasting men, and everybody else. You think you're something special because a hell of a long while ago you were a good paratrooper. And now all you want is security, and life insurance, and money in the bank to send the kids to college twelve or fifteen years from now, and you're scared because for six months you'll be on trial on a new job, and you always look at the dark side of everything, and you've got *no guts!*"

Suddenly she broke into tears. "I love you, Tommy," she said between sobs. "I just had to say it."

For several minutes the room was quiet.

"You're partly right," he said suddenly.

"I exaggerated," she said. "And, Tommy, you've got more guts than any man I ever saw. Do you know why I love you, Tommy? It's a funny thing — it's childish. It's because I never saw a man I thought could get away with making you really angry."

"Plenty have," he said.

"It's not just strength," she said. "It's something in you. When you really want something, I don't think anything in the world can stand in your way. That's why you were so damned good in the war."

"It was luck," he said. "Whether you get

out of a war or not is ninety per cent luck."

"Maybe," she said, "but since you've gotten back, you haven't really wanted much. You've worked hard, but at heart you've never been really trying."

"We'll have a go at this real-estate thing if you want," he said. "I still doubt like hell that it will work. If we wind up broke, can you take it?"

"I can take it," she said. "And you can too. I know what you're thinking about."

"My father."

"I know. But it's better to think of Barbara and Janey and Pete, and a new life. I haven't been really trying, either. From now on I'm going to change."

11

When Tom awoke in the morning, Betsy was already dressed. Her hair was combed and she had put on lipstick.

"What time is it?" he asked.

"Six-thirty."

"Good God," he said. "Go away. I've another hour to sleep."

"No you *don't,*" she said. "No more rushing for the train."

"What?"

"This is the new regime. We're going to have a leisurely breakfast before you go to work."

"Oh, God!" he said.

The three children came in and stood by the bed staring at him. Their hair was all combed, and they had on freshly ironed clothes. "Momma got us up early," Janey said mournfully. "Are you going to get up too?"

"He certainly is!" Betsy said. "Tom, I've got a lot of important things I want to say to you. Get up this minute!"

There didn't seem to be much chance of getting any more sleep, so Tom climbed out of bed, groped his way to the bathroom, and started to shave. When he went downstairs, he heard a coffeepot percolating. The coffee smelled good. In the kitchen he found the breakfast table fully set and waffles cooking. "What's going on?" he asked Betsy.

"Breakfast," she said. "No more instant coffee. No more grabbing a piece of toast to eat on the way to the station. We're going to start living *sanely.*"

He sat down and poured some maple sirup on a waffle.

"No more hotdogs and hamburgers for dinner," Betsy said. "I'm going to start making stews and casseroles and roasts and things."

"Just watch the grocery bill," he said.

"No more television."

"What?"

"No more television. I'm going to give the damn set away."

"What for?"

"Bad for the kids," she said. "Instead of shooing them off to the television set, we're going to sit in a family group and read aloud. And you ought to get your mandolin fixed up. We could have friends in and sing — we've been having too much passive entertainment."

Tom poured himself a fragrant cup of coffee. "I'll need the television for my work," he said.

Betsy ignored him. "No more homogenized milk," she said. "We're going to save two cents a quart and shake the bottle ourselves."

"Fine."

"And we're going to church every Sunday. We're going to stop lying around Sunday mornings, drinking Martinis. We're going to church in a family group."

"All right."

"*Peter!*" Betsy said.

Pete had just slowly and deliberately poured half the bottle of maple sirup over his waffle. The sirup had overflowed the plate and was now dripping on the floor. "You *know* you shouldn't do that!"

"Don't be cross," Janey said. "It was an accident."

"It was *not* an accident," Barbara said. "He did it on purpose. I saw him."

"Don't be a tattletale," Betsy said, wiping

up the sirup with a damp rag. "You children are going to learn some table manners. No waffles for you, Pete."

Pete immediately began to howl at the top of his lungs. "Give him his waffle," Tom said hastily. "It was an accident."

"No," Betsy said. "We're going to start having some consistent punishment around here."

Pete put his thumb in his mouth and stared at her solemnly.

"It's almost time for me to catch my train," Tom said. "Are you going to drive me to the station, or can I take the car?"

"You're going to walk!" she said. "It's time you started getting some exercise."

"I'm going to take the car," he said. "Unless you want to drive me."

"*Can't* you walk?"

"I'm tired this morning," he said. "Are you going to drive, or shall I take the car?"

"I'll drive," she said judiciously. "Get in the car, kids!"

The children scrambled into the car. All the way to the station, Betsy sat uncomfortably erect. Hardly any cars were at the station when they got there, and they saw they had ten minutes to wait for the train. They sat in silence.

"You think I'm being silly, don't you?" Betsy said suddenly.

"I'm just a little startled."

"We ought to start doing the things we believe in," she said. "We've got a lot of hard work ahead of us, and we better start now."

He kissed her and went to buy his paper. On the train it was both cool and quiet. He sank down in a blue plush-covered seat. All up and down the aisle men were sitting, motionless and voiceless, reading their papers. Tom opened his and read a long story about negotiations in Korea. A columnist debated the question of when Russia would have hydrogen bombs to drop on the United States. Tom folded his paper and stared out the window at the suburban stations gliding by. He wondered what it would be like to work for Ogden and Hopkins, and he wondered whether Betsy's schemes could possibly turn out successfully. What would happen if he got fired by Hopkins and Betsy's real-estate deals turned into a fiasco?

"It doesn't really matter." The words came to his mind so clearly that he half thought someone had spoken them in his ear.

"Here goes nothing."

The sentence sounded in his mind, flat and emotionless. Suddenly the tension drained out of him, and he felt relaxed. It will be interesting to see what happens, he thought. Then he had a sudden impulse to laugh. The man across the aisle from him peered over his paper suspiciously, and Tom turned his face toward the window. A railroad track alongside the ones on which he was speeding gleamed brightly in the sun.

"It doesn't really matter." During the war that had been a kind of key phrase for him, almost a magical charm, an incantation. He had always been tense before a jump. He had always started worrying about Betsy — that was the first stage, as soon as he learned he had another jump coming up. He had had a clear picture in his mind of a Western Union boy delivering a telegram to her beginning, "The War Department regrets to inform you . . ." Betsy would open the telegram, and then she'd go upstairs to the big bedroom in Grandmother's house, and she'd show it to Grandmother, and Grandmother would say, "You should be proud. He died for his country." And then Betsy would start to swear — he had always been able to see her staring at his grandmother, crying and swearing, exactly as his mother had long ago.

That vision had always given way to another, on the eve of a combat jump. He'd start thinking about how he'd never go to bed with Betsy again. And he'd start thinking about all the cold beer he was never going to drink, and the rare steaks he was never going to eat. Then he'd start getting mad.

By the time he'd got his parachute on, or had "chuted up," as they had called it in the 'troops, he had usually widened his self-pity to embrace all the others aboard the plane. The poor bastards, he had thought. The men had sat in their bucket seats on each side of the aisle of the plane, as expressionless as the men on the commuter train — about the only difference was that during the war they had had no newspapers. Tom had often sat there, expressionless as the others, thinking of a whole platoon of Western Union boys delivering the War Department's regrets. He had heard men talk about premonitions of death before a battle, and often when someone was killed, it would turn out that he had told someone about a premonition, but Tom had had premonitions all the time.

The worst part of the whole nightmare had always come just a few minutes before the jump. A sharp image of a compound fracture of the right thigh would suddenly flash into his mind. During his first combat jump the man beside him had landed wrong and suffered a compound fracture of the right thigh. A long jagged splinter of bone had come through the trouser leg, and the man had sat there staring at it until someone had given him a shot of morphine. Tom had never seen him again, because the Germans had started moving in on them, and it had been necessary to abandon the man with the broken thigh, lying there doped up, still staring at the splinter of bone. Tom had never been able to forget it, and almost every time after that he'd catch himself gripping his own right thigh a few minutes before he had to jump. It was at such times that this silly sentence would come into his mind, and he'd start to relax.

"It doesn't really matter."

The words had had a marvelous effect on him. He had often repeated them to himself, until they began to sound like some kind of revelation. By the time it had been necessary to stand up and walk toward the open door of the airplane, he had always been able to move as casually as though he were just going to step into the next room.

"Geronimo!" a lot of the men used to yell as they jumped, trying to sound fierce as hell. Tom used to yell it too when it was expected of him, but what he was really thinking, with a curiously comforting air of detachment, was

"It doesn't really matter." And then, just as Tom went through the door into the prop blast, the second part of the charm had always come to him: "Here goes nothing." And when the parachute had opened, with its terrific wallop at the back of his neck, and he found himself floating down in that curious moment of complete quiet and calm which immediately precedes a combat landing, the third part of his incantation had always come to him: "It will be interesting to see what happens."

All this seemed incredible to Tom as he looked back at it, but those three catch phrases still had the power to soothe him as he sat on the train, one of many men holding newspapers on their laps, and thought about a new job and what Betsy called "the start of a new regime."

By the time he got to New York, he felt relaxed. What the hell is all the crisis about? he thought. After the whole damn war, why am I scared now? I always thought peace would be peaceful, he thought, and laughed. As he walked through Grand Central Station, he looked up and for the first time in years noticed the stars painted on the blue ceiling there. They seemed to be shining brightly, and feeling slightly theatrical, he wondered if it were legitimate to wish on a painted star. He decided it would be all right to make a phony wish, so he wished he could make a million dollars and add a new wing to his grandmother's house, with a billiard room and a conservatory in which to grow orchids.

12

It was while he was walking up Forty-second Street from Grand Central Station to his office at the Schanenhauser Foundation that he saw the man with a leather jacket. It was an ordinary brown leather jacket with a sheepskin collar — it was only unusual that the man should be wearing it in the summer. The man was a swarthy, rather rumpled individual, wearing dungarees, a T-shirt, and the leather jacket, unzipped. Somehow the jacket nagged at Tom's mind — he had seen one like it somewhere a long while ago. It was ridiculous to have one's mind keep returning to a leather jacket when there was work to be done. The memory of the leather jacket was like a riddle, the answer to which had been half forgotten, obscurely important, as though someone had told him a secret he was never to repeat, a secret with some hidden meaning, but now he couldn't remember it.

Trying to put the jacket out of his mind, he hurried along the street. While he was waiting to cross Fifth Avenue, a man standing beside him coughed painfully. Then Tom remembered about the leather jacket — remembered everything about it as clearly as though he had never forgotten.

It had been back in 1943, not many months before Germany started to disintegrate. Only he hadn't known then that Germany would fall to pieces — it had seemed as though the war would go on forever. It had been in December, early in December, that he killed the man in the leather jacket, simply because he needed the jacket for himself.

No, it hadn't been like that at all. There was no use making it worse than it was. The man in the leather jacket had been armed, he had been an enemy, legally decreed such by several governments. He had been a German, and the Germans were different from other people, or at least it had seemed so at the time. How hard it was to remember what the Germans had seemed like then! They had been unconquerable. They had been efficient. They had been professionals at war, while everybody else was an amateur. They had been cold and pitiless. They had been

Jew beaters. They had shot, burned, and gassed millions of innocent people. They had laughed at weakness, they had taken joy in cruelty, they had been methodical, they had done things According to Plan. They had started the war, they had been infinitely guilty. The man with the leather jacket had been eighteen years old.

Jesus Christ, that doesn't make any difference! Tom looked up at the traffic light on Fifth Avenue. The man beside him coughed again. The boy with the leather jacket should not have coughed; it had been his cough which had given him away.

"Now listen. One thing you've got to get through your heads is we're not playing games!"

That was a curious sentence to remember. It had been spoken in a harsh voice, matter-of-fact rather than fierce, perhaps a little exasperated, the voice of a teacher confronted by slightly stupid pupils, the voice of the old master sergeant who had prepared Tom for his assault on the boy with the leather jacket, the old master sergeant to whom, in a sense, Tom owed his life, for if he had not learned the lesson, he himself, rather than the boy with the leather jacket, might now be only a painful memory.

"Now listen. One thing you've got to get through your heads is we're not playing games! When you're behind the enemy lines, you don't take prisoners — if you do, you have to stay awake all night to watch them, and the odds are they'll trip you up someway, anyhow. There's no use taking a chance. You see a Jerry, you don't go through this cowboy crap of telling him to put up his hands; you just shoot the bastard, in the back if possible, because you take less chances that way. We ain't playing games. And let's not have any tend-the-wounded crap. The wounded can get you with a hand grenade or a pistol — I've seen it happen a hundred times. There's no use taking a chance. Either don't go near the wounded, or finish them off before you go near them. We ain't playing games."

Well, Tom thought as he entered the office of the Schanenhauser Foundation and sat down at his desk, he had played no games back in 1943, when he had met the boy in the leather jacket. There had been no time for games. Tom and Hank Mahoney had been alone — the whole company had been busted up, it had been snafu from the beginning — situation normal, all fouled up, only they hadn't used the word "fouled" in those days; no word had been anywhere near bad enough

149

to express the way they felt. They had jumped at the wrong time at the wrong place, and a quarter of the company had been killed by rifle and machine-gun fire before they hit the ground. That had been no time to have sad thoughts about eighteen-year-old German boys. They had jumped and been jumped, by a whole damn division, it had seemed like, and Tom had had just one idea: I'm going to get out of this alive and *don't* try to stop me. No, he hadn't thought that; it had been different from that. He had thought: I'm going to try to get out of this, I'm going to try; I'm not going to die for lack of trying.

Everything had been confusion. They had jumped from the planes just at nightfall, about a hundred men dropped behind the German lines to destroy a bridge. They had been supposed to land in a field near a copse of woods without opposition and proceed to the bridge under cover of darkness, but it hadn't been like that at all. The Germans had been waiting; they had sent up flares and turned search-lights on the men dangling from the glistening white parachutes in the air. And those who survived had panicked as soon as they hit the ground. They had been green troops, many of them, boys who had never been on a combat jump before, and as soon as they saw that things weren't going according to plan, they panicked and went running across the field toward the trees, and the Germans had really had it that time; they had simply lowered their antiaircraft guns and had a real turkey shoot right there at the edge of the forest. The paratroopers had been trained to crawl like snakes at a time like that, to hide like lizards on the ground, but most of them had forgotten, and had dashed toward the woods, running scared, big as snowmen in the searchlights and the flares. It hadn't been necessary for a man to be very bright to be a soldier; all he had had to do was to remember a few basic rules, the most obvious one being to crawl when under fire, to slide like a snake, to live like a lizard, but that time the green troops had panicked and most of them, instead of living like lizards, had died like men.

Tom had gathered twelve men around him, lying on their bellies in the snow and the mud. He and Hank Mahoney and ten other men who kept their heads had crawled in a wide circle and made the woods, all right, at about ten o'clock in the evening. Going into the woods, they had crawled single file, one man thirty feet behind the other, leaving a track like a great snake through the snow and

151

the mud, with Tom as lead man, fifty feet ahead of the others, because the woods might be mined, and it would just be foolish to let a mine kill more than one man. They had been wet to the skin long before they reached the woods, and it had been cold, very cold, as a half moon climbed above the naked trees. Tom and Hank Mahoney and the other ten men had sat huddled together in the woods for a few minutes, until Tom, thinking of the great snake's trail they had left behind, had ordered them to disperse and try to get back to their own lines by different routes, traveling in pairs because it would be just foolishness to let the Germans catch them all at once.

So they had split up, and Tom had never seen most of the men again, nor heard what happened to them. Mahoney had gone with him. The two of them had walked as fast as they could through the woods, planning to circle home eventually, but hoping soon to find dry clothes, or an abandoned hut, or someway to escape the cold.

Shortly before dawn they had reached the edge of the woods and, shivering violently, had hidden behind an ice-glazed rock and looked at what they finally made out to be a German tank depot, with orderly rows of barracks topped by chimneys out of which wisps of smoke had been curling, black and velvety against the frosty sky. It had been then that they heard a man cough only a few hundred yards away from them, and they had crawled back into the trees and along the edge of the woods, keeping under cover, until they saw two sentries in leather, sheepskin-lined jackets, the dry collars turned snugly up around their ears. The younger and slighter of the two sentries had been the one doing the coughing. He had been standing about thirty feet outside the woods, looking down at his feet and coughing. With his right hand he had been negligently holding his rifle, and with his left he had been clutching his chest. The other sentry had been standing about twenty feet from him, his rifle cradled in one arm, watching his companion cough, and looking worried.

It had not been necessary for Tom and Hank Mahoney to talk. They had crawled toward the sentries over the hard crust of old snow in the dim light of the setting moon. It hadn't been difficult. They had been able to crawl within ten feet of the sentries before jumping them silently — it hadn't been difficult at all, and only one small cry had been made, not a very loud sound, the sort of noise a man might make in his sleep, not the sort of cry to alarm the whole camp. Tom hadn't even had to use his knife at first — he had choked the sentry to prevent him from shouting, and when he had taken his hands away, the boy had seemed dead. Tom and Mahoney had stripped the bodies of the warm clothes, and the sheepskin collars had felt delicious against their own cold ears and necks. Before daylight, they had effaced all signs of the struggle and dragged the bodies into the woods behind a fallen tree in the hope that the Germans would think for a little while that their sentries had just gone over the hill. They had been about to leave the bodies lying stretched in the snow when the sentry Tom had choked groaned and moved one arm.

"I made sure of mine with my knife," Hank had said. "Better finish yours off, or he'll come to and rouse the whole camp."

Tom had taken out his sheath knife and had hesitated. The young German sentry had lain at his feet, helpless as a patient on an operating table.

"Hurry up," Hank had said nervously. "We've got to get out of here."

Tom had knelt beside the sentry. He had not thought it would be difficult, but the tendons of the boy's neck had proved tough, and suddenly the sentry had started to sit up. In a rage Tom had plunged the knife repeatedly into his throat, ramming it home with all his strength until he had almost severed the head from the body.

"Come on, that's enough," Hank had said in a shocked voice. "Let's get out of here."

Trembling, Tom had stood up and followed Hank out of the woods. They had skirted the tank depot, until on the other side of the gully they found a burned-out tank which apparently had been left there to await shipment back to Germany as scrap. They had climbed into the wrecked tank and huddled in the cinders until nightfall.

In the pockets of his newly acquired leather jacket Tom had found chocolate and cough drops and a wallet with no money, and an identification card with a picture of a thin, serious-looking youth eighteen years old named Hans Engelhart, and there had also been a letter written in a fine feminine script on thin, blue, slightly scented paper, but the letter had been in German, and Tom hadn't been able to read it. On the upper-left-hand corner of the envelope had been printed what obviously was a return address. The absurd idea of writing the sender of the letter had flashed into Tom's mind. What would he say? "This morning I killed your boy, and I would like to send my condolences. He was in the wrong army, but he seemed like a nice boy, and I'm sorry it had to happen like this." Impulsively he had torn the letter into small bits, together with its envelope, and, trying to forget the feeling of the plunging knife in his hand, had lain in the ashes to sleep.

After dark, Tom and Hank Mahoney had crawled out of the wrecked tank and had begun the long, circuitous journey back to their own lines. Skirting the tank depot, they had returned to the woods. In the darkness they had tried to head west, but they had soon become confused and after about two hours had realized that they were retracing their steps.

"In a few minutes the moon will be up, and we can see better," Hank had said. "Let's sit down for a breather."

They had continued to walk until they found a tree trunk to sit upon. Through naked branches they had seen the moon climbing above the crest of a distant hill. Gradually the darkness had dissolved. They had just started to walk again when Tom noticed the two bodies they had left there that morning and realized that they had come full circle. The bodies had been lying just as they had left them, except that their faces had acquired the sardonic grin of death.

"I guess they have the last laugh," Hank had said. "I don't think we're ever going to get out of here. The dead always have the last laugh.

"Come on," Tom had replied. "We've got to try."

Together they had resumed their journey, making better progress in the moonlight. At about midnight they had come to the field where they had landed. It was still strewn with equipment, and the dead. Stealing from body to body, they had collected six boxes of K-rations and five full canteens of water. After eating and drinking their fill, they had pressed on. Just before dawn exhaustion and the continuous cold had combined to make them lightheaded, and they had staggered along, holding each other up like drunks returning from a party. There had been no more woods — only fields affording little protection. "Before it gets any lighter, we've got to find a place to hide out," Tom had said. At sunrise they had found a crater gouged in the earth by a crashing plane. Eagerly they had slid into the tangle of wreckage within it, only to be greeted by a fearful stench. "I can't stand this," Mahoney had said. "Let's keep going."

"No," Tom had said, nodding toward the endless fields which lay in front of them. "We'd be picked up sure. You'll get used to the smell."

Mahoney had gagged.

"Anyway, it's going to be a nice day," Tom had said. "We're better off than if it were raining, and we've got plenty to eat and drink. Look at those clouds over there — they look warm. It's a nice morning."

He had paused, suddenly and incongruously remembering the lines of verse carved on the bench in his grandmother's garden so far away: "The lark's on the wing; the snail's on the thorn: God's in his heaven — all's right with the world." He had started to laugh. Collapsing into the mud at the bottom of the hole, he had given himself over to almost maniacal laughter.

"You nuts?" Mahoney had said.

"No. I just thought of something — something I can't explain," Tom had replied. Mahoney had been too tired to question him further. They had curled up in the mud at the bottom of the crater full of wreckage and immediately had slept, not awakening until dusk. The sun had warmed them, and they had both felt refreshed and rested. "I think we're going to make it," Tom had said. "For the first time, I really think we're going to make it."

They had made it all right, six days later, and upon rejoining their company had been looked upon as heroes by the young recruits who replaced the men who didn't come back. There had been one young corporal who had been in the army only a few months, a thin boy of Italian ancestry, who had wanted to buy the German jacket, and Tom had given it to him. Gardella, the corporal's name had been — "Caesar" Gardella, the boys had called him. He had had a deep voice. Now, Tom suddenly froze at his desk in the offices of the Schanenhauser Foundation. Caesar Gardella! That was the elevator man at the United Broadcasting building! It was Caesar Gardella, grown fat and with a mustache! And the leather jacket wouldn't be all he'd remember; he'd remember everything that had happened after that — the jump on the island of Karkow and, before that, Rome and Maria. Tom found he was gripping his thigh and sweating.

Maria.

It is not my fault, he thought; it was not my fault; it was nobody's fault at all. It happened a long while ago.

Maria.

I have forgotten her, he thought. I haven't thought about her for a long time; I really haven't thought about her; she never entered my head for a long time.

It really wasn't my fault, he thought. It was no one's fault. I am not to blame.

How curious it was to find that apparently nothing was ever really forgotten, that the past was never really gone, that it was always lurking, ready to destroy the present, or at least to make the present seem absurd, or if not that, to make Tom himself seem absurd, the perpetuator of an endless and rather hideous masquerade.

I am a good man, he thought, and I have never done anything of which I am truly ashamed. Curiously, he seemed to be mimicking himself. "I am a good man," he seemed to be saying in a high, effeminate, prissy voice, "and I have never done anything of which I am truly ashamed." A gust of ghostly and derisive laughter seemed to ring out in reply.

It's the way things happen, he thought, and if I were to go through it all again, they would happen the same way.

It's funny, but I can think about it now, he thought — I can see what happened, after all these years, I can finally see what happened, and it's absurd to be ashamed.

Maria. The time was December 1944. The place, Rome. And everything was different. Now, as he sat behind his desk at the Schanenhauser Foundation in the year 1953, Tom felt again the blind helpless fury that had started it all, back in December 1944, when, after fighting one war and getting it almost won, he and Mahoney and Caesar Gardella and all the rest of them had got orders to go to the Pacific, without even a day of leave in the States between wars. The whole company had got those orders, after having made two combat jumps in France and two in Italy. Someone had got the idea that the way to save lives in the invasion of the islands of the Pacific was to use more paratroopers. Take the islands from the air instead of going in on the beaches, somebody had said — send us more jump boys; we want to get this thing over in a hurry and all go home.

"Another day, another war," Mahoney had said when he heard it.

Tom had said nothing. I got through one war, he had thought. I won't get through another. The odds build up against you. They throw you in once, and you fight your way out. You do it twice, you can do it three times. But sooner or later the odds catch up with you. It's like throwing dice — sooner or later you get snake eyes. If they're going to send me out to the Pacific, I won't come back.

He had had a clear picture then, as soon as he heard where he was going, of a Japanese soldier, a caricature of one, with a small evil face, grinning, and holding a bayonet poised. That's my boy, he had thought. That's the one who's waiting for me. I've had the Germans and I've had the Italians, and now the Japs are going to have me.

"Anyway," Hank had said, "they say they're going to give us a week here before we go, and it won't even be counted as leave."

"A week?" Tom had said.

"Sure! How much money you got?"

"I'm broke," Tom had said. His allotment to Betsy had never left him much. Since the beginning of the war, he had allotted her two thirds of his salary, and she had put it all into a savings bank, so that they could buy a house after the war. He had never minded being broke before.

"Don't worry," Hank had said. "I'm loaded. I got six hundred bucks I won in a crap game, and I'll give you half. This will be a week to remember!"

Betsy, Tom had thought, but somehow she

had dissolved into nothing more than an ironic and rather painful memory, something to be kept out of his mind. I've got a week, he had thought, a week in Rome, a week on the town. And to Mahoney he had said, "Okay, Hank, let's go."

It had been a week to remember, all right. They had started in a small bar in the basement of a cheap hotel. In the corner there had been a piano painted white, with a thin, bald, blind man playing old American jazz very badly. It had been there he had met Maria. She had come into the bar hesitantly with painfully obvious intention, and every man in the room had glanced up and looked at her, a pretty girl, eighteen years old, in a worn black dress and a coat that had once belonged to a soldier. She had walked over to the bar meekly and ordered a glass of vermouth. She had sat on a stool in front of the bar and had taken off her coat, which had been clumsily retailored to fit her, and she had laid it across her lap while she sipped her vermouth slowly to make it last a long time. Tom had looked at her coldly. Young, with a good figure, and a face which, if it were relaxed, could be beautiful — it might as well be this one as any other. When you've only got a week, you can't look around forever. He had walked over and sat down beside her. "Can I buy you a drink?" he had asked.

It had been real romantic. She had glanced up at him with a forced smile on her lips. "Thank you," she had said in a strong Italian accent. Her voice had been soft and timid.

"Well, I see you're fixed up," Hank had said, coming over and leaning on the bar beside Tom. "I'm going to shove on — there's nothing else around here. Let's meet here tomorrow morning."

"All right," Tom had said.

He had sat beside Maria sipping his sweet vermouth, the picture of the grinning little man with the bayonet still in his mind. "You'll be all right," Betsy had written him in her last letter. "I'm absolutely sure you'll come home to me all right."

Pretty Betsy, he had thought, as he sat sipping the sweet vermouth. Pretty Betsy, with the pretty shoulders and the soft skin tanned by the summer sun. I will not think of Betsy.

I have a week, he had thought, seven days and seven nights, the amount of time the world was created in. He had glanced then at Maria, who also had been sitting sipping her vermouth and looking down thoughtfully, and he had seen that she was prettier than he had thought, that her face, when in repose, was still the face of a young girl, and that her body was as beautiful as the body of any woman, and much more beautiful than most.

"Do you speak English?"

"A little," she had replied in her strong accent. "My father spoke English. Sometimes he used to be a guide for tourists."

"My name's Bill Brown," Tom had said, "William T. Brown from Kansas City, Iowa. What's your name?"

She had shrugged. "Maria," she had said.

"How about a meal, Maria? Let's get out of here and get a real dinner! You like champagne?"

"Yes."

They had gone to a big restaurant with white table linen and waiters in dinner coats, as though there had never been a war at all. For an enormous price they had eaten roast chicken and fried potatoes and pastries, and they had had champagne, all right, champagne which the Germans had brought to Rome from France. She had eaten greedily and drunk little. When the meal was over, and the waiter paid, she had quietly asked him to go to her room with her; he hadn't even had to hint at all. They had got into a taxi and ridden a long way, down dimly lit streets, with the silhouettes of tall buildings

165

ruined by time rather than war black and jagged against the moonlit sky. They had not talked. In the taxi he had kissed her once, finding that her lips were unbelievably soft and that he had forgotten what a kiss was like. The despair, the fury of having to fly to another war, and the cold loneliness that had been sitting in his stomach so many months, through so many battles and the intervals between battles, had left him, and somehow the sense of cheapness and sordidness had gone, and he had felt relaxed and completely happy for the first time in two years, for the first time since he had got aboard the slate-gray troopship which had carried him from New York into the fog of the North Atlantic an endless number of months ago.

"You are beautiful," he had said.

The taxi had stopped in front of a tenement house. An old woman had leaned out a window and watched them with open curiosity. After paying the driver, Tom had followed the girl through a courtyard jammed with debris, into a dark hall. There had been no light. The girl had taken his hand and led him up five winding flights of stairs, littered with cardboard boxes and bottles. Moonlight had streamed through the window at each landing. The pitch-darkness of the stairs between landings had not been like the darkness of a battlefield, an impenetrable wall concealing only danger and death. It had been a protecting darkness, friendly, warm, almost soft and caressing. She had led him to her room, and he had snapped a light switch, but no light had come on, and she had lit a candle, bending over it seriously as the flame from the match in her cupped hands grew, first showing her silhouette, and then her face, with shadows flickering in the candlelight. He had kissed her again, and with the tips of her fingers she had caressed the back of his head, and his neck and his shoulders, very gently, hardly touching him at all, and when the kiss was over, she had smiled, and the look of strain had gone from her face, and it hadn't been sordid any more. She had taken off her clothes and stood there golden in the candlelight, incredibly beautiful.

He hadn't gone to meet Mahoney in the bar in the morning. He had lived with Maria for a week, shunning everyone he knew, and in that week he and Maria had built a small, temporary world for themselves, full of delights and confidences, a completely self-sufficient world, packed with private jokes, and memories, a whole lifetime with silver and golden anniversaries, Christmases and birthdays, fifty years compressed into a week. They had kept no secrets from each other. He had told her his real name. Lying on the bed naked, taking great pleasure in nakedness even when their passion was spent, they had talked endlessly, discussing all troubles, all angers, all fears, and for that week, nothing had seemed very bad any more, even the inevitable prospect of the grinning little man with the bayonet, whom he introduced to her, and whom she acknowledged sadly, as a person she knew well. They had understood each other, the three of them, Tom and Maria and the caricature of the man waiting with a gun.

At the end of the week, Tom had said good-by to her and reported back to his unit, only to be told that transportation wasn't available yet and that he could live wherever he wanted as long as he checked in, or at least telephoned headquarters, every morning at eight o'clock. He had returned to her room, and it had been exactly as though he had returned from a long absence, the young husband coming home from the wars: they had both felt that way, they had both experienced all the happiness of a reunion, without the awkwardness which follows long absence.

He had lived in the room with her, thinking that each day was the last, thinking that tomorrow at eight o'clock the sergeant who answered the telephone would say, "Oh, yes, Captain Rath — we've got a plane leaving in two hours. You better get right down here." He had kept his bags packed, and every morning at seven o'clock he had kissed her and crept out of bed and got himself fully dressed, in case it would be necessary to hurry, and each morning for seven weeks, for forty-nine days in all, the sergeant had said, "Nothing yet, Captain — the colonel asks me to tell you to be sure to check in tomorrow."

There had been forty-nine last days, and the greatest pleasure in the world had been to walk back to her room from the restaurant where he made his telephone calls at eight o'clock in the morning, shivering a little in the dampness, and to hear her say delightedly, "Not yet?"

"Not yet!" he had said forty-nine times and, still shivering from the coldness of early morning, had jumped into the warm bed beside her.

During those forty-nine last days, they had grown old together, patient of each other's weaknesses, and they had even acquired old family friends, men in bars who nodded to them and recognized them as a couple who belonged together, old ladies on street corners who addressed Maria as a married woman, respectable as themselves. And in particular, they had acquired one friend, almost an uncle, or perhaps a brother, a melancholy man who owned a bakery, where hot coffee was served, a wonderful place to have breakfast. The man's name had been Lapa, Louis Lapa, and he had fought with the Germans against the Americans and, a little later, with the Americans against the Germans, fighting both times well, but without enthusiasm. Finally he had been wounded and had returned to his bakery with his foot in a cast, and when Tom and Maria sat down to have breakfast in his shop, he brought hot rolls and coffee, limping badly and coughing, but always smiling. After the first few days he had often sat down to join them, drinking a cup of coffee himself, of course knowing without being told a great deal about Tom and Maria, knowing that they had just met, and that they would soon part, and feeling sad about this, but also companionable. They had come to know Louis well and on one occasion had even invited him to visit them in their room, and they had had a quiet family evening together, with Louis admiring Maria's beauty the way a friendly brother or uncle might admire the beauty of a young wife. He had called her the most beautiful girl in Rome and had told Tom he was lucky, and Tom had replied that he was indeed lucky, and he had felt this to be true.

They had had many friends, other Americans living with Italian girls, and one of them had been Caesar Gardella, who had turned out to be intensely religious, who had tried to get an audience with the Pope, and who told everyone he was going to come back to Rome and marry his girl after the war was over. His girl's name had been Gina — she was a cousin of Maria's or some sort of distant relative. Tom and Caesar and Gina and Maria had sat drinking together on several evenings, and it had been almost like a suburban community, with the men all working for the same big corporation. But after seven weeks, the sergeant at headquarters had told Tom he had to hurry, transportation was available — the plane was due to leave in three hours. After hearing that over the telephone, Tom had raced back to Maria's room, and it had been then she had told him she thought she was pregnant, she wasn't sure, but she thought she probably was. There had been no recriminations. She had asked nothing, and he had denied nothing. She, knowing he was married, and knowing he was flying to the Pacific to meet his grinning little man with a gun, had assumed he could do nothing much for her and had been surprised and grateful when he borrowed five hundred dollars from his friends and gave it to her, along with a jeepful of canned goods and cigarettes and chewing gum, all of which was worth a great deal.

"If you are pregnant," he had said, "will you have the child?"

"God willing," she had replied, and he had been glad, absurdly glad that in flying to meet his evil, grinning little man with the bayonet, he was leaving a child behind, even if it were to be a child with no father to care for it; a ragamuffin child dancing in the street for pennies, perhaps, but at least a child, which was better than to die and leave nothing, as though he had never been born.

But of course he hadn't been sure about the child; it had been only a possibility. He had been sure about nothing, as he boarded the plane and sat in the hard, uncomfortable bucket seat, waiting to take off for the long flight to the Pacific. How strange to think that he might have a child, never to see, never to hold, but a child just the same! How strange that after all the long months of killing, there would be finally, perhaps, the birth of a child, and that this would be the one thing he had done in the last two years which could conceivably lead to trouble. This, of all he had done, would be the one deed which could lead to a court-martial, and stern disapproving looks on the part of commanding officers, and colonels shaking fingers in his face, and social ostracism at home, if he ever got home, and divorce, and a very bad name, instead of medals.

How strange, he had thought, as he sat in the plane: what a curious inversion, how to the despair of the chaplains is the inclination of the young soldiers to forget their job of killing and to run off and make love!

He had started to laugh as the plane took off, and above the roar of the engines Mahoney had shouted, "What the hell is funny?"

"We're all nuts!" Tom had said, with a feeling that he had at last discovered the great fundamental truth. "We're all nuts, every goddamn one of us — we're all absolutely nuts!"

"You're god-damn right!" Mahoney had replied.

"Ever hear of Karkow?" Caesar Gardella had asked an hour later.

Tom had heard of it vaguely, a small island not far from the Philippines, a very small island which the British had held for two months against strong Japanese attack at the beginning of the war, but had finally lost. "What about it?" he had replied.

"I hear," Caesar had said above the roar of the engines, "I hear they're going to drop us on it."

It was just a rumor, Tom had thought, but at such times the rumors are always right. Karkow! What a curious name for a place to die!

The plane had stopped at many places, hurrying to refuel, always in a hurry to get to its destination, until finally it had deposited Tom and Mahoney in a transient officers' camp in Hollandia, New Guinea, where there was nothing to do but lie all day on cots under mosquito netting and wait for the attack on Karkow. Lying there, drinking heavily chlorinated water or warm beer when he could get it, Tom had wondered what he would do if he were not killed at Karkow, or wherever he was going. What did one do when one had a wife in the States and a woman and maybe a child in Italy? Did one simply take one's choice? After he had been in New Guinea about two weeks, the letters Betsy had written him almost every night had caught up with him. In the first one he opened she had said:

174

TOMMY MY DARLING,

Gosh, what a day this has been! At eight-thirty this morning — *eight-thirty*, mind you — Dotty Kimble telephoned me and wanted me to play bridge in the afternoon. It seems that Nancy Gorton had promised that she would be her partner in a tournament at the club, and at the last minute Nancy got a telegram that John was getting a week-end pass, so of course she simply took off for South Carolina. That left Dotty without a partner in this tournament which she seemed to think was awfully important — you know how seriously she takes things like that. Well, anyway, I said all right, and guess who we played in the very first game? Lillie Barton and Jessie Willis! You'd die if you saw Jessie now — she's gained about *fifty* pounds, and she's worried to death that she won't be able to take it off after the baby comes. She's due next month. Anyway, I thought I'd die when I found we were going to play her and Lillie, because you know what sharks they are. Well, to make a long story short, you would have been proud of me, darling — I won't even try to be modest. Dotty and I won!

We each got a perfectly adorable majolica bowl for a prize. I've wrapped mine up and stored it with our wedding presents, and after the war, when we buy our house, I'm going to put it right in the middle of our dining-room table, and every morning you can take an orange out of it and think how smart I am!

Can't think of anything more to say now, except I miss you like anything. If I sent all the kisses I'd like to give you, this letter would have to go parcel post!

I love you forever and forever and forever and forever!

BETSY

Her other letters had been much the same. They had contained descriptions of movies she had seen, and dreams of the future, when he would have a job with J. H. Nottingsby, Incorporated, or some firm with a name which would have to sound like that. Along with the easy optimism, the cheerfulness, and long, involved jokes, Betsy had sent him pictures of herself, snapshots of a slender, fresh-faced girl, hearty, healthy, and smiling, a girl he had seen someplace sometime, long ago, a real beauty.

Perhaps I shall go back to Italy, if I go any

where at all, he had thought. If I go back to Italy I shall betray one person, but if I go home to Betsy, perhaps I shall betray two. It had been strange to lie on the narrow canvas cot in New Guinea and think of a son, perhaps, the grandson of "The Major," his own son, the great-grandson of "The Senator," the likeness of himself, dancing for pennies in the streets of Rome. If he did not go back to Rome, what would happen to such a son? He would go wandering barefoot, begging for chew-chew gum, a child without a father, the son of a harlot grown ugly and bitter. That's my boy, he had thought while lying on the hard canvas cot in New Guinea; that's my boy. If I get it on Karkow, that will be the only part of me I'll leave behind.

He had decided that if he survived the war he would go back to Italy, at least to see how Maria was making out, and he envied Caesar Gardella, who got long letters in Italian from his girl in Rome, and who considered himself formally engaged and talked constantly about getting married after the war. Maria had never written Tom at all. It had been her kind of faithfulness not to write, to allow herself to be forgotten. But apparently Gina had written something to Caesar about her, for Caesar's attitude toward Tom had changed — he had become reserved and disapproving, and with an edge to his voice, he had for the first time begun to call Tom "Sir." Now in his office at the Schanenhauser Foundation, Tom got up and stared out the window at the city below. He had not thought of Karkow for years. If Karkow had not cauterized his mind, he might not have forgotten Maria so easily, and things might have been different between him and Caesar. How had it started? He had first heard the name Karkow as a rumor, while flying from Europe. After he had lain for weeks in a transient officers' camp in New Guinea, the rumor had grown until it was substantiated by a colonel who had called Tom and Mahoney and many other officers into his matter-of-fact office, with a matter-of-fact map on the wall, to brief them.

Karkow was a small, jagged island, with steep rocky cliffs on all but one side. The Japs, like the British before them, had had many guns trained on the gravel beach on that one side, waiting for an invasion, and they had honeycombed the island with tunnels and caves. The island lay in the mouth of a large bay, and it had to be taken — no one had doubted that. The plan for taking it was simple, the colonel had explained in his matter-of-fact way: three thousand paratroopers would be dropped on it.

"Damn it to hell!" Mahoney had said that night after the colonel had explained the plan. "Don't they know anything about how paratroopers work? You don't jump on top of the god-damn enemy! You don't throw three thousand men right down on top of nests of antiaircraft artillery and machine guns and thousands of armed men, ready and waiting!"

"Well, this time I guess they do," Caesar had said bitterly. "The colonel's sure the Navy will have blasted every gun off the island before we get there. Didn't you hear him?"

"I wonder," Tom had said, "how many of us will even hit the goddamn island? It's pretty small. I bet they dump half of us in the water."

The idea had been to take off for the jump at four o'clock in the morning and to start landing troops on the island with the first light of dawn. The plan had been for the Navy to start shelling the place two days beforehand and to have landing craft approach to make the Japs think the invasion was coming from the sea.

I will be sensible, Tom had thought late on the afternoon before the invasion. I will be sensible and go to bed early, and get a good rest. He had lain down on his cot and tried hard to think of nothing, to make his mind a complete blank. He had not wanted to think of the small island, Karkow, lying now under shellfire from the Navy, with the Japs in their caves. He had not wanted to think of Betsy, and he had not wanted to think of Maria. How painful had been the memory of a kiss or of anything good he would never have again! He had lain still, pretending to be asleep when Mahoney came in and stretched out on the cot near him.

"Tom?" Mahoney had asked after a few minutes.

"Yes."

"It's funny," Mahoney had said. "I was just thinking, we got nothing to worry about. I mean, we either don't get it tomorrow, and we got nothing to worry about, or we do get it tomorrow, and we got nothing to worry about."

"That's wonderful."

"No, I mean it. I been worrying a lot about what kind of job I'll get after the war. Now I'm not worrying about it."

"No worries," Tom had said.

They had both lain there on the canvas cots, unable to sleep, and a curious light-headed mood had taken possession of them, almost gaiety. At about one o'clock they had given up trying to sleep and had gone to a near-by dispensary, where some doctors were playing poker. They had joined the game and had accepted a few drinks of medicinal alcohol from the doctors, but they had not got drunk; they would have been crazy to do that. It had not really been necessary to get drunk. The jokes had all seemed astonishingly funny, in fact everything had seemed funny. The doctors had not known that he and Mahoney were supposed to take off in a few hours for Karkow. One of them had complained bitterly about having to be on duty all night, and about what a great financial sacrifice a doctor in the Army makes, because he could be making ten times more money at home. Mahoney had sympathized with the doctor, his great face morose and understanding, without a hint of irony, and Tom had laughed inside until his stomach hurt.

At about three o'clock Mahoney had said, "Well, I guess we got to be going. How about it, Tom?"

"I guess so," Tom had said.

"Hey, you can't quit while you're ahead," one of the doctors had objected.

"Sorry," Mahoney had said. He and Tom

had left the doctors without saying where they were going, not so much because they weren't supposed to tell as because it was more bitter and more funny to hear the doctors complain about breaking up the game too early.

Tom and Mahoney had gone from the card game to the mess hall and had had a big breakfast. They had sat together, looking at the young boys, the members of their companies, fresh recruits, most of them, filing into the mess hall, the sleep still in their eyes. More than half of them had never been in a combat jump, and they had looked incredibly young, almost like schoolboys as they filed into the mess hall to get a good breakfast before taking off.

"We've got five or six years on most of them," Mahoney had said, and Tom had understood that he said it in sorrow for the young boys, for at times like that, each year of age, each year behind you, seemed like a million dollars in the bank that could never be taken away, and the old were to be envied more than anyone on earth, for they had lived their lives, but the young were vulnerable — their lives could be stolen from them.

Breakfast had been over quickly. The men had lined up outside the mess hall, and trucks had taken them to the air strip where the big planes waited, their engines quiet, their propellers motionless. The men had strapped on their parachutes and checked their equipment. It had still been dark. The moon had been almost full, a lopsided moon, and the warm tropic night had been stroked by a breeze as soft as the touch of a woman's fingertips. The sky, even before dawn, had been full of peaceful birds, and the jungle beyond the air strip had hummed with life. Tom and Mahoney had walked out on the air strip together, but they had been assigned to different planes. As they parted in the middle of the air strip, Mahoney had said, "Take it easy, boy — and when you hit, close up with my boys fast. And keep those damn kids of yours from shooting my men up — it's going to be close quarters when we get there."

"You better not be worrying about that," Tom had said. "Don't let your kids freeze up — they'll do it every time. I'm telling my boys to go in shooting and to keep shooting until nobody shoots back."

Mahoney had grinned. "You're a tough bastard," he had said. "I'm glad you're on our side."

Tom had walked up the ramp of his plane, and Caesar Gardella had helped him to check to make sure his men were all there and that they were fully equipped. Tom had been cheerful and bluff — he had learned to do that by then. And as he had told Mahoney, he had given his troops one parting piece of advice. "Just keep firing," he had said. "Start firing when you hit the ground and don't stop till the place is ours. Remember just one thing: The trouble with most green troops is they don't fire their guns, especially when things are mixed up. They remember too much about 'Safety First.' Don't shoot each other if you can help it and don't shoot up the other companies, but keep firing. You're not going to be blamed if somebody gets hurt."

Tom had sat in the airplane, like the young boys on all sides of him, chewing gum and looking out the window in a matter-of-fact way. A sergeant had shut the door of the plane. Tom had swallowed twice as the engines coughed, then roared, and had fastened his safety belt as the plane started to taxi down the runway, rushing faster and faster, until it finally soared over the gleaming sea. He had grinned at the boys around him, and they had grinned back — that had been part of the ritual. The plane had gained altitude, and gradually it had begun to grow cold. Caesar had walked down the aisle passing out blankets. Out the windows of the plane, Tom had seen the pale stars, already beginning to fade before the approach of dawn. Anyway, I will leave a child, he had thought. It had been a curiously comforting thought.

The flight to Karkow had seemed short, far too short. It had been comparatively comfortable to huddle in a bucket seat under a blanket, with the engine droning drowsily. Far below, the moon had made a path on the sea, and there had been nothing else to look at until the flash of big guns at Karkow became visible. By the time the plane reached Karkow, it had been light enough to see — the whole operation had been behind schedule from the start. Thousands of feet below, the island had looked no bigger than a pebble on the ruffled surface of the sea. What had seemed to be only a few inches from the pebble, about twenty tiny-appearing ships had lain, and from both the ships and the island puffs of smoke occasionilly lit by pale flashes of flame had floated upward. The planes carrying the paratroopers had circled at a high altitude, waiting for the ships to finish their bombardment. Suddenly the smoke from the ships had stopped. A squadron of bombers had roared in low over the island, and the whole place had seemed to explode into smoke and fire.

"Boy!" Gardella had said. "This isn't going to be so bad! By the time we get down, there isn't going to be anybody alive!"

"It won't be so bad," Tom had said, thinking of the Japs hanging on in their caves, waiting for the interval between the bombing and the landing of their enemies to come out and man their guns. He had wondered what it was like to hang on in a cave, with the bombs crashing overhead, waiting. Suddenly the Japs had not seemed so much like caricatures of little yellow men grinning and holding bayonets any more — he had found himself feeling more in common with the Japs hanging on in their caves down below, and waiting, as he was waiting, than with all the safe people in the world, the people at home, safe, and the sailors far below, safe aboard their ships, and the crews of the bombers, who were flying home right now to have hot coffee and a morning nap, their part of the invasion over. It must be tough to wait in a cave, he had thought, knowing that soon the whole works is going to be thrown at you. It must be tough, it must be like waiting up here. And yet, I will leave a child, he had thought.

The sky had begun to grow bright and blue, with an intense quality, almost like a stained-glass window. The surface of the sea had become jade green, flecked with white over the shoals to the south of Karkow. As the plane circled lower, it had become obvious that the sea was rough. It's blowing pretty hard down there, Tom had thought. I'll bet more than half of us will be blown clean over the island. I hope they have enough rescue boats down there.

A big gray transport near the north end of the island was unloading landing craft, Tom had seen, and these now began to circle as though in preparation for a landing, but the element of surprise must be diminished, he had thought, by the big planes circling overhead. Below him Tom could see the first of the planes carrying paratroopers begin to level off and head for the island. For the first time the guns on the island had opened fire, and almost immediately one of the big planes had begun to smoke and quietly, almost as if by plan, had slanted into the sea. The men in Tom's plane had already stood up, and the door had already been opened in preparation for the jump. Standing near the door as the plane slanted lower and lower, Tom had seen the men from the planes ahead bail out, had seen a few plummet down without the flutter of a parachute, had seen others drift over the island or fall short of it into the sea. He had seen hundreds land on the smoking island, which was already crisscrossed by tracers; he had seen more than one thousand men spilled into the air by the prodigal planes, and then he himself had been in the air, falling. There had been the jerk of the parachute opening, and he had swung like a violent pendulum back and forth, the great lip of the cliff down below, men all around him in the air, and, just below, one man also swinging like a pendulum in the wind had crashed into the jagged side of the cliff and was being dragged over the sea, his parachute still full of wind, like the sails of a sloop in summer. Tom had twisted, working the risers or his parachute with all the strength of his wrists, spilling wind from it, angling in over the edge of the cliff. From below tracer bullets had arched up at him, slowly, like candle flames in the air. Then there had been a sudden impact, and he had been dragged over rocks, fighting his harness, until he had found himself lying in a gully, free of his parachute, a gun in his hand, and all around him gunfire and the hoarse shouts of men.

Everywhere there had been Japs, and the paratroopers had been coming down like rain all over the island. There had been no clear line of battle, only a melee, the Japs and paratroopers all mixed up together. And as Tom had known would happen, a lot of the green troops had been afraid to fire, for fear of killing their own men. They had frozen, and Tom had crawled from his gully, rounding up his men, cursing at them and shoving their guns into their hands. The Japs had not been afraid to fire — they had taken it as a matter of course that they would kill some of their own men. It had been necessary for the paratroopers to fire too.

Hank Mahoney had been behind a rock, near the ravine where Tom had landed, and there had been three Japs with a mortar just to the left of him. Tom had found Gardella, and the two of them had got part of the company together and had just managed to clean out the Jap mortar when Mahoney ran out from behind his rock. Tom, barely seeing a moving figure out of the corner of his eye, had whirled and thrown a hand grenade. "No!" Gardella had yelled, just too late. In the instant while the grenade had been poised in midair, and Mahoney had still been running, like a schoolboy about to receive a forward pass, Tom had seen who it was, but then the grenade had exploded, Mahoney had crumpled, and at the same time a machine gun had opened up on Tom and his men.

Tom had motioned to Gardella and the others to withdraw to the shelter of a near-by shell hole. He himself had flattened his body against the earth and had crawled over to Hank. Mahoney had been lying on his belly, and no injury had been visible on his back. "Hank?" Tom had said. There had been no answer. Tom had put his hand under Mahoney's arm and turned him over. Mahoney's entire chest had been torn away, leaving the naked lungs and splintered ribs exposed. His face had been unsoiled and serene. Perhaps that, in addition to the panic-stricken torrent of self-accusation, had contributed to Tom's madness. With courage and surprising lucidity of mind, he had undertaken the rescue of a corpse. Picking up Hank's blood-drenched body, he had run, cleverly dodging from rock to rock. When confronted by a cave full of Japs, he had carefully propped Hank up in a shell hole and under heavy machine-gun fire had crawled to within fifteen feet of the mouth of the cave and tossed in two hand grenades. When the smoke and dust had cleared, he had gone into the cave with a knife, finding six Japs dead and one half alive. With grim pleasure he had finished that one off and calmly returned to Hank's body. Picking it up as if it were a child, he had continued across the island. He had fought his way almost to the beach on the opposite side when it occurred to him that he didn't know where he was going, for there was nothing on the beach, and no doctors had yet been landed anywhere on the island. Carrying Hank's body into a pillbox which had been cracked open by bombs, he had knelt astride it and had committed his ultimate act of agony and madness: he had tried to give Hank's pitifully torn body artificial respiration. Remembering fragments of lessons in lifesaving he had taken as a boy, he had pumped Hank's stiffening arms up and down relentlessly, succeeding only in forcing blood through Hank's nose and mouth. He had had no idea how long he applied artificial respiration, but after a long time he had become aware that the shooting outside the pillbox had stopped. The whole island had suddenly hummed with silence. Picking up Hank's body, which had stopped bleeding, he had run to the top of a knoll. "Medic!" he had shouted. "Medic! Medic!"

A sergeant halfway down the knoll had called to him and pointed toward a medical corpsman bandaging a man's knee a hundred yards away. Tom had run there and gently put Hank's body on the ground near the man with the injured knee. "This is an emergency case," he had said to the medical corpsman. The man had glanced briefly at Hank's body, then walked over and examined it closely.

"You don't need no medic for this guy," he had said casually. "He's been dead for hours. Put him with the other dead over there." The corpsman had gestured toward an irregularly shaped pile covered by a torn parachute. Flies had been crawling on the white cloth.

"No," Tom had said.

"He's dead," the corpsman had replied.

"He's not."

The corpsman had glanced at Tom sharply and sighed. "I'll do it for you," he had said and, leaning forward, had unceremoniously started to drag Hank's body away.

"Don't touch him. I want a real doctor for him," Tom had said.

The corpsman had straightened up and stared at Tom. Then he had called over his shoulder to a group of soldiers who had sat down in the dirt and already started a card game. "Hey, come over here," the corpsman had said. The soldiers had wearily got to their feet. Holding a knife in one hand, Tom had stood astride Mahoney's body. The soldiers had approached him slowly and stopped a few yards away.

"Captain, that man you've got there is dead," the corpsman had said. "Let these men take care of him, and you get a rest." The soldiers had spread out around him, but had kept their distance. Tom had said nothing, but his big body had been tense and alert, and some of the soldiers had started to back away. After a moment of silence Tom had said calmly and reasonably, "I just want this man here to see a real doctor."

"Let him go," a fat corporal had said to the corpsman. "The captain looks like a mighty big man, and somebody's going to get hurt if we rush him."

"The guy's psycho," the corpsman had said.

"Let him go find a doctor if he wants," the fat corporal had replied.

While they were arguing, Tom had suddenly stooped, picked up Mahoney's body, and burst through the loose circle they had formed. He had run hard, without feeling the great weight of Mahoney's body. After a few minutes he had felt gravel under his feet and had heard many voices. Looking up, he had found himself standing only a few hundred feet from the sea, surrounded by Negro troops pouring from a landing barge. "What's the matter, Captain?" a gigantic Negro master sergeant had said. "You looking for the medics?"

"Yes."

"They're taking some wounded out to the hospital ship right over there," the enormous sergeant had said, gesturing toward another landing craft several hundred yards down the beach. Tom had started off, but had felt a big hand on his shoulder. "Let me carry him for you, Captain," the sergeant had said. "You must be beat."

"I'll take him."

The sergeant had already put one great arm around Hank's body. In a shocked voice he had suddenly said, "Captain, this man's dead. Look at his chest."

"Let him alone."

"Ain't no use, Captain," the sergeant had replied in a soft voice. "Put him down and take yourself a rest."

"I'm not going to put him with the dead."

"Of course not. Let me put him right down here." The big sergeant had put gentle and respectful hands on Hank's body, and Tom had not objected. Carefully the sergeant had put Hank's body on the gravel a hundred yards from the other men. "Sit down now, Captain," the sergeant had said.

Dazedly Tom had sat down. The sergeant

had given him a cigarette and lit it for him. Tom had sat staring at the sergeant's shoes, tremendous muddy shoes, the tops of which were still highly polished. After looking at the shoes for a long while, he had brought himself to glance at Mahoney and had seen that on Hank's face was the sardonic grin of a dead man. The dead always have the last laugh, Hank had said. A wave of nausea had overtaken Tom, and he had been sick. For several minutes he had lain there retching. The big sergeant had put cool hands on his forehead, the way a mother holds the head of a sick child. Gradually the nausea had gone, and with it the madness. Tom had stood up slowly, and the sergeant had handed him a canteen. After taking a drink, Tom had poured water into his hands and splashed his face. "Thanks, Sergeant," he had said.

"Let me help you find a burial detail," the sergeant had replied. "You look mighty tired."

"I'd like to find one with a chaplain."

The sergeant had picked Mahoney up. They had walked a long while before finding a priest with a detachment of men preparing for funeral services. The big sergeant had put Mahoney down, and the chaplain had immediately come over and had gently laid a blanket over him.

"Take care of him, Father," Tom had said, and had strode across the island to rejoin his company. He had found his men lying exhausted on the ground waiting for landing craft to take them off the island. Caesar had been wounded. Seeing him being carried off in a stretcher, Tom had hurried over to him. "You're going to be all right," he had said, but Caesar had just turned his face away, as though the sight of Tom were painful to him.

Tom had helped get the other wounded to the hospital ship, and then had thrown himself on the ground to try to sleep. Only a fitful half-sleep had come, and he had been aware of men moving all around him. All kinds of things had happened that night. Some of the troops who arrived after the fighting had searched the tangled earth for souvenirs, making necklaces of teeth and fingernails from corpses. Pitched battles had been fought over Japanese swords, pistols, and flags. At two o'clock in the morning a Jap had been found cowering in a clump of underbrush and had been joyfully bayoneted and castrated by a company of supply troops who had thought they would have to finish out the war without meeting the enemy.

Finally an LST had picked up Tom and most of the paratroopers who were uninjured.

As it backed away from the island, Tom had sat in a dark corner of its hold, thinking of Mahoney running with the grenade in mid-air, poised there forever like Keats's lovers on a Grecian urn, Hank always young and alive, the grenade always outlined clearly against the sky, just a few feet above his shoulder.

A major, coming to squat beside him said, "Some of these goddamn sailors got heads. They went ashore and got Jap heads, and they tried to boil them in the galley to get the skulls for souvenirs."

Tom had shrugged and said nothing. The fact that he had been too quick to throw a hand grenade and had killed Mahoney, the fact that some young sailors had wanted skulls for souvenirs, and the fact that a few hundred men had lost their lives to take the island of Karkow — all these facts were simply incomprehensible and had to be forgotten. That, he had decided, was the final truth of the war, and he had greeted it with relief, greeted it eagerly, the simple fact that it was incomprehensible and had to be forgotten. Things just happen, he had decided; they happen and they happen again, and anybody who tries to make sense out of it goes out of his mind. Suddenly he had longed to go home, home to Betsy and the serenity of

Grandmother's house. "How long do you think they'll give us before the next jump?" he had asked the major.

Now, in his office in the Schanenhauser Foundation in the year 1953, Tom wondered whether Caesar Gardella actually had gone back to Rome to marry Gina, or whether he had simply returned to New York when the war was over and tried to forget the whole thing, as Tom had. And most of all he wondered if Gardella had recognized him, and if he were still resentful of the abandonment of Maria. It was strange that there was only Maria to worry about, Tom thought — certainly Caesar wouldn't hold the death of Mahoney against him. It had been an accident — Caesar had certainly realized that. Probably Caesar wouldn't even remember Mahoney. But if Maria had a son or a daughter, and if Caesar told her where Tom was, that conceivably could be quite another thing. A birth usually has more consequences than a death.

Suddenly Tom's telephone rang. It was Dick Haver calling from the office across the hall. "Tom, can you step in here a minute?" he asked.

"Sure," Tom said. "Be glad to."

13

"Mr. Hopkins telephoned me a few minutes ago," Dick said "and asked if I could let you start work over there next week. I take it you've reached a decision."

"I was going to tell you this morning," Tom said. "I haven't had a chance to see you. . . ."

"I understand. I told Hopkins that as far as we were concerned, you could start work over there right away."

Tom didn't like that at all — Dick hadn't made him sound very valuable. "All right," he said reluctantly. "I certainly appreciate everything you've done for me here."

"We don't have to say good-by," Dick said. "Let's have lunch together once in a while."

Tom went back to his office to clean out his desk. There are a few things I've got to get straight with myself, he thought. The fact that Caesar Gardella is running an elevator over at United Broadcasting doesn't make any difference at all. It changes nothing. The past is just as it was and I can't get myself into a state of nerves every time I step into an elevator. My nerves have held out until now, and I guess they'll keep on holding out. Whether Caesar recognizes me or not doesn't make any difference. I've got nothing to be ashamed of, or at least no more than I had before I knew Caesar was running an elevator. Mahoney wasn't the first man to be killed by mistake by his own men in the heat of battle — Old Hank would understand that if anyone would. And Maria held nothing against me. We understood each other. I wonder if she had the child, he thought. I wonder if Caesar knows. If he recognized me, why didn't he say anything?

No, Tom thought, I mustn't go on like this. Between peace and war a clear line must be drawn. The past is something best forgotten; only in theory is it the father of the present. In practice, it is only a wildly unrelated dream, a chamber of horrors. And most of the time the present is unrelated to the future. It is a disconnected world, or it is better to believe it that way if you can, and an elevator man has no business popping up to form a connecting link. The past is gone, Tom thought, and I will not brood about it. I've got to be tough. I am not the type to have a nervous breakdown. I can't afford it. I have too many responsibilities. This is a time of peace, and I will forget about the war.

It's funny, Tom thought — it's funny, the way the world goes. You take your children and with all honesty you teach them, "Thou Shalt Not Kill." You give them dancing lessons, and tennis lessons, and music lessons. You teach them Latin, and how to dress properly. You teach them self-respect, if you can. All these things my father must have learned when he was young, and all these things I learned, and if I can, I will teach all these things to my son. And if I can, I will also teach him to defend his country. If he has to, I hope he'll be a tough bastard too.

"All right, men, this is a rifle. Any of you never seen a rifle before?"

Tom remembered the sergeant who had given him basic training, a hollow-cheeked man with a flat voice, who had taught him back in the year 1942. The recruits had laughed when he said, "Any of you never seen a rifle before?" All sergeants in all generations talk the same, and all recruits laugh at the same jokes.

201

"All right. This is a rifle, and here in my other hand I'm holding a bayonet. Any of you never seen a bayonet before?"

This time, no laughter. The recruits, standing in a circle around the sergeant, had shuffled nervously.

"Now you take this bayonet and you fit it onto the barrel of your rifle like this. Shove it down until it clicks. Stand back a little. I'm going to run through this once for you now, and then you try it. There are three basic motions in the use of a bayonet. You stick it in like this, you pull it out, using your foot or knee to shove the enemy away, and then you bring the stock of your rifle down hard on his head like this, all in one smooth motion. . . ."

It is necessary to forget all that and everything it led to, Tom thought; it is as necessary to forget it now as it was to learn it in the first place. They ought to begin wars with a course in basic training and end them with a course in basic forgetting. The trick is to learn to believe that it's a disconnected world, a lunatic world, where what is true now was not true then; where Thou Shalt Not Kill and the fact that one has killed a great many men mean nothing, absolutely nothing, for now is the time to raise legitimate children, and make money, and dress properly, and be kind to

202

one's wife, and admire one's boss, and learn not to worry, and think of oneself as what? That makes no difference, he thought — I'm just a man in a gray flannel suit. I must keep my suit neatly pressed like anyone else, for I am a very respectable young man. If Caesar recognizes me, we might go out and have a drink together, and that would be that. It doesn't make any difference whether he recognizes me or not. It is ridiculous to live in fear of an elevator man. I will go to my new job, and I will be cheerful, and I will be industrious, and I will be matter-of-fact. I will keep my gray flannel suit spotless. I will have a sense of humor. I will have guts — I'm not the type to start crying now.

An hour later Tom stepped into the United Broadcasting building. The elevator operator who took him up to Ogden's office was a thin boy not more than eighteen years old.

14

A secretary in a tight pink sweater told Tom
that Ogden couldn't see him for another
hour, but that he had asked her to show him
to the office he was to occupy. Tom thanked
her and followed her down the hall. The pas-
sageway ran out of carpet by the time they got
to his door, but Tom was surprised at the size
of his quarters. He had a room about fifteen
feet square entirely to himself, and there was
a small alcove where a pert brown-haired secretary sat at a small desk copying letters.
"Mr. Rath, this is Miss Lawrence," the girl in
the pink sweater said. "She will be your secretary."

"It's nice to meet you," Miss Lawrence
said. She stood up, and smiled.

Tom's desk was fancily shaped, much like
the one behind which Walker had given him
his first interview, but he had an ordinary

swivel chair instead of a reclining one. He sat down in it. There were two telephones on the desk, an interoffice communication box, and a small panel with three red buttons on it. Experimentally he pushed one of the buttons. Almost immediately, the door to his office opened and a distinguished and statuesque blond girl in a dark-green blouse and expensive-looking tweed skirt came in. "You buzzed, sir?" she asked in a rather upstage Boston accent.

"Who are you?"

"I'm the office girl. I deliver the interoffice mail. Did you buzz for me?"

"By mistake," Tom said. "Thank you very much."

She left, and he sat examining the other buttons with interest. Maybe the second one's for a redhead and the third one's for a brunette, he thought. After a moment of hesitation, he pushed the second one. This time Miss Lawrence came in. "Yes?" she asked.

"What's the third button for?"

"Nothing," she said, grinning. "It's for men who have two secretaries. Do you know how to use the interoffice communication system?"

He said no, and she showed him. She also explained the telephone system and brought from her desk a stack of papers for him to sign which placed him officially on the pay roll and insured him against almost everything in the world but getting fired. Just as he finished signing them, his interoffice communication box uttered some ominous crackling sounds, like a radio in a thunderstorm. He flicked a switch on it, and Ogden's voice suddenly shouted at him so loudly that he jumped, "Are you there, Rath?"

Tom turned the volume down to make Ogden more polite. "Just got here," he said.

"Come up and see me in half an hour," Ogden almost whispered. There were more noises like static.

"I'll be there," Tom said.

There was no reply, and he shut off the box. For a moment he busied himself looking through the drawers of his desk, inspecting with admiration a typewriter which pulled out on a special shelf. Then he turned his chair around and stared out the window. Below him, the city stretched like a map. Far away in the Hudson River a flotilla of destroyers was getting up steam. One of them was using a signal light. Tom could still read Morse Code. "Where in hell is the liberty boat?" the signalman was asking.

Twenty minutes later Tom started toward

Ogden's office. Down the hall he took a wrong turn at a junction of corridors and wound up at the entrance to an enormous room in which about thirty clerks worked at desks in neat rows as in a schoolroom. When he found Ogden's office it was five minutes past the time set for the appointment, but that didn't make any difference because Ogden kept him waiting another hour.

"Glad you could start work today," Ogden said when he finally had the girl in the pink sweater show him in. "Is your office all right?"

"It's fine," Tom said casually.

"About a title for you," Ogden said. "I suppose we should give you a title. You'll be responsible directly to me, of course, but I think we'll call you 'Special Assistant to Mr. Hopkins.' There will be times when that title will be useful."

Ogden paused, and Tom said, "That sounds like a fine title."

"Just remember that it doesn't apply to company business," Ogden said. "You're special assistant to Mr. Hopkins on this special project — nothing else. That will be made clear inside the company, but of course there will be no need to spell it out anywhere else."

"Of course," Tom said.

"Can you have dinner with Mr. Hopkins tonight?"

"Yes," Tom said, trying not to sound surprised. "I think I can arrange it."

"Meet us at seven-thirty at his apartment," Ogden said, and gave a Park Avenue address, which Tom wrote down on a pad and put in his pocket.

"Now let me give you the pitch," Ogden continued. "There's a . . ." Before he could go on, his telephone rang. "No," Ogden said into the receiver. "Absolutely not." He listened for a full minute before adding, "I'm still not convinced. Contact me on it later. Good-by."

He hung up and shifted his gaze to Tom. With hardly a pause, he said, "The pitch is this. There's a big convention of medical men in Atlantic City on September 15. Hopkins has been asked to speak, and he figures it will be a good time for him to send up a trial balloon on this whole project. He can't mention the small group of doctors who got him interested in all this. We've got to help him with the speech."

"Does that mean you want me to write it?"

Ogden looked at Tom with distaste. "We don't write speeches for Mr. Hopkins," he said. "He writes his own speeches. We just help him with the research and try to get something on paper for him to work with."

"I see," Tom said, feeling he had made a strategic error.

"Tonight we're going to kick the speech around," Ogden said. "You better be thinking about what he should say. He'll want your ideas."

Tom didn't have any idea in the world what the president of United Broadcasting should say to a convention of physicians about mental health. "Did the doctors suggest any topic when they invited him?" he asked.

"No."

"I suppose he could talk about increasing public understanding of the mental-illness problem," Tom said tentatively. He was tired of that thought already.

"Maybe. But keep in mind the purpose of the speech. If we achieve our purpose one hundred per cent, the audience should rise as one man when he's through and demand that he start a national committee on mental health immediately. He shouldn't propose such a thing, understand — they should suggest it to him. If this is the kind of speech it should be, every newspaper in the country should have it on the front page the next morning. Requests for him to form a national committee on mental health should pour in from all over the nation."

"It'll have to be quite a speech," Tom said.

"Perhaps we can't expect to achieve our purpose one hundred per cent, but we ought to keep the goal clearly in mind. And we also must not forget the possibility of a one hundred per cent failure. Do you know what that would be?"

"No response at all," Tom said.

"No — a negative response. If the speech went one hundred per cent wrong, the doctors would all get together to *prevent* the formation of a national committee on mental health. Mr. Hopkins would be accused of meddling in things he didn't know anything about. United Broadcasting would be described as a sinister influence trying to muscle in on the doctors for mysterious reasons. People would say we want socialized medicine, or that we are reactionaries fighting co-operative health plans. Hopkins would be accused of being a publicity hound. Rumors would start that he had political ambitions. If that sort of thing happened, the whole project would of course have to be abandoned."

There goes my job, Tom thought. Bill Ogden's already chipping away at it. He said, "I don't think there's much danger of that happening. After all, the doctors invited him to speak."

"That was arranged by a small group," Ogden said. "If the speech backfired, they'd be the first to claim they had nothing to do with it."

As soon as he got back to his own office, Tom telephoned Betsy. "I've already started work for United Broadcasting and I won't be home for dinner tonight," he said. "I'm having dinner with Hopkins in his Park Avenue apartment."

"You're going up in the world fast," Betsy said. "I haven't been moving so slowly, either. I've put this house on the market. The agents are sure we can get at least fifteen thousand for it. And I've checked our mortgage — we've paid off all but about seven thousand of that."

"Don't commit yourself on anything without talking to me," Tom said nervously.

She laughed. "I don't guarantee anything," she replied.

Late that afternoon Tom steeled himself when he rang for the elevator to take him down, and he did not admit to himself how relieved he was when the operator turned out to be an old man he had never seen before. When they got to the lobby, Tom hurried to get a taxicab.

The Park Avenue address proved to be a tall apartment house with a long dark-red awning extending over the sidewalk in front of it, under which a doorman who looked like an unemployed general stood guard. The man stepped quickly in front of him, but ceremoniously pushed the button for the elevator inside when Tom explained he had an appointment with Mr. Hopkins. When the elevator, which was operated by a young girl, arrived, the doorman said, "Take this gentleman to Mr. Hopkins' apartment."

The elevator moved slowly upward for what seemed a long while. Finally it stopped, and Tom stepped into a small marble vestibule with three black doors, on one of which was a simple brass knocker. There were no name plates on the doors. Tom turned to ask the elevator operator which door was Mr. Hopkins', but the elevator had already started down. He lifted the brass knocker and let it fall. The door was opened almost immediately by Hopkins himself. He was smiling and looked more affable than ever. "Come in!" he said. "So nice of you to come!"

Tom stepped into a high-ceilinged room.

Two walls were entirely lined with bookcases. A third wall had glass shelves holding a collection of fancy hand-painted lead soldiers. The fourth wall had a large window and two glass doors leading to a neatly kept lawn on the roof, some twenty floors above the street.

"Won't you sit down?" Hopkins said. "What can I get you to drink?"

"Anything. What are you having?"

Hopkins walked over to a table near one of the windows on which stood a small forest of bottles, a trayful of glasses, and an ice bucket. "It looks as though we have quite a collection here," he said, as though that were the first time he had seen it. "I think I'll have Scotch on the rocks. Will that suit you?"

"That'll be fine."

Hopkins took a pair of silver ice tongs in his hand and delicately dropped ice cubes into a glass. After splashing whisky over them, he placed the glass on a small tray, ceremoniously walked over and handed it to Tom. "Thanks," Tom said, figuring he was getting served by the highest-paid bartender in the world. "Is there anything I can do to help?"

"Just sit down and make yourself comfortable. Bill Ogden will be along any minute."

Tom sat in a small, hard leather chair.

Hopkins poured himself a drink and, acting for all the world like an anxious housewife entertaining the rector, fussed about the room, offering Tom first a plate of crackers spread with caviar, and then a porcelain box of cigarettes. Finally he sat down near Tom and sipped his drink thoughtfully. "This is an exciting new project we're going to be working on together," he said, making Tom a partner. "I think there's a real need for it, and it certainly is a challenge!"

He sounded as though the thing he wanted most in the world was a challenge. Tom, feeling called upon to match his enthusiasm, said, "I can't think of anything more needed!"

Luckily, there was a knock on the door before he had to elaborate on that theme. Hopkins jumped springily from his chair, dashed to the door, and let Ogden in. "*Hello*, Bill!" he said, as though he hadn't seen Ogden for three months. "*So* good of you to give up your evening for this!"

"Glad to, Ralph," Ogden said urbanely, exchanged greetings briefly with Tom, and strolled over to the liquor table. "Mind if I mix myself a drink?"

"Take what you like — take what you like!"

Ogden poured himself a Scotch on the rocks and sat down on a hassock. "How are Helen and Susan?" he asked Hopkins.

"Fine! Susan is entering Vassar this fall!"

Tom glanced around the apartment. It didn't look like a place where a family lived. Did Hopkins and his family gather to play croquet on the lawn on the roof? Then he remembered that Hopkins had just built a place in South Bay. Hopkins must keep this place just for business meetings, he figured.

Ogden glanced at his wrist watch. "I've been giving a good deal of thought to this speech you've got scheduled in Atlantic City," he began. "I figure we ought to pitch it chiefly on the need for more public understanding. . . ."

For half an hour Ogden elaborated on this, saying about what he had told Tom that morning. Hopkins sat listening and nodding his head appreciatively, but saying little. His chief preoccupation seemed to be keeping everybody's glass full. At about a quarter after eight, a uniformed maid came in from the door near the shelves of lead soldiers and announced dinner. They all went into a small dining room and were served cherry-stone clams, rare roast beef, and apple pie. All through dinner, Ogden kept talking about the speech. When they returned to the living room, Hopkins cleared his throat and said, "That's very helpful, Bill. Now let me see if I can draw some of it together."

"Take notes," Ogden hissed at Tom.

Tom quickly took a pad from his pocket and sat with pencil poised. "Point number one," Hopkins said. "The medical profession has done a wonderful job on mental-health problems. Point number two: the public must supply more money and understanding. Put in a lot of 'Too few people realize this' and 'Too few people realize that.' Point out that there are special funds for polio and cancer and heart disease. Say too few realize there's no such fund for research on mental illness and that the mentally ill fill more than half the hospital beds. Mention the publicity job that made it respectable to talk about venereal disease. Talk about the amount of money a mentally ill patient costs the state a year. Say someone should start a national committee on mental health. Say it should be a doctor — use the phrase, "some fully qualified person. . . ."

He paused. "No, darn it," he said. "I think we're hitting it too directly. Maybe we could start with some sort of historical parallel. What do you . . ."

There was a knock at the door, and Hopkins leaped to his feet to open it. Two imposing-looking men carrying briefcases entered. "*So* nice of you to come!" Hopkins said heartily. "Sit down! We'll be through here in just a minute. Brandy? A liqueur?"

"Thanks, Ralph," the bigger of the two men said. "Anything you've got. Good evening, Bill."

After brief introductions, and after everyone had a drink, Hopkins said, "Now, Tom, do you think you have the hang of what I want to say in Atlantic City?"

"I guess so," Tom said.

"Would it be putting you to too much trouble to ask for a rough draft in, say, three or four days?"

"I'll have something for you," Tom said.

"Fine! Thanks *so* much for coming up. I know how hard it is to stay in town late when you live in Connecticut. I certainly appreciate it!"

Bill Ogden stood up. "Thanks for everything, Ralph," he said. "I've got to be running."

"Thank *you*, Bill!" Hopkins said.

This is the most polite damn bunch of people I've ever met, Tom thought. As he and Bill Ogden went out the door he heard Hopkins say to the other two men, "I *certainly* appreciate your giving up your evening for this! Have you got some of those promotion plans we were discussing last week spelled out a little more?"

It turned out that Ogden lived in Stamford, and he rode to Grand Central Station in a taxi with Tom. They had just missed the nine-thirty-five train, and there wasn't another one for more than an hour. They went to the bar on the lower level of the station and ordered highballs.

"I can't help being curious," Tom said. "Does Mr. Hopkins work every night?"

"He often takes long week ends on an island he has up in Maine," Ogden said.

Tom reflected upon this for a few moments. "You mean he just lives alone in that apartment and has business appointments every evening?" he asked incredulously.

"Oh, he goes out to his place at South Bay quite often," Ogden said. "He sees a lot of his family — especially around Christmas time."

Tom took a few swallows of his drink.

"He never gets tired," Ogden said. "Lots of guys work hard, but he's always fresh. I've never seen him tired in my life."

When Tom got back to Westport, the first

thing he noticed when he stepped in the front door of his house was that everything looked suspiciously neat, and a table with a large vase of hollyhocks had been moved against the living-room wall to obscure the crack in the plaster. Betsy was waiting. "How did it go?" she asked.

"Fine," he said. "I got to write a speech. I mean, I have to help Mr. Hopkins with a speech. I might as well get the terminology of this thing straight from the beginning."

To his surprise, Betsy looked hurt. "I wish you'd stop being so damn bright and cynical," she said. "It's no way to start a new job. You ought to be enthusiastic. Damn it, Tommy, try being naïve!"

"What's got into you?" he asked, looking puzzled.

"I'll bet Hopkins doesn't go around making wisecracks!" she said. "Does he?"

"No."

"Nobody does who gets anywhere. You've got to be positive and enthusiastic!"

"How come you know so much all of a sudden about how to get ahead?"

"I just *know*," she said. "I'm sick of being smart and broke."

"Okay," he said. "I'll be owl-faced. My whole interest in life is working for mental health. I care nothing for myself. I am a dedicated human being."

"All right, be witty. But I've been worried about this for a long time. You've always been talking about Hopkins' mental-health project with your tongue in your cheek, and if you feel that way about it, you ought not work for the man. You ought to be thinking it's the best idea in the world! And why isn't it a good idea when you come right down to it? What's wrong with trying to do something about mental illness? Why do you have to be so damn *cynical* about it?"

"From now on I'll be pious," he said, "if you promise to stop being insufferable."

"I just want you to start off on the right foot," she said. "Do you like Mr. Hopkins?"

"I guess so."

"You should *try* to like him! Give him the benefit of every doubt. Or quit working for him right now!"

"I love him," he said simply. "I adore him. My heart is his."

"You scare me, Tommy," she said. "I'm dead serious. You scare hell out of me when you're like that. To me it means you're going to be unenthusiastic about everything for the rest of your life."

"I'm going to try to do this job right," he

said. "You don't have to worry about that. I'm going to try."

"Sit down now and have a drink," she said. "Three people looked at the house today, and one may be coming back."

15

Just as Tom and Betsy were preparing to go to bed, the telephone rang. It was Lucy Hitchcock, who lived next door. "Hi!" she said with slightly alcoholic jubilation in her voice. "Could you and Tom come over for cocktails tomorrow night? Bob just got a wonderful raise, and we're going to celebrate."

"Congratulations," Betsy said. "We'll be there."

"I've got to call twenty other people," Lucy said. "Good-by!"

Filled with sudden distaste, Betsy put the telephone down. In this invitation tendered so late in the evening to a party for the celebration of an increase in salary received by the host, Betsy found concentrated everything she disliked about Greentree Avenue. The intensity of her displeasure surprised her, and long after she had gone to bed, she lay awake trying to analyze it.

It's not that I'm a snob — it's more than that, she thought fiercely. There are all kinds of reasons. Slowly she counted them off.

The first reason the invitation annoyed her was that she felt obligated to accept it. She and Tom had already declined invitations to two of the Hitchcocks' parties, and Lucy would interpret a third refusal as a slight, regardless of what excuse were given.

The second reason was that like most cocktail parties on Greentree Avenue, this one would be an exhausting exercise. On Greentree Avenue cocktail parties started at seven-thirty, when the men came home from New York, and they usually continued without any dinner until three or four o'clock in the morning. It was almost impossible for the owners of the small houses to provide dinner for their guests — on that street the custom of asking people in for dinner had almost disappeared. The kitchens were small, dining rooms were almost nonexistent, and after the women had put the children to bed, they were in no mood to fix company meals. Cocktail parties were an easier form of hospitality, and the only trouble was that anyone who went home for dinner was considered a spoilsport. Somewhere around nine-thirty in the evening, Martinis and Manhattans would give way to highballs, but the formality of eating anything but hors d'oeuvres in between had been entirely omitted.

It can't be true that the whole street is like that, Betsy thought — it must be just the people we know. For a long while after she went to bed, she lay thinking of the various families up and down the street. Almost all the houses were occupied by couples with young children, and few people considered Greentree Avenue a permanent stop — the place was just a crossroads where families waited until they could afford to move on to something better. The finances of almost every household were an open book. Budgets were frankly discussed, and the public celebration of increases in salary was common. The biggest parties of all were moving-out parties, given by those who finally were able to buy a bigger house. Of course there were a few men in the area who had given up hope of rising in the world, and a few who had moved from worse surroundings and considered Greentree Avenue a desirable end of the road, but they and their families suffered a kind of social ostracism. On Greentree Avenue, contentment was an object of contempt.

No one here is evil, Betsy thought defensively. In spite of all the drinking, the young couples were usually well enough behaved at the cocktail parties. Sure, there were sometimes a few kitchen kisses and an occasional high-pitched argument, but usually the men and their wives just sat talking about the modern houses they would like to build, or the old barns they would like to convert into dwellings. The price the small houses on Greentree Avenue were currently bringing and the question of how big a mortgage the local banks were offering on larger places were constantly discussed. As the evening wore on, the men generally fell to divulging dreams of escaping to an entirely different sort of life — to a dairy farm in Vermont, or to the management of a motel in Florida — but for the most part, the cocktail parties simply gave everyone a chance to prove he considered Greentree Avenue no more than a stepping stone to the same kind of life on a bigger scale. There's nothing wrong with that, Betsy tried to tell herself. This isn't a bad place to be, it's just . . .

Dull. That was the word she usually used for Greentree Avenue, but tonight she rejected it. If this were just a dull place, I wouldn't mind it so much, she thought. The trouble is, it's not dull enough — it's tense and it's frantic. Or, to be honest, Tom and I are tense and frantic, and I wish to heaven I knew why.

Betsy sat up in bed and, in the dim light from the window, glanced at Tom. He was asleep and, at least for the moment, looked entirely serene. She fumbled on the bedside table, found a cigarette, and lit it. A feeling of black pessimism and self-reproach overtook her. With Betsy, such moods were extremely rare, but when she fell victim to them, every humiliating experience she had suffered since early childhood sprang to life, and all comforting thoughts fell from beneath her, as though she had been standing on a trap door. At such times, the big brick house on Beacon Street in which she had been brought up came back to her memory not as a cheerful place, with pine logs roaring in the living-room fireplace on winter afternoons, but as a cavernous building with a long dark staircase with a creak in every step which she had been obliged to climb alone early each evening, leaving her older sister, Alice, to bask in the warmth below. Betsy had had a rather lonely childhood — her sister was eight years older than she, and her parents had been quite old when she was born and had lacked the energy, if not the will, to give much time to a small child. Almost from the beginning, Betsy had been a rather adult child. She had rarely cried, and although she had been terrified by the shadows on the wall of the stairs and the darkness in the hall above, she had never confided her fears to anyone. Instead she had hummed to herself determinedly while going up to bed, with lips compressed and fists tightly clenched as she edged along the shadows and into the blackness of the hall, where anything could lurk. Because her parents had not approved of night lights for children, she had slept in the dark, with her ears straining for the comforting sound of voices on the floor below and the occasional laugh of her older sister. Now, lying in the dark beside Tom, Betsy found herself half expecting to hear the sound of that laughter again.

"Mark my words . . ." her sister Alice had said. That had been much later, when Betsy had told her family she wanted to marry Tom. *"Mark my words,"* she had said. "If you get married now, you'll regret it. You're too young. Someday you'll remember I told you that and wish you had taken my advice. Wait till after the war. A girl your age who marries a man just about to go in the service is crazy."

"But I've known him for three years," Betsy had said.

"But you don't know how either of you will feel after he gets back."

"We'll always feel the same as we do now!"

How bravely the words came back to her! Why should I think of Alice now? Betsy thought. She leaned over to an ash tray and extinguished her cigarette. Beside her, Tom stirred restlessly in the bed.

Nothing's wrong with our marriage, or at least nothing permanent, Betsy thought. We can't be like a couple of children gaily playing house forever.

That's the way it had been before the war — *like children playing house,* she thought, but even the sarcasm of the phrase couldn't tarnish the memory. They had had only three months together before Tom went into the Army. How exciting those days had been! He had spent an absurd proportion of his savings on her engagement ring and a diamond-sprinkled wedding ring to match. At the time she had remonstrated with him, and it was curious to remember now that that jewelry, bought with a brave gesture of gallantry, had turned out to be the only shrewd investment they had ever made. The last time she had had the rings cleaned, the jeweler had offered her far more than Tom had paid for them, because diamonds had increased in value a great deal since the war.

That somehow seemed typical of the way everything had turned out, Betsy thought. The foolish gesture had turned out to be a shrewd investment, and most of their careful planning had led to nothing. I would like to go back to the beginning, and follow the years along, and find out what went wrong, Betsy thought. After she and Tom had been married, they had moved into a tiny apartment in Boston, and upon her request, Tom had immediately bought a Saint Bernard puppy and a white Angora kitten with blue eyes because in the old house on Beacon Hill, her family had never allowed her to have pets. Now her clearest memory of those three months before the war was of the great clumsy puppy and the wide-eyed kitten and Tom and herself, all rolling and tumbling and playing together on the floor, with the sunshine streaming in the window on a big red and gold oriental rug someone had given them for a wedding present.

Like children playing house, she thought. During the first two days they lived in that apartment, she had ordered milk from two milkmen, because the second one had been a very aggressive salesman, and the icebox had been jammed with milk bottles until Tom straightened the matter out. The kitchenette had been fragrant with spices thoughout those three months — she had experimented with almost every recipe in the cookbook. Meals had not seemed simply a chore to get through as quickly as possible then.

We weren't too young to be married in those days, she thought — I think the trouble is that although only twelve years have gone by, we are somehow too old to be married now. I suppose that's really why I want to move out of this house so much, Betsy thought — I don't want a bigger place so much; I want that old three months before the war back. It's as though Tom and I had been married twice, once before the war and once afterward, and what I want is my first marriage back.

"*Now mark my words,*" Alice had said.

Damn Alice, Betsy thought now. I'm still not sorry I got married, and I'm glad I didn't take her advice. Ever since the war, poor Tom has just had to work awfully hard, and he has lots of worries on his mind. And I've been tired, what with taking care of the kids and all. We're both exhausted most of the time — the Tired Thirties, the doctor called it once, the time when people have children, and have to make good at jobs, and buy houses, and all the rest of it. We're both just tired out. That's why nothing seems to be much fun any more.

There, I've said it, she thought, and it sounds absurd, but it's true. Nothing seems to be much fun any more. There's nothing wrong with our house, really, and nothing wrong with Greentree Avenue, or Tom or me. It's just that nothing seems to be much fun any more, and that's horrible, for when you've said that, there's nothing more to say.

Why? she thought.

It probably would take a psychiatrist to answer that. Maybe Tom and I both ought to visit one, she thought. What's the matter? the psychiatrist would say, and I would reply, I don't know — nothing seems to be much fun any more. All of a sudden the music stopped, and it didn't start again. Is that strange, or does it happen to everyone about the time when youth starts to go?

The psychiatrist would have an explanation, Betsy thought, but I don't want to hear it. People rely too much on explanations these days, and not enough on courage and action. Why make such a complicated thing out of selling this house? We don't like Greentree

Avenue, so we'll move. Tom has a good job, and he'll get his enthusiasm back, and be a success at it. Everything's going to be fine. It does no good to wallow in night thoughts. In God we trust, and that's that.

Betsy's fists were clenched, and her lips pressed tightly together, just as they had been when, as a little girl, she had gone up through the shadows to bed, determined not to admit her fear or her jealousy of her sister, sitting by the fire and laughing below. She glanced at Tom, and seeing that the blankets had slipped from his shoulders, she carefully covered him up. Then she went to sleep, and when she awoke in the morning, she was as energetic and cheerful as ever, humming a tuneless song under her breath as she got breakfast and drove her husband to the station.

Four days after he had visited Hopkins' apartment, Tom typed for the fifth time his final draft of a first draft of Hopkins' speech. From the first sentence (It's a great pleasure for me to be here this evening.) to the last sentence (It's a job that *can* be done.), it seemed to Tom to go quite well. True, it all had a rather otherworldly ring to it, but no matter how hard Tom tried, he couldn't make it appear quite natural for the president of United Broadcasting to be talking about mental health at all. When he had polished the speech as much as he could, he handed it to his secretary, who retyped it neatly with three carbon copies. Two of these Tom filed and took the original with one copy to Ogden. He didn't expect Ogden to throw up his hands and cheer when he read the speech, but he was totally unprepared when Ogden, after finishing the first two pages, slammed the speech down on his desk and said, "Christ! This is awful! It isn't what we want at all!"

For the first time in years, Tom felt his face turning red.

"You can do better than this!" Ogden said contemptuously, before Tom had a chance to say anything. "Take it back and do it over. See if you can have something ready by to-night. Mr. Hopkins wants to see you at his apartment at eight-thirty. And this time, really try."

"I'll try," Tom said in an unnaturally quiet voice. He had a sudden, immediately controlled impulse to kill Ogden. He knew just how he could do it — he'd clench both hands together, raise them high above his head, and, using the full strength of his back, bring them down hard on the back of Ogden's neck. Shaken by his own thoughts, he picked the speech up and walked back to his office. Glancing at his familiar, thick old wrist watch, he saw he had nine hours in which to work. He rolled a clean piece of paper into his typewriter. "It's a great pleasure to be here this evening," he began, and crossed it out. "I'm deeply grateful for this opportunity to talk to you this evening," he substituted. No, damn it! he thought, and crossed that out. "It gives me the greatest pleasure . . ."

At eight-thirty that night he knocked blearily at the door of Hopkins' apartment, clutching the retyped speech in a manila envelope in his hand. Hopkins let him in, again thanked him for coming, and gave him a drink. Tom handed him the speech and, unable to watch him read it, walked self-consciously across the room to inspect the lead soldiers. They were hand-painted, in astonishing detail. On the top shelf was a small group of knights in armor. He wondered how long it would take Hopkins to read the speech. At least he hadn't thrown it down yet, and he must have finished the first page. On the second shelf was a company of English archers, apparently aiming their long arrows at a platoon of soldiers waiting for the American Revolution. Behind him, Tom heard a page rustle, and Hopkins cleared his throat. On the middle shelf were Civil War infantrymen of both North and South, apparently teaming up against some World War I artillerymen. Behind him, Tom heard a match scratch, and Hopkins' chair squeaked. He must be half through it, Tom thought. On the bottom shelf were several squads of World War II marines, all standing at attention. Somewhere in the room a clock ticked.

"Wonderful!" Hopkins suddenly boomed.

Tom turned around.

"*Marvelous*," Hopkins said, even louder. His whole face was beaming with satisfaction. "You've really got the feel for it!"

"I'm glad you like it," Tom said modestly.

"This really *sings*," Hopkins said enthusiastically. "It's remarkable that you could do so well the first time around!"

"It's a second draft, actually," Tom said. "Mr. Ogden gave me some suggestions."

"The *heart* of the thing is just right!" Hopkins said. "Now let's just go over it together. Did you bring a copy?"

Tom took one from the manila envelope.

"Let's look at this introduction," Hopkins said. "Do you think we could make it a little more natural? How about, 'Good evening. It's good of you gentlemen to give your attention to a layman. . . .' "

Sentence by sentence Hopkins took the whole speech apart. When he finished, he had asked for changes in almost every paragraph. "Well!" he concluded. "You certainly did a grand job! Just fix up the details we've worked out and let's see it again in a few days. Would Wednesday be too early?"

"That will be plenty of time," Tom said.

"Can I fill your glass for you?"

"Sure."

"You've really got the feel for this sort of thing," Hopkins said, while putting fresh ice cubes in his glass. "You've made a grand beginning!"

"Thanks," Tom said.

There was a knock at the door, and Hopkins let in a thin man holding an enormous blueprint, rolled up like a rug.

"Good *evening,* Bruce," Hopkins said. "So nice of you to give up your evening!"

Tom gulped his drink and excused himself as rapidly as possible. He was halfway to Grand Central Station before he fully realized that Ogden and Hopkins had simply told him the same thing in two different ways: to rewrite the speech. In spite of this, Hopkins had somehow left him eager to try. Well, he thought admiringly. I always heard he could drive men and make them like it.

16

A week later just when Tom was forgetting his apprehension about meeting Caesar Gardella, it happened. He had been working late on the speech, and it was about seven-thirty when he rang for the elevator. The corridor by the elevators was empty. When he pressed the button there was the prolonged hum which always preceded the coming of the elevator. The doors rumbled open, and there was Caesar, standing alone in the entrance to the car, his big round face impassive. "Going down," he said in his deep voice. Tom stepped into the elevator. Caesar turned toward the controls, and the door rumbled shut behind him. Caesar stood with his back toward Tom. The elevator dropped sickeningly fast. Then Caesar turned toward Tom. His face was without emotion. "You're Captain Rath, aren't you?" he said.

"Yes," Tom replied, and, trying to feign surprise, added, "Why, you're Caesar Gardella!" He stuck out his hand, but just then a light flashed on the control board of the elevator, and Caesar brought the car to a halt at the nineteenth floor. The door rumbled open, and two pretty secretaries stepped in. "We'll be late, I know we're going to be late, and they'll *never* wait!" one said.

"They'll wait, all right," her companion replied. "It's a good thing to keep them waiting." The elevator started down, and both girls laughed.

When they got to the ground floor, the secretaries hurried out of the elevator. Tom stayed behind awkwardly. He wanted to say, *Did you go back to Rome? Did you ever hear what happened to Maria?* But instead, sounding foolish to himself and talking very fast, he said, "It certainly is nice to run into you, Caesar! It's been a long time! Gosh, I guess it's been almost ten years, eight or nine, anyway! You're looking good, boy! Sure looks as though civilian life is agreeing with you!"

Caesar smiled. "You're not doing so bad yourself," he said. "I seen you riding down with Mr. Hopkins. You an assistant of his or something?"

"Yes," Tom said. "I'm working for him."

There was an awkward silence, during which the smile disappeared from Caesar's face.

"I've got to be running," Tom said, edging toward the door. "Got a train to catch. Sure is nice to have seen you!"

"Could we get together sometime?" Caesar blurted out quickly. He suddenly seemed nervous and pushed his purple cap back on his head. "Just for a drink or something," he said. "I'd kind of like to talk to you."

"Sure," Tom said hesitantly. "Sure, I'd love to!" Seized with a desire to get the meeting over, he added, "How about now? I could catch a later train."

"No," Caesar replied. "I'm on duty for another two hours. Can I give you a call sometime when I'm not on duty?"

"Sure!" Tom said. "Any time! Give me a call!"

Lights were flashing on the elevator's control panel, and the starter was walking toward them. Tom hurried out of the elevator, waved cheerily, and walked rapidly toward Grand Central Station. He wants to see me, he thought. What about? To talk over old times, perhaps — that's a perfectly normal thing to do. We meet and have a drink and we make jokes about the war. That's all there is to it.

What else could he do?

Blackmail. The word flashed into his mind suddenly. That's absurd, he thought. In the first place, Caesar would never do a thing like that. He was always a decent guy. And in the second place, there's a statute of limitations. And in the third place, he couldn't prove anything, especially after all this time. When you come right down to it, I haven't done anything illegal anyway, or at least nothing anyone could do anything about. Maria wouldn't turn on me now.

Still, Caesar could make things rather awkward for me, Tom thought. Publicity — if he made any charges, the publicity alone could ruin me. And he probably thinks I'm rich, seeing me with Hopkins and all. I wonder what he's got on his mind? Maybe he knows something about Maria, something he wants to tell me.

No, Tom thought as he got to Grand Central Station, it's not that. Two old buddies meet and have a drink together, that's all — that's the convention, and Caesar's just trying to play it according to the script. It's ridiculous to worry. I've got to learn simply to relax and take things as they come. I'm tough and I'm not going to get weak-kneed now.

The next day he expected Caesar to call and

was tense whenever his telephone rang, as well as whenever he got on an elevator, but he neither saw nor heard from Caesar. The day after that nothing happened, and the day after that. Probably he never will call me, Tom thought — probably this is the way it's going to end. It's quite possible, in fact, it's probable that the poor guy was just trying to be polite. As more days went by with no word from Caesar, Tom's conviction that this was so deepened. He's probably embarrassed to call me, he thought. After all, the gulf between an elevator operator and an assistant to the president of a large corporation is greater than that between a corporal and a captain in the Army. He was trying to be polite, Tom told himself over and over, and I'll probably never hear from him again. If we meet in the elevator, we'll just nod at each other, and that will be that.

During the next week, Tom did four more drafts of the speech, each of which Ogden vilified and Hopkins praised highly before asking for a rewrite. Tom got to the point where he mumbled phrases from the speech in his sleep. "It's a great pleasure . . ." he groaned at three o'clock one morning.

"What?" Betsy asked, startled.

"A real pleasure to be here with this distinguished company this evening. . . ."

"Wake up!" Betsy said. "Wake up! You're talking in your sleep!"

The fear that he was proving an utter failure in his new job grew. He would have quit in discouragement if it hadn't been for Hopkins' praise, which grew in warmth as the number of discarded efforts multiplied, and which somehow never failed to sound utterly sincere. Maybe he just goes on like that till he definitely makes up his mind to fire you and then lets you have it between the eyes, Tom thought. But why should a guy like that lie? Maybe he *does* think I'm doing a good job. Maybe he expects a speech to be written a thousand times.

Tom didn't know. Every time Hopkins built him up, Ogden tore him down. "It's getting *worse*," Ogden said when he read the third draft. "Give it a fresh approach! Put some *oomph* into it!"

There was only one comforting thought. The speech would have to be completed before many weeks went by, if Hopkins were going to give it at all — it wouldn't really be possible to go on rewriting it forever.

A week later, when Tom was in the middle of his sixth draft of the speech, and apparently no closer to an acceptable final draft than ever, his mind was distracted by a simple event: Betsy sold the house in Westport and agreed to get out of it within two days. Tom had been falsely reassured by the fact that not many people had inspected the house, and he had figured it probably would take some time for Betsy to put her plans into action. "But why did you agree to get out in *two days?*" he asked in dismay when she told him she had accepted an offer of sixteen thousand dollars.

"He wanted to move his family in — he's just come from Chicago," Betsy said. "It was such a good price he offered, and I was afraid he'd get away."

"How can we do it?" Tom asked. "We've got to pack china, and clothes, and *everything!* And I'm going to be working day and night on this speech!"

"Don't worry about the packing," Betsy said. "I'll have everything ready. The movers will come Saturday morning, and Saturday afternoon we'll all pile in the car and drive to South Bay."

The next evening when Tom got home from New York, every room in the house was cluttered with cardboard boxes and barrels.

"Daddy!" Janey said delightedly. "Momma said not to mind about keeping things neat!"

Tom looked around the disordered house, and suddenly it was unutterably dear to him. The crack like a question mark in the living-room wall, the shabby furniture, the worn linoleum on the kitchen floor — all seemed part of something precious that was slipping fast, something already gone which never could be retrieved. He went to the kitchen cupboard where the liquor was usually kept, but it was gone, and the empty cupboard was neatly lined with clean white paper.

"The liquor's in the big red wastepaper basket," Betsy said cheerfully.

Quietly Tom poured himself a drink.

"That Mr. Howard called again today," Betsy said. "I told him we were moving into Grandmother's house. He seemed quite disappointed — and no wonder. I found something out about him."

"What?" Tom asked somberly.

"He's a professional real-estate man — that's a lot of malarky he gave us about wanting to buy the place for his own use. He's the real-estate man for that restaurant company. Mrs. Reid, the agent who sold this place for us, recognized his name and told me."

"He wouldn't want to put a restaurant way up on that hill," Tom said. "They build that kind of restaurant near highways."

"Mrs. Reid says he probably didn't want it for a restaurant — he speculates on real estate for himself on the side. He probably wanted to do just what we're going to do with it. I think that's a good sign."

A good sign, Tom thought — that's what I need. The old premonition of disaster was sneaking up on him. I've had it a million times before, he thought — it doesn't mean a thing. I'm doing all right on my job. Hopkins likes me. We're really being smart to sell this place and move to Grandmother's house. We're going to make a damn good thing of it!

He couldn't convince himself. Even if I do get fired, it won't matter, he thought. We've got a little cash now. I'll get into some kind of business for myself. I'll work full time on selling Grandmother's house.

Suddenly he had a picture of himself hanging around his grandmother's house, precisely as his father had, with nothing to do. He glanced down and found he was gripping his right thigh so hard that his knuckles were white. He hadn't done that for some time. Why the hell should I get scared in peacetime? he thought. Deliberately he stood up. It doesn't really matter, he thought. Here goes nothing. It will be interesting to see what happens.

"Betsy!" he said. "Is there any packing I can help you with?"

"Not a thing! Say, guess what I found to-day while I was cleaning out the attic!"

"What?"

"Your old mandolin — I packed it in one of the boxes. You ought to get it fixed up. It would be fun."

"I will sometime," he said.

"Daddy," Janey said, "tell us a story about Bubbley."

"All right," Tom said. "Once upon a time there was a little dog named Bubbley. He swallowed a cake of soap, and . . ."

"Don't tell it so fast!" Barbara said.

". . . every time he barked, he blew bub-bles," Tom said, spacing the words evenly. "One day a man from a circus saw him. . . ."

He told the story well and repeated it twice upon request.

17

"Will grandmother be there when we get there?" Janey asked.

It was late Saturday afternoon. They were droning along the Merritt Parkway from Westport to South Bay, with the car packed tightly with suitcases and paper cartons of clothes. Tom had just signed the deed transferring the little house on Greentree Avenue to its new owner, who had seemed overjoyed to get it.

"Grandmother is dead," Betsy said gently. She had already explained this to the children several times.

"Do dead people ever come back?" Barbara asked.

"No," Tom said.

"Do they *like* being dead?" Janey inquired.

"I don't know," Tom said.

"Grandmother is in heaven," Betsy said. "I'm sure she's happy there."

The engine of the old Ford was knocking, and the indicator on the dashboard showed it was heating up. Tom slowed down to twenty-five miles an hour and stayed at the extreme right edge of the highway. He had always had a horror of breaking down on the Merritt Parkway with the children along, and of not being able to get the old car off the pavement. Now other cars regularly blared their horns as they flashed by.

"We'll have to get a new car pretty soon," Betsy said. Tom didn't answer.

"Where is Grandmother now?" Janey asked. "What did they do with her when she got dead?"

"Her soul went to heaven," Betsy said. "Her body has been buried in the cemetery."

"Does she ever try to get out of the cemetery?"

"No," Tom said.

"She's not really in the cemetery," Betsy said. "Her *spirit* is in heaven."

"How long is it going to be before we get there?" Barbara asked.

"Get where?" Tom said.

"Grandmother's house."

"About half an hour."

"Can I have a drink of water?" Janey inquired.

The engine seemed to be knocking louder. Don't break down now, Tom thought. Not now. Somehow it would have seemed a very bad omen to have the car break down while they were moving to Grandmother's house.

When they got off the parkway, they stopped at a restaurant and had supper. By the time they reached the winding road leading up the hill to the big house, it was almost dark. The heat indicator on the dashboard of the old car touched the red line marked "danger." Tom slowed to ten miles an hour, shifted into second gear, and crawled around the sharp turns by the massive outcroppings of rock. The engine kept going. Finally he saw the stone posts, with the tall iron urns on them, turned into the driveway, and shifted into low gear as he passed the grove of oak trees, the carriage house, and the rock garden. Ahead of him the old mansion loomed, silhouetted against the sky. Tom parked the car near the house and cut off the tired engine. Old Edward opened the front door of the house and stood framed in it. "Good evening, Mr. Rath," he said.

Ever since he could remember, Tom had taken old Edward for granted — he had to think hard to remember his last name, which was Schultz. Now Tom looked at him closely, as though he had never seen him before. Edward was a tall man about sixty-five years old, thin and bent at the shoulders. Deep lines ran from the edges of his nose to the corners of his mouth, and his brow was furrowed. What kind of life has he led? Tom wondered. What has he done all these years when the supper dishes were washed? He remembered his grandmother telling him that Edward kept canaries in his room. Somehow it didn't seem possible.

Now Edward stood holding the front door open with one hand, his face stern and unwelcoming. The children, tired of being pent up in the car, dashed ahead of their parents into the big house, but, surprised by the dim and somehow eerie light of the front hall, skidded to a stop, rumpling a scatter rug. Tom and Betsy came in, carrying boxes and suitcases. Edward made no motion to help them. When they got inside, he let the front door close softly behind them. "I would like to talk to you, Mr. Rath," he said.

There was no deference in his manner — that's why he seemed like an entirely different man. There was also no friendliness. His voice was cold, almost supercilious, perhaps a little mocking, Tom thought, wondering if it were simply his imagination.

"As soon as we get these things put away," Tom said. Edward stood watching him and Betsy as they carried their bags upstairs. The children, oddly subdued, followed their parents.

"What room shall we put our things in?" Betsy asked, breathing hard.

"Grandmother's, I guess," Tom said. "We'll want the children on the same floor with us, so I guess we won't use the third floor. If the girls want to stay together we can put them in the large guest room, and Pete can have the room I used to have."

The door to his grandmother's room was not latched. Without putting his suitcases down, he pushed it with his toe. It swung open, revealing the big four-poster bed, which looked strangely wide and empty. From the walls of the room old paintings of "The Senator" and "The Major" as children stared from ornate gilt frames. Barbara and Janey, abruptly recovering their spirits, leaped onto the big bed and started jouncing up and down.

"Get off there!" Tom said sharply.

The children looked startled. "Why?" Janey asked.

"We don't want you to mess up the bed," Betsy replied kindly. She piled the boxes she

251

had been carrying on a chair.

"I think I'll go down and talk to old Edward right away," Tom said.

"What are you going to tell him?"

"I don't know — that we won't know what we can do for him for some time, I guess."

Edward was waiting for him at the bottom of the stairs. "Let's go into the living room and sit down," Tom said.

The old man followed him silently. Tom sat in an armchair, and Edward sank negligently into the rocking chair old Mrs. Rath had always used. Somehow he looked shockingly incongruous there, as he crossed one knee over the other and leaned back.

"You wanted to talk to me?" Tom asked. He thought it would be better to let Edward start.

"When are they going to read the will?"

"Read the will? I don't know that they are going to. Mrs. Rath's lawyer has it. Why do you ask?"

"Do you know what she left me?"

"Mrs. Rath spoke to me about you shortly before she died," Tom said. "She asked me to do what I could for you, and I intend to try. You weren't mentioned in the will specifically."

"I wasn't *mentioned!*" Edward said. He

leaned forward in his chair.

"I intended to talk to you about it." Tom said. "As you may know, Mrs. Rath did not leave a great deal. It will be some time before I know precisely what I can do for you, but I assure you I'll do all I can."

"I don't believe it!" Edward replied. "She said she'd remember me in her will!"

"Perhaps Mrs. Rath was a little confused . . ." Tom began.

"I don't believe it! I'll go to law! I've got proof!"

"I don't think that will be necessary," Tom said. "I don't want you to worry. I don't have much to give, but as long as we have this house, you'll at least have a place to stay, and in time I hope to work something out for you."

"I don't need your charity!" the old man said. "I've saved my money — I've probably got a lot more than you have! I only want my just due!"

"I won't be able to tell you how much I can give you until the estate is settled," Tom said.

"Never mind that! I want to see the will! I don't believe she didn't mention me. She promised she'd leave me the house."

"The *house?*"

"That's right — I've got proof!"

"You must be mistaken," Tom said. "She spoke to me often about leaving me the house. Are you sure you aren't imagining all this?"

"Of course I'm sure! Why do you think I've stayed here all these years? Why do you think I took her orders, and cooked her food, and did her laundry, and cleaned up her dirt? Do you think I loved the old woman?"

Tom stood up. He didn't mean to, but he suddenly rose out of his chair and stood towering over Edward. There was an instant of complete silence. When Tom spoke his voice was soft. "Don't talk like that about Mrs. Rath again," he said.

Edward stared up at him and said nothing. His face was white, perhaps with anger, perhaps with fear. Tom hadn't meant to lunge out of his chair so fast. Slowly Tom sat down. "Now listen," he continued quietly. "I frankly don't believe Mrs. Rath ever promised you anything. She didn't make promises like that, and if she had, she would have told me. But I'm willing to admit that you had a right to expect something, and that perhaps she said things which encouraged you. It's quite possible that as she grew older she grew confused and thought she had more than she did. Now get one thing straight: she didn't have much to leave anyone. By the time the estate is settled, and the mortgage on this house is paid, there probably won't be much more than the house and land. I intend to sell them if I can, and I intend to see you're as well cared for as possible, but I'm not going to promise you anything now. You worked here of your own free will for a salary, and you'll take what I can give you. Until I can get things organized and sell the land, you can keep your room and have your meals here if you want, and if you mind your tongue. You will not be required to do any work."

"I'll get a lawyer!" Edward said. "I'll sue! I've got proof she meant the house for me!"

"The will leaves it to me," Tom said. "The only question now is whether you're going to be reasonable and take what you can get, or whether you're going to keep on like this and get thrown out of here tonight."

"I'll leave, but you'll hear from me!"

I mustn't get angry, Tom thought. He's an old man. He had a right to expect something. Maybe she did make him promises, or at least, maybe he thought she did. I mustn't get angry. "Calm down," he said. "It's not going to do either of us any good to get excited."

"You're cheating me!" the old man said. "Either you are or she did! She was crazy!

She was filthy! She never took a bath. She was . . ."

"Stop!" Tom said. His voice was like the report of a gun. The old man drew in his breath sharply.

"Now get out of here," Tom said. "Go down and pack your bags and call a taxi, and get out of here. If you're not gone in an hour I'll throw you out."

"I'll get a lawyer," Edward said. "You think I can't afford one. I can get the best. The house is mine, and I've got proof."

"Get all the lawyers you want, but right now, get out of that chair," Tom said. "And stay in the servant quarters until the taxi comes."

Edward got up. Tom waited until he had left the room before going upstairs.

"What happened?" Betsy said. "You look upset."

Tom lay down on the big double bed and stared up at the crocheted canopy stretching like a net overhead. "I got angry," he said.

"At Edward?"

"Yes — I threw him out. He's leaving in an hour."

He told her about it then, and as he talked, her indignation grew. "Of course you got mad!" she said. "I would have hit him."

Tom didn't move. He felt limp and utterly exhausted. "I get angry too easily," he said. "Tonight I had a real impulse to kill Edward. Often I feel as though I'd like to kill Ogden, at the office. It's strange that I am permitted to kill only strangers and friends."

"What?"

"Nothing. I'm awfully tired."

"That was such a funny thing you said about killing strangers and friends."

"I meant the war," he said.

"Did you ever kill anyone?"

"Of course."

"I mean, did you personally ever kill anyone? You've never talked to me about it at all."

"Right now I'm too tired. I want to go to sleep."

He stirred restlessly and shut his eyes. In the dim light from the window, Betsy lay looking at his big hands lying quietly folded on top of the covers. "I cannot imagine your killing anyone," she said.

There was no answer. Betsy lay looking at him for several minutes before trying to go to sleep. How strange, she thought, to know so little about one's husband. I wish he would talk to me about the war, but I should know better than try to make him. After all, a good wife isn't supposed to ask her husband questions he obviously doesn't want to answer.

18

It took both Tom and Betsy a long while to get to sleep that night. They lay in the dark, separate and silent. Neither of them commented when they heard a taxi drive up to the house and the front door slam. For some reason, each felt a necessity to feign sleep. Downstairs the old grandfather's clock which had marked the passage of Tom's boyhood continued to mourn the loss of each hour.

Only a few minutes after Tom had finally got to sleep, he was awakened by a piercing scream from the next room. He leaped out of bed and, followed by Betsy, ran to the room where the two girls were sleeping, and snapped on the light. Janey was sitting bolt upright in her bed, crying. Tears were running down her face. Betsy ran to her and picked her up. "What's the matter, baby?" she said. "Did you have a nightmare?"

Janey said nothing. She hugged her mother tightly with both arms, and gradually her cries subsided into sobs. In the bed on the other side of the room, Barbara slept peacefully, oblivious to any disturbance. Betsy took Janey into the room she and Tom were using and put her down on the big bed. Tom put the lights out, and he and Betsy lay there in the dark, with the child between them. Janey's sobs stopped. She gave a long, shuddering sigh and, still clinging tightly to her mother, went to sleep.

I wonder what she dreamed, Tom thought. What does a child have nightmares about? Did she dream that wild beasts were chasing her, or about drowning, or falling through space? What does a child fear most?

"Betsy, are you still awake?" he whispered. The steady, mingled breathing of mother and child was the only answer.

When Tom awoke in the morning, he felt drugged, as though he had been drinking heavily. No one else was in the big bed. Glancing at the familiar face of his wrist watch, he saw it was almost nine-thirty. He jumped to his feet. "Betsy!" he called. "I've missed my train!"

She was nowhere in the room. In his pajamas, Tom ran downstairs, through the living room and the dining room to the big old-fashioned kitchen, where Betsy was washing dishes. "I'll be late to work!" he said. "I've got to get another draft of the speech done!"

She looked up and smiled. "It's Sunday," she said.

"Oh," he replied ruefully, "I forgot." He stood in the middle of the big kitchen, a little confused. Bright sunlight streamed through the window. "Where are the kids?" he asked.

"Outside. That old rock garden is a wonderful place for them to play."

"I think I'll go upstairs and catch another nap," he said.

"Don't you dare! I've been up since seven o'clock unpacking, and now we're going to church! And before that we're going to make a list of all the things we have to do."

"There isn't enough paper," he said. "Not in the whole world."

He went upstairs. The first thing he saw was his old mandolin in its battered black leather case, lying on top of his bureau where Betsy had put it after unpacking it. He stood looking at it a moment, then drew the instrument from its case. It was covered with dust, and the strings were rusty and slack. Slowly he tightened one of the strings, strumming it gently with his thumb. It snapped suddenly. Tom shrugged, put the mandolin back in its case, and glanced around the room. In one corner was a built-in bookcase with a wide empty shelf at its top. He reached up and put the mandolin there. Then he walked quickly to the bathroom. There was dust in the bottom of the bathtub. Impatiently he washed it out and let the tub fill while he shaved, bending almost double to see himself in the mirror.

"Hurry up!" Betsy called.

When he got downstairs, he found a plate of bacon and eggs waiting for him at one end of the big, marble-topped kitchen table. At the other end Betsy was seated, determinedly writing on a pad. "We've got to get more stuff out of the car and unpack the rest of the boxes the truck brought," she said, "and we've got to get the girls enrolled in school."

"I've got to call Sims and tell him about Edward," Tom said. "He should know, in case he makes any trouble."

"I've got to clear out Grandmother's closets," Betsy said. "Her clothes are still there. And if you want the television set in the living room, you better see about getting it hooked up."

"The main thing for me to do," he said, "is

to get the information we'll need to make some sort of decision on your housing project. I've got to get a copy of the zoning regulations, and we'll probably have to find out the procedure for getting an exception to them. We ought to have at least three contractors look the place over and give us bids on rebuilding the carriage house and putting in roads. God, Betsy, there's so much! I can't go to church today. I'm going to stay here and write letters."

"You're going to church!" she said. "We're going to church every Sunday. From now on."

"You go," he said.

"Why won't you?"

"I'm sorry," he said, feeling embarrassed. "You take the kids and go to church, and I'll stay here and write letters."

Betsy put her pencil down, picked up the plate from which he had just eaten his eggs, and put it in the sink. With her back turned to him she said, "Tommy, I'm asking you a favor. Go to church with me and the kids."

"All right," he said.

"Even if you're bored," she said, "try it. Maybe someday it would help you to stop worrying all the time."

"I don't worry all the time!"

"All right. But try it. I don't know about you, but I've been miserable for a long time. I used to think it was that damn little house, and it was partly, but it was more. We can't just go on being scared all the time, Tommy. Sometime it will have to stop."

"If you want me to go to church, I'll go," he said. "I didn't know you were miserable all the time."

"You know what I mean!"

"Sure."

"There seems to be something hanging over us, something that makes it hard to be happy."

"I know," he said.

"It isn't your fault. It's just something we both have to wrestle with."

"I'm all right," he said.

"I'm all right too. I just feel I'd like to go to church."

"Okay," he said. "Before we go, I'll call Sims."

"There isn't time."

Reluctantly Tom went upstairs and put on a blue suit. When he returned to the kitchen, Betsy was combing the children's hair. The two girls wore fluffy white dresses and Pete was in gray flannel shorts and a brown jacket. "Why do we have to wear party clothes to go to church?" Barbara asked.

"We just do," Betsy said. "Get in the car."

After leaving the children at the Sunday school in the annex of the Episcopal church, Tom followed Betsy into the church itself They sat in a back pew, and Betsy knelt gracefully to pray. Her face was drawn and serious. Tom glanced away from her, feeling somehow that he was invading her privacy. An unseen organ started to hum melodiously, and an acolyte appeared before the altar and lit fourteen candles with a long, silver-handled taper. All around Tom the pews were filled with elderly ladies, many of whom knelt. Tom glanced at Betsy and saw she was still on her knees, her eyes closed, her face rapt. How beautiful she is, he thought. He knelt uncomfortably beside her and shut his eyes.

An hour later, when Tom got home, he went right to the telephone and called Sims. When Sims heard about Edward, he swore, the oaths sounding strangely cultivated and precise as he spoke them.

"Do you think he can make any trouble for us?" Tom asked.

"It depends on what he calls 'proof' — if he has anything in writing he might make things difficult. If he tried to contest the will, it could drag on for months."

"If it were a long delay, it could break me," Tom said. "I've got to turn this place over fast — the longer we hold it, the less money anybody's going to have. Perhaps I could settle with him out of court."

"Maybe that's what he's counting on," Sims said. "I wouldn't consider it. I know damn well your grandmother meant you to have everything — we talked about it countless times. I'd hang on and see what kind of case he's got. Let him find out how hard it is to go to law before you talk to him."

"Is there anything we can do while we're waiting?"

"Not much," Sims said. "Actually, I won't be able to help you much from now on. The whole thing will be up to the Probate Judge — I've already sent him a copy of the will. He'll be the one who will have to rule on any claims Edward puts in."

"Who is he?"

"Bernstein — Saul Bernstein. He has an office on Main Street, I think — I hear he's lived in South Bay all his life. It might pay you to drop in and see him."

"Do you have any idea what kind of guy he is?"

"None," Sims said. "Never met him."

Tom thanked Sims and hung up. He decided to write Bernstein for an appointment. It was curious to think that so much depended on a man he had never met.

19

It was nine o'clock Tuesday morning. Judge Saul Bernstein, a small stout man with a large mole on his left cheek, climbed the stairs to the third floor of the Whitelock building, the second biggest office building in the town of South Bay. Puffing a little, he walked into the bare, linoleum-floored room which was his office and smiled at his secretary, a thin girl bent intently over her typewriter. "Good morning, Sally," he said. "How are you feeling today?"

Her hands stopped fluttering over the keys, and she looked up at him gratefully. "Fine, Judge," she said. "My cold's almost gone."

He sat down behind his scarred pine desk in the corner of the room and looked at the morning mail, which his secretary had opened for him. The top letter asked for an appointment the following Saturday or any evening, if that would not be too inconvenient. "I'd like to talk to you about settling the estate of the late Mrs. Florence Rath," the letter said. "I have also been told that you might be able to advise me on the possibility of subdividing her land into one-acre lots eventually. . . ." The letter referred to the will Sims had sent to Bernstein and concluded with advance gratitude for any help Bernstein could offer. It was signed, "Thomas R. Rath."

Bernstein had just finished reading the letter when the telephone on his desk rang. His secretary answered it, using an extension on her own desk and said "It's for you, Judge. He won't give his name."

"Hello?" Bernstein said.

For a moment there was no answer but the humming in the receiver.

"Hello?" Bernstein repeated.

"I want to talk to the judge!" a heavy voice replied.

"This is Judge Bernstein. Who is this calling?"

"Are you the judge that handles wills?" the voice asked.

"Yes, I'm the judge of the Probate Court," Bernstein said briskly. "Give me your name, please."

"My name is Schultz, Edward Schultz," the voice said, "and I have a claim to make. . . ."

Bernstein listened to Schultz for a long time. When he had hung up, he picked up Tom's letter and reread it. His stomach was beginning to hurt, as it always did when he saw he was going to have to arbitrate a fight.

Thomas Rath, he thought — the grandson of the old lady. Saul Bernstein remembered old Florence Rath well. He had first seen her more than thirty years ago, when his own father and mother had moved from a tenement in Brooklyn to open a delicatessen in South Bay. It had been a small delicatessen, not at all the kind of establishment that Florence Rath had patronized, except on holidays when it was the only store open. Florence Rath had often telephoned the store on Sundays to ask casually for a small jar of cheese or a can of anchovies to be delivered to her house, which had been more than six miles away from the store. More than once Saul Bernstein had bicycled up the long steep hill and around the two sharp curves by the outcroppings of rock to deliver a bottle of olives, or some other item which brought a profit of about a nickel, and often the servants who received the delivery had never bothered to see that he was tipped.

Saul Bernstein remembered many things about Florence Rath. Once she had come into his family's store. That had been in 1931, when the depression had been at its worst, and his father had been almost at the point of giving up the store and going back to New York to look for a job. The heat in the store had been turned off for reasons of economy, and Saul Bernstein's parents had stood behind the little counter all day wearing heavy coats, mufflers, and gloves and slapping their hands against their shoulders to keep warm. The store had been damp and had smelled of mildew, and a few jars had broken when their contents froze. Saul Bernstein hadn't been in the store much himself in those days, for his family had insisted that he and his two brothers spend as much time as possible in the high school, where it was warm, but on this particular Sunday when Florence Rath came in, his mother had been lying in her little room upstairs ill, with her husband taking care of her, and Saul had been in charge of the store. Florence Rath had been dressed in a long fur coat, and while she waited for him to bring her a box of mixed nuts, she had complained. "Why don't you keep this place warm?" she had said. "Are you trying to freeze your customers to death?"

"No, ma'am," he had replied and had felt obliged to add, "The furnace broke — we're having it fixed."

Saul Bernstein had a long memory. He remembered when he had been a young lawyer, only a year out of school, and a hardware merchant had come to him and asked him to collect a bill from Mrs. Rath for some expensive garden tools which the merchant said she had ordered and never paid for. That had been in the days when Bernstein had been spending most of his time sitting patiently in a tiny office, hopefully listening for the footsteps of possible clients in the hall and trying to forget the advice of his best friends, who told him that he ought to go into New York to practice law, because there was no place for a Jewish attorney in a small, hidebound Connecticut town notorious for its prejudice against Jews. The hardware merchant with his claim against Mrs. Rath had been Bernstein's first client, for the simple reason that all the other lawyers in the town had refused to handle his case. Bernstein had been glad to get it, and he had burned with righteous indignation at the thought of the rich old woman at the top of the hill ordering tools from the poor merchant and refusing to pay for them. He had almost gone charging to the top of the hill to berate her, but an innate caution had stopped him, and instead, he had made inquiries around the town and discovered that Mrs. Rath was famous for paying her bills the day she received them. He had found from the hardware merchant that a gardener of Mrs. Rath's had bought the tools, and further investigation had shown that the gardener had been discharged by Mrs. Rath two days before the purchase of tools had been made. And so Bernstein had turned the case over to the police, who eventually had extracted payment from the gardener, and he had felt that on his first case he had learned a lesson: to investigate thoroughly.

All this had happened long ago. Since then Saul Bernstein had prospered in the town of South Bay, despite the predictions of his best friends. He had grown reasonably rich, and respected, and might have been happy except for one thing: he detested justice almost as much as he detested violence or cruelty of any other kind.

He had found this out in 1940, when he had been made judge of the Municipal Court. One of the first men to appear before him had been a truck driver who had got drunk and driven his truck into a tree. The man had been about forty years old, with a red face and dismayed blue eyes, and he had pleaded for mercy. He had explained that his job depended upon his driving license, which would be taken away from him if he were convicted of drunken driving, and standing there in court, full of hurt dignity, he had said his wife was pregnant, and that he didn't want to lose his job.

"But this is your second offense," Bernstein had said. "According to the record, you were convicted of driving while under the influence of liquor only two years ago."

"That's why I can't be convicted now!" the man had replied desperately. "I'll never get my license back again!"

And he had asked for mercy, but Bernstein had been in the business of giving justice, and with his stomach aching, he had given justice, and the man had turned away with a look of utter despair on his red, forlorn face.

It is not an easy thing for a judge to find he detests justice, and Bernstein had not admitted his discovery to himself for a long while. He had not faced it until 1948, when he had had a choice between becoming Probate Judge in South Bay, or going on to a higher court. There had been some temptation to leave South Bay, for in spite of his new eminence, his wife had not been asked to join any of the women's clubs in town, but he had chosen differently for two reasons: the idea of having to judge cases involving long prison sentences, or even the death penalty, appalled him, and he had evolved the theory that justice is bearable to the judge only when it is based on complete knowledge of the disputants as well as the law. He had a horror of sentencing men he knew almost nothing about. In South Bay, where he knew almost everyone and had plenty of time to devote to each case, Bernstein was able to withhold his decisions until he had assembled complete information. Rarely was he put in the position of having to decide what was justice for strangers.

So Bernstein had chosen to stay in South Bay and become the judge of the Probate Court, which was primarily concerned with the orderly disposal of papers rather than people. And somewhat to his own astonishment, he had become enormously powerful in the town, for people had found that hating justice as he did, he dispensed it extremely well and they called him in on disputes of all kinds, even those which had nothing to do with the Probate Court, and when, after delaying as long as he could Bernstein delivered his opinion, it had a weight in the town more than that of any other man. He and his wife were rarely asked to cocktail parties or dinners, but he was almost always appointed moderator at town meetings or on any occasion, formal or informal, where impartiality was needed, and few people knew how his stomach hurt when he raised his pudgy hand and said, "Yes, yes, I understand, but let us now examine the other point of view. . . ."

Now as Judge Bernstein reread the letter he had received from Tom Rath and recalled the conversation he had just had over the telephone with Edward Schultz, the gnawing in his stomach grew worse and worse. Disputed wills were always painful, almost as painful as divorce cases. They brought out the worst in everyone, Bernstein knew from experience. On the surface this case was simple: a rich young heir was apparently trying to cut out a faithful old servant. Usually things turn out to be exactly as they appear on the surface, Bernstein had found, but not always. He wondered what young Thomas Rath was like — probably one of those commuters who did their shopping in Bermuda shorts, sporting a cigarette in a long holder, he decided — old Mrs. Rath would be apt to have a grandson like that. And this man Edward Schultz, who had sounded rather lunatic over the telephone, what sort of man was he? Which of the two men would be pleased by justice?

But more than a dispute over a will had been dropped on his desk that morning, Bernstein reflected. If Rath got the land, he apparently intended to try to subdivide it into one-acre lots. The Rath estate was in a "Triple A Zone," where no estate of less than ten acres was supposed to exist. That meant that if Rath got the land, there would be a zoning fight. Bernstein had lived in South Bay so long that he could predict the intensity of any dispute, if not its outcome, and he thought, "Not a zoning fight now — all we need is a zoning fight now!"

Sometimes it was almost a disadvantage to have lived in a town so long, because Bernstein knew all the people in the local government so well that he could foretell how they would answer almost any question, and without moving from his chair could conduct a fairly accurate public-opinion poll, a process which was often disturbing. Now he imagined what the various leaders in South Bay would say if Thomas Rath asked the Zoning Board to let him divide his land. Old John Bradbury, chairman of the Zoning Board, would explode at the very thought. He would immediately tie the whole question up with the controversy over whether to build a new public school. "Twenty acres with one house will bring in one family which will use a private school," old Bradbury would say exasperatedly. "Twenty acres with twenty houses will bring in twenty families, all of whom will expect the town to educate their children!"

And old Mr. Parkington, whose estate was near the south side of the Rath property, would have a double reason for apoplectic objections. As a member of the Zoning Board he had been one of the people who had instituted the ten-acre area in the first place, "to preserve the rural beauties of South Bay," and for more than fifteen years he had conducted a personal crusade against any effort to change the zoning ordinances. His reaction to having land so near his own converted into a housing project would be picturesque, Bernstein reflected grimly, and hoped he wouldn't have to see it.

The worst part of such a fight would be, Bernstein thought, that the arguments in favor of allowing Rath to subdivide his land would be as apoplectic as the arguments against it. Bob Murphy, who since 1931 had been a member of the Zoning Board, would use the case as an excuse to continue his unending battle against what he termed "the privileged few." And old Mrs. Allison, the fourth member of the board, would undoubtedly agree with everyone on both sides of the controversy, but would end by voting for young Rath, because she would be almost sure to judge him the underdog.

If there had been a fifth member of the Zoning Board, Bernstein could have foretold how the case would go with little possibility of error, but there was no fifth member. The post was vacant and seemed likely to remain vacant for a long time. It had been vacant ever since Harold Mathews, a tight-lipped Yankee who had decided each case on its merit, had died a month ago, for every time anyone had been suggested to take Mathews' place, a great fuss had been made by those who believed the new member would weight the board against them. Sooner or later a new member would have to be named, but meanwhile even Bernstein couldn't predict how zoning cases would be decided. All he knew was that there would be a bitter fight, the very thought of which made his stomach ache worse than ever. How violent Schultz had sounded over the telephone! *"I want justice,"* he had said. I wonder how many murders have been committed, and how many wars have been fought with that as a slogan, Bernstein thought. When they say they want justice, they always want someone else to get the sharp end of it. Justice is a thing that is better to give than to receive, but I am sick of giving it, he thought. I think it should be a prerogative of the gods.

20

That Tuesday morning, Tom perfected the latest draft of the speech he was writing for Ralph Hopkins. The whole text, which was now about thirty pages long ("We can cut it later," Hopkins said), had come to seem a sort of penance from which he would never escape, an endless tract, a meaningless life-work.

At noon Tom took the speech up to Bill Ogden. He thought he knew precisely what would happen next. Ogden would read it and say it was terrible. Tom would then rewrite it again and be asked to dinner in Hopkins' apartment. Hopkins would say it was wonderful and tell him to do it over again, and this whole process would doubtlessly be repeated over and over again until September 15, when Hopkins would presumably walk out on the speaker's platform in some big hotel in Atlantic City and tell everybody how delighted he was to be there.

But it didn't happen that way at all. Tuesday when Tom took the speech up to Ogden, Ogden laid it negligently among some other papers on his desk without even glancing at the first page.

"Thanks, Tom," he said casually. "We're going to take you off this now and give Gordon Walker a crack at it."

Tom waited, thinking there would be some other assignment for him, but apparently there was none. Ogden picked up his telephone and placed a call to someone in San Francisco. Tom got up uncertainly, thinking Ogden would tell him to wait, but Ogden just sat there, holding the telephone receiver negligently to his ear, saying nothing. I shouldn't dislike the guy so much, Tom thought. After all, he's awfully good at his job. He went back to his own office and sat down. Why had they taken him off the speech? Did that mean he had failed at it? Or was it normal procedure to pass the speech around among several of Hopkins' assistants? Tom didn't know.

There was nothing for him to do. Only a few minutes ago he had dreaded the prospect of coming back to his office and starting to rewrite the speech, but now he would have welcomed it. There was nothing for him to do. How long would Hopkins pay him to sit in a neat little office, with a secretary outside, with nothing to do? Maybe that was the way Hopkins got rid of people. In this strange, polite world high in the sky above Rockefeller Center, maybe nobody ever really got fired. Maybe all Hopkins did was to give a man nothing to do, absolutely nothing to do, until he started to go out of his mind sitting uselessly in his office all day, and resigned. Maybe that was the polite, smooth way to get rid of a man nobody wanted.

It wouldn't work, Tom thought. If they tried that on me, I'd buy magazines and just sit here having a good time, making nine thousand dollars a year. It wouldn't be so bad to get nine thousand dollars a year for doing absolutely nothing. I'd find something to keep me busy. By God, I'd work on selling Grandmother's land.

But that state of affairs wouldn't last long — of course Hopkins would fire a man if he insisted on staying, after he had been given nothing to do for a few weeks. Giving a man nothing to do would just be a warning; it would be offering him an opportunity to get out gracefully.

Maybe that isn't it at all, Tom thought.

Maybe they're just clever enough to know that a man goes stale on a speech after he's worked it over a few times. This is probably routine, and because this mental-health thing is a new project, they just don't have anything else for me at the moment. That's all it is — just routine. He got up and started pacing up and down his office, feeling much as he had during the war when he heard of another jump coming up. He glanced at his watch and nervously wound it.

I wonder if old Edward really has any proof, he thought; I wonder if Grandmother did write a later will and give it to him, but that's impossible; she wouldn't have done that without telling me. I wonder if we really will be able to sell off the land in small lots. This man Bernstein will be able to tell me — I wonder what he's like.

I shouldn't be thinking of private business, he thought. I should be showing initiative on this mental-health project. I shouldn't expect Ogden to keep giving me assignments; I should dream up assignments of my own. I bet Ogden never has to be told what to do. I'll think of what has to be done, and I'll do it. How the hell *do* you start a national committee on mental health? You get a list of big shots for members — Hopkins undoubtedly has that in his mind already. You get the thing financed — and I bet Hopkins already has some understanding with the foundations about that. He could pay for the thing himself as another tax deduction, but he'll need the prestige of the foundations, and he wouldn't have gone this far if he didn't have it all lined up. He'll need the cooperation of the medics, and that's why he's working so hard on this speech. What else will he need? A little knowledge of what the problems in the field really are — that's the only thing nobody seems to be bothering about. If we're going to figure out a program, we ought to have a list of what the experts think the basic problems are. I ought to interview the top medics. I ought to see what the public library has on the subject. I ought to become well informed.

I can't start interviewing people without Ogden's permission, he thought — that might be tipping Hopkins' hand too soon. But I can start getting books to read, and I can ask Ogden for permission to interview people — that at least will let him know I'm on the job.

Tom pressed a button on his desk, and when his secretary came in, he dictated a memorandum to Ogden requesting permission to visit the state mental hospitals and several leading psychiatrists to gather information about mental-health problems. He added that he was planning to get together a bibliography on the subject — he thought that sounded quite impressive. He had just told his secretary he was going out to lunch, and that he would spend the afternoon at the public library, when the telephone rang. He picked up the receiver.

"Hello," a familiar deep voice said. "Is this Mr. Rath?"

"Hello, Caesar," Tom replied with sinking heart, and he thought, Here it comes. So Caesar wasn't just embarrassed at seeing me — he was biding his time. I wonder if he's been in touch with Maria.

"I'm off duty now, and I thought maybe we might have lunch together," Caesar said.

"Sure!" Tom replied with forced cheer. "Where will I meet you?"

"In the lobby by the information booth," Caesar said. "What time would be best for you?"

"Right away," Tom replied. "I'll be right down."

Caesar, still dressed in his plum-colored elevator operator's uniform, was leaning against the wall by the information booth, smoking a cigarette. He grinned diffidently when he saw Tom coming toward him.

"This is a swell idea!" Tom said heartily, ashamed that in addition to all the other strains involved in their relationship, he should find it awkward to have lunch with a man in an elevator operator's uniform. "I know a swell little place on Forty-ninth Street, up toward Sixth Avenue."

"Fine," Caesar replied, and fell in beside him. They walked rapidly across Rockefeller Plaza. Actually, Tom had no restaurant clearly in mind — he simply wanted to find a place where they wouldn't be seen. The impulse to keep his connection with Caesar completely private was overpowering. They walked in silence for several minutes. When they finally came to a dingy little Mexican restaurant and bar on Sixth Avenue which looked like an establishment none of his acquaintances ever would frequent, Tom said, "This is the place. I like Mexican food, don't you?"

"Sure," Caesar replied.

They went in and sat down at a dimly lighted table. A waiter in a stained apron came to take their orders. Over the bar a radio was playing a song in which a girl kept saying over and over again, "I love you."

"The drinks are on me," Tom said. "Order

anything you want."

"I'd like Scotch," Caesar replied. "Some Black and White."

"Make it two double Black and White's," Tom said to the waiter.

"Funny, the way we just happened to run into each other," Caesar said.

"I'm falling for you," the woman on the radio sang. "Falling, falling, falling, head over heels in love."

"It is funny," Tom said. "I sure was surprised to see you."

The waiter put their drinks before them, and Tom lifted his to his lips eagerly.

"Well, this is better than that old jungle juice we used to drink in New Guinea," Caesar said.

"It sure is!" Tom replied. The phrase "jungle juice" sounded antique to him — he didn't really remember drinking any at all.

"You've sure done all right for yourself," Caesar said. "Assistant to Ralph Hopkins!"

"The breaks," Tom said. "It isn't as much of a job as you might think."

"Mind you, I'm not complaining," Caesar said. "Things have gone pretty good for us."

"You married?"

"Sure. Are you?"

"Yes," Tom said. "I was married before the war."

The girl on the radio finished her song. "And now the news," an announcer said. The bartender turned the radio off.

"Did you go back to Rome after the war?" Tom asked.

"Sure — as soon as I got out of the hospital. Gina and I got married in forty-seven. We got three kids now."

Tom said nothing. He finished his drink and motioned to the bartender to bring two more.

"Three kids," Caesar repeated. "Things were pretty tough for us for a while, but I've got a twenty per cent disability because of my back, and Gina is working now. We're making out all right. She runs an elevator over in the Empire State building. Sometimes she takes a night shift and sometimes I do — we got it worked out so one of us is always home with the kids."

"Sounds like a pretty good arrangement," Tom said.

"We got a nice apartment," Caesar replied. "It's a hell of a lot better than we'd have had if we'd stayed in Rome, the way Gina's folks wanted us to."

"I guess things are pretty tough back there," Tom said.

"I'll say! We hear from Gina's old lady every once in a while. Those people don't have it easy."

Tom took a long sip of his drink. "Caesar," he said "did you ever hear anything about Maria?"

Caesar looked down at the table. "I did," he said. "That's what I wanted to talk to you about."

"How is she?"

"I haven't heard anything lately — not for more than a year. You knew she married that guy who had the bakeshop, Louis Lapa?"

"No!" Tom said. "When?"

Caesar seemed embarrassed. "She married him about two months after we left," he said.

"I'm glad to hear it," Tom said. "I certainly am glad to hear it. Louis was a nice guy."

Caesar glanced up. "You knew she had a son?" he said. "She had a son a little while later."

"No," Tom said. "I didn't know that."

"She's got a boy," Caesar said, "and things weren't going well for them. You know Louis had a bad leg, and it's given him a lot of trouble."

"I'm sorry to hear that," Tom said.

"He was in the hospital for a long while trying to get that leg fixed and they lost the store."

"I'm sorry to hear that," Tom repeated.

"Gina's folks helped them out for a while," Caesar said. "I don't know how you feel about these things, Mr. Rath, but when I saw you, and found you were doing so well and all, I got to thinking about Maria and her boy, and I wondered whether you could do anything for them."

Tom said nothing.

"Of course, I haven't heard from them lately," Caesar continued, "but if you wanted, I could find out about them — Gina's mother could tell me easy. Maria is a cousin of Gina's."

Still Tom said nothing.

"What I mean is," Caesar continued earnestly, "things are so much easier for us here than they are for them. Gina and I manage to send a little back every month. And I thought the way things worked out for you and Maria . . ."

"I've got a wife here!" Tom said. "A wife and three kids!"

"I'm not trying to make any trouble for you," Caesar said hastily. "I just thought that if you had a little money you didn't know what to do with . . ."

"But . . ." Tom began.

"I'm just trying to say it would be a blessing," Caesar interrupted. "Anything you could do would be a blessing."

"But I don't even know whether Maria would want me to do anything!" Tom said. "Maybe Louis wouldn't like it."

"I'm not even sure Louis is still alive," Caesar said. "The last I heard, he was pretty sick. And even if he is alive, it's hard for a sick man to get work in Rome."

"You don't really know, though, do you? For all you know, they might be doing fine."

"I haven't heard for over a year," Caesar said, "but I could find out."

"You don't understand," Tom said. "I'm practically broke. And I never could send Maria much of anything without my wife finding out about it, and how could I ever expect her to understand a thing like that?"

"I'm not trying to make trouble for you," Caesar said. "I just thought I'd talk to you about it. You ought to know that things are pretty tough back there."

"I can't promise anything," Tom said. "I'd like to hear how they're doing, but I can't promise anything."

"I'll write a letter," Caesar said. "It may take a little time to hear. . . ."

"All right!" Tom said. He was breathing hard. "Let's not talk about it any more now.

Let's have something to eat."

"Okay," Caesar said.

Tom beckoned to the waiter, and they ordered hot Mexican chile con carne which burned their tongues. Hank Mahoney's name was in Tom's mind constantly, but Caesar never mentioned it. Maria was obviously his only concern.

An hour later Tom returned to his office, feeling exhausted. "Mr. Ogden called while you were gone," his secretary said. "He asked you not to do anything more now."

"What?" Tom asked.

"He said he'd just gotten your memo, and he wanted you to know right away that he doesn't want you to talk about the mental-health committee with anybody. Not now, he said."

"All right," Tom replied. "Thank you." He sat down at his desk and stared out the window. After a few moments he got up and went to the library. In spite of everything, it was necessary to succeed at his job, he thought — maybe it would be more necessary than ever now.

21

"How did it go today?" Betsy asked when she met him at the station that night.

"Fine," Tom said, just as he always did. There's no point in carrying your troubles home with you, somebody had said. You're supposed to leave them in the office.

"There's a man named Bugala coming to see you," she said. "He's a contractor. He spent all morning looking at the carriage house."

"Bugala?" Tom asked. "He's not one of the contractors I wrote to."

"I don't know about that," she replied, "but he wants to see you. And he looks to me like a man who can get things done."

When they got back to the house, Antonio Bugala was waiting, sitting in a battered Chevrolet pickup truck. He was stocky, dark-haired, and had once been told by a girl that he looked like pictures of Napoleon as a young man. This was a compliment he had never forgotten — he much preferred it to the dubious distinction conferred upon him by his nickname, which was "Buggy." "Buggy Bugala" had been brought up in South Bay and for the past five years had been astonishing everyone by becoming almost as successful as he had always predicted. Already, at the age of twenty-eight, Bugala was a contractor with thirty-four men, including his father, on his pay roll.

Now Bugala jumped out of his pickup truck and walked cockily over to Tom. "I'm Tony Bugala," he said. "I hear you got some building and road work to be done."

"How did you hear about it?" Tom asked.

Bugala glanced at him sharply. There's no use in giving this guy a lesson in business, he thought. In point of fact, Bugala had cultivated the affections of a secretary in the office of the leading contractor in South Bay, and she obligingly told him about all jobs on which her boss was asked to bid, but obviously this was a trade secret which could not be divulged.

"Friend told me," Bugala said honestly. "Said you wanted that old barn made into a house."

"I just want some estimates," Tom said. "I won't be in a position to do anything about it for some time."

"I looked at it this morning," Bugala said. "You can't do much with it — it's just a shell. You could build a house from the ground up for what it would cost you to make anything out of that place."

"Are you sure?" Betsy asked.

Bugala thought, You figure I go around discouraging business for the fun of it? Aloud he said, "There's no basement — just a dirt floor. That stone is only a façade, and the wood under it is rotten."

Well, there goes what we thought would be a sure initial profit, Tom thought. He said, "If we divided this land into one-acre lots, how much would it cost to run in a road that would give access to all of them?"

"You figuring on doing that?"

"I'm just looking into it."

"You got permission from the Zoning Board?"

"I haven't even asked. I don't have title to the place yet."

"Your land go to that row of pines over there?"

"That's right. The stone fence marks the other boundaries."

"Let me take a look at it," Bugala said. He wanted time to think, for he had immediately perceived there might be more to do here than run in a road or convert a barn into a house. The light was fading, and the row of pines was dark against the sky. Bugala plunged into the grass, which was growing knee high, and walked rapidly toward the pines, darting quick glances in all directions. He took in everything — the astonishing view of the Sound, the gradual slope of the land which would provide a view from every lot, and the outcroppings of rock, which probably would mean expensive blasting, but no drainage problems. Putting in a road would be easy, he figured — the driveway to the old house could probably be continued right along the west boundary of the property. With a view like that, why sell acre lots? There was no place else in South Bay, almost nowhere else within commuting distance of New York, where a man could buy such a view of the Sound. Bugala's imagination, which was always at a slow simmer, suddenly began to boil over. Why not put up a whole housing project on quarter-acre lots? All right, you'd have to jump over the Zoning Board somehow, but if it could be done — the prospect was fantastic!

Bugala's mind did not plod, it soared, and he abruptly arrived at a picture of the way the land could be developed, complete with all financial details and photographs in national magazines showing what Antonio Bugala, *Mr.* Antonio Bugala, *Esquire*, had done. You'd start by running in a crooked road along the west boundary — a straight road would be cheaper, but everybody in Connecticut was crazy and liked crooked roads better. In all, Bugala judged with a practiced eye, there must be more than twenty acres of land. You wouldn't put in straight rows of houses, you'd stagger them, about eighty houses on quarter-acre lots, each with a view of the Sound — you'd set them in just like seats in a theater, the back row the highest, and the front row the lowest, only you'd be careful to avoid straight lines. You'd put planting around each house and perhaps push up some earth between houses, so in time you couldn't see one house from another, at least in the summer — maybe it would pay to transplant some fairly big bushes. The houses would be modern, very low to preserve the view, with big windows overlooking the Sound, and no cellars, to save having to blast through that ledge. It might pay to go arty and get a fancy architect to figure out enough variations on a few simple modern designs to prevent the place from looking like a low-cost housing development. The houses wouldn't have to be much — what you'd be selling would be the view. With just an adequate house, you might get twenty-five thousand dollars for a quarter acre of that view. If you brought in your materials and heavy machinery to build all eighty houses at the same time, you might be able to put up something pretty good for a base cost of no more than fifteen thousand dollars per unit, for labor and materials.

Tony Bugala began to sweat. That meant there was a potential profit of ten thousand dollars on each quarter acre of land, he figured — a possible take of $800,000 before taxes, if it were handled right, and if you could raise the initial money for labor and materials. He wondered how much money Tom Rath had, and whether Tom had any clear idea of the potentials of the place. Quickly a lot of facts came together in his mind. Tom drove an old car; the land was obviously run down; people were saying old Mrs. Rath had died broke. Obviously Tom Rath didn't have much. Bugala wondered whether Tom would sell him the land cheap — maybe the thing to do was to tell him a road couldn't be put in, the whole venture was impractical, but he'd take the place off his hands for twenty or thirty thousand dollars. No, that wouldn't work — in the long run it never paid to try that stuff, not if you planned on getting big. If you wanted to become really tops in the business, you had to forget that small-time cleverness and play it straight. Anyway, Rath had already asked other contractors for estimates on roads, and one of them would be sure to tell him he had a potential gold mine in the view.

The thing to do, Bugala decided, was just to talk the whole idea over with Rath, maybe try to form some kind of partnership, even a stock company to raise the money to put up the houses all at once. After all, there was no reason to try to cut Rath out — there would be plenty of profit to go around, a long way around, and it was more important to get part of it than to fail in a try to get it all. Tony Bugala, a man of quick enthusiasms and fast decisions, immediately made up his mind to drive some sort of bargain with Tom. For five years he had been looking for something big, something into which he could throw all his energies, one great calculated risk that would take him out of the small stuff and put him into the big time, where no one had thought "Buggy" Bugala could go. This was it, he figured — there would have to be lots of talking and fussing around and figuring and paper signing, but if the Zoning Board didn't block them, this was it.

Bugala had jumped so far ahead in his thoughts that when he reached the row of pines and looked up to find himself standing in a bare field, with the light almost gone, he was surprised. He turned and started walking rapidly back toward Tom. If I can't get Rath's co-operation, the whole deal's off, he thought — that's the first step. His mind, however, refused to wait for the first step — it kept bounding ahead. The financing wouldn't be hard. Rath could probably raise fifty thousand dollars on the land alone, once it was re-zoned, Bugala figured. As each house went up, more could be borrowed on it. On his own heavy construction equipment, Bugala figured, he could raise twenty thousand, and maybe he could get more on a personal note — the banks were already beginning to keep a friendly eye on Antonio Bugala. It wouldn't be difficult to find a partner to throw in another twenty thousand, maybe, and with a hundred thousand in the kitty, construction could begin. Put a down payment on the materials for all eighty houses, but concentrate on completing the first four. Sell those at twenty-five thousand apiece, and you've got your initial investment back!

While he was thinking all this, Tony Bugala was walking rapidly, almost running with enthusiasm, back to the house, where Tom and Betsy were standing with the three children. Tom watched Bugala's hurried movements with astonishment. It was growing chilly, and an evening breeze was starting to ruffle the distant waters of the Sound, which lay gray and nebulous in the last glow of twilight. Bugala came striding up to Tom, perspiring with excitement.

"Mr. Rath," he said bluntly, "I've got a proposition to make."

They sat in the kitchen of the old house talking until midnight. "Buggy" Bugala slammed the table with his small thick hand and, talking a mile a minute, described the houses he wanted to build so minutely that Tom could almost look out the window and see them. Betsy leaned forward, her face flushed and her lips parted, drinking it all in. "Eight hundred thousand dollars!" she said.

"Wait a minute," Tom said. "This is all fine, but before we go any farther, there are a few hard facts we got to take into account. In the first place, the estate isn't settled yet, and the will may be contested — it may be months before we have a clear title on this land. In the second place, the whole plan depends on our getting permission from the Zoning Board. I'll know more about that Saturday when I see Judge Bernstein, but meanwhile I wouldn't count on anything too much — it's never easy to put quarter-acre lots among a lot of big estates. In the third place, even if everything else goes all right, we're going to have to look for somebody to put up more cash. Even if I can raise fifty thousand on the land, and even if you can throw in twenty or thirty thousand, we've still got twenty or thirty thousand to go — and that's assuming that a hundred thousand is enough to start a project like this. And in the fourth place, Mr. Bugala, I don't mean to be discourteous, but I just met you for the first time tonight, and I don't want to commit myself on going into a venture like this with you. Have you ever done anything like this before?"

Bugala flushed. "I built six houses last year," he said. "I can do it. I built fifteen houses since the war. And you know what? During the war I put an air strip across Kiwan in eight days! Eight days! You ever seen Kiwan?"

"Yeah," Tom said. "I've seen it. Did you put that air strip in?"

"You're damn right! In eight days! And with the Japs bombing us every night!"

"You didn't have to pay your men for overtime on Kiwan," Tom said practically. "This is a different deal."

"All right," Bugala said. "I'll tell you something else I've done. You know that big place a guy named Hopkins just put up down where the old yacht club used to be? I built almost half of that. Now let me level with you — I wasn't the contractor, but plenty of it was subcontracted to me. I did most of the outside construction work, and damn near all the landscaping. You want to see what I can do, go down and look at the place. I'll give you a list of all the people I've done work for! Ask the bank about me. Ask anybody around here about me — I got a good name!"

"I don't doubt it," Tom said. "I just don't want to have to commit myself tonight."

"You wouldn't take my ideas and go to a big outfit with them, would you?"

"I don't plan to, but I don't want to commit myself," Tom said. "There are a lot of wrinkles to be ironed out of your ideas yet. Do you really think we can make a profit of ten thousand dollars on each house and quarter-acre lot?"

"Maybe — and what if we only make half that? Would that be so bad?"

"No, but how are you going to pay interest on a hundred thousand dollars while we're building? And there'll be taxes. It might be a year before we had anything to sell. We'd be operating on an awfully slim margin."

"Hell, we can borrow a hundred and ten thousand and use ten of it to pay the interest and taxes — that would last us almost two years!"

"I don't know," Tom said. "You make it sound awfully easy. What if you run into unexpected delays? What if you can't get your materials on time, or a storm washes us out when everything's half done, and what if a depression sets in, and we can't sell our houses when we finish them? This might be an easy way to make a pile, but it's also an easy way to go bankrupt!"

"Tom always looks at the dark side of everything!" Betsy said impatiently. "Tommy, sometimes I think you just look for reasons why nothing can ever get done."

"You got to gamble," Bugala said. "Hell, everything's a gamble! It's the guys who take the chances who make the dough! If I hadn't been willing to gamble, I'd still be on a pick and shovel gang!"

"I'm willing to gamble," Tom said. "I just want to make sure we've got the odds on our side."

Bugala laughed and stood up. "We'll make it work!" he said confidently. "Get in touch with me after you've talked to Judge Bernstein about the zoning."

The next morning on the way to the train, Tom asked Betsy to circle around by the waterfront, where the old yacht club had been, so he could look at the house Hopkins had built. Involuntarily, Betsy stepped on the brakes when they saw it. Hopkins' house was low, long and enormous. The old yacht club wharf had been removed, and in its place was a carefully buttressed sea wall and an elaborate artificial harbor, in which a tall white yawl was anchored. One wing of the house reached out over the edge of the harbor. At least twelve acres of green lawn separated the house from the road. Betsy whistled. "You mean you work for *that* guy?" she said.

22

That same morning Ralph Hopkins awoke in his Park Avenue apartment at precisely seven o'clock. He had been working on his speech about mental health until after midnight, and as soon as he opened his eyes, his thoughts were full of it again. The latest draft written by Ogden wasn't right, and Hopkins was beginning to wonder whether he was ever going to be able to devise a speech on mental health he wanted to give. Maybe the whole idea of starting a mental-health committee was a mistake. Glancing at his wrist watch, he saw it was quarter after seven. No time to worry about the speech now, he thought — there was a busy day ahead. He jumped lightly out of bed, stepped briskly across his small, simply furnished bedroom, and slid open a door leading to a large tiled shower room. Stripping off his white silk pajamas, he stepped into a booth and pulled a curtain. He turned an elaborate chromium dial on the wall in front of him, and hot water shot against him at a high velocity from a dozen nozzles placed in the booth above and on all sides of him. Gradually Hopkins turned the dial until the water was lukewarm — the doctor had forbidden him to take cold showers. He stood there in the lukewarm water for thirty seconds before turning the shower off and stepped out of the booth. From a special slot in the wall he drew an enormous, warm turkish towel. Wrapping himself in this, he walked to the other side of the room and stepped on a set of scales which had been built into the floor. He weighed a hundred and thirty-eight pounds, including the towel. That was three pounds too much, he figured, and made a mental note to cut down on his eating. It was stupid to get fat, he thought — half his friends were eating themselves into their graves.

After he had brushed his teeth and shaved, Hopkins went into his dressing room, where his valet had laid out his clothes. The valet was not there — Hopkins liked to have his clothes laid out for him, but hated to have people fussing about him. He dressed himself.

At quarter to eight Hopkins walked downstairs to the living room of his apartment, just as his personal secretary, Miss MacDonald, the elderly gray-haired woman Tom had observed in Hopkins' outer office, was arriving. She always began her working day at a quarter to eight in Hopkins' apartment and went to the office with him.

"Good morning, Miss MacDonald," he said cheerily. "What have you got on the docket for me today?"

"Mr. Albert Pierce is coming in to have breakfast with you," she said. "Mr. Pierce owns three television stations in Texas and two in Oklahoma. He has some programming suggestions he wants to discuss with you — remember his letters?"

"Yes," Hopkins said.

The breakfast business appointment was routine; it had been routine for ten years. So many people wanted to see Hopkins that it was necessary to fit them in wherever possible. First there were all the people who wanted to see him on company business — production people, research men, the top entertainers who had to be flattered, advertising executives with big contracts, the owners of affiliated stations, promotion men, publicity experts, sponsors, writers who were great artists and had never written for television, but now were going to. There were also bankers, real-estate men, investment experts, and lawyers who, under Hopkins' guidance, administered the holdings of the United Broadcasting Corporation. And in addition to all these people who wanted to see Hopkins, there were executives of the many corporations of which he was a director, and the men and women connected with the good works of which he was a trustee. Hopkins was a trustee of two universities, five hospitals, three public libraries, one fund for orphaned children, two foundations for the advancement of the arts and sciences, a home for the blind, a haven for crippled children, and a snug harbor for retired seamen. In addition to that, he was a member of committees and commissions studying, variously, conditions in South India, Public Health in the United States, Racial Segregation, Higher Standards for Advertising, the Parking Problem in New York City, Farm Subsidies, Safety on the Highways, Freedom of the Press, Atomic Energy, the House Rules of the City Club, and a Code of Decency for Comic Books.

"After Mr. Pierce, Dr. Andrews is coming up — it's time for your quarterly check-up," Miss MacDonald said.

Hopkins frowned slightly. It was only common sense to have a quarterly check-up, but he detested it. "All right, what next?" he asked.

"Because of Dr. Andrews, I haven't scheduled you for anything at the office before ten o'clock this morning. At that time Mr. Hebbard wants a conference with you — he's got some new cost estimates and time schedules. At eleven there's a board meeting, lasting through lunch. . . ."

She was interrupted by the doorbell. Hopkins opened the door. Albert Pierce, a large potbellied man wearing a wide cream-colored sombrero, walked in.

"Hello!" Hopkins said, shaking his hand heartily. "*So* good of you to come so early. I had hoped to have lunch with you, but my board is meeting today, and you know how it is! I *certainly* appreciate this chance to see you!"

The big man beamed. "Right nice of you to put yourself out for me!" he said.

Miss MacDonald slipped out a side door, and Hopkins led Pierce to the dining room. A waitress served Pierce a bowl of fresh fruit, waffles, and sausage patties. Hopkins had only a bowl of dry cereal with skim milk and a cup of black coffee. "I wish I had your appetite!" he said to his guest. "It's this city air that takes it away from a man!"

Throughout the meal Pierce expounded his views on television programs, which consisted mostly of the thought that more *old-fashioned* shows, such as square dances, rodeos, and hymn sings, would be welcomed by rural audiences. Hopkins agreed with him heartily. At a quarter of nine, the doorbell rang again, and Hopkins jumped up to answer it. That was one of the advantages in not having a servant open the door — it gave Hopkins an opportunity to conclude interviews without being impolite. Dr. Andrews, an urbane man with prematurely white hair, walked in, carrying a small black bag. *"Thank you for coming up,"* Hopkins said. "I'll be with you in a few moments. Mr. Pierce, this is Dr. Andrews — *don't* go, Mr. Pierce — I had hoped to chat with you longer. Well, if you *have* to go, I understand. I *certainly* do appreciate your advice on the programs, and you can be sure it will have effect!"

When Pierce had left, Hopkins and the doctor sat down in the living room. "How have you been feeling?" the doctor asked.

"Fine — better than ever!"

"Trouble getting to sleep?"

"Not a bit!"

The doctor opened his bag and took out a stethoscope. Hopkins took off his coat and opened his shirt. The doctor listened to his heart intently for several seconds. "It sounds pretty good," he said finally. "Had any more dizziness lately?"

"Not a trace of it!"

"Difficulty breathing?"

"No."

The doctor put his stethoscope back in his bag and took out his equipment for measuring blood pressure. Hopkins rolled up his sleeve and looked out the window at the green lawn on the roof while the doctor strapped the device to his arm. There was an interval of silence. "It's up a little," the doctor said finally. "Not badly — nothing to worry about."

"That's good," Hopkins said, relieved.

"It's a warning, though," the doctor continued. "I guess there's no use in my repeating it: you ought to slow down."

"I've been getting plenty of rest," Hopkins said.

"I'll say it to satisfy my own conscience," the doctor continued. "You ought to take a long vacation — a couple of months, just lying in the sun. You ought to get yourself a hobby, something to help you relax."

Hopkins looked at him intently, but said nothing.

"You ought to cut way down on your schedule," the doctor went on. "Start getting into your office about ten-thirty or eleven and leaving about three or four in the afternoon — there's no reason why a man in your position can't do that. In the long run, you'd be ensuring yourself more working hours. And cut out all these outside activities of yours — take it easy for a few years. You've got to slow down!"

"Are you advising me to retire, Doctor?" Hopkins asked dryly.

"No — I'd be satisfied if you just followed a normal, human routine!"

"I will," Hopkins said courteously. "I certainly appreciate your advice, Doctor, and I'll take it. Thanks *so* much for coming up so early this morning!"

When the doctor had gone, Miss MacDonald called for Hopkins' car, a black Cadillac five years old, driven by an aging Negro chauffeur. They started driving toward the United Broadcasting building. Before they had gone three blocks the car got caught in a bad traffic jam and could barely crawl. Hopkins put his head back on the soft gray uphol-

314

stery and closed his eyes. "You've got to slow down!" the doctor had said. It seemed to Hopkins that people had been telling him that all his life.

It had started when he was a boy in public school. He had been editor of the school paper, and though he had been too small to excel at athletics, he had been manager of the football and basketball teams. He had stood at the top of his class scholastically, and whenever there had been a dance or a school play, he had always been chairman of the arrangements committee. "You've got to slow down!" the teachers had told him. "Take it easy, boy — you'll wear yourself out!"

At Princeton, where he had gone on a scholarship, it had been more of the same. He had headed the debating team, managed the football team, and engaged in a dozen other activities in addition to maintaining an almost straight A average in his studies. "You've got to slow down!" his faculty adviser had told him. "Take it easy!"

But he had not slowed down. Summers he had worked at all kinds of jobs, always astonishing his employers with his energy. After college had come a brief stint in the Army, a period during which his friends had kidded him about wanting to be a general. Upon being released from service in 1919, he had worked for a few years at a brokerage house before going to the United Broadcasting Corporation, which had just been started. A year later he had met Helen Perry, who had at the time been a fashionable beauty in New York. He had pursued her with all the zeal he always devoted to anything he wanted, and on June 3, 1921, he had married her. Up to that time, Hopkins had never had a failure in his life.

"You've got to slow down!" Helen had started saying, even before they were married, but unlike the teachers and faculty advisers, she had not let it go at that. As she discovered that it was Hopkins' habit to spend most of his evenings and week ends at his office, she had become first annoyed, then indignant, and finally hurt and bewildered.

"Life isn't worth living like this," she had said. "I never see you! You've got to slow down!"

He had tried. Especially when their first child, Robert, had come, during the second year of their marriage, he had tried. He had come home every evening at six o'clock and conscientiously played with the baby and sat talking with his wife, and he had been genuinely appalled to find that the baby made him nervous, and that while he was talking to his wife, it was almost impossible for him to sit quietly. He had felt impelled to get up and pace up and down the room, jingling his change in his pockets and glancing at the clock. For the first time in his life, he had started to drink heavily during those long evenings at home. Gradually he had started staying late at the office again — by that time he had already had a fairly important job at the United Broadcasting Corporation. Helen had remonstrated with him. There had been recriminations, high-pitched arguments, and threats of divorce.

All right, it's a problem, he had said to himself after a particularly bitter scene — it's a problem that must be met head on, like all other problems. To Helen he had said, in a quiet voice, "I don't want to have any more scenes — they wear us both out. I'm prepared to admit that whatever is wrong is entirely my fault. I am preoccupied with my work — I've been that way all my life, and it is nothing for which you should blame yourself."

She had gone pale. "Do you want a divorce?" she had asked.

"No," he had said. "Do you?"

"No."

They had never talked about divorce again,

but she had begun to refer to his preoccupation with work as a disease. "You've got to do something about it," she had said, and had suggested a psychiatrist.

For two years Hopkins had submitted to psychoanalysis. Five times a week he had lain on a couch in the psychoanalyst's apartment on Sixty-ninth Street and recalled his childhood. His father had been a cheerful, rather ineffectual man who, each afternoon upon returning from his job as assistant manager of a small paper mill in an upstate New York village, had spent most of his time rocking on the front porch of their shabby but comfortable house. His mother had been disappointed by the modesty of her husband's achievements and aspirations and had been bitterly condescending to him. Leaving her family to fend for itself most of the time, she had thrown all her energy into working for the local garden club and a bewildering variety of social and civic organizations. As she gained positions of leadership in these groups, her resentment at her serenely undistinguished husband had grown. Finally she had established herself in a separate room on the third floor of their house and, throughout most of Ralph's boyhood, had conducted herself like a great lady temporarily forced to live with poor relatives.

Hopkins was not an introspective man, but in recounting all this to the psychoanalyst, he had said, "I always felt sorry for my father because my mother treated him so badly. She never gave me much time, either, except when I did something she thought was outstanding. Whenever I got a particularly good report card, or won anything, she'd take me up to her room to have tea alone with her. 'We're two of a kind,' she used to say. 'We get things done.' I suppose I got the impression from her that achievement means everything."

Hopkins had felt quite proud of his efforts at self-diagnosis and had been surprised when the psychoanalyst had disgarded his suggestions in favor of much more bizarre "explanations of neurosis." He had said that Hopkins probably had a deep guilt complex, and that his constant work was simply an effort to punish and perhaps kill himself. The guilt complex was probably based on a fear of homosexuality, he had said. To Hopkins, who had never consciously worried about homosexuality, or guilt, this had seemed like so much rubbish, but he had tried to believe it, for the psychoanalyst had said it was necessary for him to believe to be cured, and Hopkins had wanted to be cured, in order to make his wife happy.

The trouble had been that every time he left the psychoanalyst's office the temptation to return to his own office and bury himself in work had been irresistible. At the end of two years he had become the youngest vice-president of United Broadcasting and had told his wife he simply wouldn't have time for psychoanalysis any longer.

It had been shortly after this that he had rented an apartment to use for business meetings in New York and had drifted into the habit of staying away from his home, which had then been in Darien, for weeks at a time. His wife had not objected. She had gone in for horses for a while and, tiring of that, had become a relentless giver of parties. After Susan had been born in 1935, she had abruptly stopped the parties and had thrown herself into motherhood with abandon, firing the nursemaid who had taken care of her son and surrounding herself with *avant-garde* parents who discussed their children the way psychiatrists discuss their patients. Hopkins had never complained — he had been too grateful to her for letting him alone and, as he saw it, making up for his deficiencies as a parent.

Things had gone pretty well until 1943,

when Robert, their son, had been killed in the war. Hopkins had hurried home when his wife telephoned to tell him and had tried to sympathize with her, but all she had said was, "You never knew him! You never knew him!" Hopkins had stayed with her for three days, at the end of which time he had returned to his office and thrown himself harder than ever into his work.

"Slow down!" the doctors had been saying regularly ever since. "You've got to slow down!" But Helen, his wife, had stopped saying that to him. After Robert had been killed, she had gone for a brief time to a sanitarium, leaving Susan, her daughter, with the servants. After returning from the sanitarium, Helen had started to give parties again, and had begun to plan the great show place in South Bay, and had bought the yawl, and had seemed happier than she ever had in her life.

"This traffic!" Hopkins said now, as he sat in his limousine and looked out the window at the pedestrians on the sidewalk, who were making better time. "This traffic is terrible!" He sat back and consciously tried to relax, but it was impossible. A policeman blew his whistle sharply, and a taxi driver ahead started to curse. Hopkins shut his eyes. It was ridiculous to worry, it was unproductive. It would be better to think of the future, of things to be done. There was, for instance, the mental-health speech to revise. Hopkins took a cigarette out of his pocket and lit it. "Miss MacDonald," he said, "it looks as though we're going to be stuck in this traffic for quite a while. Would you mind taking dictation?"

23

"They want to use the top of the tower for sky watchers," Betsy said to Tom when he returned from work Friday night.

"What?" he asked in astonishment.

"It's Civilian Defense — they're making a plan for Civilian Defense here. They want to use our tower for airplane spotters until they get a permanent place for themselves."

"Oh, Lord," Tom groaned.

"Don't you approve?"

"I guess so," he said. "I don't know, it sounds so absurd. What do they want us to do?"

"Just let them use the tower for a few weeks. It's the highest place in South Bay, they said, and has the best view. Why is it absurd?"

"It's not," he said. "I'm just tired, and I don't like thinking about another war. I have a million other things to do."

"Sit down and have a drink," Betsy said. "Dinner will be ready in a few minutes."

That night Tom lay awake a long time worrying about Maria, about old Edward's claim on the estate, about zoning laws, and about the meeting he was to have with Bernstein in the morning. When he awoke he felt exhausted and so irritable that the high-pitched voices of the children at the breakfast table annoyed him. "Be quiet!" he said sharply to Janey when she said, "Daddy, can I have the milk? Can I have the milk? Can I have the milk?" She looked so hurt that he hastily added, "I'm sorry," gave her the milk, and himself kept quiet for the rest of the meal.

"I'll drop you off at Judge Bernstein's office," Betsy said after he had finished his second cup of coffee. "I'll take the kids with me and enroll the girls at school."

"I don't want to go to school," Janey said. "I *never* want to go."

"It's not so bad," Barbara said thoughtfully. "I only hate it a little."

"Can I go?" Pete asked.

"Nobody has to go for another month," Betsy said.

They got in the car and drove slowly to the main street of South Bay.

"Now don't take any nonsense from him," Betsy said as Tom got out of the car in front of the building in which Bernstein had his office. "We ought to have our first ten houses for sale next spring, and if we're going to do that, we should start right away."

Bernstein was sitting behind his scarred pine desk when Tom came in. He glanced up at Tom sharply — somehow he hadn't expected Mrs. Rath's grandson to be so tall. "Sit down, Mr. Rath," he said cordially. "What can I do for you?"

"I want to get some idea of how long it will take for Mrs. Rath's estate to go through the Probate Court," Tom said, "and I want to learn about zoning laws around here. We've got an idea we may want to put up some kind of a housing development."

"I see," Bernstein said, and waited.

"How long does it generally take for an estate to be settled?"

"Not long, if there are no complications. A man by the name of Schultz was in here to see me a few days ago. Edward Schultz. Name mean anything to you?"

"He used to work for my grandmother. I want to do what I can for him, but I have to wait until the estate is settled."

"Mr. Schultz tells me he believes Mrs.

Rath meant the entire estate to go to him," Bernstein said quietly.

"That's absurd! My grandmother talked to me about him shortly before she died."

"Apparently he believes he's entitled to the house," Bernstein said dryly.

"That's ridiculous!"

"Why do you suppose he thinks he has a claim?"

"I think he must be a little crazy," Tom said. "I don't know — I feel pretty badly about this. Mrs. Rath was ninety-three years old when she died, and possibly she gave him some reason for hoping she would leave him everything."

"Do you think she could have promised him the estate in return for his services for the rest of her life?" Bernstein asked mildly.

"No! She would have told me! Just before she died she told me she was leaving everything to me, and that's the way the will is written."

"Mr. Schultz claims that he asked Mrs. Rath for a salary increase about a year before she died, and that she said she couldn't afford to give him one, but that if he'd stay as long as she lived, she'd leave everything to him."

"I want to try to be fair about this," Tom said. "We can't prove whether she said that or not. She was old and confused, and I suppose it's possible she said that and forgot it. All I know is she used to talk all the time about saving the house for me, and that's the way the will is written."

"Mr. Schultz seems to feel an attempt is being made to cheat him."

"I can't help the way the old man feels!" Tom said. "I can't afford to have the settling of the estate delayed indefinitely! How can he hold things up? He hasn't got any proof!"

"He says he has," Bernstein said.

"What kind?"

"He told me he has everything in writing from her, postdating the will Mr. Sims sent me."

"I don't believe it!"

"That's what he says. I have asked him to have a photostat of his document sent to me, and he agreed to."

"Have you received it yet?"

"No — there hasn't been time."

"I can't understand it!" Tom said. "She wasn't like that. She never would have done a thing like that without telling me!"

"The court will have to examine both documents and make a decision."

"How long will it take?"

"That depends on a lot of things. It may be

necessary to get a lot of information together. It could be a matter of months, or even more."

"Meanwhile, I'm living in my grandmother's place. What would happen if the court awarded it to him?"

"He could dispossess you and perhaps charge you rent retroactively, I suppose."

"Is it legal for me to be there now?"

"When a property is in dispute, it's hard to tell what to do with it. I don't think Mr. Schultz is trying to dispossess you before the court makes a decision."

"That's nice of him," Tom said bitterly. There was a moment of silence before he added, "I guess I should ask Mr. Sims to represent me — I'll need a lawyer, won't I?"

"That would be advisable."

"You wouldn't take the case for me?"

"Hardly. I'm the judge."

"Has Edward, I mean Mr. Schultz, got a lawyer?"

"Yes. A big outfit in New York is representing him. Frankly, I don't think he could have got them to take the case if he didn't have a legitimate claim in their opinion."

"That's fine," Tom said.

"All you can do is put the case in the hands of your lawyer and wait," Bernstein said.

Tom looked at him helplessly for an instant before getting to his feet abruptly. "I guess there's nothing more I can do," he said. "There doesn't seem to be much point in asking about zoning laws now."

"You're in a ten-acre zone," Bernstein said. "If you wanted to put a housing development there, you'd have quite a fight on your hands. I wouldn't go into it until the estate is settled."

"Thanks," Tom said, feeling a rush of unreasonable resentment against Bernstein. "Anyway, thanks." He left the room.

As soon as he had gone, Bernstein walked to the window of his office and stood looking down at the street, where Betsy and the children were waiting in the parked car. His stomach was beginning to ache.

"Why, that school is *terrible!*" Betsy said as soon as Tom got into the car, before he could say anything. "It's dingy and overcrowded, and I don't think it's safe. I *hate* to send the kids there! When we get going, I'm going to send them to a private school!"

"Betsy," Tom said, "I've got some news that isn't very good."

"What?"

"Edward has put in a claim for the whole

estate, and he says he has a will Grandmother signed after she wrote the one we have. He's got a big firm of lawyers working on it."

"Oh, no! She *told* you . . ."

"I know."

"What's going to happen?"

"We just have to put Sims to work on it and let the court decide."

Betsy said nothing. "What's the matter?" Janey asked.

"Everything's all right, baby," Betsy said.

"What did Daddy say?"

"Nothing important," Tom said. "We're going home now."

He started the car. On the way up the hill to the old house they were all silent. When they came to the rock ledge against which his father had slammed the old Packard, Tom stared at it deliberately — it was ridiculous to look away. The rocks were massive and craggy, some of them tinged with a dull red hue, which was probably iron ore.

"Either Edward or your grandmother lied!" Betsy said suddenly, as Tom stopped the car in front of the house. "I know it was Edward! Everything's going to turn out all right!"

"Don't count on it, baby," he said.

For some reason he didn't want to go into

the dim old house. Instead, he walked alone into the tall grass toward the distant row of pines. In the distance the smooth surface of the Sound glittered. The children bounded after him until Betsy called them back. "Leave your father alone," she said.

It's funny, he thought. I'm always sure things are going to turn out badly, and, damn it, they usually do.

"Everything's going to turn out all right!" Betsy always said.

Sure, he thought, we'll live here a year or so while this case is being decided, and then Edward will get the house and slap a bill for back rent on us. And we'll have lawyers' bills and court costs to pay. And the only job I've got now is sitting all day behind a desk doing nothing.

What will happen if we lose this place, and run up a lot of bills, and I get fired? he thought. What will we do? And what will happen if Maria makes trouble?

I can always get a job, he thought. Dick Haver would give me a job again. I can always get a job somewhere.

Maybe, he thought. If Hopkins fired me six months after I was hired, people would want to know why. And if there were any publicity about Maria — if she made any charges — none of the foundations would touch me. And what the hell other kind of work am I trained for?

I could go back in the Army, he thought. They'd make me a major. Good pay, travel, education, and security. Grandmother could look down from heaven and be real proud of me — she could talk to the angels about the family major and be honest.

Grandmother, he thought — by God, what kind of woman was she? Did she promise Edward her estate just to make sure she would have service the rest of her life? And was she afraid to tell me, unwilling to suffer the slightest unpleasantness? Did she play it both ways, getting the fun of telling me she was leaving me everything and at the same time wringing the last drop of ease out of life? Was she, when you come right down to it, only an evil, pretentious, lying old woman who could be expected to beget nothing but evil, a suicide, and a . . .

This is ridiculous, he thought — that's one thing I won't do. Money isn't that important. I'm tough. I can always get a job. I can go back to the Army. Travel, education, security. Times like these are made for me — a tough bastard who knows how to handle a gun. And I wouldn't even have to do that. If worse came to worst, I could dig a ditch, I could operate an elevator like Caesar, and in heaven Grandmother could say, "My grandson is in the transportation business."

It's absurd to think of these things, he thought. I could get a job in an advertising agency. I'll write copy telling people to eat more corn flakes and smoke more and more cigarettes and buy more refrigerators and automobiles, until they explode with happiness.

I shouldn't get excited, he thought. It doesn't really matter. Here goes nothing. It will be interesting to see what happens.

Maybe it will turn out all right, he thought; maybe it really will. Betsy says you have to believe everything will turn out all right, even if it doesn't. You can't go on worrying all the time; it has to stop someday. You can't really believe the world is insane; you have to believe everything's going to turn out all right. The Lord is my Shepherd, I shall not want. I shall grow old gracefully, and my children will all grow up happily and healthily, and everything's going to be fine; it is ridiculous that optimism should always sound false.

He wondered suddenly whether the young German in the leather jacket who had stood negligently holding his rifle and coughing had been an optimist. And he wondered whether the girl or woman who had written the man in the leather jacket the letter on thin, blue, faintly scented stationery had had faith that everything was going to turn out all right. And how about the other men he had killed? How about the man who had run zigzagging across the beach, while Tom moved the machine gun up on him, the bullets kicking up the sand behind him, until the man had sagged with the blood pouring out of his mouth like a long tongue? Had he had faith? In what? And how about Mahoney? And Maria, who right now, perhaps, might be trying to raise her son alone?

Maybe they had no faith, Tom thought. Maybe they were like me, always expecting disaster, surprised only when it doesn't hit. Maybe we are all, the killers and the killed, equally damned; not guilty, not somehow made wise by war, not heroes, just men who are either dead or convinced that the world is insane.

He felt someone pulling his trouser leg and looked down. Janey was there, telling him that lunch was ready. She had a worried expression on her face. Her hand was soft as a dove in his as he led her into the house.

24

The important thing is to make money, Tom thought as he took the train into New York on the following Monday. The important thing is to create an island of order in a sea of chaos — somebody very bright had said that, somebody whose name he had forgotten, but whose writings he had studied at college. And an island of order obviously must be made of money, for one doesn't bring up children in an orderly way without money, and one doesn't even have one's meals in an orderly way, or dress in an orderly way, or think in an orderly way without money. Money is the root of all order, he told himself, and the only trouble with it is, it's so damn hard to get, especially when one has a job which consists of sitting behind a desk all day doing absolutely nothing.

On his way up to his office in the elevator

that morning, he did not see Caesar — he was grateful for that. And he hadn't been sitting behind his desk doing nothing for more than fifteen minutes when the interoffice communication box crackled and buzzed. He switched it on.

"Rath?" Ogden's voice whispered hoarsely.

Tom turned up the volume control. "Good morning," he said. "What can I do for you?"

"Can you fly down to Atlantic City this afternoon — the Stockton House Hotel? I've just heard that the place is filling up with conventions, and I want to make sure we have the proper accommodations for Mr. Hopkins on the fifteenth."

"Sure I can go," Tom said. He was so grateful to be given something to do that his voice sounded ridiculously eager.

"I want you to make all the arrangements, both for the rooms and the speech. Check the speaker's platform. Find out just what room his speech is scheduled for, exactly where it is, and what door he should enter."

"I will!" Tom said. He found himself speaking with exclamation points, like Ralph Hopkins.

"Check the amplifying equipment, and if it isn't good, make the hotel fix it. Be sure there's a lectern — Mr. Hopkins likes to stand behind a lectern with enough space on it to open a ten-by-twelve-inch notebook. Are you taking notes?"

"Right!" said Tom, scribbling furiously.

"He likes the lectern four feet five inches from the floor," Ogden continued, "and he likes the mike the same height, to the right of the lectern, not in front of it. There will be only the mike for the loudspeaker — this won't be broadcast."

Tom was not surprised at that. For the president of a broadcasting company to have his speech broadcast, even if he wanted maximum publicity, would be shooting fish in a barrel. The executives of broadcasting companies yearn for space in magazines and newspapers, and the publishers of magazines and newspapers yearn for radio and television coverage.

"I've got it," Tom said.

"Now about his rooms. Get a suite of three. He likes a hard mattress. Try out the mattress — he hates a soft one."

"Right," Tom said.

"But it shouldn't be lumpy. Don't hesitate to make the hotel get you a good one — hard but smooth."

"Check," Tom said.

"Immediately after the speech, a bartender

should be on duty in the living room of Mr. Hopkins' suite, and he should be equipped to serve fifty people anything they want. He should remain on duty for the rest of the evening if necessary."

"Got it," Tom said.

"Now about flowers. Mr. Hopkins sometimes gets hay fever, so be sure there's no goldenrod or anything like that around — sometimes they put it in fall decorations. And he detests chrysanthemums. He likes roses — long-stemmed roses. Be sure there are several dozen around his rooms."

"Right," Tom said.

"And be sure he gets a good bedroom suite. Mr. Hopkins' rooms all should be facing the sea. Three rooms, with the living room big enough to hold fifty people comfortably — he detests crowded rooms. We'll also need single rooms for you, me, and Miss MacDonald on the same floor, all reserved for September 15."

"Fine," Tom said.

"Another thing. Mr. Hopkins will want an electric refrigerator and a few bottles of Scotch in his bedroom. He doesn't like to have to keep calling room service."

"I've got it," Tom said.

"There should be a large-screen television

set and a radio in his bedroom."

"I'll get them."

"We'll want a man with a wire recorder to record Mr. Hopkins' speech — he likes to hear it played back."

"Will do."

"Make sure the local press is alerted. Our public-relations department will be sending them advance releases, but it helps to drop in and chat with them."

"I'll do it," Tom said.

"I guess that's about all — in general, make sure everything's set for Mr. Hopkins. Call me when you get back. Tell the travel department to get you a plane ticket."

Before Tom could say "Right" again, Ogden snapped off his voice box. Tom started to telephone Betsy to say he wouldn't be home that night, but before he got the call through, the voice box sputtered again. This time it was Hopkins. "Tom," he said, "could you come up to the apartment for dinner tonight?"

"Bill Ogden just asked me to go to Atlantic City to arrange hotel accommodations for your speech," Tom said.

"Oh, fine, but see me when you get back, will you?"

"Sure," Tom said, hoping Hopkins would

tell him what he wanted. Instead, Hopkins said cheerily, "Have a good trip," and the voice box was silent.

That afternoon Tom boarded a plane and sat down in one of the comfortably uphol-stered seats. As the plane gunned its engines and began the familiar headlong, all or noth-ing, rush down the runway, he fastened his safety belt and leaned back, still wondering what Hopkins wanted to see him about. Any-way, I won't have to jump this time, he thought — this time I'm on my way to test a mattress and arrange for long-stemmed roses. He started to laugh. I'll get roses with the longest god-damn stems in the whole world, he thought.

The hotel was a large one, twenty stories high, without a room to rent for less than twenty-two dollars a night, and please make reservations well in advance. Tom looked up the manager and found him eager to co-oper-ate in making things satisfactory for Ralph Hopkins. The right sort of lectern was pro-cured, and the loud-speaker system proved suitable. The manager felt that a bridal suite, ornately furnished with pictures of French courtiers on the wall, was just the thing for Mr. Hopkins. Ceremoniously Tom lay down on the large double bed and pronounced the mattress too soft. Four housemen quickly brought another. Feeling like Goldilocks in the house of the Three Bears, Tom pronounced it too lumpy. Grumbling, the four housemen brought a third mattress, which Tom decreed just right.

"I want the stems *really long*," he said to the hotel florist. "There ought to be about four dozen roses on a table in the living room and two dozen in the bedroom."

"You can rely on me," the florist said.

By seven o'clock in the evening Tom had completed his arrangements. He went to the hotel bar and ordered a Martini. It was an ornate circular bar, in the center of which a lighted pyramid of bottles revolved slowly. Somewhere in a near-by room an orchestra was playing dance music. Suddenly a group of young people in evening clothes swept into the bar and sat down at tables near Tom. "I don't *really* believe you, Harry," a young girl not more than twenty said to her escort, "but I thank you just the same."

The sight of the young couples and the sound of the dance music made Tom feel suddenly old. He looked at the couple nearest him. They're not more than twenty, or at the most twenty-one, he thought. My God, when Pearl Harbor was attacked, they couldn't have been more than ten years old! And when Betsy and I met, back in 1939, they were seven years old!

The band in the next room began to play a waltz. It had been in a hotel that Tom had met Betsy, a hotel in Boston with a big bar and a dance band and crowds of young people in evening clothes. It had been in the fall of 1939, just a few weeks before the Christmas holidays, in the best hotel in Boston, in the grand ballroom of which Betsy had had her coming-out party.

"When the deep purple falls over sleepy garden walls . . ." That had been the song that year. He had never liked it much at the time and could never have expected that his mind would choose it as one of the things to remember, probably for the rest of his life.

Nineteen thirty-nine! My God, the world has changed since then, he thought — it's enough to make a man feel a million years old! In the fall of 1939, Hitler had just invaded Poland. The experts had been saying that the Polish Lancers and General Mud would stop him, but by the time Betsy had had her coming-out party, Poland had fallen, and the experts had turned to saying that now France would stop Hitler, the French Army was the finest in the world. The experts had also been saying that the United States would not get into this war. It had been then Tom had started to acquire a permanent disrespect for all experts and to equate pessimism with wisdom. Almost ever since he could remember, he himself had been sure there would be a war, and that the United States would get into it. At Covington Academy, way back in 1935, the boys had even had an organization called "The Veterans of Future Wars" which had demandcd soldiers' bonuses before death instead of after. The pacifists had been printing pictures in magazines showing a wounded soldier, and the caption had said, "Hello Sucker!" But the boys had not been confused. They had known for a long while that regardless of what anyone said, war was coming. They had been offended by the picture of the wounded soldier with the caption calling him a sucker, and they had also been horrified at a picture book in the library with the grim and then prophetic title, "The First World War," but they had not talked about it much. They had played football and baseball, they had organized a mandolin club and gone to see Ginger Rogers in the movies, and they had waited without any confusion at all. Only the experts had been confused.

But the night Tom had gone to Betsy's

coming-out party he hadn't been worried about the war. He had received the formally engraved invitation about three weeks before. "Mr. and Mrs. Mathew A. Donner cordially invite you to a dance in honor of their daughter, Miss Elizabeth A. Donner," it had begun, and he had answered, "Mr. Thomas R. Rath cordially accepts . . ." Dozens of such invitations had arrived every month during those years at college, because his name had been on the right lists — old Florence Rath had seen to that.

He had never met Betsy when he got the invitation and never had heard of the Donners. The afternoon before the party he had made up his mind not to go, because he had too much studying to do, but along about eight o'clock he had grown bored with his history book and, throwing it down in disgust, had put on his dinner coat and driven his second-hand car into Boston. "Might as well get some free champagne," he had said to his roommate.

The hotel had been crowded when he came in — it was a big party, he had seen at a glance. He had pushed through the groups of young people in evening clothes who crowded around the entrance to the ballroom and made his way to the long table in an adjoining room, where the champagne was being served. It had been good, imported champagne. Sipping his drink, Tom had stood just inside the door to the ballroom surveying the dancers in a mildly predatory way. At the time, he had considered himself an expert on women; he had thought he could just glance at them and tell which ones were passionate, which were cold, which would expect a lot of money to be spent on them, and which would not. His eye had skipped over Nina Henderson, who already had become a professional beauty, pictured on a magazine cover as the debutante of the year, a girl who later, as things turned out, married the fat orchestra leader who played at most of the dances that year and bore him a son before divorcing him. Tom's eye had also passed over the plain girls sitting on the side lines or dancing with their brothers. His glance had traveled across the floor until he saw Betsy.

How strangely comforting it was to look back now and realize that the enchantment he had felt that night at the first sight of her had been, after all, as unsentimentally real and factual as any ugly emotion or truth he could recall. And it was also comforting to reflect that what he had felt that night still defied analysis. Sure, Betsy's figure had never been calculated to calm a young man's pulse, but certainly there had been other girls in the room as admirable in measurement. The grace with which Betsy moved, the way her sparkling white dress had accentuated the warm colors of her skin and hair, the curve of her cheek, the flash of her smile — of course, all these things had had their effect, but there had been more, much more which could never have been caught by a camera, even if it used all the Technicolor in the world. The moment he had seen her he wanted to marry her, a fact which sounded so banal when he told it to her months later that they both had laughed, feeling suddenly ridiculous. But it was a true fact, and that night he had felt so bewildered by it that he stood for a long while watching her dance with others before mustering the courage to make his way across the dance floor and cut in on her.

"Who are you?" he had asked.

"Betsy Donner."

"The lady of the evening!" he had replied, hoping that his voice sounded light and sophisticated. "It's a nice party."

"It's a *beautiful* party!" she had said. "I suppose I shouldn't say that, but it is."

She had seemed to be floating. He had never been a good dancer, but her feet hadn't seemed to touch the floor at all, and he had felt suddenly graceful. Then a hand had touched him on the shoulder, and she had gone to someone else.

It's natural, he had thought — she's a pretty girl, and it's her party, and everybody has to dance with her at least once. But he had been disturbed to find he was unable to be with her for more than a few minutes.

That's when it all had started. For three years after that they had gone to movies and football games and college dances and night clubs, and performed the whole ritual of entertainment preparatory to marriage. He had played the mandolin for her — she had considered it a quaint, old-fashioned instrument. They had talked. At the time, Tom had been sure he would be rich a few years after the war was over, although he hadn't given much thought to what he would get rich at. They had kissed. At the time, they had known much less about each other than any personnel man knows about a prospective stenographer, but almost casually, certainly without anything which could be described as thought, on the strength of a kiss, she had agreed to marry him and had not considered it strange at all.

I was lucky, Tom thought now, as he

stared at the slowly revolving bottles in the center of the bar in the hotel at Atlantic City. That was one time I was lucky. At that age I could have fallen in love with any empty-headed girl with a good figure, but I was lucky — that's one time when everything turned out all right.

How strange it is to remember, he thought. Poor Betsy, she could have married somebody with money, somebody who would be taking her to Florida every winter now, somebody who would never worry, who would smile and be cheerful while the cook cooked dinner, and the waitress served it, and Betsy sat smiling. Back in 1939, there had been several rich young men pursuing Betsy, and without thinking, apparently, she had turned them down, because they had not appealed to her at the moment, and she had chosen Tom on the strength of a kiss and had never thought about money.

How incredibly naïve we were, he thought now as he stared at the revolving pyramid of bottles. How incredibly innocent, as we parked my car and worried because we couldn't stop making love to each other! Once while they had been parked, a police-man on a motorcycle had shone the bright beam of his flashlight on them, and Betsy had jumped as though she were burned. The policeman had grinned and said, "All right, kids, break it up!" and had gone on, patrolling his beat, his light disappearing around a bend in the road.

I wonder if she's sorry, Tom thought. It isn't just the money — I wonder if she wishes she had a husband who could be cheerful around the house.

It's funny what happens to people, he thought. We were alike in those days, Betsy and I, all our experiences had been the same, and there was nothing we found impossible to explain to each other. We were confident — my God, we never worried at all! With the whole war in front of us, we never worried at all. We were sure that I would go through the war and become a hero. He remembered a mental picture he had had of himself, a clear image of himself, a soldier in a foreign land, sad and tired-looking, but clean and unwounded, thinking of Betsy on Christmas Day, writing sad, brave letters about his friends who had died.

It wouldn't be too bad to be a soldier, he had thought — he had seen himself sitting in some jolly French tavern, or perhaps in the corner of some romantically Spartan barracks, singing Army songs — things like

"Pack Up Your Troubles in Your Old Kit Bag, and Smile, Smile, Smile." Probably he'd take his mandolin along, he had thought — it would make him popular in the Army.

The future had seemed perfectly predictable in those days. Betsy would weep in a genteel way when he sailed overseas, with his mandolin, but he would come back unhurt and march up Fifth Avenue, and she would throw herself into his arms and say, "Darling, you have come back to me!" and it would all be sad and brave and happy, like a movie of the First World War.

And the funny thing was, it had all happened, more or less; at least in the beginning, it had followed the script. He had gone off to his basic training carrying, among other things, his mandolin, and he had actually played it a few times, and several of the men had gathered around to sing. But when he had learned he was going overseas, he had shipped the mandolin home along with other surplus gear — somehow the idea of a paratrooper arriving in Europe with a mandolin had already begun to appear ridiculous. That had been the beginning of the destruction of the script, although to a surprising degree the outline had been followed. He had been a hero, all right, and had been awarded three medals to prove it. He had not been wounded. He had come home, and Betsy had met the transport at the wharf. She had run out of the crowd as he came down the gangplank, thrown her arms around him and said, "Darling, you have come back to me!"

That's what she had said, meaning it from the heart, and it had not been her fault that the words sounded satirical to him. He had held her away from him a little, seeing that she was a woman any man would want. That day she had been wearing a new dress specially bought for the occasion, a gay red dress that closely followed the lines of her figure, a flamboyant dress which she had bought in a flamboyant mood the day she heard he was actually on his way home. She had kissed him passionately, and he had felt precisely as though a beautiful woman he had never seen before had rushed out of the crowd and begun making love to him. He had felt incredulous, awkward, abashed, and unwillingly lustful. The feeling of lust had appalled him, making him feel unfaithful to Maria, and also to Betsy as he remembered her from long ago, a young girl to be taken in love, not with the sort of feeling he would have for a pretty stranger unbelievably embracing him in the street.

"I've got a hotel room all reserved," she had said. "I'm not going to take you back to Grandmother's house tonight."

They had gone to the hotel, and the love-making had been intense and brief and unsatisfactory, leaving him with a profound feeling of confusion and shame. When it was over, her cheerfulness had surprised him. She had poured drinks, and, sitting down in a big armchair with a cigarette in her hand, she had leaned back and said, "Do you mind talking about the war? There are all sorts of questions I'm dying to ask."

"There's not much to tell," he had said. "What do you want to do tomorrow?"

Betsy had never been insensitive. She had not pursued the matter, and with gratitude he had felt he would never have to tell her anything about the war, not about Maria, not about Mahoney, not about anything. It would be better that way, he had thought, far better for both of them.

She had not seemed to mind his reticence. That night she had begun to talk brightly about the future. As he listened to her, he had gradually realized that here in this pretty girl sitting across the room from him in a pair of silk pajamas was himself as of 1939. Here was a kind of antique version of himself, unchanged. Here was the casual certainty that he would get a job which would soon lead to the vice-presidency of J. H. Nottersby, Incorporated, or some firm with a name which would have to sound like that. Here was all the half-remembered optimism, the implicit belief that before long they would move into a house something like Mount Vernon, with nice old darky servants nodding and singing all the time, a place where they would grow old gracefully, no getting fat, but becoming only a little gray around the temples, a mansion where they would of course be happy, real happy for the rest of their lives.

The trouble hadn't been only that he didn't believe in the dream any more; it was that he didn't even find it interesting or sad in its improbability. Like an old man, he had been preoccupied with the past, not the future. He had changed, and she had not.

That night he had listened to her almost paternally. "I don't know what I want to do," he had said when she asked if he had any definite ideas about a job. "We'll have to figure that out."

"I know you'll succeed, no matter what you do," she had said, her whole happy dream of the future hanging almost palpably in front of her, like the pictures of dreams people have in cartoons.

But of course her dream had not come true — that seemed sad to him now for her sake. Instead of getting the house like Mount Vernon, they had moved into the little house on Greentree Avenue in Westport, and Betsy had become pregnant, and he had thrown the vase against the wall, and the washing machine had broken down. And Grandmother had died and left her house to somebody, and instead of being made vice-president of J. H. Nottersby, Incorporated, he had finally arrived at a job where he tested mattresses, was uneasy when his boss said he wanted to see him without explaining why, and lived in fear of an elevator operator.

I hope Betsy isn't sorry, he thought. If I lose this job and have to take whatever I can get, I hope she still won't be sorry. I hope she never has to learn about Maria.

"Hello," someone said.

He turned and saw a pretty, dark-haired girl in a copper-colored evening gown sitting at the bar next to him. "You look preoccupied," she said.

He smiled. "I was thinking," he replied.

"Bad practice," the girl said. "Very bad practice. My name's Marie. Want to come to our party?"

"Thank you," he said hastily. "No, I can't." He got up and walked out of the room, feeling oddly perturbed.

25

After dinner that night, Tom went to his room in the hotel and lay down. It isn't fair to Betsy, he thought, to keep remembering the weeks with Maria as the happiest of my life. It wasn't the difference between two women — it was simply the difference in circumstance. When he and Betsy had first met back in 1939, they had been children, and their happiness had been the pale, fragile happiness of children, full of little anxieties about getting home on time, and doing the proper thing. And after the war, there hadn't really been time for happiness — there had been budgets and bills from obstetricians and frantic planning for the future. That had been the trouble with him and Betsy: what with his brooding about the past and worrying about the future, there never had been any present at all.

But with Maria it had been different; they had both been reconciled to having no future, and the past had been something which had to be forgotten. With Maria there had been only the moment at hand, completely unshadowed, unexpected, something to be grateful for. Perhaps, Tom thought, it's a matter of expectations — he and Betsy had always expected so much! Everything would be perfect for them, they had expected from the beginning. They would be rich, they would be healthy, and they would do no wrong. Any deviation from perfection had seemed a blight which ruined the whole. But he and Maria had expected nothing; they had started with hopelessness and had been astonished to learn that for a few weeks they could be happy.

Lying there in his hotel room, Tom suddenly remembered the day of the picnic with Maria, and he smiled — even the distant memory made him smile. It had been a ridiculous day from the beginning. After having wangled the use of a jeep, he and Maria had started from Rome at nine o'clock in the morning, with a large basket full of groceries and a bottle of wine. The sky had been gray, with feathery wisps of white cloud blowing across darker, blacker clouds billowing up from the horizon, and it had been cold — the mud puddles beside the road had been crusted with ice. At nine-thirty, just as they got outside the city, it had begun to rain. It had been a ridiculous day for a picnic, but the thought of going back had not even occurred to them. He had stopped, and she had helped him to put the side curtains on the jeep, and it had been snug and warm inside, with the world appearing eerie through the dripping windshield. They had headed south and driven aimlessly — there had been a delicious sense of freedom in coming to a crossroad and turning to the left or right completely at random, without caring at all where they were going. Maria had turned up the collar of her old soldier's overcoat, but she had not worn a hat, and her dark glossy hair had got wet while they were putting the side curtains up and had stayed damp all day. She had looked contented sitting there on the hard uncomfortable seat of the jeep. She had not smiled — her face had so often been serious — but she had hummed a song almost inaudibly under her breath, and he had kept glancing at her, receiving enormous satisfaction from the sight of her sitting there beside him so serenely.

"What are you singing?" he had asked. "Sing louder, so I can hear."

She had shaken her head modestly. "I can't sing," she had said. "I know no music."

"I do," he had said. "You happen to be sitting beside the star baritone and mandolin virtuoso of the entire United States. Want to hear me?"

"Yes." She had laughed.

"You'll have to imagine the mandolin in the background," he had replied. "Pling, pling, pling — does that set the proper mood?"

"Yes."

"All right!" At the top of his lungs he had sung "Old Man River" and the "Saint Louis Blues," both of which had seemed absurdly doleful. Her laughter had formed a sort of accompaniment to the songs, and he had gone on to sing, "Way down upon the Swanee River, far, far away — there's where my heart is turning ever, there's where the old folks stay. . . ." He had been briefly conscious of the irony of the fact that at the moment he wasn't worrying much about the old folks at home, but he had brushed that thought away. He had sung all the songs whose words he knew that day while they drove aimlessly around in the rain. She had not tried to sing with him — she had just sat there and from time to time had put her hand on his knee with curious hesitation, almost as though it were dark and she were trying to make sure he was still there. Once, when he stopped at a crossroad, she had leaned over and kissed him on the mouth with almost painful intensity. That had been a curious and wonderful thing about her that he had understood only gradually: her almost constant eagerness to make love. At first, he had been surprised, and then he had thought that she was simply an ideal and probably practiced soldier's girl, and he had been a little cynical about her ardor. But after he had known her a few days he had realized that physical love was the only form of reassurance she knew, and that she was completely happy and sure of him only when she was caressing him and giving him pleasure, and that it was chiefly this that caused her constantly to entice him. She was scared, just as scared as he was, he had realized. On that day while they were driving in the rain she had told him a little about her past. The village in which she had lived with her parents had been one of the first hit by the invasion. The Germans had made a brief stand there, and the planes had dropped bombs of white phosphorus. Her parents had refused to go to a bomb shelter for fear that their house would be looted if left empty, but they had forced her to go. Crawling up from the shelter after a bomb had burst near by, she had seen her house in flames, seen her father stagger out carrying her mother, both their bodies enveloped in flames. The other people from the bomb shelter had not let her run to them. Her father had fallen after taking only a few steps, and she had seen the bodies of her parents lying at right angles to each other, burning like a fiery cross. As she told Tom about this, she had been objective, almost matter-of-fact. The tears had not come until he had impulsively stopped the jeep and put his arms around her, feeling in himself an overpowering need to try to comfort her, in spite of the knowledge that for such things there is no solace. She had cried hard for about ten minutes, and her sobs had been all the more agonizing because they came silently through clenched teeth and taut lips. After regaining control of herself, she had taken from her battered handbag a cheap imitation gold compact, opened it, and put powder on her face. For several seconds she had stared at herself in the tiny, clouded mirror. "Do you think I am beautiful?" she had asked.

"Very beautiful."

"Not beautiful enough to keep you. Everyone dies or goes away."

Not wanting to lie or to be cruelly truthful, he had not contradicted her. He had said nothing, but had kissed her, and she had returned the kiss with all the passion which had been suppressed in her silent tears. "Tell me again that I am beautiful," she had said.

He had done so. She had sighed and said, "All right. Let's drive some more."

For an hour they had driven in silence. At about noon they had grown hungry and had turned up a narrow road in hilly country, seeking a place where they could get out of the rain and eat. They had driven for perhaps another half hour before coming to an abandoned villa, the east end of which had been destroyed by artillery fire. The ground all around the villa had been badly cut up, and the buff-colored stucco walls pockmarked with machine-gun bullets. He had driven the jeep slowly around the driveway which encircled the building, past a swimming pool choked with fallen masonry. On impulse he had twisted the steering wheel suddenly and driven between two shattered pillars, across a tiled courtyard littered with rubble, under a part of the roof which projected over what must once have been an anteroom. There he had stopped, and, wondering at the marvelous convenience of the ruin which allowed them to drive out of the rain, they had stepped out of the jeep. He had lifted the hood and taken part of the distributor with him, as well as the ignition key, to make sure no one would steal the car. Carrying their picnic basket and shivering a little in the dampness, they had walked through an enormous jagged hole in a charred wall and entered a huge living room. The glass in the high windows along the righthand side of the room had been shattered, and tattered damask draperies were being blown inward, arched by the wind into the shape of wings. There had been a puddle in the middle of the polished oak floor, and everywhere there had been bits of glass and countless pieces of paper, as though an office had exploded. In one corner there had been the wreck of a grand piano, the board with the ivory keys lying separate from the rest, like the jawbone of a prehistoric beast, and the big brass-colored frame with most of the strings still taut resting on edge, like a harp. They had crossed this room and, after walking through two utterly bare rooms, had found what must once have been a small library, with a white marble fireplace at one end. The walls had been lined with bookcases, all empty now, except for many scattered leaves and detached leather bindings. There had been only two windows in that room, and, miraculously, only a few of the lower panes had been broken. Through one of the windows they had been able to see a small circular pool, in the middle of which a white marble nymph, slim waisted and full breasted but now headless, rose, holding in one upraised arm a cornucopia, out of which a fountain must once have spouted.

"Here," he had said, putting the picnic basket down. "We'll see if the chimney works." Gathering some of the book leaves which lay on the floor, he had struck a match, ignited the paper, and dropped it into the fireplace. The smoke had gone straight up. "We can build a fire," he had said.

She had stood, holding her coat collar close around her neck and looking small and lost, while he had gone to the great living room and brought back an armful of polished fragments from the splintered top of the piano. After she had helped him to gather more paper, he had built a fire carefully, setting the sharp splinters of wood on end like a wigwam. The smoky orange flame had climbed them swiftly. Suddenly the room had been full of the acrid smell of burning varnish. She had knelt by the fire and held her hands out to it, and he had noticed for the first time that her hands were the hands of a nervous child, that she had bitten her fingernails to the quick. Her hands had been surprisingly small, fragile, and finely tapered. She had glanced up at him, and upon seeing that he was looking at her hands, she had quickly doubled them into fists, so that the finger-nails were hidden, and had put them into the pockets of her coat with exactly the gesture of a child caught stealing cookies. Then she had stood up, looking flustered. Impulsively he had taken her right hand out of her pocket, smoothed it in his own hands, and kissed it. She had buried her face in his shoulder, and he had felt that she was shivering.

"You're too beautiful to worry about your hands," he had said. "Come on, you're cold — let's get more wood on that fire." He had gone to the living room and come back carrying a heavy amputated leg of the piano, the foot of which had been carved to resemble the claws of a lion clutching a round, shiny ball. This he had placed on the fire, and the flames had immediately embraced it, licking greedily at the varnish. He had returned to the living room and, grabbing one of the tattered damask draperies, had given it a hard pull and brought it down in a cloud of dust and a clatter of falling curtain rods. This he had dragged to the library and had ripped pieces from it to stuff the broken windowpanes. The remainder he had spread on the floor as a tablecloth, and she had begun to unpack the basket, placing sandwiches done up in brown paper and the bottle of wine and a cold roast chicken carefully in a row. Gradually the roaring fire had warmed the room. They had taken their overcoats off and folded them by the tablecloth to serve as pillows on which to sit.

That day she had been wearing a worn black skirt, a white blouse cut almost like a man's shirt with an open collar, and a dark-green jacket which she had made herself, trying to copy a picture in a magazine advertisement. They had eaten greedily, wiping their hands on the damask tablecloth and passing the bottle of wine back and forth between them. When they were through, she had packed the remnants of the picnic away in the basket. Carefully lighting two cigarettes, he had handed her one, and she had sat down comfortably, edging a little toward the fire and holding her hands out to the flames, this time unabashed. Outside, the rain had started coming down faster, and the rags he had stuffed in the broken windowpanes had started to drip on the floor. Far overhead a squadron of bombers had droned, going somewhere, high above the clouds. The unbroken glass in the windows had trembled. Content to sit and stare into the fire, which was already reducing the great claw of the piano leg to embers, he had said nothing. Glancing at his wrist watch, he had seen it was not yet two o'clock. That meant they would have eighteen more hours until eight o'clock the next morning when he would have to check in with the sergeant at the transportation desk. Eighteen more hours, he had thought gratefully, and slowly had calculated: the big sweep hand on his watch would have to tick off one thousand and eighty minutes, a marvelously long time. He had glanced at her and to his surprise had found her looking hurt and forlorn. Suddenly he had realized that she had expected him to make love to her long before this, and that she was afraid that he had grown tired of her, or that she had displeased him in some way. He had smiled at her. "Come over here," he had said. Quickly she had gone to him and lain with her head in his lap, looking up at him, his smile mirrored on her face. He had stroked her hair and forehead softly, feeling, for the moment, oddly calm. Overhead another squadron of bombers had droned, followed by more and more, until the whole building trembled. He had glanced over his shoulder and through the rain-streaked glass had seen the headless nymph outside, holding her empty cornucopia high, silhouetted against the rain-drenched clouds. After a few moments he had looked back at Maria, lying with her head on his lap in the yellow firelight, and he had seen that to invite his affections, she had unbuttoned her jacket and opened the blouse, partly exposing her breasts and the deep valley between them. He had kissed her then, the kiss beginning almost as an act of kindness, but quickly becoming much more than that. "Oh, God, I love you," he had said.

They had left the villa just in time to get back to Rome before dark. When they had returned to her room, she had started cooking supper on a small primus stove he had given her, and he had lain down on the bed and glanced at his watch again. It had been only six o'clock — still fourteen more hours, eight hundred and forty more revolutions of the sweep hand before he had to check in. He had stretched out on the soft bed, full of an incredible sense of luxury, thinking of the minutes ahead as a king might think of his empire. Maria had sat, looking wise and contented, stirring a pan of soup, which slowly had begun to steam, giving a fragrance to the air.

Only a few days after that he had bought a mandolin in a little music store they had happened to pass while walking home from a restaurant, and he had spent many afternoons lying in Maria's room strumming it idly, not really trying to play it, but finding great relaxation in the feel of the smooth steel strings under his fingers. Maria had loved it — her father had played the mandolin, she had said. The mandolin had been one of the things Tom had left her, along with the jeepload of canned goods and twelve cartons of cigarettes.

Now, lying alone in his hotel room in Atlantic City, Tom involuntarily glanced at his watch, with the same old sweep hand emptily ticking off the minutes. It was just youth, he thought, and the war, which, if it did nothing else, taught the value of time. Somebody should make me and Betsy check in at a transportation desk every morning and give us just one more day — that might teach us not to waste time. How different Betsy and Maria are, he thought. Betsy's parents had not died — instead of dying, they had retired to a modern bungalow in California, from which they sent their daughter pictures of themselves smiling and picking oranges. Nobody whom Betsy loved had ever died or left her for long. Ever since she was twelve years old, Betsy had been told she was beautiful — she did not like to hear it any more. I wonder if anyone tells Maria she is beautiful now, he thought. I wonder what kind of word Caesar will bring me about Maria after Gina writes her family in Rome. I wonder what Maria will do if Caesar tells her where I am, and that I look rich.

26

The first thing Tom did when he got back to his office the next day was to call Hopkins on the interoffice communication box.

"Glad you're back!" Hopkins said cheerily, as though Tom had just returned from a voyage around the world. "Have a good trip?"

"Fine," Tom said. "Did you want to see me?"

"Yes," Hopkins replied. "I'll send a girl down with the latest draft of my speech for Atlantic City. Let's have lunch tomorrow, and you can tell me what you think of it. Would one o'clock be all right?"

So that's all he wanted, Tom thought. He said, "Fine! I'll meet you in your office tomorrow at one."

An hour later an exceptionally pretty office girl arrived and with a dazzling smile handed Tom a large manila envelope from Hopkins.

Tom opened it and extracted the speech, which had grown and changed since he had worked on it. "It's a real pleasure to be here this evening," he read. "I tremendously appreciate this opportunity to discuss with this distinguished gathering what I believe to be the most crucial problem facing the world today." Having made this point, the speech went on — in fact, it went on and on and on for thirty pages, saying over and over again in different ways that mental health is important. The last ten pages were devoted to the thought that mental-health problems affect the economy of the nation. "Our wealth depends on mental health," this section concluded. "Yes, our wealth depends on mental health!"

Tom put the speech down, feeling slightly ill. Good Lord, he thought, they're going to sell mental health the way they sell cigarettes! He left the speech on his desk, walked over to the window, and stared out over the city. Standing there, he shrugged his shoulders in an oddly hopeless way.

"Let's have lunch tomorrow, and you can tell me what you think of it," Hopkins had said.

"Well, of course I'm just talking off the top of my head, but I think this draft has some fine

things in it, and, on the other hand, I have some reservations," Tom imagined himself saying. That was the way it was done — always feel the boss out to find what he thinks before committing yourself. Tell the man what he wants to hear.

"I'm sorry, but I think this speech is absurd. It's an endless repetition of the obvious fact that mental health is important. You've said that over and over again and finally turned it into a cheap advertising slogan. If you want to form a mental-health committee, why don't you find out what needs to be done and offer to help do it?"

A few years ago I would have said that, Tom thought. Be honest, be yourself. If the man asks you what you think of his speech, tell him. Don't be afraid. Give him your frank opinion.

That sounds so easy when you're young, Tom thought. It sounds so easy before you learn that your frank opinion often leads directly to the street. What if Hopkins really likes this speech?

Tom shrugged again. The thing to remember is this, he thought: Hopkins would want me to be honest. But when you come right down to it, why does he hire me? To help him do what he wants to do — obviously that's why any man hires another. And if he finds that I disagree with everything he wants to do, what good am I to him? I should quit if I don't like what he does, but I want to eat, and so, like a half million other guys in gray flannel suits, I'll always pretend to agree, until I get big enough to be honest without being hurt. That's not being crooked, it's just being smart.

But it doesn't make you feel very good, Tom thought. It makes you feel lousy. For the third time, he shrugged. How strangely it all works out, he thought. The pretty girl smiles as she hands me the innocuous manila envelope with the speech. I'll go with my boss for luncheon to a nice restaurant somewhere, with music playing in the background, perhaps, and people laughing all around, and the waiters will bow, and my boss will be polite, and I'll be tactful, and there in such delicate surroundings, I'll not be rude enough to say a stupid speech is stupid. How smoothly one becomes, not a cheat, exactly, not really a liar, just a man who'll say anything for pay.

Tom remained by the window a long while, looking down at the cars crawling along the streets below. It was queer to be suspended motionless so far above the city. It was almost as though his parachute had got stuck in mid-air, halfway between the plane and the ground.

That night when Tom went home he put the speech back in the manila envelope and on impulse took it with him. Betsy and the children met him at the station in South Bay. "What's that?" Janey said, eying the big envelope. "Is it a present for us?"

"No," Tom said, and handed the envelope to Betsy. "This is Hopkins' speech. I'd like you to read it and tell me what you think of it. Hopkins wants me to have lunch with him and give him my opinion on it tomorrow."

"I'll look at it after dinner," Betsy said, and casually put the envelope down on the front seat of the car.

"Mother has a surprise for you," Barbara said. "She got it for you today."

"Hush!" Betsy said. "How is it going to be a surprise if you talk about it?"

"I can hardly wait to find out what it is," Tom said, and, realizing he had been so preoccupied that he hadn't kissed Betsy, leaned over and patted her on the shoulder. "It's good to get home," he said.

She turned toward him with a quick, vivid smile. "It's not much of a surprise, really," she said. "Don't get your hopes up."

The surprise turned out to be a large leather armchair with a matching hassock for Tom to put his feet on. Betsy had put a small table by it, with a box of cigarettes, matches, and an ash tray. She had also placed an ice bucket there, two glasses, and the mixings for cocktails. "You looked so tired when you got back from Atlantic City last night," she said. "I figured you ought to have a place where you can just sink down and rest when you get home. I'm going to try to organize things so we have a half hour of quiet before supper. Kids, go upstairs, the way you promised you would!"

Janey grinned, and with unusual obedience led the others up the stairs. "I put ginger ale up there for them," Betsy said. "They're going to have a quiet period in their room, while we have ours down here. We're going to try to do it that way for a half hour every night."

"That's wonderful," Tom said. "It's a marvelous chair." He sat down in it gratefully, put his feet up on the hassock, and lit a cigarette. Betsy mixed the cocktails and handed him one. He took a sip and said, "Did you bring that speech in from the car?"

"Yes. It's on the hall table. Why?"

"I'm anxious to see what you think of it."

"Sure," she said. "I'll go get it."

She sat in a chair across the room from Tom and took the speech from the envelope. He watched her face while she read it. Her expression was serene. At first she read slowly, but soon began to flip rapidly through the pages. Tom poured himself another drink. "What do you think of it so far?" he asked.

"Did you write this?"

"I helped. Do you like it?"

"Well," she said hesitantly, "I don't know much about the subject. My opinion wouldn't mean much."

"Come on. What do you think of it?"

"It's kind of boring," she said. "Maybe it's just me, but I find it pretty hard to keep my mind on it. It seems to keep saying the same thing over and over again."

Tom laughed. "Any other comments?"

"To be honest, some of it sounds pretty silly," Betsy said. "Is this what Hopkins wanted you to write?"

"I didn't really write it," Tom said. "I think Ogden did most of it, or maybe Hopkins himself. And now Hopkins wants me to tell him what I think of it."

"What are you going to say?"

Tom laughed again. "There's a standard operating procedure for this sort of thing," he said. "It's a little like reading fortunes. You make a lot of highly qualified contradictory statements and keep your eyes on the man's face to see which ones please him. That way you can feel your way along, and if you're clever, you can always end up by telling him exactly what he wants to hear."

"Is that what they do?" Betsy asked. She didn't laugh.

"That's what they do. For instance, I'll begin by saying, 'I think there are some *wonderful* things about this speech. . . .' If Hopkins seems pleased, I'll finish the sentence by saying, 'and I have only the most minor improvements to suggest.' But if he seems a little surprised at the word *wonderful*, I'll end the sentence with, 'but as a whole, I don't think it comes off at all, and I think major revisions are necessary.' "

"Is that what you're going to do?" Betsy asked. She wasn't even smiling.

"As I say, it's standard operating procedure," Tom replied. "The first thing the young executive must learn."

"I think it's a little sickening," Betsy said bluntly.

"Damn it, have a sense of humor. What's the matter with you?"

"Nothing's the matter with me. I'm just interested in knowing the answers to a few questions. What do you really think of that speech?"

"I think it's terrible," Tom said. "My business education, you see, is not complete. In a few years I'll be able to suspend judgment entirely until I learn what Hopkins thinks, and then I'll really and truly feel the way he does. That way I won't have to be dishonest any more."

Betsy put the speech neatly back in its envelope, handed it to Tom, and without a word went to the kitchen.

"Betsy!" he said. "Come back. I want to talk to you."

"I'm getting dinner," she said.

"What's the matter? It's not time for dinner yet."

"I've got some things that have to be put on the stove."

He went to the kitchen and found her filling a kettle with water. "You're angry with me," he said. "Can't you take a joke?"

"I don't think you were joking."

"Of course I was. I was knocking myself out with humor."

"What are you going to tell Hopkins tomorrow?"

"I don't know. Why's that so important all of a sudden?"

She put the kettle on the stove and turned toward him suddenly. "I didn't like the look of you sitting there in that big chair talking so damn smugly and cynically!" she said. "You looked disgusting! You looked like just the kind of guy you always used to hate. The guy with all the answers. The guy who has no respect for himself or anyone else!"

"What do you want me to do?" he asked quietly. "Do you want me to go in there tomorrow and tell Hopkins I think his speech is a farce?"

"I don't care what you tell him, but I don't like the idea of your becoming a cheap cynical yes-man and being so self-satisfied and analytical about it. You never used to be like that."

"All right," Tom said. "I'll tell him I think his speech is absurd. And he'll decide I'm a nice honest guy who just happens to be no use to him at all."

"How do you know? Maybe he doesn't like the speech either."

"Sure, it might turn out that way. I've got a fifty-fifty chance if I play it straight, but if I feel my way along, I have a ninety per cent chance of giving him what he wants."

"Maybe he just wants an honest opinion."

"That sounds real nice," Tom said bitterly. "You don't know how guys like Hopkins are."

"No, I don't," she said.

"You haven't even met him."

"No, I haven't. What's he ever done to convince you he's dishonest?"

"I didn't say he is dishonest."

"He is if you have to agree with him all the time to keep your job."

"That's not true. A guy who disagreed with him most of the time simply wouldn't be useful to him."

"Not if you were right and he was wrong — if it were that way, you could be damn useful by disagreeing. There's no two ways about it: either you think that he'd fire you for disagreeing, even if you were right, or you're not sure you're right. Either you've got no confidence in him, or none in yourself. Which is it?"

"Don't be so righteous," Tom said. "If you really want to know, I'm not too damn sure of either him or myself. I don't really know whether that speech will do whatever he wants it to do or not — maybe all the slick advertising guys will think it's wonderful, and maybe that's what he wants. I don't know how he'd feel about a guy who disagreed with him. The point is, you'd have to take an awful chance to find out."

"And you don't want to take a chance."

"You're talking like a typical American woman," Tom said disgustedly. "You want it both ways. 'Don't play it safe,' you say, 'and can we get a new car tomorrow?'"

"You can't imagine being honest and getting a raise for it."

"My Boy Scout days are over," Tom said doggedly.

"And so you're going in there tomorrow and lie to the man if you figure that's what he wants."

"You're damn right I am."

"How long will it be before you decide it isn't necessary to tell the truth to me?"

The truth, Tom thought. The truth about what? The truth about Maria? Shall we all sit down now and tell each other the truth? Suddenly he felt immensely angry. "You've had an easy life, Betsy," he said in a deadly quiet voice. "You just stay here and take care of the kids and enjoy your moral indignation while I go in town every day to wrestle with guys like Hopkins. But don't read me lectures. The truth is I'm doing the best I can with the world as I see it."

"*Go to hell,*" Betsy said with passion.

"Thanks," Tom replied. "Is that the last of your moral advice?"

Betsy didn't answer. She was pale and

quiet all through dinner. After she had put the children to bed, Tom said to her, "Haven't we been making an awful lot out of nothing?"

"I guess we have," she said. "If you don't mind, I think I'll turn in. And if you're going to see Hopkins tomorrow, you better get a good night's rest yourself."

27

Saul Bernstein walked into the First National Bank, which was the biggest building in South Bay. As a boy he had thought "the bank" a frightful monster, for he had often heard his parents worrying about whether it would take their store away, as though it were a giant who could reach out and rip the building from its foundations, but for two years now, he had been a member of the bank's board of directors, and he no longer thought of it as anything but a rather tired group of men trying to meet their responsibilities. He walked to the rear of the bank, opened a gate in a low partition there, and approached the desk of Walter Johnson, the president. "Good morning, Walt," he said. "I'd like to find out the bank balance of two men: a Mr. Thomas R. Rath and a Mr. Edward F. Schultz."

"Just a minute," Johnson said, and picked up his telephone. Bernstein sat down. That morning he had received in the mail from Edward Schultz a photostat of a document written on the personal stationery of Mrs. Florence Rath. "To Whom It May Concern," the document said. "In exchange for his services for the rest of my life, and in place of paying him a regular salary for same from this day forward, I hereby bequeath my entire possessions, including my house and land, to Edward F. Schultz, who has served me faithfully for more than thirty years." This was typewritten, with the date, June 10, 1953. Florence Rath's signature followed, written by a quavering hand.

Bernstein had studied this and had carefully reread the long, precisely phrased will which Sims had sent him, a document which was dated January 18, 1948. Edward's document was not a legal will like the one which left everything to Tom, Bernstein saw, but it might be considered a legal contract, and quite a case might be built on that. And regardless of the legal technicalities, what had old Mrs. Rath intended?

As he waited for Johnson to get him the figures he had requested, Bernstein reviewed for the hundredth time the possibilities, the different combinations of circumstance, which theoretically could have led to contradictory documents. It was possible that old Mrs. Rath had simply been forgetful, had made her bargain with Schultz and forgotten to tell her lawyer or grandson. It was possible she had deliberately refrained from telling them, for fear that their objections might be painful. On the other hand, she might have told her grandson of the change, and young Rath might have decided simply to say nothing about it to anyone, confident that his grandmother's agreement with Schultz would be thrown out of court because of legal technicalities — because it bore the names of no witnesses to the signature. And theoretically it was just as possible that the document presented by Schultz was in some way a fake, although Bernstein was quite sure that Schultz's lawyers would have had the signature examined before accepting the case. His real responsibility, Bernstein felt, was to discover which of these circumstances had actually happened. Until he knew that, it would be impossible to tell what paragraphs in the thick law books which lined the walls of his inner office should be chosen to justify a decision in the case. It was, of course, difficult to ˜esurrect the past, but not impossible. In a small town the past clung to the present more permanently than in a big city. People's footprints lasted longer before they were stamped out.

The bank president wrote several figures on a pad. "Mr. Rath has a savings account with approximately nine thousand dollars in it, deposited on September 2, all in one check from a real-estate outfit in Westport," he said. "Mr. Schultz has a savings account of approximately seventy-eight thousand dollars, deposited here over a period of thirty years, in varying amounts on the third of each month."

"Are you sure?" Bernstein asked in astonishment.

"Those are the figures."

"Thank you," Bernstein said.

"Not a bit," Johnson replied. He knew he was not supposed to give out such figures, but in South Bay a man who had demonstrated good intentions and the ability to keep his mouth shut could get any information he wanted.

Bernstein walked slowly up Main Street. It was surprising how often bank balances helped to point the way toward justice. The figures he had just learned might mean anything or nothing, but they at least rid his mind of the picture of the faithful impoverished old servant being cheated by a young heir. Here the servant was richer than the heir, all of which went to show, Bernstein reflected, that a man must guard himself against his own prejudices. And another thing: how could old Schultz have continued his deposits if he had had no salary for several months? And why were his monthly deposits of "varying amounts"? Wouldn't an employee with a regular salary tend to deposit the same sum every month? Perhaps he had cashed his checks, spent varying amounts, and deposited the remainder, Bernstein thought, but it would be strange if such a haphazard plan enabled a butler to save so much. How much had Mrs. Rath been paying him? Suddenly Bernstein had an idea. He hadn't worked in a delicatessen all during his boyhood without learning anything.

Quickening his pace, Bernstein walked to Hopeland's Grocery Store, which specialized in luxury items. That is where Mrs. Rath would have been almost sure to order her groceries. He went to the room on the second floor where Julius Marvella, the manager, was busy reckoning his accounts. "Morning, Julius," he said.

"What are you doing up here, Judge?"

Julius replied, grinning. "Have you come to take me in?"

"Not today. I wondered if you could tell me something. Did old Mrs. Rath trade here?"

"Nope — she went to Fritz's place."

"Why?"

Julius shrugged.

"Did she ever trade here?"

"A long time ago, when I was a kid. Then she changed."

"Do you know why?"

Julius shrugged again.

"Nobody's going to get into trouble if you tell me," Bernstein said. "And you won't have to appear in court. I won't mention your name."

"Okay, Judge," Julius said. "This guy Schultz did all her buying for her, and he wanted kickbacks. He asked Pop to pad Mrs. Rath's bill. Not just a little, mind you — Schultz wanted him to add twenty per cent every month and kick back fifteen per cent to him. You know how Pop was on that stuff. He threw the bastard out."

"Thanks," Bernstein said.

"I don't know what Fritz did for him," Julius said. "I'm making no charges — I'm just telling you what happened here. I don't want to get Fritz into trouble. You know how it is, Judge — Fritz might get a chance to put me in a jam someday. It don't pay to start things in a town like this. Wouldn't be long before he found some way to knock me."

"I won't even have to talk to Fritz," Bernstein said. Six years before he had successfully represented a man bringing suit against Fritz for padding bills. He thanked Julius again and continued on his way down Main Street. That clears up one thing, he thought — Schultz is dishonest. A piece of knowledge like that was a lot more help to Bernstein than the legal reviews that came to his office each month.

Bernstein strolled around the town, chatting casually with shopkeepers, the manager of the movie theater, the keepers of taverns, the man who sold tickets at the railroad station and many others. Within two hours he had accumulated a fairly complete dossier on Schultz. Five shopkeepers had reported that Schultz had tried to get them to pad bills. These five all had good reputations, and Schultz had not traded with them regularly. He had done most of his purchasing at stores whose proprietors Bernstein suspected, some because of rumors he had heard, others because of their record. All this was perhaps less strange, Bernstein thought, than the fact that virtually no one could remember ever having seen Schultz spend money on himself, or buy any entertainment. In the thirty years Schultz had lived in the house on the top of the hill, the taxi company had rarely been called to bring him to town. He had never been seen in the movies or taverns and had not taken regular trips on the train. What had he done on his days off? Perhaps he's a miser, Bernstein thought; perhaps he did nothing but save money. One couldn't refuse to allow a man to inherit a house simply because he had padded bills and saved money, but Bernstein felt he was beginning to see the tortuous road to justice more clearly.

28

It was a little after ten o'clock in the morning. "Mrs. Hopkins is on the wire, Mr. Hopkins," Miss MacDonald said. "Will you take the call now?"

"Of course!" Hopkins said. "Put her through."

"Ralph?" Helen's voice broke in.

"Hello, dear," he said. "What can I do for you?"

"Ralph, can you come out here? I want to talk to you."

"Sure," he said. "Sure! I have some appointments, but I can break them. What time do you want me to be there?"

"Try to get here for lunch. This is important, Ralph. It's about Susan."

"Susan? What's the matter with her?"

"She just told me she refuses to go to college. I'm worried about her, Ralph. I'll talk to you about it when I see you."

"I'll come right out," he said.

After telephoning Tom to postpone their luncheon date, Hopkins had his chauffeur drive him to South Bay. As the car turned into his driveway, he tried not to look at the enormous low house, with one wing extending over the edge of the artificial harbor. His wife had had it built, had directed the architect herself, and Hopkins did not like the place — he detested anything which seemed to be made mostly for show. He had never complained about the house, however, and did not intend to.

A butler let Hopkins in, and a maid took his hat — that was another thing which bothered him about the house: there were always too many servants hanging around. He walked through the enormous living room, the entire east side of which was made of glass, to the library. Helen was sitting there alone. She was a short woman who had grown rather stout, but her face retained its delicate shape. Her graying brown hair was carefully arranged in a style a little too youthful for her, and she wore a severe black cocktail dress which had been designed for a much slimmer figure. She got up a little nervously when Hopkins came into the room. She hadn't seen him for more than a month.

"Hello, dear," he said. "You're looking grand!" He kissed her lightly.

"Thanks for coming," she said. "I've been terribly worried."

"Sit down," he said. "Let's have a drink. Do you have any liquor in here?"

"Just pull the bell cord."

He pulled it, and a moment later a maid who had never seen Hopkins before came in. She was extremely nervous. "You rang, sir?" she asked. "Did you ring?"

"Yes," Hopkins replied. "Scotch on the rocks, please."

"I'll have a Manhattan," Helen said.

The maid withdrew.

"Is Susan here?" Hopkins asked.

"No — she's at some party out on Long Island. That's what I want to talk to you about, Ralph. She's at parties all the time."

"That's natural," Hopkins said easily. "She's young. I don't see anything to worry about."

"Well, I do!" Helen paused as the maid came in to set up a stand for a tray of drinks.

"After this, please try to have a closet or something in here with some liquor in it," Hopkins said to her. "I like to mix my own drinks."

"All right," Helen said. "Anna, please see about that in the morning."

"Yes, Madam," the maid said, passed the drinks, and withdrew.

"I don't think you understand the situation," Helen said. "Have you ever *thought* about it?"

"About what?"

"About Susan! About the problems she's going to have."

"It doesn't seem to me that she's in very difficult circumstances," Hopkins said dryly. "When I was her age . . ."

"You haven't thought about it, then," Helen interrupted. "It's time you did. What do you think is going to happen to her?"

"Happen to her?" Hopkins said. "Nothing, I hope. I hope she marries and has a nice family."

"What chance do you think she has for that?"

"Not bad, I'd say. She's pretty, and she won't be exactly a pauper."

"No, she won't be a pauper," Helen said. "I'm glad you've thought about it at least that much!"

"What do you mean by that?"

"To put it bluntly, your little daughter is probably going to be one of the richest young women in the country, and we haven't done anything at all to prepare her for it. And if she keeps on the way she's started, she's going to get into a lot of trouble."

"I think you're exaggerating," he said. "Money is no reason why she has to get into trouble."

"What do you think would happen if you and I died tomorrow?"

"Susan would inherit a lot of money, but she wouldn't have to worry about it. My lawyers would take care of all that."

"For the rest of her life?"

"If she wanted."

"You're awfully willing to write her off as an incompetent," Helen said. "The fact is that sooner or later the child's going to have tremendous responsibilities, and she has enormous temptations right now. It's our job to help her handle them."

"It's too early for that," Hopkins said. "Wait till she gets older. Then I'll see that she learns something about investments and all the rest of it."

"It's not investments I'm worried about!" Helen said. "Don't you see what a difference that money makes for her already? For one thing, everything she does gets in the newspapers! 'Miss Susan Hopkins seen at the Stork

Club last night.' My God, any little joke she makes gets in the gossip columns. Don't you read the papers?"

"Not the gossip columns."

"Well, try them! You'll learn a lot about your daughter. At the age of eighteen, she's a celebrity!"

"That's inevitable," he said. "She'll learn to take it in her stride."

"And the men she goes out with!" Helen said. "They're not just nice healthy school-boys — you should see them. A man called for her here the other night who's older than I am!"

"Who?"

"Byron Holgate, his name is. He drives a ridiculous-looking automobile, he's had two wives, and he sails in ocean races."

"I know Holgate," Hopkins said. "He's a fool. What's she running around with him for?"

"She's not just running around with him in a casual way — she's with him half the time. I wouldn't be surprised if she were thinking about marrying him. And the other people she sees aren't much better — it's the whole café society crowd. Do you know what she said to me the other day? She came in here dressed in some horrible thing she'd just bought, and she said, 'Mother, do you think I'm old for my age? I think boys my age are children.'"

"All girls go through a stage like that."

"Nonsense! Most girls would like to, but they don't get the chance. You have no idea what's been going on. The other day a man who had a play opening on Broadway took her to the opening night with him. How can a college boy compete with that?"

"Who was it?"

"Michael Patterson, his name is. He's forty-three years old and has three children. His wife divorced him last year."

"His play folded after three nights," Hopkins said. "You shouldn't let her run around with a crowd like that."

"How can I stop her? Do you want me to lock her in her room?"

"Have you had a talk with her?"

"Sure I've talked with her! She says I'm old-fashioned and she says . . ." Helen paused before she finished the sentence. "It's rather funny," she continued. "She says I'm nobody to talk, because my own marriage has been a failure."

"That's not true," Hopkins said quietly. "I consider our marriage a success."

"Let's not go into that," Helen said. "The

point is, I can't do anything with her. And I'll tell you exactly what's going to happen if she keeps on: she's going to be one of those women who's in and out of the divorce courts most of her life."

"I think you're being an alarmist," he said. "She's young and high-spirited. Give her a few years, and she'll straighten out."

"*How* is she going to straighten out?" Helen demanded. "What kind of training is she getting? In the mornings she sleeps until lunch. She spends half the afternoon getting dressed. Most of the time she's awake she's getting entertained. Is that going to straighten her out? My God, she's already complaining that she's bored all the time. Bored, at eighteen!"

"She ought to go to college," Hopkins said.

"Yesterday she flatly refused. College is for children, she said. She claimed most of the men she knows are more brilliant than college professors — I suppose she's thinking of her playwright."

Hopkins finished his drink. "Tell that girl to bring a bottle and an ice bucket in here," he said.

Helen touched the bell pull, and a moment later the maid appeared. "You rang, Madam?" she asked. "Did you ring for me?"

"Bring a bottle of Scotch and an ice bucket for Mr. Hopkins," Helen said.

"Certainly, Madam," the girl replied, and scurried from the room.

"That girl makes me nervous," Hopkins said. "Where did you get her?"

"She's just inexperienced. I think she's a little overawed by you."

"I like to mix my own drinks!"

"Don't get irritable, dear," Helen said. "It isn't like you."

"I'm sorry," Hopkins said.

After the maid had brought the bottle of Scotch and the ice bucket, Hopkins filled his glass and took a long drink. "I think you better tell Susan she simply has to go to college," he said.

"I have, and she told me not to be medieval. That's exactly what she said."

"Maybe we've got to get a little tough with her. Tell her if she doesn't go to college we'll stop her allowance."

"I've already told her that," Helen said patiently. "She said to go ahead. She said she's already been offered a job singing with a band, and that she thinks she could get a screen test. And the funny thing is, she's right: plenty of people would be willing to hire your daughter, and you might as well understand that. Simply because she's your daughter, she's not the same as other people. You've given her a problem, and it's time you started helping her to handle it."

"I don't see what I can do," Hopkins said. "She's not a child any more. If she wants to ruin her own life, there's not much either of us can do about it. All we can do is watch, and if she runs wild, I'll set up a small trust fund for her and put the rest into my foundation."

"The Ralph Hopkins Foundation!" Helen said bitterly. "That and the headlines about your daughter's divorces will perpetuate your name."

"Let's not get emotional," Hopkins said.

"I'm not emotional!" Helen replied, her voice rising. "I just want to discuss a few facts. Since they were born, you've left the upbringing of the children to me. I've done it alone, and up to now, I haven't done a bad job. Bobby was a good boy — you were never particularly aware of him, but he was. He got good marks in college, and he never got into any trouble, and he enlisted in the Marines because he thought it was the right thing to do. He didn't even want a commission — he wanted the hardest job he could get, and no favors from you!"

Tears suddenly came to Helen's eyes, as they still did quite often when she talked about her dead son. Hopkins got up and awkwardly put his arm around her. "You've done a wonderful job," he said.

"But Susan has me licked, and I need your help!"

"I'll try," he said. "I don't know what I can do. You know I'm no good at this sort of thing."

"You're not stupid! This is a problem. All I'm asking is that you *try* to do something about it. It would help if Susan just knew you were trying. Don't go back to that office of yours and just forget about her. By God, if it will help you, think of her as a business problem!"

"I'll do anything you want," he said.

"It's not anything *I* want. I don't know what to ask you to do. I just want you to figure something out for yourself."

"I'll try," he said.

He handed her a clean handkerchief, and she wiped her face. When she straightened up in her chair she was completely composed. "I just want to tell you this," she said quietly. "I'm asking you for help. I haven't done that for twenty-five years. I've got to admit I don't think I'll get it. What I really think is that you'll go back to New York, and maybe have a talk with Susan, and then forget all about her and me too. What I want you to understand is this: if that happens, I'm through. I'll get a divorce, on grounds of desertion."

"I'm going to try," he said.

"Trying isn't enough. I don't mean you've got to succeed with Susan, but you've got to do more than just make a halfhearted effort to get yourself interested. And don't come back to me and tell me you're sorry, but you are what you are, and nothing can be done about it. You've got to give her *time*. Put her down on your calendar. Treat her as though she were something you were a trustee of!"

29

At noon of the day finally set for Tom to have lunch with Hopkins to discuss the speech, Tom's secretary came into his office and rather incredulously said, "There's an elevator man here to see you. He says his name is Gardella. Shall I tell him to come in?"

"Yes," Tom said.

A moment later Caesar entered, shut the door behind him, and rather self-consciously took off his purple cap.

"Hello, Caesar," Tom said. "Nice to see you."

"Good morning, Mr. Rath," Caesar replied. "We heard from Gina's mother. It's funny — I thought you'd want to know about it. She doesn't know where Maria is."

"Doesn't know?"

"What I mean is, Maria and Louis and the boy — they've gone somewhere. They're not

in Rome any more, or at least they're not anywhere where Gina's mother can find them.
She hasn't heard a word from them for six
months."

"What do you think happened?"

"I don't know. Things had been pretty
hard for them for a long while. Louis was out
of the hospital, but with his leg and all, he
couldn't get any work. Gina's mother had
been helping them out, and I guess that bothered Louis a lot. Louis's a funny guy — he's
proud."

Tom glanced out the window. He found it
hard to look at Caesar.

"Gina's mother thinks they may have gone
to Milan to look for work, and that they
didn't tell anybody they were leaving because
they owed so much money," Caesar continued. "Anyway, there's no sign of them now. I
thought you ought to know."

"Thanks," Tom said.

"Gina's mother has an aunt in Milan, and
she's asked her to look for them," Caesar
added. "She'll let me know if they find
them."

"I guess there's not much we can do now,"
Tom said.

"They'll turn up eventually," Caesar replied. "I'm sure of that. Gina has an awful

lot of relatives over there. Louis's funny — if he made some money, he'd come back and pay his debts. And if things went real bad, Maria would have to go to some relatives for help. Sooner or later she'll turn up. I'll let you know."

"Thanks," Tom said.

"Well, so long," Caesar concluded, awkwardly put on his cap, and went out the door.

Tom got up and walked over to the window. So they've disappeared, he thought. I wonder if this is the way it will end — with no ending at all, with me never knowing what happened to them. They'll turn up, Caesar said. Somewhat to his own surprise, Tom found himself hoping they would — soon. The implications of that startled him a little, and he turned quickly to sit down at his desk. What would I do? he thought: what would I do if right now I knew they were starving and knew where to reach them? I couldn't do anything without telling Betsy — we've got joint bank accounts, both the saving and the checking, and Betsy keeps much closer track of the money than I do. I could take a few dollars out and make up some kind of excuse, sure, but not much and not regularly. And even if I could find a way to get the money without her knowing, it wouldn't be fair to her. I'd have to tell her, he thought. I'd have to tell her and pray to God she'd understand.

How would you tell your wife a thing like that? he asked himself. Would you go up to her and say, "Look, honey, I'm sorry to have to say this, but during the war . . ."

What would she do? It suddenly seemed to him that his wife was a stranger whose actions he could not predict at all. I don't know her, he thought with a kind of panic, I don't really know my own wife at all. Poor Betsy! Betsy had never had anything happen to her which could possibly help her to understand a thing like that. Would she accuse him of being immoral? Would she cry? Would she be angry, jealous? Would she figure that the whole time they had spent together since the war had been a kind of living lie, and would she want a divorce? He simply could not imagine what she would do — he couldn't picture himself telling her about Maria at all. Maybe I'll never have to, he thought. Maria has disappeared as completely as though I had wished her away. She isn't there any more, or at least no one can find her — it is as though she never existed. I should be glad Caesar can't find her, he thought; I should be glad, I should feel immensely relieved. He put his hand up to his face and suddenly realized he

407

was praying like a child: Dear God, I want Maria to be all right.

His thoughts were suddenly interrupted by the buzz of the interoffice communication box on his desk. He turned it on, and Ralph Hopkins' cheery voice said, "Good morning, Tom! Ready to go to lunch now? Bring along a copy of the speech!"

"I'll be there in a few minutes," Tom said.

Carrying the speech in its manila envelope, Tom stepped into one of the golden elevators. The secretaries in Hopkins' office all smiled at him, and he smiled back. Hopkins came out almost immediately. "Glad you could make it, Tom!" he said. "How have you been?"

"Fine," Tom said. "The hotel accommodations are all set for you in Atlantic City."

Hopkins started toward the elevators. "Did you read the speech?" he asked.

"Yes."

"I'm looking forward to talking to you about it," Hopkins replied. An elevator door rumbled open, and they both stepped in. The elevator was crowded, and on the way down they both remained silent.

"How about the University Club for lunch?" Hopkins asked when they got out on the street.

"That would be nice."

"Let's walk — it's a grand day," Hopkins said, and strode rapidly up Fifth Avenue.

I hope he doesn't ask me what I think of the speech now, walking along Fifth Avenue in the sunshine, Tom thought. It would be very difficult for me to play games with him here and now.

"Did you get a chance for a vacation this summer?" Hopkins asked.

"No — I haven't been on the job long enough," Tom said.

"I just got a couple of week ends myself," Hopkins replied. "Put in some good fishing, though. Have you ever tried landlocked salmon?"

On the way to the University Club, Hopkins continued a pleasant line of chatter about fishing. They sat at a table in the corner of a high-ceilinged dining room. All around them earnest-appearing businessmen ate and talked. A waiter bowed and took their order for cocktails.

It isn't quite as I pictured it, Tom thought. Such a respectable place for me to lie about a speech, and there really should be music.

"Well, what do you think of the speech?" Hopkins asked mildly.

Parts of it are wonderful, Tom started to

say, but on the other hand . . .

He didn't say it. Instead, he glanced at Hopkins and saw that he was watching him intently. On his face was an expression of courteous attention, nothing more. There was a pause.

"Would you care to order your luncheon now, sir?" a waiter asked. He spoke in a thick Italian accent.

"I guess we might as well," Hopkins said. "What will you have, Tom?"

"Anything," Tom said. "I guess I'd like some cold salmon."

"Scrambled eggs for me," Hopkins said. "And a cup of tea."

The business of ordering luncheon took a few more minutes. A man at a near-by table laughed explosively. The hell with it, Tom thought suddenly, so clearly that he half thought he had said it. It doesn't really matter. Here goes nothing. It will be interesting to see what happens. In defiance of his intentions, he heard himself saying aloud in a remarkably casual voice, "To tell you the truth, Mr. Hopkins, I read the latest draft of your speech, and I'm afraid I question it pretty seriously."

"You do?" Hopkins asked. His face did not change expression.

"I'm afraid I just don't think it's a very good speech," Tom said flatly.

"What do you think is the trouble with it?"

"It doesn't say anything," Tom replied. "That's the main trouble I had when I was trying to write it. The only point you really make is that mental health is important, and you can't repeat that for thirty pages. And frankly, I don't think an audience of physicians will react very well to slogans."

"I see," Hopkins said. "What do you recommend that I do?"

"I think you should come up with some concrete recommendations on how to solve mental-health problems," Tom heard himself booming confidently.

"I believe that at some point Ogden already has me asking for more mental hospitals and research," Hopkins said dryly.

"But everybody knows that's necessary — it's another repetition of the obvious," Tom said. "Couldn't you give some ideas about how to get the research and the hospitals?"

"Wait a minute," Hopkins said with a trace of impatience. "Don't let's forget that I don't know anything about concrete solutions for mental-health problems, and I don't want to pretend that I do."

"But . . ." Tom began.

"Wait a minute. I think you've put your finger on something. This draft of Bill Ogden's rings false because it confuses the job of starting a mental-health campaign with carrying it out. As you say, my audience at Atlantic City certainly won't need convincing that mental-health problems are important. But it would be just as phony for me to do a little quick research and come up with all kinds of recommendations in a field I don't know anything about. Let's go back to the original purpose of this speech. What I'm trying to do is to form a committee to publicize mental-health problems — that's a subject I do know something about. I'm going down to Atlantic City, not to convince a lot of doctors that mental health is important, but to show them I know it's important. I'm trying to make myself a rallying point, to bring the doctors and a committee of publicity boys together. Somebody's got to do it if anything's ever really going to get done about mental health, and it looks as though the finger's been pointed at me. It won't be an easy job, but it's a necessary one."

"I see," Tom said.

"Now, I can't stand up and propose a committee right off the bat — that would be pushing it too hard and would invite misinterpretation. Never forget that there are always a million cynics ready to read the worst motives into anything we do. Before I try to start a committee, I have to demonstrate my interest and my availability. What this speech should say, in effect, is that I know the problem, and Barkus is willing if wanted. That's all. Do you get the picture?"

"I think so," Tom said.

"All right. We've been way off base on this speech. Try it for me from scratch, will you?"

"Be glad to," Tom said.

Hopkins turned his attention toward his scrambled eggs. Well, that's that, Tom thought, feeling a peculiar sensation of letdown. It all happened awfully fast, and I'm not sure where it leaves us. Hopkins finished his eggs and glanced at his watch. "Say, I've got to hurry — some people are waiting for me in my office," he said. "Can you have something for me by the end of the week?"

"I'll certainly try," Tom said, paused, and added, "I was wrong in advising you to make specific recommendations — I can see that."

Hopkins smiled. "You've helped me cut through a lot of fog on this," he said. "Can't thank you enough!" Waving cheerily, he pushed his chair sharply backward, and at his usual brisk gate almost trotted from the room.

That night when Tom got home to South Bay, Betsy immediately asked, "Did you see Hopkins?"

"Yes," Tom replied.

"I suppose you told him his speech is great," she said bitterly.

"No, I didn't."

"You didn't?" Betsy asked, her voice quickening.

"It didn't go the way I expected it to at all," Tom said. "I was completely honest with him, and I think he was with me. And what's more, he cleared up a doubt I've always had in the back of my mind — he showed me he's completely sincere about wanting to do something about mental-health problems. All this talk about his starting this committee just for a publicity build-up is a lot of nonsense — I'm sure about that now."

"You seem so astonished," she said, laughing. "You sound almost disappointed."

Tom grinned. "I don't know," he said. "Maybe I've been worrying too much about Hopkins' honesty and not enough about my own. Anyway, from now on I'm going to play it straight with him, and we'll see how it goes. I'm rather looking forward to fixing up that speech."

"Thank God!" Betsy said. "You know, for

414

a while there, I wasn't sure *what* kind of a man I had married."

Tom glanced at her sharply. "Don't let's go into that," he said. "Let's have a drink. How about mixing up some Martinis?"

30

Hopkins had tried to arrange to have lunch with his daughter the day after he had talked to his wife, but Susan had been busy. Now he was due to meet her in his apartment in half an hour. At quarter after twelve he said to the motion-picture producer with whom he had spent the morning, "I'm sorry, but I've got to be going. Can I see you tomorrow?"

"I've got to fly back to the Coast," the producer said. "How about lunch?"

"I'm sorry, I just can't today," Hopkins said. "I'll be in touch with you by phone."

The producer was an important man in the business, and he looked a little hurt. Hopkins shook hands with him, apologized effusively, and dashed for the elevator. Miss MacDonald had a taxi waiting for him. He gave the driver the address of his apartment and said, "Hurry."

When he got to his apartment, he let himself in and looked quickly around the big living room. No one was there. He walked through the dining room and poked his head into the kitchen, where the cook was fixing luncheon for two and the waitress was filling a silver bucket with ice cubes. "Has Miss Hopkins called?" he asked.

"No, sir," the waitress said. "No one's called all morning."

He returned to the living room and sat down. When the waitress brought in the ice, he mixed himself a drink and glanced at his watch. It was a quarter to one. He had talked over the telephone to Susan two days ago, and she had said she would be there at twelve-thirty. Well, anyone could be a quarter hour late. He glanced out the window and was suddenly seized with the fear that she simply would not come. Impatiently he got up, walked to his desk, and took out a draft of a promotion brochure. Picking a pencil from his pocket, he sat down and began to edit it.

A half hour later there was a timid knock on the door. He sprang from his chair, dashed across the room, and opened it. Susan stood there. "Hello," she said. "I'm sorry I'm late. The traffic . . ."

"It's all right!" he said. "Come in! Come

417

in and sit down!"

She walked hesitantly into the room, which she had seen only once before, long ago, after her father had taken her and her mother to the theater. She was a slight, dark-haired girl with a good figure, who in a curiously elderly way leaned a little forward as she walked. Her face was beautiful, more because of an intense quality than any unusual symmetry of feature. She sat down and nervously lit a cigarette. "You wanted to talk to me?" she asked.

"Yes," he replied. "Have a drink. Ginger ale? Coca-Cola? Or something else? I guess you're old enough to drink now, aren't you?"

"It seems so," she said, smiling. "I'll have bourbon on the rocks."

He mixed her the drink, fussing perhaps a little too long with the silver ice tongs and the little tray on which he put the glass. After handing it to her and passing her a plate of canapés, he returned to his chair. She was glancing down into her glass with an abstracted look on her face, as though the glass were a crystal ball in which she could see her future. She is beautiful, he thought, and she's no child any more. I've got to handle this thing carefully.

"I suppose Mother told you I don't want to go to college, and now you're going to try to persuade me," she said suddenly without looking up.

"Of course I'm not!" Hopkins said without hesitation. "I don't want you to go to college if you don't want to!"

He had answered automatically, from instinct and long training in the handling of people, in spite of the fact that he had of course intended to try to persuade her. She glanced up at him, surprised. "What do you want to see me for, then?"

The arguments he had planned could not be used now. "I just want to talk to you in general about your future," he said. "Obviously, there's no point in our trying to send you to college if you don't want to go, but what are you going to do?"

"I don't know," she said, appearing a little confused. "I want to get married. Maybe before long."

"Anybody particular in mind?"

"I'm not sure yet."

"After marriage, what?"

She shrugged. "I'd like to travel," she said.

He sipped his drink slowly. "I've got a problem I've never discussed with you," he said. "It's a rather hard one to talk about, but perhaps we should."

"What kind of a problem?"

"It's difficult to describe. You are aware, I suppose, that the world has treated me pretty well. Over the years, I have gradually accumulated a good many responsibilities. I have been lucky, because they came to me gradually, and I had plenty of time to learn how to handle them. The curious thing is that all these accumulated responsibilities, or at least, a good many of them, could easily fall upon your shoulders quite suddenly, and you've had no opportunity to get ready for them. . . ."

"Are you talking about money?"

"In part."

"I'm not interested in money. I think it's a bore."

"No sane person is interested in money as such," he said.

"You've always seemed to be. I always thought it was all you were interested in. That's what everybody says."

"I'm sure they do," he said. "Susan, what's a million dollars?"

She shrugged.

"Go on — think about it and tell me."

"A lot of money, I guess."

"You'd be surprised how little. A million dollars is about half a small hospital. With a million dollars you could give all the children in a place like, say, South Korea, maybe one cupful of milk at each meal for two days. It isn't much, really, when you come to think of it, yet it represents the entire life earnings of about six average men — the whole working energy of six men during their entire lives. A million dollars is a lot of things. It's a college education for maybe a hundred boys. It's a home of their own for maybe seventy-five people. It's a pursuit plane for the Army, it's a new television station, but one thing it's not: it's not something any intelligent person can consider a bore."

"You're saying it's power," she said. "I'm not interested in power, either."

"Of course not. Neither am I. I wasn't trying to say money is power. I'm saying that when you hold a million dollars in your hand, you are in a very real sense holding the entire working lives of six men, and you better be damn careful what you do with it!"

"Are you trying to tell me you're going to leave your money to charity?"

"I don't know. I'm saying that we've got a problem we ought to start working on together, a responsibility that is mine, which someday may be yours. I got a lot of training before I was given any responsibility, and I am appalled to think what you may have to do without any training at all. Susan, do you know I have a bad heart?"

"No! No one told me."

"I never told your mother — there didn't seem to be any point in worrying her. It's not very bad, but it's at least conceivable that I could die any time. And frankly, Susan, leaving a lot of money to you would be like giving a gun to a baby!"

"I'm not going to let that part of it worry me," she said. "I hope nothing happens to you, but I'm not going to worry about money. I'm not going to let money ruin my life the way it's ruined yours and Mother's."

"Let's at least be accurate," he said dryly. "Money has not ruined your mother's life, and it has not ruined mine. I'm not willing to concede that either your mother or I have been more unhappy than most people, but if we have been, it's not because of money. The money has come as a by-product."

"It's stupid, the way you work all the time!" she said. "You don't know how to live. If I'd been Mother, I would have divorced you long ago. I don't know why you have to work all the time — ever since I can remember! I think you must have a guilt complex. You're a masochist!"

"Which of your friends is an amateur psy-

422

choanalyst? The playwright?"

"He understands people," she said in confusion.

"Tell him to stop trying to give pat explanations of men and women," Hopkins replied. "If he had learned that, his play might not have closed down so quickly."

"It was a great play!" she said. "The public just doesn't . . ."

". . . appreciate great art," Hopkins finished wryly for her. "I know. But Shakespeare didn't do badly in his time, and not many good plays today shut down as soon as they open. If you want to know what the public wants, I'll tell you: great art on the extremely rare occasions when it's available, but no phony art — they'd rather have good honest blood and thunder. The public doesn't like fakers, and neither do I. If you want to meet some playwrights, tell me, and I'll get some good ones up here for you."

There was a brief silence during which he got up and poured himself another drink. While his back was turned she said passionately, "I want to get some happiness out of life! I don't want to be like you and Mother. I want to have a good time. And no matter what you say, there's nothing wrong with that!"

He turned toward her slowly. "Of course there isn't," he said. "I just want to see that you set about it properly."

"I don't need any help. Not from you, anyway. I don't think you're anyone to be giving lessons!"

"I'm not trying to give you a lesson," he said. "I think we're getting a little off the subject. I'm talking about learning to handle responsibilities."

"I don't want to handle responsibilities. I want to get some fun out of life. It's time somebody in this family did!"

"How would you set about getting fun out of life?"

"I'd give parties. I'd give beautiful parties. I wouldn't try to change the world. I don't have any God complex. I just want to have a good time!"

"You'll get tired of parties," he said.

"Maybe. But by then I'll have had a good time!"

She was breathing hard, and he saw that she was upset. "Believe me, I want you to have a good time," he said gently, "but people who have that primarily in mind rarely accomplish it."

"What do you want me to do? You must have asked me up here alone for some reason.

You never did anything like this before!"

"Look, Susan," he said. "I don't want you to continue accusing me and your mother. I'm quite ready to admit that I've made a great many mistakes, and that a great many things are the matter with me. I'm not apologizing to you — there would be no point to that. And there's no point in continuous accusations. The main thing is for us to see if we can start working together on what really are common problems. I can't undo the past, but I'm going to try to be of more help to you in the future."

"How?"

"I don't know yet. Let's think it over. I have a number of ideas. If you'd like, it might be nice if you moved into this apartment for a while — we could see each other evenings. Perhaps it would be fun for your mother and you and me to take a trip together somewhere. Someday it might be possible for me to arrange for you to get some sort of job working closely with me, if you'd like that. We both should think this whole matter over."

"I don't want to work with you!"

"You don't have to. I'm just trying to think of ways in which you might get some training if you don't want to go to college, and ways in which we might grow closer together."

"Why don't you leave me alone? You always have!"

"Susan," he said quietly, "when I was your age, I didn't have much money, and nobody paid much attention to me. I had a good chance to grow up. Now I've made a lot of money — I've never thought about it in this way before, but I suppose that if everything I have were liquidated today, there would be more than five million dollars. I know this talk of money shocks you — undoubtedly you think it vulgar. But I think this is a time for plain talking. For better or for worse, you're rich. It's nothing for you to be ashamed of, or proud of, or to worry about — it's just a fact. Now there are two kinds of rich — foolish rich and responsible rich. I've hated the foolish rich all my life, and I've never seen anybody who was foolish rich and happy for long. It seems to me that you're getting a good start on the way to being foolish rich. If you keep on the way your mother says you have been, you're going to make yourself miserable. You're going to get involved in a lot of half-baked marriages and divorces, and by the time you're thirty, you're going to find there's no way in the world for you to have a good time. A lot of this is my fault, but I refuse to go into that now. What I'm trying to do is help you and myself too. This is just as much my problem as it is yours, and I plan to do something about it. I'm asking your help."

She stared at him a moment. "Why are you doing this?" she asked finally. "Why the long speeches all of a sudden?"

"Because you're my daughter," he said. That sounded strangely inadequate, and he added awkwardly, "Because I love you."

"That's not true!" she exclaimed. "Don't be a hypocrite! You've hardly bothered to see me since I was born!"

He was shocked at her vehemence. "People love in different ways," he said.

"Why can't you be honest? You don't love me and you don't love Mother. To tell the truth, I don't think you love anyone — I don't think you love anyone in the whole world! And I don't want to be like that!"

Before he could say anything, she got up and fled from the apartment, slamming the door behind her. "Susie!" he called, getting up and following her. *"That's not true!"*

Frantically she rang for the elevator. He stood in the door of his apartment and said, "Come back and sit down. Let's be reasonable."

"I don't want to be reasonable," she

replied. "You and Mother have been reasonable all your lives. I'm going to try something else."

Before he could answer, the elevator doors slid open, revealing the calm and aloof face of the girl who operated them. "Going down," she said. Susan stepped into the elevator, and the doors rumbled shut behind her. Hopkins was left alone.

31

Edward Schultz walked up to the stairs to Judge Saul Bernstein's office. He wore a shabby raincoat over his uniform. He had always had his uniforms provided by his employer and for years had refused to buy a suit to wear on his day off. He walked into Bernstein's office boldly, without knocking, and stared for a moment at a man sitting in a wheel chair there. Then he turned and looked at Bernstein, who was sitting behind his desk. "You wanted me?" he asked harshly.

"Yes," Bernstein said calmly. "Sit down, Mr. Schultz."

Edward remained standing. "Who's he?" he demanded, jerking his thumb toward the man in the wheel chair.

"This is Mr. Sims, Mr. Rath's lawyer," Bernstein said. "Sit down, Mr. Schultz. We have some things we wish to talk over with you."

"Why isn't my lawyer here?"

"This isn't a trial, and you are at liberty to call your lawyer whenever you want," Bernstein said. "I suggest that you hear what we have to say first."

"We want to do you a favor," Sims said icily.

"A favor? What kind of a favor?"

"We think we can save you money."

Edward sat down in the nearest chair. "What do you mean?" he asked.

"We want to give you a preview of the hearings on this document you brought in signed by the late Mrs. Rath," Sims said quietly. "We think that might save you money — lots of it."

"She signed it!" Edward said.

"We know that," Sims replied. "But by a curious coincidence, she never told anyone about it, and there are no witnesses to her signature. Do you know why the law generally requires witnesses to a signature?"

"It doesn't always!" Edward said. "I read that any document can be considered a will if in the opinion of the court it represents the intention of the deceased." He spoke in a monotone.

"That's true," Sims replied gravely. "But there usually is some reason even for technicalities in the law. The reason that witnesses to a signature are generally required is that theoretically — theoretically, mind you — it would be possible for a man to trick an elderly woman into signing something without knowing it. I don't say that happened in this case, mind you — I just say it's theoretically possible."

"You can't prove that."

"Of course not," Sims replied soothingly. "Of course not. But if you persist in pressing your claim against the estate, there are a few facts I can prove, and I intend to bring them all before the court. For one thing, I intend to show it was part of your job to type up the checks Mrs. Rath used to pay her bills and to submit them for her signature. I also intend to prove that her eyesight was extremely poor during her later years. And finally, Mr. Schultz, I will prove that you are dishonest."

"How?"

"By presenting at least five witnesses who will swear that you asked them to pad bills," Sims said mildly.

Bernstein, who had been looking at Schultz's face, glanced away. His stomach was hurting badly.

"They're lying," Schultz said.

"I doubt that the court would think so,"

Sims continued evenly. "Our witnesses happen to be the most respected tradesmen in town. And there are other things we could look into. It might be interesting, for instance, to compare your bank balance with your income tax returns — that too might show you are dishonest."

Edward's face went white. "You can't . . ." he began.

"Just keep quiet a moment," Sims said. "I'm going to give you a chance to save your neck. If you withdraw this document of yours and sign a release giving up all claim to the Rath estate, you can get out of this by paying only a small fee to your lawyer for the trouble you've already caused him. It's entirely possible, of course, that your lawyer will sue you for giving him a fraudulent case, but that will be between you and him. If you continue your suit he'll be much more likely to sue you himself, and that won't be all. We may reconsider and sue for all the bills which you've been padding during the last thirty years. If you pursue this fraudulent claim, you'll walk out of here without a cent, and you may go to jail!"

"Wait a minute," Bernstein said. "You understand, Mr. Schultz, that we don't want you to sign any sort of release if you feel further investigation would clear you of the suspicions Mr. Sims has formed. If you have a clear conscience, I suggest you sign nothing and that you call your lawyer immediately. If, on the other hand, you know that Mr. Sims's suspicions are justified, you will probably be saving yourself and everyone concerned a lot of trouble if you drop your case here and now."

"I have prepared those papers," Sims said, pointing to some neatly typed documents on Bernstein's desk. "It is an ordinary release, and by signing it you will give up all claim to the Rath estate. I'd like you to sign all five copies, and we'll have a witness come in from next door."

Edward said nothing.

"If you don't sign, we'll go ahead with our case," Sims said. "I think I'll start by impounding your bank account."

"You're cheating me!" Edward said.

"Then don't sign and get out of here," Sims shot out. "If you think you're being cheated, call your lawyer, and we'll get on with the case. In the long run I think we might get more out of you that way, anyhow. We might collect forty or fifty thousand dollars."

Without a word, Edward walked to Bernstein's desk and seized the papers lying there. Standing like a speaker about to deliver an address, he read them, his lips moving slowly. Then he reached for a pen.

"Wait a minute," Bernstein said. "We want to call a witness."

He picked up the telephone, and a moment later an elderly woman who served as a Notary Public and worked in an insurance office next door stepped in. With a trembling hand Edward signed his name to all five documents. When he had finished, he stood watching the Notary impress her seal on them. Then he suddenly turned and bolted out the door.

When the Notary Public had gone, Sims said, "That's that."

"I'm glad it's over," Bernstein said, and sighed.

"I'll tell Tom Rath," Sims said. "I'll also tell him you deserve the credit for figuring this thing out."

"Oh, no!" Bernstein said in real alarm. "Don't do that — in conducting my own little investigation, I really exceeded the prerogatives of a judge. It wasn't ethical at all!"

Sims laughed. "Now if you'll help me down the stairs, I'll go up and see the Raths," he said. "I imagine they'll be happy to hear about this."

"Wait," Bernstein said. "You might as well give them the bad news with the good. I've just been appointed a member of the Zoning Board, and although I can't speak for the other members, I personally would not like to consider a housing project unless the town votes for a new school. If the people here won't build schools, we can't bring in a lot of new families. Ask Rath to hold up on his housing project, at least until the vote on the school next month."

That same morning Tom finished a new, much shorter draft of the speech. For the first time he himself liked what he had written, and he was anxious to find if Hopkins approved. Only an hour after he had sent the speech up to Hopkins, the voice box on his desk buzzed, and when Tom flipped it on, Hopkins' voice boomed, "Well, you've really done it, Tom! That's just what I wanted. Let's have lunch today by way of celebration."

"Thanks!" Tom said. "I'm glad we finally got it right."

"Come up in about ten minutes," Hopkins said. "Bill Ogden will join us, and we can talk about plans for following up the speech."

Only about five minutes after Tom had

learned of this success, his telephone rang. It was Betsy, with the news that Edward had withdrawn his claim from the estate, and that in due time the house, land, and a small amount of money would be theirs. The two pieces of good news, arriving so close together, seemed extraordinary to Tom. "That's wonderful!" he said several times to Betsy, and to himself thought, Let this be a lesson to me. Sometimes things really do turn out all right. Grandmother was perfectly honest, and I never should have doubted her.

"There's only one thing for us to worry about now," Betsy said after he had told her that he had successfully completed the speech. "Bernstein says we shouldn't do anything about our housing project unless they pass a bond issue for a new school. If they vote that down next month, it may be ages. To tell the truth, I don't understand much about it — Bernstein says that in a few days there's going to be a public hearing on the whole thing that we ought to go to. Anyway, don't let's worry about that now. Tonight we're going to have a *double* celebration."

"That will be swell," Tom said. "I've got to see Hopkins now. Don't cook anything tonight — let's all go out somewhere."

He started up to Hopkins' office. As soon

as he got in the elevator, he saw Caesar at the controls. "Going up," Caesar said in his deep voice. "Going up. Face the front, please."

The elevator was crowded. Tom edged toward Caesar. On this day of good luck, it seemed that anything could happen, and he half expected Caesar to tell him that he had just heard from Maria, that she was doing fine and didn't need any help at all. Instead, Caesar, who had a strong sense of propriety, barely glanced at him, and all he said was, "Floor, please. Going up. Face the front."

He couldn't have heard anything about Maria, Tom thought. If he had, he would have nodded to me or something. He hurried to Hopkins' office, feeling somewhat subdued.

Hopkins led the way to a taxi and told the driver to take them to the River Club, where they were going to meet Ogden. It was cold — the first cold day of autumn. Many of the women on the street were already wearing their fur coats. When they passed St. Patrick's Cathedral, Tom saw on the wide stone steps a worn woman with a shawl around her head leading a thin child, a little boy wearing only a light summer coat, which the wind was whipping around his legs. The cathedral looked like one which was not far from

Maria's apartment in Rome. Tom remembered the first time Maria had taken him there, two days after he had met her, and before he had known her very well — he had been surprised that a girl he had picked up in a bar wanted to take him to church. She had been insistent about going, and he had agreed, feeling, if anything, indulgent. The moment he had stepped into the cathedral that had changed. Somewhere an organ had been playing softly. The ceiling had arched up so high that it disappeared in the shadows. The air had smoldered with incense. Along the walls had been life-sized statues of saints, their faces exalted and serene. In front of the saints had been racks holding tiers of many short thick candles — at first glance, the whole interior of the cathedral had seemed to be sparkling with innumerable small flames. He had never been in a Catholic church before and had watched, entranced, as one person after another stepped up to the statues of the saints, lit a candle, placed it carefully on the rack among all the others, then knelt in prayer. Taking him by the hand, Maria had led him to the statue of the Virgin and had made him kneel beside her. He had glanced from the simply carved but compassionate face of the statue to Maria, kneeling beside him with her lips moving silently, and he had felt no irony and no hypocrisy in kneeling before the Virgin with a girl he had picked up in a bar. After that he and Maria had gone to the cathedral often. He had said good-by to her there. After he had received his orders to go, and after she had told him she expected a child, she had insisted that they go to the cathedral one more time together. And she had not prayed for herself — she had prayed for him. Knowing how scared he was of death, she had knelt with him before the Virgin, and she had prayed for him. "After you have gone, I will come here often and light a candle for you," she had said. And he had cried — for the first time in his adult life he had cried when he said good-by to her.

Now, riding past St. Patrick's Cathedral in New York on this day of his good luck, Tom wondered whether she had lit many candles for him. Now he was safe, and everything was turning out beautifully for him, but where was she? He had a sudden impulse to leap out of the moving taxicab, run into the cathedral, and light a candle for her.

At luncheon Hopkins was effusive in his praise of the speech, and Ogden gave even more satisfaction by seeming pained at the compliments Tom got, but the thoughts set in motion by the glimpse of the worn woman with a thin little boy in the cold wind on the steps of St. Patrick's Cathedral robbed Tom of a feeling of victory. It is strange, he thought, that almost always there is so much irony in success.

"*A fundamental responsibility* . . ." Hopkins was saying.

"What?" Tom asked, bringing himself back to the luncheon conversation with difficulty.

"We people in the business of communications have a fundamental responsibility to bring key issues to the attention of the public," Hopkins continued. "I think this speech we've worked out is an excellent example. . . ."

Tom couldn't concentrate, and Hopkins' voice seemed to fade away. *Maria,* Tom thought, *Maria.* Somehow the very name sounded heartbreakingly lonely and forlorn. He felt as though he had been awakened suddenly in the night by the distant echo of a cry for help.

32

It was eight-fifteen on the evening of the fifteenth of September. The Grand Ballroom of the big hotel in Atlantic City had been changed into an auditorium by filling it with rows of chairs. About fifteen hundred physicians were sitting there holding printed programs on their laps. The room hummed with conversation, which gradually subsided as a tall, white-haired doctor in a dinner coat stood up behind the lectern at the head of the room. The tall man stood there smiling until the room was quiet. "Gentlemen," he said, "we have a distinguished speaker here tonight, a man whose influence is felt in almost every home in America — every home which has a radio or television set. This is a man who without ever seeking personal fame has been behind almost every public-service advertising campaign which has taken place in the past twenty years. He has been one of the leaders in marshaling public opinion in the fight against polio, heart disease, and cancer. He is not a physician himself, but I think it fair to say that indirectly he has been responsible for saving more lives than any of us. Gentlemen, I present to you Mr. Ralph Hopkins, president of the United Broadcasting Corporation!"

There was mild applause. Ralph Hopkins, who had been sitting in one of the front rows, walked to the platform and stood behind the lectern. He looked astonishingly small, almost frail. He placed a black notebook containing the speech Tom had written for him on the lectern, looked up, and coughed apologetically. Tom, sitting in a back row, thought with astonishment, He's nervous — the poor guy doesn't like to make speeches, and he's scared. Hopkins waited until the applause died down. Then in a small, unassuming voice, he said, "Dr. Stutgarten, and other distinguished physicians: it is a great pleasure for me to have this opportunity to talk to you tonight. As a layman, I feel peculiarly honored to be invited to address this gathering of doctors. I will not keep you long. . . ."

He paused. The audience waited without a sound.

"Now, we laymen look at disease somewhat differently than you doctors do," Hopkins continued in a firmer voice. "In the first place, we're scared of disease and don't like to talk about it much. When something goes wrong with us, we go to a doctor and put the whole burden on his shoulders. We don't tend to believe that there's anything *we* can do about disease ourselves, and almost the last thing which occurs to us is that the doctor might need help. Of course, there actually isn't much a patient can do to help his doctor, except to follow his advice, but there is, I think, a legitimate responsibility the public as a whole has toward its physicians. We laymen must make sure we have a broad understanding of the problems the physicians face and that the physicians have the tools they need to find solutions."

Hopkins looked up from his notebook to smile hesitantly at the audience, then glanced down again. "Now, the medical profession," he went on, "has done wonders with the conquest of the physical diseases — we all know how the human life expectancy has been extended. But while this progress has been going on, the incidence of mental illness has been rising, as we all know. The question I want to pose here tonight is whether there is anything the public could do to help the doctors conquer this problem. It is my belief that the public has failed the medical profession worst in this area, because the public is the most scared of mental illness and understands it least of all. I am wondering if something couldn't be done to bring the problem of mental illness into the open and get together the funds necessary to make a major frontal attack upon it."

It was an odd sensation, Tom found, to sit in the audience and hear the words he had written come back to him. He did not feel very proprietary about the words. If I myelf said them, they would mean little, he thought, but coming from Hopkins, they mean a lot. He listened as Hopkins continued to develop his theme. At the end of precisely twenty minutes, Hopkins concluded by saying, "There is a possibility that some organization might be formed, similar in purpose to the March of Dimes, to subsidize research on mental disease, but, beyond that, to banish unreasonable fear. In such an effort, the medical profession would have to take the lead. I think you can be sure that those of us whose business it is to transmit information to the public will do everything we can to help."

He stopped abruptly and folded his notebook. The audience clapped politely, almost enthusiastically, and several doctors walked up to the lectern to congratulate him. Hopkins stood in the middle of a small circle of physicians, shaking hands and smiling. Then he moved slowly toward the lobby and, followed by a growing group of physicians, headed toward the elevators.

Fifteen minutes later, Tom walked into the crowded living room of Hopkins' suite and found Hopkins drinking with a group of the leaders of medical associations. Several of them were urging him to start a mental-health committee. "It's nice of you to suggest it," he said. "I'm not at all sure I'm the man to take the leadership and I'm so pressed for time. . . ."

"How do you think it went?" Tom asked Ogden, who was standing in a corner sipping a highball, next to a vase of long-stemmed roses.

"Fair," Ogden said. "Just about fair, I'd say. The advance publicity wasn't much. We'll see what the morning papers do with it."

As it happened, the morning papers played the story up. Some of them put it on the front page, but Hopkins barely glanced at the clippings Ogden handed him. He seemed much more impressed by the many requests he got from doctors to start the committee. "I didn't sense a bit of opposition," he said to Tom. "I know that speech was a lot of work, but I think it's done exactly what we intended."

33

Without warning, on September 16, Susan Hopkins eloped with Byron Holgate, an aging playboy with an affectionate smile. Ralph Hopkins heard about it in his office on one of his own company's three o'clock news broadcasts soon after he returned from Atlantic City. He immediately called his wife in South Bay. She answered the telephone herself. "Hello," she said, and her voice sounded so dead that he knew she had heard about it and had not hurried to let him know.

"I just heard about Susan," he said. "I'll be right out."

"No," she said dully.

"I want to."

There was no response.

"I want to," he said again.

"I know."

"I'll be right out."

"I'm tired," she said. "I'm terribly tired."

"Of course. Go to bed and I'll see you in an hour."

No answer.

"I think I'll stay out there with you, Helen," he said. "I think I'll give up the apartment here in town."

There was a pause, and then, as though he hadn't spoken, she said, "Ralph, will you do me a favor?"

"Of course!"

"Have one of your secretaries get me a ticket on one of those cruises that go around the world."

"I'll go with you," he said.

There was another long pause before she said, "That's awfully nice of you, dear, but I think I want to be alone for a few months. I'm awfully tired."

"Of course," he said.

"One more thing. Could you get rid of this place out here? I don't know — with Susan gone, there doesn't seem to be much point to it any more. I don't want to have to worry about it."

"Leave it to me," he said. "I'll have it put on the market, or think of something to do with it."

"Thank you, dear," she said, and there was

448

still another long pause.

"I'm going to start driving out now," he said. "I'll see you in an hour."

"Ralph," she replied, "would you mind waiting? I don't know, I don't want to talk to anybody right now. I just want to go to bed."

"I understand," he said.

"I'll see you in a few days. Get me on a boat that leaves as soon as possible, will you?"

"I'll make all the arrangements."

"Thank you, dear," she said quietly. "Good-by."

Later that afternoon Miss MacDonald told Tom that Hopkins would like to see him that evening at seven o'clock. At two minutes after the hour, Tom knocked at Hopkins' door. Hopkins opened it. He was alone, and to Tom's surprise, he looked tired. He was pacing restlessly up and down the room jingling the change in his pockets and gesticulating as he talked. The first thing he said after greeting Tom was, "I've definitely decided to go ahead with this mental-health committee. I want to get rolling on it now fast."

"Maybe we should start by . . ." Tom began.

"Wait a minute," Hopkins said. "Here's what I want to do. I'm going to expand it beyond the publicists — I want a really representative group. Begin by asking about a dozen people to form an Exploratory Committee — choose the people we'll eventually want as trustees. For labor, Bill Krisky. For a Catholic, Fred Bellows. For a Jew, Abraham Goldberg. For a liberal, Mary Harkins. For a hard-shelled businessman, I'll do. For a Democrat, Pete Cronin. For a Republican, Nat Higgins. How many is that?"

"Seven," Tom said. He was taking notes furiously.

"All right. For a Negro, Herbert Shaw. For radio and television, I'll do. Sam Peterson for newspapers. Ted Bailey for mass circulation magazines. We should have an intellectual: make it Harold Norton, up at Harvard."

"What are we missing? Oh, somebody from the movies. Ross Pattern. Make that the first twelve. Write letters of invitation to them tomorrow for my signature and find out a convenient day for all of us to meet at the Waldorf next month."

"Right," Tom said.

"Now an advisory medical panel. Make it seven members. The heads of all the major medical associations, and fill up the rest of it with the best psychiatrists — make sure you don't get the crackpots."

"I've got a list all made up," Tom said.

"Fine — show it to me tomorrow. Now a tentative program — enclose it with your letter of invitation. We'll start with a broad publicity barrage aimed to make people more aware of mental-health problems. We'll want spot announcements on both television and radio, all networks. Have films and records made to send out to the local stations. Get the agencies to work on the copy and bring me samples as soon as possible. I'd play up the theme, 'An enemy in the dark is more dangerous than one in the light — bring the problem of mental illness into the open!' That's not the wording, of course — I'm just thinking out loud."

"I'll get the agencies to work on it," Tom said.

"Start getting the National Mental Health Committee incorporated."

"I've done the spade work on that already."

"Good — make sure the lawyers have it done as soon as the Exploratory Committee meets."

Hopkins continued to pace as he spoke. He ordered drafts of the preliminary program readied for the foundations, lists of possible members, bylaws, and news releases announcing the formation of the committee.

"Now the program," he said. "First, your general publicity barrage — and while you're on that, make sure that mats are sent to all newspapers and that plates are made up for the magazines. See if the Advertising Association will foot the bill. The advertising boys ought to arrange for outdoor posters and car cards for buses and subways, too. Second, we'll want a small study group to develop a long-range plan for attacking the problem. I've already got foundation support lined up for that. Don't worry about the money on this — all the foundations are interested in the study part of it."

He paused, walked over to a table, and poured himself a drink. "Now Tom," he said, "I want you to carry the ball on this. You did a grand job on that speech — I think I can count on you. You've got the signal. I'm not going to be able to give this project much time, other than to arrange the financing and look over your plans just before they're final. I've got several new projects underway. Wrap this whole thing up for me. Figure out the details for yourself. Just remember that nothing can go until after the Exploratory Committee meets, but you've got to be ready to jump the next day. The Exploratory Committee won't do anything but approve what we submit to them, and you can't expect any work from them."

"We'll get everything ready," Tom said.

"And while you're making your publicity plans, don't forget the outdoor advertising boys. I want this campaign to break in all media within a week after the full committee is formed, and I want the full committee formed within a month after the Exploratory Committee meets. So you've got to work fast."

"We can do it," Tom replied.

Hopkins smiled. "Thanks, Tom," he said.

Tom stood up to go. He was surprised when Hopkins added, "Don't rush. Sit down and have a drink."

"Sure," Tom replied, sitting down again. "Sure." Expecting more directions concerning the mental-health committee, he took his pad out of his pocket and held it ready.

"Put that thing away," Hopkins said, and then with unusual hesitation in his voice, "I don't know, I just thought it might be fun to sit and talk a little while."

"Of course," Tom said, feeling curiously embarrassed. There was a moment of silence. Hopkins got up, mixed two strong highballs, and handed one to Tom. Tom was astonished to see him drink his very fast. The silence became painful.

"Do you have any children?" Hopkins asked suddenly.

"Yes," Tom said.

"How many?"

"Three."

"That's a nice family," Hopkins said. He mixed another drink for himself and to Tom's surprise stretched out comfortably on the couch. He seemed to be staring at Tom — he never turned his eyes away from him. On his face an expression Tom had never seen there before: a look of exhaustion, confusion, and, incongruously, great kindness.

"Do you like working on this mental-health committee?" Hopkins asked after an awkward interval of silence.

"Yes," Tom said. "I like it very much."

"What are your plans?"

"I don't know," Tom replied. "I want to do my job here as well as I can, I guess, and see where it leads."

"That's the best way. When I was your age, I didn't have any plans — I was just thinking about the job at hand."

There was another interval of silence, during which Hopkins apparently was thinking, but he never took his eyes off Tom's face.

"I had a son once," Hopkins said suddenly. "He was killed in the war."

"I'm sorry to hear that," Tom said, although he had heard it before.

"Were you in the war?"

"Yes."

"Back in the First World War, I was a lieutenant, but I never got overseas. The war ended about two days after I got my commission."

"You were lucky."

"I guess I was," Hopkins said.

Tom sipped his drink. He was tense and wary, terribly conscious that it was important for Hopkins to like him.

"How did you happen to get interested in working on this mental-health project?" Hopkins asked abruptly.

Tom started to say, "I've always been interested in mental health," but he remembered how ridiculous that had sounded the last time he said it. I made up my mind I was going to play it straight with him, he thought, and I will. Aloud he said, "I was working over at the Schanenhauser Foundation. I needed more money, and a friend told me there was an opening in your public-relations department. I applied for it, and Mr. Walker steered me into this."

"That's the way I got started in radio," Hopkins said. "After I got out of the Army, I worked a few years for a brokerage house, and I hated it. A friend told me a magazine was hiring people. I walked over there, and they didn't have a place for me, but the personnel man said a new broadcasting company was being started in the same building. I walked in and was hired."

There was a pause. "When I was a boy, I wanted to be an actor," Hopkins continued, "a Shakespearean actor. That was my ambition for about five years. I used to try out for all the high-school plays, but I wasn't much good, and they always got me to be stage manager."

"I don't think I ever knew what I wanted to be," Tom replied.

"I wonder whether this mental-health project is right for you," Hopkins said contemplatively. "I think you have a lot of capabilities. You look at things straight — I like the way you brought that speech down to the ground. And you're at an important stage of your career. How old are you?"

"Thirty-three."

"That's an important age. In the next six or seven years, you should really be on your way."

"Do you think there will be many opportunities with the mental-health committee?"

"Yes — of a kind. Of course, there's always a limit to that sort of thing. Organizations which don't make money never pay much, and the top planning is done by volunteers. There's a limit to how far you can go as a staff member on that sort of thing."

"What do you think I should do?"

"I don't know," Hopkins said thoughtfully. "It depends on what you want, I guess. Is money important to you?"

"Yes."

"I could look around the company and see if I could find a spot for you."

"I'd appreciate that," Tom said. Under Hopkins' kindly but steady gaze he felt as tense as though he were waiting for a parachute jump.

"The business world is different than it was when I was young," Hopkins said. "It's tougher and more competitive."

"I guess it is."

"A young man has to get started right. The ideal thing is to find a job which always expects a little more than you can deliver, but not so much that you get snowed under. A job should always keep you straining at the limits of your abilities. That's the way men learn."

"I guess it is," Tom repeated.

"How do you assess your own abilities? What do you *like* best? If you could choose any branch of the business, what would you take?"

There was a pause while Tom wondered whether honesty should be pushed to the point of self-depreciation. I can't fool him, he thought — he's not a guy who can be fooled. I'd better go on telling him the truth. "I don't know what my abilities are," he said. "I'd like to find out. I'm afraid that the branches of the broadcasting business I'd really enjoy are probably the ones I know least about and if I got into them, I might not like them as much as I think."

"What are they?"

"I'd like to analyze the news," Tom said, entirely to his own astonishment. "I'd like to study the news and give my views on it. I know I don't have any qualifications at all for that kind of job."

Hopkins smiled wryly. "That's like me wanting to be an actor," he said. "If you wanted to be a news commentator, I'm afraid you'd probably have to put in a long apprenticeship on a newspaper, and there might be a good deal of voice training involved. There aren't many jobs for news commentators —

there are at least a hundred applicants for every opening."

"I know," Tom said, "but you asked me what I'd really like, and that came into my mind. It's not a thing I've thought about. To tell you the truth, I've always just gone along taking what I could get."

"If you really wanted to broadcast news, and were willing to devote the time and effort to it, you probably could," Hopkins said. "I'm afraid the job isn't as good as you think it is. It pays comparatively little, and unless you're something special, it's pretty routine."

"I know," Tom said. "With me, it's probably just a case of far fields looking greener."

There was a pause, during which Tom regretted his frankness. I've made a fool of myself, he thought. I should have told him what I really want to be is a good administrator. That's a field in which he could really help me. Hopkins eyes were still upon him. It was disturbing, that steady, unabashed gaze, the eyes tired, the whole face exhausted, yet so curiously intense and kind.

"How would you like to be my personal assistant?" Hopkins asked suddenly.

"What?"

"I mean, not just on this mental-health thing — someone to help me with everything

I do. I don't really have a personal assistant. Walker is in public relations, and Ogden is going to be a vice-president before long. I've never had a personal assistant — I've never wanted one. But I like the honesty of your approach, and it strikes me that you might be able to help out in many ways. The job would give you a chance to watch lots of operations in the company and see what you're best fitted for. Who knows? Maybe you could learn something." These last words were said with an attempt at jocosity and self-disparagement which was utterly unlike Hopkins. Seeming ill at ease, he got up and poured himself another drink.

"I'm sure I could learn a lot," Tom said. "It would be a great opportunity."

Hopkins stood with his back toward him, putting ice in his glass. When he turned around, his briskness had returned, and he seemed his old self again. "I'll talk to Bill Ogden about it in the morning," he said. "We'll see what we can work out. I'm afraid it's getting late — your wife will be angry at me. Thanks for coming up. It's *so* nice of you to give up your evening."

When Tom got to Grand Central Station that night, he bought a paper to read on the train home. On the front page he saw a story about the marriage of Susan Hopkins to Byron Holgate, whose age was given as forty-eight, but who, in an accompanying photograph, looked much older. After reading the article, Tom folded the paper and sat thinking about Hopkins all the way home to South Bay. When he got to his house, he found Betsy waiting up for him. "Hopkins wants me to leave the mental-health committee and become his personal assistant," he said.

"Why, that's wonderful," she replied. "What a marvelous opportunity! It must mean he likes you."

"I guess it does."

"You don't sound very excited about it."

"I don't know," Tom said. "I'm trying to figure it out. It *is* a marvelous opportunity — there's no doubt about that. But I'm not sure I want to be given a job simply because a man likes me. I'm not sure it's good business."

"What do you mean?"

"I don't want to have to depend on somebody's friendship. I want to feel that any time I want to quit a job, or any time my boss dies or retires, I can walk two doors down the street and get something as good or better. It's not smart business to depend on friendship — it's too risky."

"What makes you think he's hiring you because of friendship? He liked that speech you wrote. He must think that you're simply the best man for the job."

"I don't know," Tom said. "He's never had a personal assistant before. And the way he was tonight — it's hard to explain. He was trying to do something for me."

"Is there anything wrong with that?"

"No — I should be grateful. But I don't know what he *can* do for me. For a child, yes — a man can make sure a child gets a good education, and all the rest of it. But for another man, no. After all, what could Hopkins do for me? Keep me on as a ghost writer? I'd hate that as a full-time career. There's nothing dishonest about ghost writing, really, but the whole idea of it makes me uncomfortable. I don't like being the shadow of another man. Should I ask him to give me a top administrative job? I wouldn't know what to do with it if I had it. I must be getting old or something — I'm beginning to realize my limitations. I'm not a very good administrator — not compared to guys like Hopkins and Ogden. I never will be, and the main reason is, I don't want to be. This sounds like a silly way to put it, but I don't think you can get to be a top administrator without working every week end for half your life, and I'd just as soon spend my week ends with you and the kids."

"Some good administrators don't work all the time."

"A few — damn few. It's the fashion nowadays for them to pretend they don't work as hard as they do. After all, running any big outfit is incredibly hard work. You know what a good administrator has to do? He has to keep a million details in his mind all at the same time, and he has to know how to juggle people. Why do you think Hopkins is great? Mainly, it's because he never thinks about anything but his work, day and night, seven days a week, three hundred and sixty-five days a year. All geniuses are like that — there's no mystery about it. The great painters, the great composers, the great scientists, and the great businessmen — they all have the same capacity for total absorption in their work. I like Hopkins — I admire him. But even if I could, I wouldn't want to be like him. I don't want to get so wrapped up in a broadcasting business that I don't care about anything else. And I'm afraid that in asking me to be his personal assistant, he's trying to make me be like him, and I know that's foolish. I never could do it, and I don't want to."

"Aren't you making this awfully complicated?" Betsy asked. "He's offered you a better job. Maybe a raise will go with it."

"Maybe. But this *is* complicated! What it all comes down to is, what do we want? He asked me that tonight: what do I want? I tried to answer him straight, but I was too confused to think. He asked me whether money is important to me, and I said yes, but I forgot to say why. I want money to help us enjoy life, but that's not what a guy like Hopkins wants. He doesn't care any more about money than a good violinist does. He's totally absorbed in his work — nothing else matters to him. You could pay him in medals or in beans, you could put him in the middle of the Sahara Desert, and he'd still find some way to go on working day and night. Something about the way he acted tonight scared me. It sounds crazy, but I think he wants to try to create me in his own image and I don't want any part of it."

"What makes you think that?"

"Figure it out for yourself. Hopkins doesn't need a personal assistant — he has three secretaries and Ogden and Walker helping him already, and he's always been careful to keep his relationship with all those people anything but personal. The whole time I've known him, he's never had the slightest personal interest in me. And now all of a sudden he wants me to be his personal assistant. Why?"

"Because he likes that speech you did for him," Betsy said.

"Partly. But you know something? His daughter got married today — I read it in the paper on the way home. And his son got killed in the war — I'd heard that, and he told me about it tonight. I think the poor guy's just lonely, and he's trying to hire a son."

"If that's the way he feels, it could still be pretty good for you," Betsy said.

"I don't think so. When he found I couldn't get to be like him, he might get sick of me — he might get sick of me pretty soon, anyway. You can't tell. Playing with a guy like that is like petting a tiger — any time he wants to turn on you, he can. I don't want to be in a position like that."

"What are you going to do, turn him down?"

"No — that might hurt his feelings. As I say, this is like petting a tiger — you have to be awfully careful. And the funny part of it is, I'd like to be his personal assistant for three reasons: I might learn something, it would be a good recommendation for anything else I wanted to do later, and I like the guy. I think I better take the job, but I'm going to have to keep my fingers crossed — nobody can tell how it's going to turn out. When he finds I have no idea in the world of trying to be like him, he may get mad — and then he may fire me altogether."

34

At quarter to seven the next morning Betsy came into the bathroom while Tom was shaving and said, "I don't know what to do. Janey says she won't go to school."

"She give any reason?"

"No. She just woke up and announced that she wasn't going. I told her that she had to, and she said she simply wouldn't."

"Why don't you let her stay home a day or two," Tom said. "At her age it wouldn't matter."

"If I let her stay home, Barbara will want to stay too — she's not very happy about going herself. As a matter of fact, I wouldn't be surprised if she wanted to go even less than Janey does, but she's different. She does what she thinks she has to do."

"I'll talk to Janey," Tom said.

"The trouble is, I really don't blame the

child," Betsy said. "It's such an awful-looking school!"

Tom wiped the soap off his face and walked to the bedroom his daughters shared. Janey was sitting on her bed, still dressed in her pajamas. Her face was set in a determined expression, and her hands were folded stubbornly in her lap. On the other side of the room Barbara was slowly getting dressed. Her face looked strained.

"What's the matter, kids?" Tom asked. "Janey, if you don't hurry up and get dressed, you're going to be late."

"I'm not going to school," Janey said.

"Why not?"

"I'm just not going."

"You have to go," Tom said. "There's a law. Anyway, you wouldn't want to grow up without knowing anything."

"I'm not going," Janey said. From her face he saw she was about to cry.

"Did something happen at school yesterday?"

"No."

"Was someone cross to you?"

"No." She paused before adding, "I'm afraid."

"Afraid of what?"

"The hall."

"The hall? What do you mean?"

Janey said nothing.

"What's the matter with the hall?"

"Nothing," Janey said.

"I'll take you to school today and you can show me the hall. Will that help?"

Janey looked down at the floor, her face hopeless. She said nothing.

"School is fun when you get used to it," Tom said hesitantly. Still Janey said nothing.

"If you're a good girl and go nicely, I'll bring you home a present tonight. I'll bring you a surprise."

"All right," Janey said woefully. "If you'll go with me."

"I'll take you down," Tom said, and began to help her get dressed.

At breakfast Betsy said, "I can take her — you'll miss your train if you go."

"I'll take a later train," Tom said. "There's something about a hall that bothers Janey. I want to see this school."

Leaving Betsy at home with Pete, Tom put both his daughters in the car and started down the road toward the school. He remembered being driven down the same road by a chauffeur during his own boyhood, only they had not stopped at the public school; they had gone beyond it to the South Bay Country

Day School, where both Tom and his father had gone. The tuition had been six hundred dollars a year, even in the nineteen twenties. Tom wondered what it was now. It was ridiculous to feel that he had to send his children to a private school, he thought. In Westport, the public schools had been just as good as the private schools.

The traffic got heavy as they neared the public school. It was a weather-beaten brick building of Victorian design set in the middle of a black asphalt-covered play yard, part of which had been marked off to form a parking area. The school and its yard was surrounded by a high iron fence, as though it were a zoo. Tom drove through a gate and found a parking place adjoining the play yard, where children of widely varying age were running, jumping, and shouting together. He and his daughters walked up the front steps of the school and entered a narrow, high-ceilinged hall, the walls of which were painted a dull chocolate brown. The indefinable smell of an old school building was strong — sweat, chalk dust, and an incongruous trace of cheap perfume.

Suddenly an electric bell rang, reverberating harshly against the bare walls. Immediately a horde of children rushed through the door which Tom had just entered and dashed down the hall. They continued to funnel in from the playground, jostling and pushing each other. The hall quickly became overcrowded, and someone said, "Don't push!" in a high shrill voice. The children continued to jam in, and Tom felt a flash of claustrophobia. Janey clung tightly to his hand. She looked scared. "This is the hall," she said.

"Yesterday she got knocked down here," Barbara volunteered.

"It won't happen again," Tom said, his voice sounding false to himself.

"I guess I better go now," Barbara said. "My room's upstairs." She let go of Tom's other hand and was immediately swept away in the crowd. A few minutes later Tom caught a glimpse of her going up the stairs at the end of the hall, her small figure very erect.

"Stay with me," Janey said.

"I'll take you to your classroom," Tom said. "Where is it?"

Janey led the way to a crowded doorway and paused. Inside, Tom could see a small room with many desks jammed together. With so many children jostling by, it was hard to stand still. Janey suddenly let go of his hand. "Thanks," she said. He saw her go and sit at the very back of the room.

When Tom got outside, the fresh air felt good. He drove to the station and walked up and down the platform waiting for his train.

They shouldn't have a school building like that, he thought. They shouldn't have a school like that for *anybody's* children. It wasn't like that in Westport. It's not just that I can't afford to send my children to private school.

I wonder what kind of schools they have for the children of the poor in Rome, he thought. Suddenly he remembered how easy things had been for him in his boyhood. The old South Bay Country Day School had had ten or, at most, fifteen children in a class, and often the teachers had met with the pupils in the big living room of the old mansion which had been made into the school, and they had all sat in overstuffed chairs. How soft everything was made for me, he thought. Because his father had gone to the South Bay Country Day School, and because his grandmother had given generously to the school in the past, old Miss Trilly, the head mistress, had been especially kind to Tom and had once given a teacher a stern lecture for reprimanding him too harshly. Maybe it's better for my kids to begin the way they are, he thought, as he paced up and down the platform of the railroad station. Maybe they'll have less to learn later.

"Rowdies! Young Rowdies! They come from the public school!"

He remembered those words being spoken in a high, slightly nasal, indignant voice by Miss Trilly — she had said them often. The public-school children had frequently invaded the playground of the Country Day School to play on the slides and swings. Occasionally they had picked fights with the Country Day children, and this is what had inspired old Miss Trilly's anger.

"They're from the *public school!*" she had said, incorporating a sly slur in the words which none of her pupils had missed.

Tom wondered whether Janey and Barbara would ever sneak into the playground of the Country Day School to play on the slides and the swings, and whether Miss Trilly, or her successor, would say, "They're from the *public school!*"

It doesn't really matter, he thought now, as he reached the end of the station platform and started to pace in the other direction. People are tough, even children. But good Lord, I ought to be able to do something. There's no particular democratic virtue in jamming so

473

many children into a school like that. Janey isn't going to learn much by being knocked down in the hall.

Money, I need money, he thought. If they don't build a new public school, I should be able to afford a private school. I should get everything but money out of my head and really do a job for Hopkins. I ought to be at work now. He glanced at his watch and saw it was quarter after nine — the train was late.

Money, Tom thought. The housing project could make money, but it depends on re-zoning, and Bernstein says we shouldn't ask for that until they vote on a new school.

A new school, he thought — so much depends on that! Bernstein says there's going to be a hearing on it and that a lot of people are against it. I should find out all the details. I should work for a new school, and I should work harder for Hopkins, and I should be making plans for our housing project. Where did I ever get the idea that life is supposed to be anything but work? A man's work should be his pleasure — I shouldn't expect anything more.

Far up the track the train blew its whistle. He joined a throng of men pushing to get aboard the train and, with chin on his chest, sat thinking about his daughters' school.

35

Two day later, Tom moved into Hopkins' outer office. He sat at a desk in a corner — it had been necessary to move Miss MacDonald's desk and those of the two typists to make room for him. Hopkins' office had not been designed with accommodations for a personal assistant. Miss MacDonald seemed flustered by the change. She sat at her desk nervously thumbing through correspondence, and whenever Tom said anything to her, she answered with an exaggerated politeness which was almost worse than the coldness which Ogden displayed. The two stenographers kept glancing from Miss MacDonald to Tom, as though they expected a battle to start between them. Tom missed his private office and his own secretary. In its exterior aspects, the change seemed more like a demotion than a promotion.

A half hour after Tom arrived at his new desk, Hopkins came out of his inner office. "Good morning, Tom!" he said briskly. "Good to have you here!"

"Good to be here!" Tom said. He had developed a hesitancy about whether to call Hopkins by his first name. "Mr. Hopkins" now sounded impolitely formal, and "Ralph" sounded brash. He avoided using either name whenever possible.

"I've got some correspondence I'd like you to answer for me," Hopkins said. "Miss MacDonald, you can give Mr. Rath the morning's mail after I've looked it over and let him rough out the replies."

"Yes, sir," Miss MacDonald said.

Hopkins returned to his inner office. An hour later Miss MacDonald brought Tom a wire basket containing about thirty letters. Some were requests from charities, some suggested various new projects for United Broadcasting, and others concerned complex business transactions already underway. On the latter Hopkins had written in his small, neat handwriting, "See me." On some of the simple requests he had written, "Tell him no," and on others, "Tell him yes." On still others he had written, "Maybe — don't commit us."

Tom was not surprised at all this — he

476

knew that the stage after having a girl to take dictation is to have someone to do the dictating. He had often written letters for Dick Haver at the Schanenhauser Foundation. Calling one of the stenographers over to his desk, he began the letters for Hopkins' signature. In reply to a letter from a newly formed charity on which Hopkins had scribbled, "Tell him no," he said, "I was most interested to see the information you sent me, and I certainly agree with you that this is an important and worthy endeavor, but it is necessary for us to plan ahead on this sort of thing, and I'm afraid that we've already committed ourselves so heavily on other similar projects that we won't be able to include this one on our list of contributions now. I certainly hope your program is successful, however, and at some later time we would be glad to give your needs thorough consideration. Sincerely, Ralph Hopkins, president, United Broadcasting Corporation."

When he had several similar letters typed up, he sent them into Hopkins' office. To his surprise, they came back almost immediately with carefully inked corrections on them. Most of the letters had been made a little more gracious, a little more informal, but on the letter saying no to the charity, Hopkins had written to Tom, "Don't agree with him that project is important and don't wish him success. I never heard of this outfit. They might use my letter as an endorsement, and they might be phonies."

Tom glanced up, and, seeing that Miss MacDonald was looking at him smugly, he realized that she had been the one who had answered the letters before and that she was pleased to see his work needed correction. He called the stenographer to his desk again and redictated the letters.

A few moments later, Hopkins spoke to him through the interoffice communication box. "Come in and bring the rest of the mail," he said. Tom picked up the letters on which Hopkins had written, "See me," and entered the inner office. Hopkins was pacing back and forth, looking ill at ease. "The reason I'm having you start out on this mail is that I think it's the best way for you to learn how I work and to get an idea of some of the projects we have underway," he said. "Now, take that letter from Richardson at the Henkel Manufacturing Corporation. That's a long story. They manufacture television sets which go out under various brand names. For some time we've been trying to work out a deal that will let us market our own sets —

United Broadcasting Corporation sets. We've got two or three other companies interested in supplying the sets, but this is more than a matter of just getting bids. We're trying to work out a deal where we tie in with some big retailing outfit. . . ."

He talked on for a long time. To Tom, the whole subject seemed hopelessly complicated. "Anyway," Hopkins concluded, "the point is, we've got to stall Richardson now without letting him think we've lost interest. Tell him that several other people here want to study the specifications he sent us and that he'll hear from us in a few days."

Hopkins went on to discuss this and other letters, while Tom took notes. By the time Tom got back to his desk, his head was whirling.

"Mr. Ogden called you," Miss MacDonald said. "He wants you to call him back."

"Thanks," Tom replied, and immediately called Ogden. "Oh, Tom," Ogden said. "Can you drop in at about ten tomorrow to review what you've done for the mental-health committee?"

"Sure," Tom said. "I'll be there."

"There was another call for you," Miss MacDonald said as soon as Tom had hung up. "A Mr. Gardella. He said it was personal."

"Gardella?"

479

"Yes. He left his number. He wants you to call him back."

Miss MacDonald handed him a slip of paper with an outside telephone number written on it. Tom dialed it himself. "Hello," Caesar's deep voice answered.

"This is Tom Rath. Did you call me?"

"Yes, Mr. Rath," Caesar said. "I just thought I ought to tell you. . . ."

"Did you hear anything?" Tom interrupted.

"No — not yet. I just thought I ought to tell you that I've got a new job. Gina and I got a job taking care of a new apartment building over in Brooklyn — we're going to be custodians. We get an apartment for ourselves with the deal and everything. Anyway, I probably won't be around the United Broadcasting building much any more, but I wanted to tell you that when we hear from Maria, we'll let you know."

"You think you will hear?"

"Sure, sooner or later. When Louis gets on his feet, they'll get in touch with Gina's mother. Anyway, I'll let you know."

"Thanks," Tom said, and hurriedly added, "I'm glad you've got a good job. I wish you luck."

"Same to you," Gardella said. "Good-by."

Tom put the telephone receiver down. Miss MacDonald was looking at him curiously. Quickly he picked up a letter lying on his desk and started to read it. So Caesar's got a new job, he thought — I won't be running into him on the elevators any more. Suddenly he felt sure he would never see or hear from Caesar again. So that is my punishment, he thought — I probably never will know what happened to Maria and the boy. Maybe this is just retribution. The hardest thing of all for me is going to be never to know. She and the boy could be starving. They could be dead. Or they could be getting along fine. How strange it is never to know. He picked up the piece of paper on which Miss MacDonald had written Caesar's telephone number and carefully put it in his wallet.

The next morning Ogden said to Tom, "For the time being your duties as Mr. Hopkins' personal assistant will be in addition to your work on the mental-health committee. We'll start looking for someone else for that, but until we find someone, it's still your responsibility."

Tom hoped he'd go on and discuss an increase in salary. Instead, Ogden said, "As you know, Mr. Hopkins wants to get cracking on

481

the mental-health committee. Fill me in now. Where are we?"

"I've been getting some tentative bylaws drawn up to show the exploratory committee when it meets," Tom said.

"Good. How about a statement on the background of this committee — something to tell how it got started."

"We haven't discussed that," Tom said.

"You mean you haven't even thought of it? It's the first thing Hopkins will want. How did this whole thing begin, anyhow? Everybody's going to be asking that. You've got to answer it."

"I'll work something out," Tom said.

"Have you got sample news releases announcing the formation of the committee?"

"Yes."

"Suggested budget?"

"Nothing yet," Tom said. "We haven't discussed that."

"Haven't discussed it! Hasn't it ever occurred to you that someone might inquire how much this whole operation is going to cost? What's Mr. Hopkins going to say: 'I'm sorry, but we hadn't thought of that'?"

"I'll get some cost estimates together," Tom said.

"How about plans for staff? How much of a

staff is this committee going to need when it gets going? You're going to have to answer that before you can make out a tentative budget."

"I'm sorry," Tom said hotly, "but I've never been able to get a very clear idea of just how big a project Mr. Hopkins is planning!"

"We're supposed to do the planning for him! That's what we're paid for. Get some data together! How much of a staff does the polio outfit have, and what did it start with? How about the cancer outfit? What are their budgets? You've got to think these things out for yourself!"

"I'll get some data together," Tom said.

"You better get cracking. This should have been done two months ago."

"I'll do my best," Tom said.

There was an instant of silence before Ogden said, "Now listen, Tom. You wrote a darn good speech for Mr. Hopkins — I know that. And I know you're Mr. Hopkins' personal assistant now, but that doesn't mean you can forget about this mental-health committee. It's going to grow. Mr. Hopkins can't be worrying about it all the time. He's got to be able to rely on you."

Ogden paused, and Tom waited without saying anything.

"Up till now," Ogden continued, "there

hasn't been much we could do, but in the future, things will be different. There's a big administrative job to be done, and a big job of promotion. I of course won't be the one to determine where you will fit into the structure — ultimately, that will be up to you. It will depend on what you've shown us you can do. But if you're going to be Hopkins' personal assistant, you should get to the point where you anticipate his needs. Don't wait for me to tell you."

"I understand," Tom said. His face was hot.

"Thanks for coming up," Ogden said, and swung around in his swivel chair. Picking up the receiver of his telephone, he said, "Now, Miss Horton, you can put that call through to Denver." He remained with his back turned while Tom got up and walked out of the room.

When Tom returned to Hopkins' outer office, the first thing he saw was a pile of about fifteen thick leather-bound books on his desk.

"Mr. Hopkins asked me to give you those," Miss MacDonald said. "They're the company's annual reports — there are two to a volume. He said he thought you'd like to go through them."

"Thanks," Tom said. He sat down, picked up one of the books, and leafed through it. The pages were full of graphs and statistics showing the progress of United Broadcasting. Of course, he thought — I should be studying these. I should have asked for them myself. I bet Hopkins knows these by heart. Anyone who seriously intended to make this company his career should study its history. I should be spending every spare minute on these. He tried to read one of the pages describing a complicated division of stock. His mind wandered — it was difficult material. I should be getting that work on the mental-health committee done first, he thought — my background reading should be done on evenings and week ends. Work in the office on Saturdays and do your background reading on Sundays — hundreds do it. He glanced at his watch. It was only eleven o'clock. Suddenly he longed for the day to be over — he was ashamed to find that for no particular reason he felt exhausted, and he wanted to go home and relax. An hour and a half until lunch, and then another five and a half hours before he could reasonably catch the train to South Bay. The big sweep hand on his wrist watch seemed to crawl with maddening slowness. Hopkins rarely left his office before seven o'clock, and Tom had sensed he was annoyed to find that Tom usually left earlier. It was embarrassing to have to compete with Hopkins' hours — it was like taking a Sunday-afternoon walk with a long-distance runner. The stereotyped notion of the earnest young man arriving early and leaving late, and the complacent boss dropping in for a few hours in the middle of the day to see how things were going was completely reversed.

Tom rolled a piece of paper into his typewriter and began to write a brief statement describing the origins of the mental-health committee. After finishing it, he glanced at his watch again. Almost an hour before lunchtime — it was ridiculous to be so restless. I'll bet Hopkins never was a clock watcher, he thought.

"Don't wish time away."

The sentence came abruptly to his mind. Who had said that? It's just an old saying, he thought. "Don't wish time away." Suddenly he remembered sitting with Maria in the abandoned villa so many years before, looking at this same wrist watch and counting each second the way a miser might count his money.

We didn't wish time away, he thought. I've got to stop thinking about Maria. Time, he thought — I need more time. I've got to get this work done for the committee, and I've got to read the annual reports, and I must get our housing project going. I've got no business wishing time away.

Time, he thought: I wonder how much more time I've got? I'm thirty-three years old; that's the halfway point, really — I'm probably halfway through my life. What am I going to do during the other half, ride the commuters' train, and read annual reports, and write endless letters for Hopkins or someone like him, and pride myself on working every week end? Shall I make a full-time career of being Hopkins' ghost? Is that what I want?

I don't know, he thought — who the hell knows what he wants? It's ridiculous to think of the next thirty-three years stretching ahead like an endless uphill road. Don't wish time away.

There's something wrong, he thought. There must be something drastically wrong when a man starts wishing time away. Time was given us like jewels to spend, and it's the ultimate sacrilege to wish it away. He glanced at his watch and again found himself thinking of Maria. She had not liked the watch. "Take it off," she had said. "I hate to hear it ticking."

That had been in her room, only a few days before he had left Rome. "Tick tock!" she had said derisively. "Tick, tick, tick, tick, tick! I would like to break it! And the buckle scratches me."

He had taken it off and put it on the floor beside the bed. The room had been very dark, and the luminous dial had glowed like the eyes of a cat.

"I can hear your heart beating," he had said.

"Kiss me. I don't want you to hear my heart beating."

"I love the sound of your heart and the sound of your breath."

Tom's thoughts were suddenly interrupted by the telephone ringing on his desk in the United Broadcasting building. He picked up the receiver. It was Betsy. "Hello," she said cheerfully. "Can you get home a little early tonight?"

"Why?"

"The PTA is having a meeting in advance of the public hearing on the new school. We ought to go — Bernstein says rumors about our housing project have got around, and we may get involved in the discussion tomorrow. We should get boned up on all the facts tonight."

"I'm afraid I won't be able to make it tonight," Tom said. "I'm going to have to stay here and work late this evening. I may not be home until after midnight. And don't count on me for week ends for a long while."

"Why? What's happened?"

"Nothing. I just have a lot of work to do."

"Can't you do it some other time? This meeting is *important.*"

"No. Don't count on me. I'll go to the hearing tomorrow, but I can't go anywhere tonight."

"All right," Betsy said resignedly.

Tom put the receiver down and turned toward his typewriter. That school thing is important, he thought — I should be helping to work for it. How interconnected everything is! If we could get the school, maybe we could get the housing project through and really make some money. Then maybe I could find and help Maria, and maybe I could work something out with Hopkins. Maybe I could find a good honest job with him which would pay me a decent living, but not require me to work day and night, pretending I want to be some kind of a tycoon. What could I say to him? Could I say, look, when you come right down to it, I'm just a nine-to-five guy, and I'm not interested in being much more, be-

cause life is too short, and I don't want to
work evenings and week ends forever? Could
a guy like Hopkins ever understand that?
Damn it, Tom thought, I'm not lazy! If there
were some cause worth working for, I might
not mind so much. But what's the great mis-
sionary spirit in United Broadcasting? It
seemed to Tom suddenly that he had managed to get himself into a position which
made it necessary to keep secrets from both
his employer and his wife — that both, if they
knew the truth about him, would abandon
him. Maybe that's why I'm on edge all the
time, he thought — I have to keep pretending. Maybe if I could tell Betsy about Maria,
and if I felt that Hopkins really understood
that I don't want to get as wrapped up in my
work as he is, then maybe I might relax. It's
no damn fun to keep the truth from people.
And it's not fair to them. Damn it, I'm really
cheating Hopkins — by agreeing to become
his personal assistant at all, I in effect promised him something I have no intention of delivering. Of course he'll be angry when he
finds out! And I'm cheating Betsy too. I bet
she doesn't like this kind of life any better
than I do. It must not be much fun to have
a husband as incommunicative as I've been.
It's funny how hard it is for us to understand

each other! But how could I ever expect her really to forgive me for Maria and her boy? What would she say: "That's all right, dear, don't give it a second thought"?

I'm wasting time, he thought — I've got to get to work. The next thing to do, he decided, was to write some introductory remarks for Hopkins to use at the first meeting of the exploratory committee on mental health. "It's very kind of you to accept my invitation to meet here to discuss one of the great problems of the day," he wrote. "It is my hope that from this meeting will stem . . ."

36

On the evening of October 8, Tom and Betsy Rath went to the Town Hall in South Bay to attend the public hearing on the proposed new school. The town hall was stuffy, and the people filing in from the commuting trains looked bored. The chair on which Tom sat was hard, and he was tired. He squirmed restlessly. Why is it that important public issues always have to be decided in places like this? he thought. Somehow the hard chairs, the smoky room, and the rumpled coats of the weary commuters didn't seem to be the right props for stirring decisions about anything. "How long do you think this meeting will take?" he asked Betsy.

At five minutes after eight, Bernstein, who had been appointed moderator, walked out on a raised platform at the front of the hall. He foresaw an evening of bitter argument, and his stomach was already beginning to ache. Sitting behind a wooden table, he picked up a gavel and tapped it lightly. Gradually the big auditorium quieted down. "Good evening," Bernstein said. "We have gathered here for a hearing on an eight-hundred-thousand-dollar bond issue which has been proposed for a new elementary school, and which we will vote on a week from today. The call for this meeting has been duly published in the newspaper, and I hereby make a motion that we dispense with reading it."

"Motion seconded," someone from the audience called.

"All in favor say 'Aye,' " Bernstein said.

"Aye!" the audience thundered.

"Nay?" Bernstein asked.

"No!" a lone, derisive voice called, and the audience laughed.

"The Ayes have it," Bernstein said, and thought, They seem good humored, but a crowd's laughter can be a symptom of tension. He cleared his throat and said, "To begin the proceedings, Dr. Clyde Eustace, Superintendent of Schools, will tell why he believes a new elementary school is necessary."

Eustace, who had been sitting in the front row, climbed to the platform. He was a large man, but his voice was surprisingly soft. "Ladies and gentlemen, it's very simple," he said. "Although the present elementary school building is badly overcrowded, the welfare of our children is only one question to be discussed tonight. Another basic issue is whether this town should be allowed to grow any more. If you build houses you have to build schools. The main thing I want to point out is that if you decide to vote *no* on this school, you are voting against any further development of this community, and . . ."

A tall, gray-haired man in the front row stood up. "I'm willing to fight it out on those grounds," he said.

Bernstein banged his gavel. "Dr. Eustace has the floor!" he said sharply.

Betsy glanced at Tom. "Who's that?" she asked.

"Parkington's his name," Tom replied. "He was an old friend of Grandmother's — they used to feud all the time."

"Eustace doesn't have to say any more," Parkington persisted. "He's named the basic issue."

"Dr. Eustace will have the floor until I as moderator recognize someone else, and I have not yet recognized you, Mr. Parkington," Bernstein said firmly, and banged his gavel again. "Dr. Eustace, please continue."

Parkington sat down. Eustace went on to give many facts and figures about the need for a new school. He talked too long, and the tone of his voice became monotonous. As soon as he was through, Parkington stood up again.

"All right, Mr. Parkington, you may have the floor now," Bernstein said.

"Let's just go back to what Dr. Eustace said a few moments ago," Parkington began in a deep voice. "If you vote *no* on this school, you vote against further development of this community — and, if I may say so, against further deterioration. What I'm trying to tell everyone here tonight is that's exactly what you should do."

"That's bad for our housing project," Tom whispered to Betsy. "Parkington's nuts, but he's pretty powerful around here."

"This has always been a good town, a beautiful town," Parkington continued passionately. "I was born and brought up here. I've never been able to understand why people move here because they like the place and then start to change it. This new school will send taxes up. That will drive the owners of big estates out. If the big estates are broken up, housing projects will come in. Housing projects bring more children than they do money. The average small house owner pays the town only about a third of what it costs to educate his children. Who's going to make up the difference?"

There was a rising murmur from the audience, and several people tried to speak at once. Bernstein slammed the table with his gavel. "Mr. Parkington still has the floor," he said. "Do you wish to continue, Mr. Parkington?"

"Yes," said Parkington. "I just want to point out that if this school is built, it won't be six months before another one is needed. I've heard a rumor that the old Rath estate is going to be made into a housing development. I'd like to come right out and ask Mr. Rath about that now. I know he's here tonight, because I saw him come in. He's sitting right there in one of the back rows. How about it, Tom? Aren't you just waiting for this school to go through, so you can get permission from the Zoning Board to cut up your land?"

"Mr. Rath, would you care to comment?" Bernstein asked. His stomach was hurting quite badly now.

Slowly Tom stood up. There was a rustling sound throughout the auditorium as people twisted in their seats to see him. He glanced at Betsy and saw she looked nervous. Mechanically he smiled at her. The hall seemed astonishingly quiet, and all faces were turned toward him. His mouth felt dry. "I didn't come prepared to give a talk . . ." he began lamely.

Somewhere in the crowd there was a snicker, which quickly grew into laughter. Bernstein tapped his gavel. "Mr. Rath, please step to the front of the hall," he said.

Awkwardly Tom edged his way to the aisle. The walk to the front of the auditorium seemed endless. Then he was on the platform facing the crowd, and the laughter subsided. The upturned faces blurred. It doesn't really matter, he thought. Here goes nothing. It will be interesting to see what happens. "All right," he said suddenly in a firm voice, "the rumor is true. I plan to ask the Zoning Board for permission to start a housing project."

He paused, and the hall was utterly silent. He couldn't find Betsy's face in the crowd. He took a deep breath. "I don't want my plans for a housing project to hurt the chances for this new school," he said. "They ought to be decided as separate issues. A new school is needed right now. I've got two children in the old one, and I've seen it — it's terrible. Let's get the new school first and fight the battle of my housing project later."

"But the school is an opening wedge!" Parkington interrupted. Bernstein banged his gavel.

"Mr. Parkington," Tom continued, "I think I see your point of view. I was born in South Bay too, and I like the town the way it is. As a matter of fact, I liked it even better the way it used to be, didn't you? It was prettier before the houses went up on the golf course. What I'm trying to say is, the town *is* changing, and we can't take a vote to stop change. If the Zoning Board lets me start a housing project, I'll do everything possible to keep it from being unsightly, or a financial drain on the town, but I don't promise to keep my grandmother's house and land unchanged. That's impossible. And I hope you won't leave the school we have today unchanged. As it stands today, it's a disgrace to all of us."

There was mild applause as Tom stepped down from the platform. Almost immediately Parkington was on his feet. "I just want to warn everybody here that breaking up the Rath estate is just the beginning," he said. "If we don't hold taxes down, other big estates will go. I've just heard that the big place the president of a broadcasting company built down by the water has been placed on the market."

"I know a little about that, and it doesn't have anything to do with schools or taxes," Tom said quickly.

"Maybe," Parkington replied, "but if the big estates go, and we keep on building schools, our taxes will be doubled!"

"I don't think the big estates will go just because we build a new school, and even if they do, I don't think we're so poor and so helpless we can't educate our children," Tom said.

"That sounds fine," Parkington retorted heatedly, "but I'm telling you here and now that if we replace the big estates with housing projects, South Bay will become a slum within ten years — a slum, I tell you, a slum!"

He paused, and the silence was impressive.

"I don't agree with you," Tom said quietly. "We won't let the town become a slum." He started walking toward the back of the hall to rejoin Betsy. Immediately a dozen people were on their feet asking Bernstein for permission to be heard. Antonio Bugala, the contractor, began an impassioned plea for increased business opportunities. For more than an hour the argument raged back and forth, the voices becoming louder and more strident. Tom glanced at Betsy. She looked scared. How curious, he thought, that we should be so dependent — that so much of our future should depend on what all these shouting people decide. His head started to ache, and he longed for the cool air outside.

Finally there was a pause. "Does anyone have anything more to add about the construction of a new school?" Bernstein asked wearily.

Parkington jumped to his feet again immediately. "To sum it all up, a vote for a school is a vote for a housing project Tom Rath admits he's planning," he said. "That's a vote to make this town a slum!"

Bernstein raised his gavel. "If there are no more opinions to be heard . . ." he said.

"A slum!" Parkington repeated portentously.

"I hereby declare this meeting at a . . ." Bernstein began.

"Wait a minute!" Betsy called impetuously, and suddenly found herself on her feet. Tom looked at her in astonishment and saw that her face was flushed.

"Mrs. Rath has the floor," Bernstein said.

For an instant Betsy hesitated. "I'm sorry," she said. "I just didn't want this meeting to end with the word *slum*."

The audience was attentive.

"The children need a new school," Betsy continued. "Don't let our housing project be used as a weapon against . . ."

"This will be only the beginning . . ." Parkington interrupted.

"Mr. Parkington!" Betsy cut in with remarkable self-possession. "I don't think that growth will necessarily hurt the town. And although I may be taking advantage of being a woman, I refuse to let you have the last word!"

The audience laughed, and although Parkington said something, no one could hear him. Bernstein banged his gavel. Gradually the hall quieted. "I think we've heard the full expression of all relevant opinions," Bernstein said. "I remind you that a week from today we vote on this issue. This meeting stands adjourned!"

On the way out of the Town Hall, Betsy clung tightly to Tom's arm, and he saw that she had been shaken. "I was proud of you," he said.

She smiled up at him. "I was proud of you too," she replied. "You were wonderful."

Going home in the car she sat very close to

him. After leaving the car in the old carriage house, they walked up to the house, arm in arm. The sitter they had left with the children met them at the door. "There was a telephone call for you, Mr. Rath," she said. "A Mr. Hopkins called from New York. He left his number and wants you to call him back."

Tom put the call through immediately. Hopkins answered the telephone himself. "Hello, Tom!" he said. "Sorry to bother you so late, but I just decided to fly out to Hollywood tomorrow, and I thought you might like to go with me."

"Hollywood?"

"Yes. We're thinking of organizing a subsidiary company out there to produce some of our programs on film, and I have to go out. I thought it might be a good chance for you to come along with me and learn something about that end of the business."

"Thanks," Tom said. "I'd love to. How long will we be gone?"

"Only four or five days. I've had reservations booked on Flight 227 leaving La Guardia at ten in the morning. Meet me there."

"Certainly!" Tom said. "Certainly! Thanks very much."

He put the telephone down and said some

what bewilderedly to Betsy, "Hopkins wants me to fly out to Hollywood with him."

"What for?"

"I don't know. He thinks I should learn something about the company's operations out there."

"He really is trying to do something for you," Betsy said. "This is a fantastic opportunity."

"I guess it is," Tom replied. "I hope I'll be back in time for the school election."

"That's not as important as this," she said. "How long do you think you'll be gone?"

"Just four or five days, according to Hopkins. I hope it won't be any longer."

Betsy sat down, looking suddenly solemn. "Gosh, it's going to be lonely around here," she said. "Do you realize that we haven't been away from each other that long since the war?"

"It will be lonely for me too," Tom said, and sat down beside her. She had dressed up for the school meeting and was wearing a dark-blue dress with silver buttons. How young she looks, he thought — she looks almost as young as she did before the war.

"I wish we had more time together," she said. "Things have been so hectic lately."

"I know."

"When do you think you can get your vacation?"

"I guess I could get a week off any time I wanted."

"If things go well," she said, "let's see if we can get somebody like Mrs. Manter to come in and take care of the kids. I'd love to go off on a trip somewhere — just you and I alone together. We wouldn't have to go far."

"It would be fun," he said.

"Maybe we could get a cottage up in Vermont. We could just go there and swim in a lake, maybe, and talk. The way things are going now, we hardly see each other, Tommy! I hate this business of your working every week end. You're always running for a train. We ought to just go off somewhere alone together. We haven't done that for ages."

"Maybe we can." He glanced at his watch. "It's almost midnight," he said. "We better get to bed — I'll have to leave here at eight in the morning to make that plane."

"Eight hours," she said. "We've got eight hours — that's still quite a lot of time."

He glanced at her, startled. She smiled hesitantly at him. It was true: time had become precious again.

37

The next morning Tom got to the airport before Hopkins did. He waited at the gate where Flight 227 was posted. In a few moments he saw Hopkins walking toward him. Hopkins looked small — a short, almost frail-appearing man hurrying across the terminal, holding a huge hard leather briefcase in his hand. "Good morning, Tom!" he said briskly. "It's good of you to come on such short notice as this!"

"No trouble at all," Tom replied, still avoiding the use of Hopkins' name, because he couldn't make up his mind whether to call him "Ralph" or not. They walked aboard the plane, and Hopkins politely resisted the efforts of a stewardess to put his briefcase in the luggage compartment — it was so big that she thought it was a suitcase. No one aboard the plane recognized Hopkins. Tom had grown so used to seeing him deferred to in the United Broadcasting building that it was a shock to see him treated like anyone else. Hopkins obviously didn't mind — if anything, he appeared more confident and more anxious to be polite than anyone else on the plane. He meekly allowed himself to be jostled away from the seat he was heading for, and when the stewardess offered him some chewing gum, he said, "Thank you — thank you very much, but I think not. I don't chew gum," and smiled apologetically, being almost absurdly careful not to hurt her feelings. She smiled back at him. What a nice little man, she thought.

Tom sat next to Hopkins. Even before the plane took off, Hopkins opened his briefcase, took out a thick report in pale-blue covers, and started to read. When the plane's engines roared, and they taxied toward the runway, he glanced up briefly. "This might interest you, Tom," he said, leaned over, and took another report from his briefcase. "This is something Bill Ogden roughed out on our plan for a subsidiary company to put programs on film — it's still just in the tentative planning stage, of course."

"Thanks," Tom said, accepting the document. As the plane rushed down the runway and lunged into the air, he opened the report. "On the basis of all available data, which is as yet incomplete, there might be considerable advantage in organizing an affiliated company, rather than trying to do the job directly ourselves," he read. He glanced out the window of the plane. Already they were at an altitude of about a thousand feet. He flexed his shoulder muscles, unconsciously trying to see if the parachute harness were strapped tight enough, then realized what he was doing, and smiled at himself. Sitting back, he tried to concentrate on Ogden's report.

After reading for two hours, Hopkins placed his briefcase on his lap and started writing memoranda with a pencil. He worked steadily throughout the long trip. When the plane finally landed in Hollywood, Tom felt tired, but Hopkins seemed energetic as ever. "We're right on time," he said with satisfaction, glancing at his watch. "Let's go to the hotel and wash up. Then we've got some meetings scheduled."

At the hotel a suite of large rooms had been reserved for Hopkins with an adjoining private room and bath for Tom. It was late, but Hopkins didn't mention dinner. They left their bags and hurried to the executive offices of the United Broadcasting Corporation's

Hollywood building. Hopkins introduced Tom to a succession of men, all of whom talked fast and with apparent urgency about matters Tom could hardly understand at all. He was glad when they went into a private dining room adjoining one of the offices and sat down around a long table. In all, there were eight men present, and they all kept talking to Hopkins at once. A pretty waitress brought cocktails.

"I'll tell you, Ralph," a tall but rather paunchy man with the oddly apt name of Potkin said. "Like it or not, live shows are going out. In another ten years, the whole television business will be right here. You ought to be thinking in terms of moving your whole operation. If you don't, it's not going to be long before the tail out here starts wagging the dog in New York."

I'm not convinced of that yet," Hopkins said. "And that's not the only consideration involved in setting up a subsidiary company. There are some legal angles to this. . . ."

On and on the conversation went. It was nine o'clock in the evening before it was over. "Come on over to my house for a drink," Potkin said.

"No," Hopkins replied. "I'm a little tired. I think I'd better go back to the hotel and get some rest. Want to come, Tom?"

"Sure," Tom said.

A taxi took them to the hotel. In the elevator Hopkins said,

"Want to stop in for a nightcap before you turn in?"

"That would be fine," Tom replied.

When they entered Hopkins' suite, Tom saw that someone in the company's Hollywood office had made all the arrangements he had made at Atlantic City the month before. On a table was a large vase of long-stemmed roses, and in the bedroom was an electric refrigerator and a cabinet holding a small bar. Tom suspected suddenly that Hopkins had never asked for such elaborate fixings, that they were all the idea of Ogden or someone else trying to please him, and that Hopkins was simply too polite to object. He wished he could find out, but there didn't seem to be any way to ask. Hopkins fixed two glasses of bourbon on the rocks and sprawled out on a sofa the way he had the night he and Tom had talked in his apartment. To his increasing discomfort, Tom found that Hopkins was staring at him again. There was the same mixture of tiredness and kindness on his face, the same steady gaze. Tom sipped his drink nervously.

"Well, what do you think?" Hopkins asked suddenly.

"About what?"

"About this whole operation we've been talking about. Do you think we ought to set up a separate but affiliated organization?"

"I don't know," Tom said. "There's so much involved. . . ."

"Of course — we can't make a decision yet. How would you like to move out here and work on this end of things for a year or so?"

"What?" Tom asked in astonishment.

"You could work with Potkin. He's right about one thing — this end of the business is going to get increasingly important. If you put in a year or two on it, I think you might pick up a lot that would be useful when you came back to New York."

Several thoughts immediately flamed up in Tom's mind. This is his way of getting rid of me, he suddenly knew — this personal assistant business is making him as uncomfortable as it's made me. But he's still trying to do something for me — now he just wants to do it at a distance, by remote control. It's a great opportunity, he thought, but what would happen to our housing project? He was suddenly filled with the confusion of moving, putting his grandmother's house on the market to sell the quickest way possible, and looking for a place to live in Hollywood. Out of this welter of impressions came one word: no. He didn't say it. Instead, he said,

"Gosh, that's a pretty big step. . . ."

"Don't you like the idea?"

Wait a minute, Tom thought. If I say no, he's going to wonder what the devil to do with me in New York. I'll be upsetting his whole scheme. If I buck him, he's liable to turn on me. This is like petting a tiger. "I don't know," he said carefully. "I'd like to have a little time to think it over."

"Don't you want to learn the business?" Hopkins asked quietly, but with obvious import.

"Of course . . ." Tom began. Then he paused and took a sip of his drink. The hell with it, he thought. There's no point in pretending. I've played it straight with him so far, and I might as well keep on. Anyway, he's a guy who can't be fooled. He glanced up and saw that Hopkins was smiling at him with great friendliness. Here goes nothing, Tom thought, and the words came with a rush. "Look, Ralph," he said, using the first name unconsciously, "I don't think I do want to learn the business. I don't think I'm the kind of guy who should try to be a big executive. I'll say it frankly: I don't think I have the willingness to make the sacrifices. I don't want to give up the time. I'm trying to be honest about this. I want the money. Nobody likes money better than I do. But I'm just not the kind of guy who can work evenings and week ends and all the rest of it forever. I guess there's even more to it than that. I'm not the kind of person who can get all wrapped up in a job — I can't get myself convinced that my work is the most important thing in the world. I've been through one war. Maybe another one's coming. If one is, I want to be able to look back and figure I spent the time between wars with my family, the way it should have been spent. Regardless of war, I want to get the most out of the years I've got left. Maybe that sounds silly. It's just that if I have to bury myself in a job every minute of my life, I don't see any point to it. And I know that to do the kind of job you want me to do, I'd have to be willing to bury myself in it, and, well, I just don't want to."

He paused, out of breath, half afraid to look at Hopkins. And then it happened — Hopkins gave a funny, high, indescribable little laugh which rose in the air and was cut off immediately. It was a laugh Tom never forgot, and it was followed by a moment of complete silence. Then Hopkins said in a low voice, "I'm glad you're honest. I've always appreciated that quality in you."

It was Tom's turn to laugh nervously. "Well, there it is," he said. "I don't know what I do now. Do you still want me to work for you?"

"Of course," Hopkins said kindly, getting up and pouring himself another drink. "There are plenty of good positions where it's not necessary for a man to put in an unusual amount of work. Now it's just a matter of finding the right spot for you."

"I'm willing to look at it straight," Tom said. "There are a lot of contradictions in my own thinking I've got to face. In spite of everything I've said, I'm still ambitious. I want to get ahead as far as I possibly can without sacrificing my entire personal life."

Hopkins stood with his back turned toward Tom, and when he spoke, his voice sounded curiously remote. "I think we can find something for you," he said. "How would you like to go back to the mental-health committee? That will be developing into a small, permanent organization. I'm thinking of giving my house in South Bay to be its headquarters. That would be quite nice for you — you

513

wouldn't even have any commuting. How would you like to be director of the outfit? That job would pay pretty well. I'd like to think I had a man with your integrity there, and I'll be making all the major decisions."

"I'd be grateful," Tom said in a low voice.

Suddenly Hopkins whirled and faced him. *"Somebody has to do the big jobs."* he said passionately. "This world was built by men like me! To really do a job, you have to live it, body and soul! You people who just give half your mind to your work are riding on our backs!"

"I know it," Tom said.

Almost immediately Hopkins regained control of himself. A somewhat forced smile spread over his face. "Really, I don't know why we're taking all this so seriously," he said. "I think you've made a good decision. You don't have to worry about being stuck with a foundation job all your life. I'll be starting other projects. We need men like you — I guess we need a few men who keep a sense of proportion."

"Thanks," Tom said.

Hopkins smiled again, this time with complete spontaneity "Now if you'll pardon me, I think I'll go to bed," he said. "It's been a long day."

38

The next morning Hopkins was friendly, but brisk and a little distant. "Good morning, Tom!" he said when they met for breakfast. I find that I've got to stay out here a little longer than I thought. There's no reason why I should hold you up, though — you can fly back to New York any time you want."

"Thanks," Tom said. "I guess I might as well take the first plane I can."

"Certainly!" Hopkins replied, "and thanks so much for coming out with me. Don't worry about anything. In a couple of months we'll have that mental-health committee set up, and I'm sure we can work out something good. I really meant it when I said we can use a man like you. I won't keep you on the mental-health committee more than a few years — we'll work out lots of new and exciting projects. I think the two of us will make a good team."

"I'm grateful," Tom said.

"By the way," Hopkins concluded, handing him a large manila envelope. "Give this to Bill Ogden when you get back, will you? It's just a few notes I've made on some projects he has underway, and I know he's waiting to get my reaction."

"Sure," Tom said. "Glad to. See you later, Ralph — see you when you get back to New York."

Tom went to his room to pack. He glanced at the telephone. Half the night he had lain awake wanting to call Betsy to tell her about his conversation with Hopkins. He didn't know why, but he didn't want to wait any longer. Without knowing whether she would be disappointed or glad, or even whether she'd understand what had happened at all, he had an intense urge to communicate with her. On impulse, he picked up the receiver and placed the call.

"It'll be a few minutes," the operator said. "I'll ring you."

He sat down on the bed and waited. In a shorter time than he had expected, the telephone rang. "I have your call to Connecticut," the operator said. "Go ahead, please."

"Betsy?"

"Yes!" she replied, sounding marvelously

close. "Is everything all right?"

"Yes. I'm flying home today."

"Today? That's wonderful! But why?"

"Something's happened," he said. "I had a really frank talk with Ralph and I'm going back to work on the mental-health committee. I'm going to be its director, at least for a while. Then I'll probably go on to something else with Ralph."

"Are you glad about it?" she asked, sounding bewildered.

"Yes. I think it's going to work out fine. Ralph is a good guy, Betsy — an awfully good guy. Guys like that never get appreciated enough. I'm going to go on working with him, but he understands that I'm not built the way he is. You and I will have plenty of time to ourselves. No more working every week end."

"It sounds grand," she said. "Tell me all about it when you get home. And hurry back. I miss you."

"I'll hurry," he said.

To his disappointment, he found he couldn't get a plane until evening. He was tired, and after sending a wire to Betsy to say he wouldn't be home until the next morning, he spent most of the day sleeping in his hotel room. As a result, he had difficulty sleeping on the plane. It was not a direct flight, and every few hours they landed at some big airport. During the night Tom had four cups of coffee in four different states. The plane wasn't due in La Guardia until six-thirty in the morning, and head winds made it an hour late. Tom shaved with an electric razor provided by the stewardess. It would be almost nine o'clock by the time he got to Grand Central Station, he figured, and he better stop at the office at least long enough to give Hopkins' envelope to Ogden before doing what he wanted to do, which was to rush home.

Ogden seemed surprised to see him, but accepted the envelope without comment. Tom stopped at his desk in Hopkins' office to see if there were any calls for him. Miss MacDonald also seemed surprised to see him. "There's a message on your desk," she said. "I didn't expect you back until the end of the week."

Tom went to his desk. There was a typewritten memorandum from Miss MacDonald with yesterday's date. "A Mr. Gardella called," she had written. "He said it was important and asked me to have you call him as soon as you returned." Caesar's telephone number followed. Tom dialed it.

"Hello," a woman with an Italian accent answered.

"Is Mr. Gardella there?"

"Just a minute," the woman said, and Tom heard her calling, "Caesar! Caesar! Telephone for you!" She added something in Italian. There was a moment of silence, followed by the sound of heavy footsteps approachng the telephone. "Hello," Caesar said in his deep voice.

"This is Tom Rath. Did you call me?"

"Yes, Mr. Rath. I heard from Maria. I'd like to see you."

"Is she all right?"

"Things aren't very good, Mr. Rath. Louis is dead. They went to Milan, just as I figured, and he got killed there, only a couple of weeks after he found a job. They had a strike in the plant where he was working. They've got a lot of Commies in Milan, and they make a lot of trouble — there was a riot, and Louis got killed. With that leg of his, he couldn't fight and he couldn't run."

There was a pause. "Did you hear me, Mr. Rath?" Caesar asked.

"I heard. I'm very sorry that Louis died. Are Maria and the boy all right?"

"They're back in Rome with Gina's folks. They need help bad, Mr. Rath. I'd like to see you and kind of talk it over. Gina and I do what we can to help, but you know how it is.

We've got three kids of our own. We'd all sure appreciate it if you could do something."

There was a moment of silence before Tom said, "When can I see you?"

"How about lunch today?"

"I'll meet you here in the lobby by the information booth, where we met last time," Tom said. "Twelve-thirty for lunch. Will that be okay?"

"Sure, Mr. Rath. I'll be there."

"Thanks," Tom said, and hung up. I'll have to tell Betsy after all, he thought. I hope this housing project goes through. Then we'd have plenty of money, and it would be easier to tell her.

I won't tell her now, he thought. Not tonight. I might as well wait until the school vote goes through. It would be easier to tell her then, when we knew we were going to be all right ourselves.

What will I do if the housing project fails? he thought. If it doesn't work, we'll just have my salary, and is it fair to ask Betsy to share that with some woman I met during the war? She'd never do that — no woman would!

Tom glanced at the telephone. He wished he didn't have to see Betsy until he could tell her about Maria — he didn't want to have to keep secrets from her any more. The eagerness to go home had left him. He telephoned Betsy and told her he had to stay in town for a business lunch.

"Oh!" she said, sounding disappointed. "Do you really have to?"

"I'm afraid so."

"You sound funny. Is everything all right?"

"Yes."

"Are you angry at me or something? You sound so funny."

"I'm not angry," he said. "I just have to see a guy. This is a thing I simply have to do."

At twelve-thirty Tom got into one of the golden elevators and rode down to the lobby of the United Broadcasting building. Caesar Gardella, dressed in a dark-blue business suit, was waiting for him at the information booth. Caesar smiled embarrassedly when he saw him. "Do you want to go to that Mexican place again?" he asked.

"I guess so," Tom said.

They walked across Rockefeller Plaza in silence. When they got to the restaurant, they sat down in the same booth they had occupied before.

"Two double Black and White's," Tom said to the waiter. When the drinks arrived, he said to Caesar, "Is there anything more you can tell me about Maria?"

"It's just that she and the boy are living with Gina's folks," Caesar said. "I guess they're well enough. I don't know whether I should have done it or not, but there didn't seem to be any point in calling you unless . . ."

"What did you do?"

"I told Gina's mother that I had run into you here in New York, and I asked her to talk to Maria about it and see if Maria would take any help from you if you were willing to give it."

"What did Maria say?"

"She sent me a letter to give you. I didn't open it, but Gina's mother says . . ."

"You have a letter for me?"

"Yes." Caesar put his hand in his breast pocket and took out a rather soiled envelope with Tom's full name written in black ink across the front in large, slanting letters. Tom tore it open. He took out a single-page letter folded around a snapshot wrapped in tissue paper. He looked at the snapshot first. It showed a plainly dressed woman, quite stout and almost middle-aged, whom he dimly recognized as Maria, and standing beside her was a boy, a thin little boy all dressed up, with a cap on his head, and a shirt with a wide collar, and a little tight-fitting jacket, and short trousers. With his queer old-fashioned clothes, and his slender big-eyed face, and with his shockingly familiar forehead and nose and mouth, he looked like one of the faded photographs Tom's grandmother had kept of "The Senator" as a child. Tom stared at the snapshot and then with trembling hands quickly stuffed it back into the envelope and unfolded the letter. Apparently Maria had dictated it to someone — the grammar and spelling were all correct.

"Dear Tom," the letter said, "I do not like this, but I don't know what to do. For myself I do not need help, but there is the boy. Anything you could do for him would be from heaven. I am ashamed to ask you, but we were never proud with each other, so perhaps you will understand. The boy needs help. He is a good boy. He studies well. I am sending you this picture that Louis took last year. Do not think we are trying to make trouble for you. I leave this in the hands of God."

The letter was signed, "Maria Lapa." Tom took a drink before folding it carefully and putting it back in the envelope with the photograph. He put the envelope in his inside coat pocket, glanced up, and saw that Caesar was discreetly staring at the wall. There was a heavy silence.

"Caesar," Tom said suddenly, "can I have some time to think this over?"

"Sure, Mr. Rath," Caesar replied. "Nobody's trying to hurry you. We don't want you to do anything you don't think should be done."

"How much do you think I should send?"

"Anything would help. Gina and I have been sending ten dollars a month to her mother. Ten dollars a month is a lot of money in Rome."

"How much would Maria need to raise that boy decently?"

Caesar shrugged his shoulders. "Maria will probably go on living with Gina's mother," he said. "If you sent her a hundred dollars a month, she could do an awful lot with it. She could send the boy to a pretty good school, and everything."

"I've got to have time to work this out," Tom said. "Look, Caesar, you've always been a decent guy. I've got to tell my wife — you can understand that. And it's not going to be easy. I've got to have time."

"Sure, Mr. Rath," Caesar said earnestly. "Maria's all right for now — Gina's mother can take care of her. You've got no need to hurry."

"It might take me a few weeks," Tom said. "I've got to pick the right time to tell my wife."

"It's none of my business, Mr. Rath, but aren't you going to make a lot of trouble for yourself? By telling your wife, I mean."

"Could you send money somewhere every month without telling your wife?"

"No, I guess I couldn't. I sure hope this doesn't make trouble for you, though. I know Maria wouldn't want that."

"I've got a good wife," Tom said. "I don't think there's going to be any trouble. I've just got to pick the right time."

"Mr. Rath, I'd like to say this," Caesar replied awkwardly. "We're grateful to you — Maria and Gina and I. We know you don't have to do it, there's nothing that could make you. I don't know whether it will mean anything to you or not, but Gina and I are going to pray for you, and I know Maria will."

"Maria already has," Tom said. "Now listen. You may not hear from me for quite a while. But I'll get in touch with you, and I'll make some kind of arrangement for Maria. I'll probably do it through a bank or a lawyer. I'll write her a note, but I want to make some kind of permanent arrangement." He paused in confusion. "It would be kind of difficult for everybody if I had to write her every month," he concluded.

"What if your wife won't let you do anything? I better not tell Maria until you're sure."

"No, you better not. We better wait and see."

There was an interval of silence before the waiter came to take their orders.

"You want anything to eat?" Tom asked Caesar.

Caesar shook his head. "I got to be getting back," he replied.

"Me too," Tom said. He paid the check for the drinks. They left the restaurant and hurried off in different directions.

That afternoon Tom had a vicious headache. He threw himself into his work and missed his regular train home. While he waited for another train in Grand Central Station, he went to a drugstore and swallowed two aspirins. Finding that they didn't help much, he went to the Hotel Commodore bar and drank too many Martinis. When he finally got home, Betsy looked at him with astonishment and concern. "Tommy," she said, "what's the matter with you? You look terrible."

"I guess I just got a little stomach upset,"

he said. "I think I'll go upstairs and lie down."

Without saying more, he walked up to the big bedroom. Taking off only his shoes, he lay down on the wide four-poster bed. All the objects in the room seemed to swirl before his eyes. The paintings of his father and grand-father as children, the old mandolin in its cracked leather case on the top shelf of the corner bookcase, and an electric clock on the bureau blurred and wavered. He shut his eyes. In the quiet room he could hear his wrist watch ticking. A few moments later Betsy came in and looked at him worriedly. "Should I call a doctor?" she asked.

"No," he replied, shaking his head. "I guess I just drank a little too much. I was tired, and when I missed my train, I stopped at the bar in the station."

"You shouldn't," she said. "It's not adult, Tommy! And when you drink like this, I feel as though we were in different worlds. You haven't even told me about your trip to Cali-fornia, and now the kids and I will have to eat supper without you. I wish you'd quit drinking, if only because it makes me feel so lonely."

"I'm sorry," he said. He stretched out and stared up at the crocheted canopy overhead.

Betsy left the room. A moment later she came back, and he felt something cool on his forehead. He put his hand up and found a damp towel she had placed there. "Thanks," he said.

"Would an ice bag help?"

"This is fine."

"Did Hopkins say anything to you that worries you?"

"No — everything is fine with Ralph. I'm not worried about my job at all. I'll talk to you about it later."

"Please don't drink any more," she said.

"I won't."

"I don't like to see you like this. It makes me feel awful."

"I'm sorry."

"We've got so much work to do. I promised I'd help mail pamphlets for the school."

"After the school election can I talk with you?"

"What about?"

"Never mind now. It's funny you said you were lonely. We've both been lonely so long."

39

It was Indian summer. The day of the school election turned out to be warm and clear. After an early breakfast, Tom and Betsy took the children with them and went to the Town Hall to vote. Ahead of them waited a long line of commuters, the young and ambitious, the old and successful, and the tired of all ages, standing in line to vote yes or no on whether to tax themselves for the construction of a new school. They were polite, excusing themselves elaborately when they jostled each other and pointedly refraining from commenting on the issue at hand.

On the way home after they had voted, Tom and Betsy passed a white sound truck. "Vote *no* on the school!" it was blaring. "Vote against high taxes and poorly planned school programs!" A block ahead was another sound truck shouting, "Vote *yes* on the school! Our children deserve the best!" Apparently the two trucks were following each other around town, blatting like moose in the mating season.

Tom left Betsy and the children at the house and hurried to the station to go to work. On the train he looked once more at the photograph of Maria and her son. Then he read his newspaper, all of it, from headlines about wars and incipient wars to the comics. When he got to his office, he worked all day, getting together plans for the first meeting of the mental-health committee.

At six o'clock he took the train back to South Bay and again examined the photograph, which was becoming stained and creased. Before going home he stopped at the Town Hall, where Bernstein and a group of other officials were about to close the polls and announce the count on the voting machines. A quiet crowd was assembling in the building. Tom saw both Parkington and Bugala. A few last-minute voters hurried in, and then there was a hush while an elderly town councilman consulted his watch and declared the voting at an end. Three rather self-conscious officials began to inspect the voting machines, and there was a long wait. Bernstein walked to the head of the hall, and a small man handed him three pieces of paper. Bernstein cleared his throat. "On machine number one," he announced, "the vote is seven hundred and forty-two *yes* and four hundred and forty-three no."

There was a ragged cheer from the crowd. Bernstein read the counts on the other two machines, which did not differ markedly from the first. "It looks as though the vote on the school is *yes* by a margin of almost two to one," he said.

There was another cheer, and a rising hum of conversation. Old Parkington headed toward the door without comment. Bugala grinned at Tom and shouldered his way through the crowd toward him. "It looks like we got it made," he said.

"I hope so," Tom replied. "Let's get together tomorrow." Hurriedly he headed home. Just as he reached the sidewalk, Bernstein caught up with him. "Say, Tom," he said. "Have a beer with me?"

"Sure."

They went to a bar across the street. When two glasses of beer were before them, Bernstein said, "Well, we got the school. The people in this town have more sense than they're given credit for."

"I guess they do."

"Now about this zoning problem of yours. I'll be glad to call a meeting of the board next week if you want to submit your petition."

"Do you think they'll approve it?"

"I can't tell you that. As a friend of yours, all I can say is that, in my opinion, now would be a good time to submit it."

"Thanks," Tom said. "If you don't mind, I think I'll hurry back and tell Betsy."

The old Ford knocked as he drove it fast up the steep winding hill, past the great outcroppings of rock. When he got to the house, Betsy came to the front door to meet him. She had brushed her hair until it shone and had put on a crisp white blouse. She smiled, and he found he didn't want to keep secrets from her any more. Now is the time, he thought. The housing project's not sure yet, but nothing's ever sure. Now is the time I'll have faith.

"Did we get the school?" she called as he came toward her.

"Yes," he said.

"Wonderful!" she exclaimed. "If Bugala is right . . ."

"I want to talk to you," he said.

"What about?"

"I've got something important I want to talk over with you. Let's go up to our room."

"Is something the matter?"

"Its nothing about the project."

"Can you wait a minute? I'll put the kids to bed."

"I'll wait in our room," he said.

"Is it anything serious? You're acting so strange!"

"I'm all right. I don't want to worry you. It's just something we've got to talk over."

"I've fed the kids, but I've got dinner waiting for you," she said. "Don't you want anything to eat?"

"Later. Come to our room when you can."

As he went upstairs Barbara and Pete, already in their pajamas, ran to meet him. He kissed them and went in to say good night to Janey, who was already half asleep.

"Come on, kids," Betsy said. "To bed!"

"We haven't had a story yet!" Janey said, waking up.

"I'll read you a short one."

Tom went into the big bedroom and sat down nervously on the edge of the bed. He could hear Betsy in the next room quietly reading a story about Winnie the Pooh. He put his hand in his pocket, took out the letter from Maria, and for perhaps the hundredth time examined the photograph. There was the child, big-eyed, serious, dressed with that pathetic and grotesque gentility, staring out at him solemnly, the image of "The Senator" as a young boy. Beside her son, Maria looked proud and serene. He stuffed the photograph and the letter back in the envelope and put them in his pocket.

It was about fifteen minutes before Betsy came in. She was pale and suddenly seemed to him to be as fragile as a girl in her teens. He realized he had scared her. Getting to his feet with clumsy politeness, he said, "I don't want you to be frightened," and immediately realized that those were hardly the words to reassure her.

"Why are you being so mysterious?"

"I don't know if I should talk to you about this. I don't know what else to do. It isn't just the money — I don't like to do things behind your back."

"Behind my back?"

"It was all such a long time ago," he said helplessly.

"What was?"

He had an impulse simply to give her Maria's letter and the photograph, but decided that would be cruel. There was an awkward silence which he realized must be painful to her.

"There was a child," he began.

"A child?"

"During the war. In Rome."

"What child?"

"A child of mine."

"You had a child?"

"Yes."

She said nothing. He had the strange feeling that he had not spoken, that the secret was still his. "I wasn't sure," he said. "I didn't know where she was. I didn't know for sure until I got this letter."

"A letter?"

He gave her the letter. Her face was pale but expressionless as she read it. Then she took the photograph out of the envelope and stared at it.

"Was this the woman?"

"Yes."

"Did you love her?"

"I can't explain it. You can't possibly have any idea what the war was like."

"We've never talked about it."

"I can't. Do you want me to tell you horrors? I wouldn't have brought this up at all if it weren't . . ."

"What do you want to do?"

"I'm going to support this child," he said. "I've thought it over, and I'm going to send him a hundred dollars a month. I guess what I want is your blessing."

"My *blessing!*" she said, her voice rising suddenly.

"Betsy, do you want me to apologize for this child? So much happened during the war! It's strange I should have to apologize for this. I killed seventeen men. I cut the throat of a German boy eighteen years old, and I killed Hank Mahoney, my best friend, because I threw a hand grenade too fast. I'm not ashamed of it, but for having a child I feel terrible. What do you want me to tell you?"

"All of it," she said. "I want you to tell me all of it. You can't just come and tell me you had a child in Italy, and that's that. If you don't tell me now, I'll wonder about it the rest of my life. Where did you meet the girl in that photograph?"

"In Rome."

"*Where* in Rome?"

"In a bar."

"Was it a formal introduction, or did you just pick her up?"

"Goddamn it," he said. "Don't let's make this any harder than it has to be."

"I'm not making it harder than it has to be! Was she just an ordinary pickup? Were you drunk, Tommy?"

"I wasn't drunk. I was scared. And so was

536

she. She was eighteen years old. Her parents had been burned to death before her eyes. She was broke and hungry. Now let this thing alone."

"No," she said. "I want to know. How many times did you sleep with her?"

"I lived with her," he said. "I lived with her for two months."

"When?"

"In 1944."

"When in 1944?"

"December and part of January of the next year."

"The turn of the year," she said. "You know something, Tommy? I almost went crazy worrying about you those months. I suppose that's rather funny. You didn't write. It was the first time I'd gone that long without letters. I didn't hear from you for three months. I'll never forget that. I was so worried that I got your grandmother to try to pull some strings in Washington and find out where you were. It didn't work — we couldn't find out a thing. I used to jump every time the telephone or doorbell rang, for fear it was a telegram for me from the War Department. I can remember trying to write you letters during those months. It isn't easy to write letters when you're not getting any, and when you're sure in your heart that the man you're writing is dead. There wasn't much for me to write about. I can remember trying to be cheerful, not to let you know I was worried. What did you do with my letters when you were living with her? Did the two of you lie in bed and read them together for laughs?"

"Don't," he said.

"No, I want to know. What did you do with my letters when you were living with her?"

"I don't think I got them until I got to New Guinea. The mail was pretty mixed up for us while we were on the move."

"Was she pretty, Tommy?"

"Not as pretty as you. Look at the picture and see for yourself."

"Was she better in bed than I am?"

"Stop it."

"Did she have a good figure? Were her breasts better than mine?"

"Why do you torture yourself?"

"I want an answer."

"I did not love her as much as I love you."

"You're lying a little, aren't you ? Do you catch yourself wishing for her when you're making love to me?"

"Try to be adult about this," he said. "I'm

not the only man to leave a child behind during the war. There are hundreds of thousands of war children in Japan and Italy and Germany. There are more in France and England and Australia. Anywhere the men were sent out to fight, quite a few ended up becoming fathers. Call it a practical joke of nature. The human race goes on, in spite of itself. That's a dirty thing, I suppose. Wars are full of dirt."

"You sound almost righteous when you talk about it."

"I find it hard to be really ashamed. When I met Maria I thought I was never going to see you again. Do you know what it's like to be scared right down to the bottom of your guts? Do you know what it's like to be sure beyond the shadow of a doubt that you'll be killed on the next jump, or the jump after that? And do you know what it's like to be half afraid of yourself, to know in your heart that the last man you killed was killed with pleasure? Do you know how a corpse grins? When you see enough of that grin, everything decent in the world seems a joke. The dead always have the last laugh — Mahoney, a man I killed, told me that once when we were in Germany together. The dead always have the last laugh. I'm not trying to shock you, Betsy, but you've got to understand that having a child doesn't seem to me to be so bad. Maybe I've got everything twisted backward. Ever since the war, it's been as though I were trying to figure something out. I've never been able to get it quite clear in my mind, but I keep feeling just the way I did when I was about to make a jump and knew a lot of us were going to get killed. I keep having the same feeling I had when I killed Hank Mahoney, the feeling that the world is nuts, that the whole world is absolutely insane."

"And now you've done your bit to straighten things out," Betsy said. "A few more illegitimate children, and everything will be fine."

"All right — I don't make sense. But love, even when it's three quarters lust, does not seem to me to be as bad as lots of things I've seen. I don't love Maria any more — you don't have to worry about that. But she was with me when I didn't have a hope in the world. She was the only good thing that happened to me in the whole war, and we had a child. Dirty or not, that still seems a kind of miracle to me. What do you want me to do, forget it? Maria hasn't got any legal hold on me. I can just tell her to go to hell. Probably if worst came to worst and she sued me, I could prove she was a prostitute. Would that make you feel any cleaner? I can write her now and tell her I don't believe this child is mine. One more act of brutality wouldn't change the world. But I'm not going to do it. I can't do anything about the state of the world, but I can put my own life in order. The only really dirty part about an illegitimate child is that usually the father doesn't support it. This is one decent thing I'm going to do, if I never do anything else, and I hope you'll help me."

"Go ahead and send him money," she said. "I'm not trying to stop you. You have my blessing. That's what you want, isn't it?"

"I didn't think you'd be bitter."

"I'm not bitter, but things haven't been very good since you got out of the service, have they? Is Maria the reason? Let's be honest about it. We haven't had much of a life together. You and I seem to have learned a lot of things since the war — a lot of things I don't want to know. We've learned to drag along from day to day without any real emotion except worry. We've learned to make love without passion. We've even learned to stop fighting together, haven't we? We haven't had a real good fight since you threw that vase against the wall a year ago. We used to fight a lot when we were first married, but we don't really care enough to fight any more, do we? I haven't even cried for months. I think I've forgotten how to cry. All I know how to do nowadays is be responsible and dutiful and deliberately cheerful for the sake of the children. And all you know how to do is work day and night and worry. You give a good sermon on love, but I haven't seen much of it around here. It's a great life, isn't it? Was it that way with Maria?"

He began pacing nervously up and down the room. "I know things haven't been good since the war," he said. "I think they're going to be better. We're not going to have to worry so much about money."

"Did you worry about money when you were with Maria?"

"Maria was part of the war. I can't explain that to you."

"Sure, I don't know anything about war. All I know is the wife's side of it — four years of sitting around waiting, believing that faithfulness is part of what you call love. All I know is that I lived on the belief that everything would be marvelous after the war, and that we've both been half dead ever since you got home."

"Stop it," he said. "We're going to have a good life together." He put his arm around her, but suddenly she twisted free and fled from the room and down the stairs. He followed her. She ran out the front door. There was brilliant moonlight on the tall grass and on the distant waters of the Sound. She ran through the dark shadows of the rock garden toward the old carriage house, where the car was parked. He caught her just before she got there, but she whirled and hit him on the mouth with her clenched fist. He kissed her and she bit him hard. He put his hand up to his mouth. When he took it down, there was blood on it.

"Did Maria kiss like that?" she asked.

Without saying anything, he grabbed her. She twisted away, tearing open the shoulder of her blouse. He caught her around the waist, pulled her down in the tall grass, and lay beside her with one arm imprisoning her.

"We can still fight, can't we?" she said, struggling to free herself. "Is that the one thing we've got left?"

He stroked her hair. "Hush," he said. The grass smelled sweet.

"Let me go," she said, almost wrenching herself free. He threw himself across her and, feeling her fingers digging into his back, kissed her hard. Suddenly she burst into tears and, burying her face in his neck, clung to him like a child. Her whole body was quaking.

"It's all right," he said over and over again. "Everything's all right."

There was no answer but her sobs. It took a long time for them to subside. After an instant of complete silence she said, "Now let me go."

He released her and she lay full length in the grass. Her face, still tear streaked, was bright in the moonlight. Her blouse was shredded at one shoulder, and on her other shoulder there was a dark blood stain on the white cloth, where he had held her. She was breathing hard. "Leave me alone for a little while, will you?" she said. "Go in the house and let me be by myself for a while. I've got a lot to think out."

"Come in the house with me."

She propped herself up on her elbows slowly. "No. I'm not sure what we should do. Maybe you should take a few weeks off and fly over to Italy and see Maria. When you came back, we could decide what's right."

"I don't want to go to Italy. I want to stay here with you."

"Perhaps I should go off by myself for a few days. It might help me to get things clear in my mind."

"I've got a better idea. Let's get Mrs. Manter to take care of the kids for a week. We could buy a new car and take a drive up through Vermont together."

"I don't know. Give me some time to think. Go in the house — I'll be in after a while."

"I don't want to."

"Please."

"All right." He kissed her gently and walked slowly through the moonlight toward the shadows of the house. Just before he went inside, he turned and saw her walking forlornly through the long grass toward the distant row of pines, like a ghost in the moonlight. He started to go after her but thought better of it. After sitting in the living room and smoking a cigarette, he went to the front door and looked out. There was no sign of her. Restlessly he went to the kitchen and put some ice in a glass. He poured a drink, carried it upstairs, and lay down on his bed. Maybe when I finish this drink she'll be back, he thought, and sipped it slowly. He had just drained the glass when he heard the car start. He dashed down the stairs and ran outside. In the moonlight he saw the old Ford back violently out of the carriage house. He ran toward it, but before he got there, it jerked ahead, its lights flashed on, and with its engine roaring in second gear, it careened down the hill. The thought of his father speeding down that same hill toward the waiting rocks at the turn so many years before gripped his mind, and he started running. Ahead of him the red tail light winked in the night. Abruptly it disappeared as the car rounded the first turn. There was no crash. He climbed the great red rocks glistening in the moonlight and could see the car continuing down the road more slowly. He watched until it vanished into the darkness. After standing there a long while to see if she would come back, he returned to the house and lay fully dressed on the bed. There was nothing to do but wait. Maybe she'll telephone and tell me what she plans to do, he thought, but the only sound was the somber striking of the grandfather clock downstairs.

40

It was two o'clock in the morning when the telephone finally rang. He leaped to answer it. "Hello," he said. "Is that you, Betsy?"

"Yes," she said in a small voice. "The car broke down."

He started to laugh with relief. "That's a good old car," he said. "It won't take you away from me."

"I was trying to get home — I was trying to get home as fast as I could. I just wanted to get away by myself and drive for a while. I got everything figured out in my mind and was on my way home when the engine made an awful noise and stopped."

"Where are you?"

"A little way beyond Westport."

"Where are you calling from?"

"The police station. The car broke down on the Merritt Parkway. I was walking along the road trying to find a telephone, when a patrol car stopped and picked me up. I showed them where I had left the car, and they wanted to see my driver's license and registration. I don't have them with me."

"Tell the cops to have the car hauled to a garage, and we'll turn it in on a new one tomorrow. And take a taxi home as soon as you can."

"I don't know if the cops will let me go."

"That's ridiculous. Are there any charges against you?"

"They say they're just holding me for driving without my license and registration, but they seem to think there's something suspicious about me. I guess I'm not very well dressed at the moment. They keep asking me where I got this blood stain on my sleeve and how my blouse got torn."

"They probably think you've been in an accident," he said, laughing.

"Don't laugh. I want to come home. I feel awful and I want to come home."

"Let me talk to the cops," he said.

"Just a minute."

There was a short delay before a gruff voice said, "Sergeant Haggerty speaking."

"My name is Rath, Thomas Rath in South Bay," Tom said. "I want you to call a cab for my wife and let her come right home. If there's any difficulty about it, I'll have Judge Saul Bernstein here get in touch with you immediately and straighten it out."

"No difficulty," the voice said. "We just thought it was peculiar, girl walking along the road alone late at night like that. We just wanted to make sure everything was all right."

"Everything's fine. Please have the car towed to a garage and call her a cab."

"Be glad to. You a friend of Judge Bernstein's?"

"Sure am."

"Give him my best when you see him — name's Haggerty. And tell your wife to bring her license and registration with her after this when she goes out driving alone late at night."

"I will. Let me talk to her again, will you?"

"Okay," Haggerty said. "Just a minute."

"You're out of hock," Tom said when Betsy came on the line. "They're going to call you a cab. Come home. I can't wait to see you."

"I'll be there as soon as I can. I've been an awful fool, Tommy. I know that."

"Anybody can forget a driver's license," he said. "Hurry home and we'll talk then."

He went outside and sat down on the front doorstep. The moonlight was still bright on the long grass and on the water of the Sound, lying ruffled by a rising morning breeze. He lit a cigarette and watched the smoke float lazily off in the moonlight. After about a half hour, he heard a car approaching. Bright headlights flashed across the driveway, and a taxi stopped in front of the house. The back door swung open, and Betsy jumped out. She ran immediately to him. Neither of them spoke. The silence was broken after about thirty seconds by the taxi driver clearing his throat. Tom paid him. When the taxi had gone, he turned to Betsy. "Don't let's go in yet," he said. "It's too nice a night out."

They walked over to the stone wall and sat with their backs against it. He kissed her. "There are some things I have to say," she said. "Don't kiss me again, or I'll never say them."

"Nothing has to be said now."

"This must be said. Tonight while I was driving alone, I realized for the first time what you went through in the war, and what different worlds we've been living in ever since. I'm sorry I acted like a child."

"I love you."

"You're right about helping your boy in

Italy. Of course we should do all we can."

"I love you."

"He should have a good education and everything he needs. Do they have trouble getting enough food and medicine and clothes over there? We should find out what he needs and send it. We shouldn't just send money."

"I love you more than I can ever tell."

"I want you to be able to talk to me about the war. It might help us to understand each other. Did you really kill seventeen men?"

"Yes."

"Do you want to talk about it now?"

"No. It's not that I want to and can't — it's just that I'd rather think about the future. About getting a new car and driving up to Vermont with you tomorrow."

"That will be fun. It's not an insane world. At least, our part of it doesn't have to be."

"Of course not."

"We don't have to work and worry all the time. It's been our own fault that we have. What's been the matter with us?"

"I don't know," he said. "I guess I expected peace to be nothing but a time for sitting in the moonlight with you like this, and I was surprised to find that this isn't quite all there is to it."

"I disappointed you."

"Of course you didn't. I was my own disappointment. I really don't know what I was
looking for when I got back from the war, but
it seemed as though all I could see was a lot of
bright young men in gray flannel suits rushing around New York in a frantic parade to
nowhere. They seemed to me to be pursuing
neither ideals nor happiness — they were
pursuing a routine. For a long while I
thought I was on the side lines watching that
parade, and it was quite a shock to glance
down and see that I too was wearing a gray
flannel suit. Then I met Caesar, running an
elevator. He's the one who knew about Maria
— he went through most of the war with me.
There was Caesar in his purple uniform, staring at me in my gray flannel suit and reminding me, always reminding me, that I was
betraying almost everyone I knew."

"I wish I could have helped you."

"You did help me — you and Caesar. I
needed a great deal of assistance in becoming
an honest man. If you hadn't persuaded me to
play it straight with Ralph, I would be thinking differently now. By a curious coincidence, Ralph and a good deal of the rest of
the world have seemed honest to me ever
since I became honest with myself. And if I
hadn't met Caesar, I don't think I ever would

552

have had the courage to tell you about Maria. I would have gone on, becoming more and more bitter, more and more cynical, and I don't know where that road would have ended. But now I'm sure things are going to be better. I've become almost an optimist."

"I'm glad we're going to have a week to ourselves. Where are we going in Vermont?"

"I know a place where we can rent a cabin by a lake a thousand miles from nowhere. The foliage on the mountains will be beautiful this time of the year. If we get a few more days of Indian summer, it may not be too late for a swim. The nights will be cold, and we'll sleep by an open fire."

"Do you love me?"

"A little."

"Don't tease me. Do you like the way I look?"

"You're beautiful. You never used to like to have me tell you that."

"I want to hear it now. Often. Tell me again that I am beautiful."

"Every time I look at you, you are a delight to me. Every night when I get off the train and see you, I want to tell you that. I haven't for years, because you told me once that you would rather have other compliments."

"I guess when I decided to be a fool, I

had to play it big."

"You've not been as foolish as I," he said, and pulled her down beside him in the fragrant grass and kissed her. A sudden puff of wind set the long ends of the grass shivering all around him. She shuddered. "You're cold," he said. "I'll take you in now."

"No. Hold me tight."

"You're trembling. Why?"

"I don't know. I feel as though we almost died and have just been rescued."

"We're not going to worry any more. No matter what happens, we've got a lot to be grateful for."

"When I think of all you've been through, I'm afraid."

"Don't be. The dead don't have the last laugh. It's the children left by the dead and the survivors who laugh last, and their laughter is not sardonic. Ever since you came back to me tonight, I've been remembering a line from a poem that used to sound ironic and bitter. It doesn't sound that way any more. Tonight, for a little while at least, I feel it's true."

"What is it?"

" 'God's in his heaven'," he said, " 'all's right with the world.' "

41

At eleven-thirty the next morning Judge Saul Bernstein got a telephone call from Tom Rath. "I'm just about to leave town for a week, but I'd like to drop down and see you first," Tom said. "I want your help on a very personal problem."

"Come ahead," Bernstein said. "I'll be expecting you." He hung up and tried to concentrate on the tax form he was completing for a client. Tom's call troubled him. He had had many people telephone to ask immediate help on "a very personal problem," and the approaching trip Tom mentioned was also a bad sign. To Bernstein it all sounded like the usual preliminaries to a divorce case. Divorce cases always saddened Bernstein, and the thought of Betsy and Tom Rath dissolving their marriage especially bothered him. He liked them and he thought that with three young children they had no business splitting up. I wonder what I might do to talk them out of it, he thought, and felt a few warning twinges of pain in his stomach.

Ten minutes later when Tom walked into his office, Bernstein was surprised to see that for a man presumably on the verge of divorce, he appeared indecently cheerful. "Good morning!" Tom boomed heartily. "Beautiful day, isn't it?"

"Yes," Bernstein said uneasily. "What can I do for you?"

"Mind if we go into your inner office?" Tom asked, glancing at Bernstein's secretary.

"No," Bernstein said. "Go right ahead." His stomach began to ache quite badly now. People who wanted to go to the inner office even before naming the nature of their business quite often wanted to discuss divorce. He followed Tom into the small book-lined room, and they both sat down.

"I came to you with this because it would be a little embarrassing to discuss with strangers, and I'm sure you'll understand," Tom began.

"I hope so," Bernstein said dubiously.

"The situation is simply this. During the war I had an illegitimate child in Italy. He's been on my mind a lot, but I haven't been absolutely sure of his existence until recently. Now I want to send his mother a hundred dollars a month for his support — they're in real need. When this housing project of ours goes through, I'm going to establish a trust fund, but right now I want to take it out of income. I think it would be less awkward for everyone concerned if we set up some mechanism for having the checks sent regularly by a bank, or perhaps you could do it."

"Are you trying to make this an anonymous gift?" Bernstein asked somewhat guardedly.

"For the sake of propriety I don't want it talked about all over town, and I don't particularly trust the discretion of the local bank, but the person who will get the money will know who it's from. There's no need to keep anything a secret from her."

Bernstein cleared his throat. "You intend this to be a permanent arrangement?" he asked.

"Certainly. At least until the boy has finished his education."

"It might be possible for you to receive considerable tax benefits by having the child legally declared a dependent," Bernstein said. "You ought to look into that if you plan anything permanent."

"I hadn't thought of that," Tom replied.

"Fix it up for me if you can, will you? Might as well get all the tax benefits I can."

"It might be necessary for you to admit paternity," Bernstein said. "That might leave you open to further claims by the child's mother, and it might pose certain problems for you in filling out your tax returns."

"I'm not worried about further claims. What would the difficulty be with the tax returns?"

"It might be hard to keep the matter a complete secret here," Bernstein said somewhat embarrassedly. "Especially if you file joint tax returns which your wife has to sign."

"Betsy already knows all about it," Tom said. "She and I are doing this together."

"You are?" Bernstein said, unable to preserve his professional air of detachment any longer.

"I know this must sound a little odd to you," Tom said, "but I met a girl in Italy during the war, and I've told Betsy all about it. The child the girl had needs help, and Betsy and I are going to send it. I suppose that may be a little unconventional, but to us it seems like simple justice."

For a moment Bernstein didn't say anything. Misinterpreting his silence as censure, Tom said a little stiffly, "This is a matter of

558

conscience with me, and I don't intend to try to justify it to anyone. Betsy and I are driving up to Vermont this afternoon, and I would appreciate it if you could arrange to have the checks sent. In this envelope I've brought the money for three months and the name and address I want it sent to. What will you charge me for handling the matter?"

"Nothing," Bernstein said.

"What?"

"No charge."

"Why not?"

Bernstein smiled. "I like what you call 'simple justice,' " he said. "The kind I generally deal with is so complex."

"Thanks," Tom said. Suddenly the air was charged with emotion. Bernstein got up and Tom grabbed his hand. "Thanks!" he said again. "I've got to be running. Betsy's been shopping, but she's probably waiting outside for me now. We're heading up to Vermont!"

He dashed out the door. Bernstein's stomach wasn't aching any more. He walked slowly to the window of his office and stood looking down at the street. Betsy, with her arms full of bundles, was just coming down the sidewalk. Bernstein watched as Tom hurried toward her. He saw them bow gravely toward each other as she transferred the bundles to Tom's arms. Then Tom straightened up and apparently said something to her, for suddenly she smiled radiantly. Bernstein smiled too.